Also by Will Wight

CRADLE

Unsouled

Soulsmith

Blackflame

Skysworn

Ghostwater

Underlord

Uncrowned

Wintersteel

Cradle: Foundation

Cradle: Path of Gold

THE TRAVELER'S GATE TRILOGY

House of Blades

The Crimson Vault

City of Light

The Traveler's Gate Chronicles

THE ELDER EMPIRE

Of Sea & Shadow

Of Dawn & Darkness

Of Kings and Killers

Of Shadow & Sea

Of Darkness & Dawn

Of Killers & Kings

*For the most up-to-date bibliography, please visit **WillWight.com***

BLOODLINE

CRADLE : VOLUME NINE

WILL WIGHT

HIDDEN GNOME PUBLISHING

PROLOGUE

ITERATION 246: COMMANDMENT

From far away, Suriel watched a rain of orange lightning fall across the eastern hemisphere of the planet, scorching it to bare rock in seconds. Dull gray vessels drifted away, bearing most of the people and objects of any significance.

Around the planet, war raged.

Vroshir defended their ships' retreat with protective workings, barriers, guardian beasts the size of moons, and shields that could block exploding stars.

Abidan attacked to seize the ships, lances of blue as they drew on the Way to reinforce their attacks with absolute authority. But it was too late; millions had died in the planetary barrage, and the Iteration's relationship to the Way was weak.

Color-swirling portals bloomed in front of the ships as they prepared to leave through the Void.

Drifting in endless sapphire light outside the Iteration, Suriel tapped into her mantle and reverted the world towards a state of order.

A dozen Abidan blinked back to life from where they had been struck down. A hundred others found their armor repaired, their minds restored, their weapons returned.

The charred planet blossomed to blue and green once again, the dead population finding themselves whole and alive. Commandment's relation to the Way strengthened again, so the Abidan attacks punched through Vroshir defenses.

The ships carrying the captives lost their connection to the Void, their portals fading.

Suriel felt the exultation from her people like a wave of cheers. Their morale surged, a warm heat inside her, as the tide of power turned.

But she couldn't bask in the sensation.

Half her attention was elsewhere.

ITERATION 247: JESTER

Six Silverlords, platinum-crowned men and women, coordinated a barrage of attacks against Jester's primary planet.

Positioned in orbit all around the globe, they unleashed a synchronized bombardment, each attack entirely different from the others. One released a storm of razor-sharp rose petals to scour a continent, another sang a song that drifted all through that reality, eating away at opposing workings. Yet a third summoned titanic spires of dense metal, hurling them into the planet.

The four remaining Abidan of Sector Twenty-Four Control held the world. They maintained a triple-layered shell around the atmosphere, a shield of blue Way-power that wouldn't falter even if the planet beneath it exploded.

But the Silverlords were elites, powerful figures even by the standards of Judges. Their combined wills eroded the barrier like moths eating away fabric.

Suriel added her power to the Abidan, and the shell restored itself.

The Silverlords redoubled their efforts, pushing back against her...

...and Suriel found herself stretched to her limit.

The instant she released her attention from Commandment, the Vroshir ships would re-open gateways to the Void and escape with the captured population.

But if she took an ounce of focus from Jester, the Silverlords would crack the barrier like an egg.

In one world, time was on her side. The longer she stalled in Commandment, the more likely her forces would defeat their opponents and reclaim the enemy transports.

In the other world, time was against her. The longer the siege of Jester lasted, the more opportunities the Silverlords would have to break open the shield.

And there were a dozen other worlds calling for a Judge. She didn't have time.

[All forces halt,] her Presence called to the Abidan in Commandment. [Secure the remaining population of the planet. Allow the enemy to withdraw.]

In Commandment, the Abidan halted their assault. Multicolored portals swirled in front of the blocky spacecraft, which vanished one by one into the Void, soon followed by their Vroshir guardians.

Only a handful of millions were left on the planet, but at least it was whole. She had protected as much of the Iteration as she could.

Now it was time to focus on Jester.

With a brief effort of will, Suriel passed through the Way and into the Iteration.

The instant she manifested in reality, the Silverlords cut off their attack and retreated. They stepped through portals of their own, several of them looking toward her and touching their silver crowns in mocking salute.

They knew better than to fight a Judge directly, but that meant only that they were cautious. Not afraid.

She couldn't hunt them down, and they knew it. If she chased them too far, eventually they'd overwhelm her with numbers.

A saying passed down among Judges: "There are always more Silverlords."

She felt that external surge of relief and elation crash over her again as the Abidan in the world celebrated her arrival. Suriel only wished she felt the same.

From their perspective, she had just won two great victories, but she knew better. In her head, a distress call from a far-off world went silent. There was no longer anyone left to cry out.

She hadn't won anything.

She had only delayed defeat.

CHAPTER ONE

Mercy sat at her brother's bedside, carefully peeling a fruit. She offered him a slice with trembling fingers.

"Pride..." she said softly. "Would you like this? Only if you feel up to it, okay? Don't strain yourself."

Pride snatched the rest of the fruit from her hand, leaving her holding only the slice. He bit into its flesh with an audible crunch.

He was trying to prove how strong he was, and that effort touched her. She almost teared up again, thinking of the suffering he'd been through when she failed to protect him. Juice dribbled down his chin, and she reached out with a napkin.

He slapped her hand away. "What are you doing?"

She spoke in a quiet, soothing tone. "You don't have to prove yourself to me. It's okay. You can relax."

"That's enough. Get out of the way." He tossed the fruit aside and slid out of the bed.

"No! Aunt Charity said you have to rest!"

She wrestled him down, and initially she overpowered him. Until four Enforcer techniques flowed through him, and then he broke her grip, seized her by the shoulders, and shoved her back down into her chair.

Now that he stood over her for once, he glared down. "How injured do I look to you?"

Not at all, she had to admit. Her brother was a compact and heavily muscled man, which fit his Book with its many Enforcer techniques. He looked healthy as ever, ready to wrestle a bear, and his purple eyes had a sharp gleam.

He *wasn't* injured anymore, and she knew that. In fact, as she understood it, Charity had restored him to the point that he had never been hurt in the first place.

"She still told you to rest," Mercy insisted, and it sounded like a plea.

"Not to strain myself," Pride corrected. "*Straining* myself is fighting two Overlords at once." His voice caught on that sentence, darker emotion bleeding through, but he continued as though he didn't notice. "I don't need someone spoon-feeding me."

Mercy hung her head. She knew all that, she just didn't know what else she could do for him. Charity had emphasized that, while his physical and spiritual wounds were gone, the mental and emotional consequences were difficult to determine.

Coming from the Sage of the Silver Heart, that warning had sounded dire indeed.

More than just a shadow on his heart, this experience could impact his willpower and slow his future advancement. And it was all Mercy's fault.

She had apologized over and over, until Pride had hit her on the head to stop her from talking. Now...she only wanted to help her little brother. She just didn't know how.

Shakily, she offered him the one remaining wedge of fruit.

He sighed before taking it.

A shadow passing over the room was all the warning they had before Uncle Fury popped into existence between them, screaming loudly enough to hurt their ears.

Mercy was on her feet, readying Suu with an arrow of madra, and Pride fell back onto his bed with hands raised defensively.

Fury's scream trailed off. "Sorry, sorry!" He rubbed the back of his head sheepishly, his hair drifting like black seaweed caught in an unseen current. "Not used to that yet. I thought I was about to fling myself into the center of the earth."

Mercy straightened to meet his eyes, though she wasn't quite tall enough. She ground the butt of her staff into the floor, and the dragon-headed Suu hissed. "What were you *doing?* Do you see what you did to Pride?"

Pride had already straightened and was brushing off his clothes. "I'm fine."

Fury looked more embarrassed. "I didn't mean to. It's not as easy as Charity makes it look. How you feeling, Pride?"

"Perfect."

"Oh, great!" He glanced at Mercy's face before coughing and continuing to speak. "Ah, yeah, but wounds can be deeper than you realize. Even when the healing is done exactly right, sometimes time is still the best cure."

"I think he's pushing himself too much," Mercy insisted.

Fury blinked. "By standing up?"

Pride gave her a look of superiority.

"He can handle it." A trace of rage crept into Fury's face, and his crimson eyes burned. "I came to let you know that we've captured Seishen Daji."

Pride ground his teeth, and even Mercy felt a cold anger. She had known it was only a matter of time before the family found the Seishen Lords, but they had produced results even faster than she expected.

Now they would face justice.

"The trial's in a few hours. Mercy, *she* wants you to sit in judgment."

Mercy's first instinct was to say that Pride was the one who deserved to pass judgment, as he was the one who had almost died. But she knew better. This was to get her used to determining the lives and deaths of others.

Pride gave her a nod. He understood too.

"I will hear them out," Mercy said. "As fairly as I can."

Fury reached out and placed a hand on each of them. "You know, I'd given up on my brothers and sisters until you two. Your father would be proud."

Pride and Mercy both stared at their oldest half-brother. He tended to wax sentimental even less often than his daughter.

"Uncle Fury..." Mercy began. "...is everything all right?"

"What? Yeah! Of course, yeah, everything's fine!" His red eyes slid up to the ceiling. "But I *am* going away."

"Where?" Pride asked.

Fury pointed one finger to the ceiling, and the bottom dropped out of Mercy's stomach.

"You're ascending?"

He scratched the side of his neck without meeting her eyes. "I don't really have a choice. It's not a surprise, though. This was always part of the plan."

"What about Aunt Naria?" Fury's wife was an Archlady, but she almost never fought anymore. Mercy hadn't seen her in years.

"She's coming with me!" Fury said brightly. "The little ones are coming too, and a few families from my branch. I guess it's embarrassing to ascend unless you're bringing a whole parade with you." He rolled his eyes, but she knew he didn't really object.

He was unreliable in many ways, but he would hate the idea of leaving the world forever if it meant abandoning his children before they grew up. His youngest was only eight.

This was all too much for Mercy to take in so quickly after returning from the battlefield. It had been less than a day since she'd fought Sophara outside Sky's Edge.

Pride seemed to be taking it all in stride. He folded his arms. "What about Aunt Charity?"

It was a good question. If the Akura clan lost two of their three pillars at once, they would be vulnerable. Even considering that their biggest rival had been killed.

By Yerin.

Mercy still couldn't quite wrap her mind around that one.

"Charity's staying," Fury said, and he sounded a little

regretful. "She has her own responsibilities. But she saw this coming a long time ago, and we made our peace with it."

"When are you leaving?" Mercy asked.

"Now."

He said it so matter-of-factly, but to Mercy it was another heavy blow in a long string. "You mean...today? You're not even going to wait until we get home?"

Fury looked down on her sadly. "Well, tonight. I wish I could wait longer, but another Monarch staying in Cradle causes all sorts of problems. Especially now."

She blinked back tears to focus on the implications of what he said, but Pride asked the question she wanted to.

"What does that mean?"

"Mother will explain it to you." Fury's shoulders slumped and he gave a heavy sigh. "I wish I could, but I don't want to fight with her before I leave. Don't worry too much, though; it won't be too long before you join me yourself, Pride. Herald, Sage, doesn't matter. Even some Archlords make it out by their own power."

Mercy noticed that Fury didn't include her in those words, and she knew why. If she succeeded Malice, she would stay in this world for the rest of her life. Which could stretch on for centuries.

Why did that make her sad? She *liked* this world.

But it did mean that she would probably never see Fury again.

"Did Mother..." Pride started speaking, but hesitated and visibly changed what he was about to say. "Is she going to come see you off?"

Mercy knew what he had started to ask. Pride wanted to know if she had come to see him when he was on the verge of death.

Fury answered the real question. "She would have come if we really needed her," he said, though he didn't sound very convincing. "Charity was plenty able to heal you. And Mother's busy. There's a Dreadgod, not to mention a bunch of dragons to kill."

He sighed wistfully. "At least I got to finish off Xorrus. What a nice going-away present."

"So she's *not* going to see you off?" Mercy said.

"We said our good-byes a long time ago."

Silence fell heavily over the room, and Mercy knew they were all thinking about their mother.

Fury finally broke the quiet by clapping his hands together. The entire room shook, and someone down the hall screamed.

"Not leaving until sunset, but I've got a lot of people to see before then. I'll see you with the rest of the family then, all right?" He looked off into the distance. "In the meantime, you should probably go see your friends. I think Charity's about to lock them in a box and sit on them."

"What do you mean?" Mercy asked.

"Where are we supposed to go at sunset?" Pride added.

In an implosion of wind and a swirl of shadow, Fury vanished.

Mercy stopped herself in the doorway as she was about to leave, leaning back to check on Pride. "Are you going to be okay by yourself? Do you need anything?"

He gave her a flat look. "If you ask me that one more time, I'm going to pick a fight with Yerin."

"Do..." She hesitated to say anything, but she couldn't let that go. "...do you think you *can?*"

Pride folded his arms and sat back down on the bed. "Shut up."

The cloud fortress that Lindon shared with Yerin had a control panel similar to those that he had used before. It was a raised, polished podium that looked like it had been designed to hold a book, but was instead covered in script-circles.

These controls were more elaborate than those he'd used

in the past, and there were several secondary panels to his left and right. The main control panel was situated in the highest room of their home, and broad windows gave him a clear look outside even as projection constructs showed him glimpses of other angles.

It was designed to be as easy to pilot as possible, which would come in handy whenever he was allowed to do so.

The Ninecloud Soul's feminine voice filled the inside of the control room. "We regret that we still cannot allow any air travel away from Ninecloud City at this point. We will inform you as soon as our security procedures change."

"Apologies, but I don't need to fly out of the city. I need a portal."

"Sadly, our spatial travel is even more restricted at this time, and I cannot guarantee that we will ever be able to accommodate that request. If you would like to make an appointment with one of our Heralds, I can submit your petition into the queue, but we are experiencing a higher-than-normal volume of requests."

Lindon was finding that even his polite tone was becoming strained. "I *understand* that, but as I said before, I don't need you to provide me a portal. I would like you to connect me to the Akura clan."

Every Akura he'd found had been more than happy to speak to him, but none of them were able to help him find Charity. Or Fury. Or Malice, for that matter.

In short, he couldn't find anyone who could actually get him out of here.

He couldn't even get to Mercy; the last time he'd tried, he had been told—politely, and with more than a few fearful glances—that she had asked not to be disturbed while she cared for her brother.

Under normal circumstances, he would have waited for her. He didn't want to leave the city without letting her know, whether he needed her help or not.

But the Dreadgod was on its way to Sacred Valley. The ending that Suriel showed him had come at last.

No matter what assurances Eithan gave him, he couldn't waste another second.

And now his seconds were being wasted for him.

"I apologize, but I have been unable to contact any Sages or Heralds from the Akura clan myself," the Ninecloud Soul said. "I will pass along your message when it is appropriate; until that time, please return your cloudship to the dock."

"Ram them," Yerin said.

She stood at his shoulder, arms folded, two metallic red sword-arms poking out from over her shoulders. The fresh crimson streak in her otherwise-black hair still struck him as unexpected, as did her scarlet eyes.

"Who?" Lindon asked.

There were other cloudships in their view, but none of them were the ones trapping them in. It wasn't as though he could ram the Ninecloud Soul.

Yerin shrugged. "Anybody. That ought to perk up their ears."

He knew she wasn't serious, but it was a measure of his frustration that he considered it for a moment.

The Ninecloud Soul's voice gained an edge of panic. "Please, do not do anything in haste. You are valued guests of the Court, and I assure you, your requests will be considered with due importance."

That was quite a sudden shift in attitude. Maybe threatening to ram someone had worked after all.

Dross popped onto Lindon's shoulder, scowling with his one purple eye at the nine-colored flame that represented the Ninecloud Soul. [Don't listen to her. She was going to lock us up.]

"I never said that," the Soul corrected. "I said that if you continued to sabotage Court property, you would be punished to the extent of Ninecloud City law, but those circumstances were entirely different. We are now dealing with an unprecedented disaster, and at the time, you were acting well above your station. You did not have the status you have now."

Dross' eye narrowed. [That's not what you said before. You said...]

He spun into a twisted copy of the Ninecloud Soul, but his colors were duller, and he was shrouded by a haze of oily smoke. He spoke in a version of the Soul's voice, but he spat every word out in a vicious, spiteful tone.

[Lindon Arelius, if you don't stop, I will *ruin* you. I will hunt you down to the ends of the earth! I swear I will *destroy* you, and even if you become some kind of Sage, I will never be satisfied until my vengeance shreds you to pieces!]

Dross' form shifted, and he returned to his usual form of a round, purple, one-eyed creature. He stroked his bottom lip with one of his pseudopod arms and spoke in his normal voice. [Yeah, that sounds about right.]

For a moment, the Ninecloud Soul was stunned speechless.

"...is that how you remember my words?"

[I'd say I captured the core essence. The spirit of the message, you know. Better than you did, even. Not to brag.]

"We do not have time for this," Lindon said. "Please. I recognize that you have a crisis to deal with, and I apologize, but there are lives at stake for us as well. I would be grateful if you could put me through to *anyone* that can authorize spatial travel."

"I am truly sorry, but it is beyond the scope of my—" The Ninecloud Soul cut off mid-sentence. "Ah, it seems I spoke too soon. A representative of the Akura clan has arrived. Please contact me if you have any further requests. The Ninecloud Court values your friendship."

The rainbow flame winked out as the Soul escaped, leaving Lindon to view one of his projection constructs. It displayed the image of the woman who had just stepped onto the edge of his cloud fortress.

She had a slight build and looked to be about twenty, her slick black hair tied into a neat bun. Her sacred artist robes were layers of black and white and violet, and her purple eyes had an ageless serenity.

Akura Charity stood at the base of their home.

Wards over the entire fortress made entering via spatial travel...not impossible, but more difficult. Lindon had requested that security measure to stop Sages from popping in unannounced.

He suspected that one day soon, Eithan would be able to teleport. Best to plan for that early.

Sages could most likely overpower those protections, and Monarchs certainly could, but it would be better than nothing. Evidently that script had kept Charity out, or he was certain she would have appeared at his elbow instead of knocking on his front door.

When she did knock, the entire castle shook.

She was already unhappy. Lindon didn't think that was fair.

Lindon's pure madra slipped into the control panel. Opening the doors remotely required an intricate process of chaining madra from script to script, which recently would have strained his concentration.

Now, it was as though his madra did as he wished without his input. On the ground floor, the door swung open.

Once she was through the threshold and inside the protective script, Charity stepped into shadow. She emerged at Lindon's side a second later.

"You can't leave," she said flatly.

Lindon pressed his fists together to salute the Sage of the Silver Heart. "I am grateful for your attention, but we have no time to wait. My homeland is in imminent danger from the Dreadgod. If you would provide us with travel there and back, it would greatly speed our return."

She moved her gaze from Lindon to Yerin and back. "It was risky enough to allow you to move as you wished when you were only a talented young Underlord. Do you expect me to permit an Underlord Sage and the world's first...pseudo-Herald...to willingly place themselves in the path of the Wandering Titan?"

That sentence raised Lindon's curiosity on a number of points.

"Pseudo-Herald," Yerin repeated. "Would have thought they'd give me a shinier name."

"Do I count as a Sage, officially?" Lindon asked.

Charity flicked one hand. "This is why you must stay with us. You need guidance now more than ever. You are—*both* of you—playing with forces beyond your comprehension, long before you are ready to do so. Now that we're losing my father, we cannot afford to stretch our resources any thinner."

Lindon's heart froze. *Losing her father?*

Dross gasped.

Even Yerin rested a hand on her sword. "Are the Heralds still on him?" she asked, as though she could do something to influence that fight.

He startled himself as he realized that she potentially *could.*

While she wasn't a full Herald, and he didn't expect her to be blotting out the sky with her techniques yet, they hadn't found the time to test out the full extent of her abilities. If Fury was still alive and fighting, maybe Yerin could turn the tide in his favor.

But if he *was* still fighting, Charity wouldn't be here. Fury must already be gone.

"He's ascending," Charity said. There was an edge of bitterness to the words.

[Ooohhh, that sounds fascinating!] Dross said. [And sorry for your loss. Can we watch?]

"If you stay," the Sage responded.

The passing seconds pressed in on Lindon, but he needed Charity's cooperation. "Losing your father will be a loss to us all, and I'm sorry to hear it. I will be happy to comply with anything you wish...*after* I've done this one last thing."

Everything he'd done, all the pain he'd suffered, all the long hours he'd put in, it had all been to save Sacred Valley. He refused to fail now.

"Your homeland is in the path of the Dreadgod. If there are individuals you wish to evacuate, I'm sure we can arrange that. Carefully. With planning. There are reasons we don't enter that territory."

Lindon defied his long-standing instincts by steadily meeting her eye and asking her a direct question. As though they were equals. "And what are those reasons?"

She matched him for a long moment.

"It's too dangerous," she said at last. "There are ancient protections in place that...dampen...the powers of anyone above a certain threshold. The field affects you more strongly the more powerful you are, and for some it can be lethal. Large cloudships can't even fly in such thin aura."

"A security measure for the labyrinth," Lindon said.

He had learned a *few* things. Most recently from a careful inspection of some documents from the Ninecloud City records.

Charity gave him a short nod. "We don't avoid that place because we hate it. It's dangerous, and a hundred times so now that there's a Dreadgod on its way."

Yerin stood stiffly at Lindon's side. "Feed that to me one more time."

"Surely I'm not the first to inform you that the Wandering Titan is on the move," Charity said, with a glance at Lindon.

"Not that. You're talking about a boundary field that smothers sacred arts." Lindon could read tension in every inch of her body. Even her sword-arms were poised, like scorpion tails.

When he realized what she was talking about, he felt it like a slap to the face. This field must have led to the death of her master. He should have seen that immediately and prepared her for it, but he had only been thinking about the implications to his homeland.

Charity spread her hands. "If you'll dock your cloudship, I would be delighted to explain what little I know about this restricted area."

"Rotten deal for me, isn't it? I'm about to see it with my own two eyes."

Yerin had relaxed somewhat, but Lindon reached out and rested his left hand on her shoulder. Her madra spun restlessly through her body.

To him, the mystery of the Sword Sage's death was just a

small question, a distant itch. As he'd advanced, he'd wondered how it could be possible, but it had never been urgent enough to demand his attention.

To Yerin, it must be far more important. That deserved real investigation.

Once Sacred Valley was safe.

"There are people living in that field," Lindon said. "Surely they're entitled to the protection of the Akura clan, or at least the Blackflame Empire."

"I don't wish to speak ill of your homeland," Charity said, "but we only allow them to remain because they aren't worth our time. They're like fleas living in an armory. We could sweep them out, but why bother?"

Lindon felt a little guilty that he found Charity's perspective reasonable.

The Sage's attachment to him and Yerin made sense as well. They now represented a significant force for the Akura clan. She didn't want that slipping through her fingers.

But if he had value, he had leverage.

"Did I not contribute enough to our cause during the fight for Sky's Edge?" he asked quietly. "Have I not done as you wished all this time? Have I not exceeded your expectations over and over again? How about Yerin?"

"I know your worth better than you do. It is precisely *because* of that—"

Lindon cut her off. "Apologies, but I wasn't finished."

If he was going to use his value, he may as well act like it.

Though his heart hammered, and he could feel Charity's will focusing on him.

It felt strange, like her intentions were pressing down on him from the outside. She was frustrated, and she wanted to *force* him to see things from her perspective, but knew she couldn't.

Before he lost his nerve, he continued. "All of that, I've done to spare my family from *this* fate. I desperately want your support, but if I don't have it, we will fly there ourselves, no matter how long it takes. If we must, we will walk."

It felt wrong to speak for Yerin, but she stood at his side and nodded along.

A voice echoed from the floor below. "We won't make it if we walk!" Eithan shouted up.

"So we won't walk," Lindon allowed. "We can find other transportation if we must."

"It won't be as fast!" Eithan called again.

Lindon spread his hands. "Which is why I would like your help." And, because he couldn't resist, he added, "...and I apologize for interrupting you."

He was hoping that his resolve would make an impression on the Heart Sage, but her face was still placid. She did, however, let out a long breath.

"Lindon. Yerin. I will do anything in my power to keep you as allies. So instead of forcing you, I will *beg* you."

To Lindon's surprise and discomfort, Charity bowed deeply at the waist.

"Please, do not go yourselves. There is too much that may go wrong, and humanity will be worse off for your deaths. Please stay here."

Even Yerin shifted uncomfortably, and she flicked a glance up at Lindon to gauge his reaction.

At that moment, the script-circle on a panel to Lindon's right lit up with a new figure made of light. Mercy was running up to their front door, waving a black-clad hand.

"Can you hear me? Open up!"

Lindon triggered the door without thought, and Mercy's projection beamed as she ran through. "Thank you!" she called.

Charity straightened from her bow, folding her hands in front of her and waiting as though she had expected Mercy to arrive with exactly that timing.

When Mercy reached the top floor and joined them in person, she spoke immediately. "Don't hurt them, Aunt Charity!"

Mercy's appearance was sloppier than usual. Her hair had been tied back unevenly, with strands escaping here and there, and her black-and-white robes were rumpled and loosely tied. There were unexplained smudges on her face, and Lindon wondered if she'd had a chance to rest.

Overlords didn't need much sleep, but they'd all had an exhausting few days.

Charity's eyebrows tightened. "What makes you think I was going to hurt them?"

Lindon absolutely thought Charity would use violence to make them listen, but he didn't say so.

Mercy ground her staff and raised her chin, as confident as if she were giving an order. "They've earned the right to go where they want."

Maybe she *was* delivering an order, though Charity still outranked Mercy in their family hierarchy.

The Sage was unmoved. "Even if we ignore the Dreadgod, there are other threats. If an enemy Monarch or Sage finds them, they will be slaughtered."

"Then aren't they going to the safest possible place?"

"Not from the Wandering Titan."

Yerin waved one crimson-tinted sword-arm. "Malice owes me a prize."

"The Monarchs *collectively* do," Charity pointed out. "Our clan owes you a debt of gratitude that we will gladly repay, but it is poor compensation to send you into certain death."

"Then help us," Lindon said. "You said we could organize something to evacuate Sacred Valley without us going in person. Why don't we do both?"

He had pushed her for help before, but now he felt he had an opening. "It can only be faster than going alone. And safer."

Charity looked to Mercy, who eagerly nodded. The Sage searched the faces of Lindon and Yerin, and then she closed her eyes.

Lindon couldn't tell if she was communing with her Monarch, looking through her own memories, or even gazing into the future, but he sensed nothing.

After a few breaths, she opened her eyes.

"I can only mobilize perhaps two dozen passenger cloud-ships," she said. "They have a maximum capacity of six thousand apiece, so depending on the size of your valley, you may need to make multiple trips, and that may not be possible if the Dreadgod is too close."

Lindon's spirits soared, but before he could thank her, she continued.

"Furthermore, the cloudships cannot operate inside the valley's security field. The ships will have to wait at the border. I will leave their crews under your command, and they can help you evacuate, but they will have standing orders to leave *immediately* at the first sign of the Wandering Titan. Even if they have no passengers aboard.

"Finally, in order to reach the territory in question, we will need to pass through the portal to Sky's Edge. Where the Dreadgod is currently feeding."

A chill passed through Lindon's spine. He remembered the massive humanoid figure of dark stone, its shell rising from the ocean like an island.

He had felt its thoughts crashing over his mind in an avalanche of hunger.

He could imagine what it was like when it was awake, active, and focused on destruction. He could imagine it all too well.

"I will enter the portal first," Charity continued. "If I believe the situation is too dangerous, I will not allow you to pass. Once I have escorted you through, if the situation is too risky for the other cloudships to follow, then I will leave them behind and you will be on your own. Even if everything goes perfectly, I expect you to be wise enough not to throw your lives away and to return as quickly as possible. If these conditions are not acceptable, then I cannot allow you to go at all."

She spoke as though she expected resistance, but Lindon couldn't understand why.

Not acceptable? That was *perfect*. She was offering more support than he had hoped for, much less expected.

Now, he had a real chance of success.

Dross folded his arms. [That seems convenient, don't you think? *Awfully* convenient. You've got some kind of plan for us, don't you? A secret Sage plan. I'd trust you a lot more if you gave me a peek inside your memories. Just a quick—]

"It's perfect," Lindon said in a rush, forcibly cutting off Dross. He bowed as deeply as he could. "My sincere gratitude. I cannot thank you enough."

[Something I've noticed about you,] Dross said to Lindon from inside his head. [You're so agreeable once you get what you want.]

"Thank me when you come back alive," Charity muttered. "It will take some time to arrange the cloudships, and my father is about to ascend. The earliest we can leave is tomorrow morning, so in the meantime I will put you to work. Disembark your cloudship and return to the tower. Dress for a formal occasion."

Lindon chafed at the delay, but ultimately this should save him time. If it meant two dozen more cloudships with which to evacuate the population, then he could wait.

Charity rubbed at the center of her forehead as though to soothe a headache. "Now, do you have any other business with me?"

If he said he did, Lindon thought Charity might transport him to the bottom of the ocean. "Apologies for taking up so much of your time, honored Sage. We will see you tonight."

She waited a moment longer, purple eyes looking him up and down. "You're a Sage yourself now," she said at last. "Even if you have a long way to go. Call me Charity."

Mercy sputtered while Lindon tried to formulate a response, but the Sage didn't wait.

In a fold of shadow, Charity vanished.

第二章

CHAPTER TWO

The cold weight of Lindon's wintersteel badge hung against his chest as he stood witness in the trial.

This room in the Akura tower of the Ninecloud Court had been shrouded entirely in shadows. The edges were totally black, creating the impression that the circle of people in the center existed in the one well-lit island in a sea of endless dark.

Purple eyes glowed in the darkness, all filled with rage, all focused on the three figures bound and kneeling in the middle.

Meira, Underlady of the Seishen Kingdom, looked largely unharmed. Her gray hair, unfitting for her age, hung messy behind her, but her skin was untouched. Her pink flower Goldsign shone over one ear.

Her eyes were weary, fearful, and resigned over the gag that trapped the entire lower half of her face. It was a contraption of metal and scripted leather, and it suppressed almost as much power as the halfsilver cuffs that encircled her wrists.

An older man, built like a noble bear, was bent and bound next to her. Unlike her, he bore obvious wounds, with blood trickling from his salt-and-pepper hair to stain his short beard.

King Seishen Dakata breathed heavily through his nose, obviously trying to keep up a breathing technique, but Lindon had seen the Akura Overlords carrying him in.

They had not been gentle.

In the worst shape by far was Dakata's remaining son, Seishen Daji. One of his eyes was swollen shut, his clothes were torn and looked to be somewhat burned, and instead of handcuffs, both his arms were wrapped in halfsilver chains. That had to be spiritual agony.

He wore no complex scripted muzzle, but had a dirty rag stuffed in his mouth to gag him. While he trembled in fear and pain, Lindon would call his expression sullen, even defiant.

Whatever fate the Akura family was about to decide for him, it would be no worse than he deserved.

Akura Charity stepped forward, her young-looking face cold as usual. "Kingdom of Seishen. You stand accused of conspiracy to assassinate members of the Akura head family." She pulled a scripted spike from a void key and held it up.

It resembled a long tent stake made of stone and ringed with runes, and Lindon had seen it before. It was the spatial anchor Daji had tossed into Lindon's team to summon the Blood Sage. Leading directly to their deaths.

The anchor would be dangerous to carry around, lest someone else use it to teleport into their midst, except that Charity had sealed off the runes with scripted straps. Only once the straps were removed could the device be used again.

"A trusted witness testified that one of you used this device to summon assassins," the Sage continued. "The traces of madra remaining in the script have aspects similar, possibly identical, to your Paths."

Seishen Dakata looked to his left, and the horror that slowly crept over his face was enough to tell Lindon he was innocent.

Because his son surely wasn't.

Meira's eyes drifted shut, and she heaved a deep sigh.

Charity continued to speak quietly. "Your guilt is beyond

doubt. We are gathered here to decide the extent of that guilt and the severity of your punishment. Your fate lies not in your hands...nor in mine."

She extended the spatial anchor to her right, where Mercy hesitated before taking it. She looked from the scripted spike to her aunt's face...then, with obvious resolve, she seized the anchor.

When she stepped forward, she quivered with a cold fury of the sort that Lindon had never seen on her. "Underlady Meira," Mercy said, "I will address you first."

The script on the leather over Meira's mouth dimmed, but she didn't speak.

"Swear to answer my questions truthfully," Mercy commanded.

There was a long moment before Meira's voice came out, heavy as a tomb door and quiet as a whisper. "I swear on my soul to answer you with the truth and tell you no lies."

Lindon felt the oath between Mercy and Meira as a distant quiver in the air. He had a whole new set of senses now. He would have to get used to them.

Sometime after Seishen Daji got his justice.

"What do you know of the attempt on my brother's life, my life, and the murder of three other young sacred artists of the Akura clan?"

It was strange to hear Mercy speak with such gravity and hidden anger, and indeed she looked furious, grieved, and uncomfortable in equal measure.

Meira shook her head, her eyes still closed. "I knew of no plot against you or the Akura clan until this moment."

"Do you believe it plausible that one among the Seishen Kingdom did carry out such a plot?"

"Yes."

"You know who it was, don't you?"

"...I suspect I do." Meira tilted her head slightly in Daji's direction, though her eyes were still closed. "I warned you, Daji. I warned you and warned you."

King Dakata lunged against his manacles, coming up short

at the chain holding him to the ground. He screamed into his muzzle, only a muffled sound coming from him.

"Thank you, Meira," Mercy said softly. "King Dakata, you may—"

The instant the script around the king's mouth stopped shining, his shouts resolved. "Me! It was me! I'll kill you! I'll kill you *all!*"

He shrieked in rage, making a show of fury, even snapping his jaws behind his muzzle as though he wished he could bite out Mercy's throat, but Lindon was certain the anger was just a front.

It was nothing spiritual or supernatural, no working of madra or willpower. The king's desperation just seemed more like fear than anger.

Mercy's hand trembled on the anchor. "King Dakata, will you swear—"

"GET OVER HERE!" He craned forward, growling and pulling against his restraints. "RELEASE ME! I'LL DO IT MYSELF!"

"Swear to tell the—"

"KILL ME! KILL ME, YOU COWARDS!"

"Your Majesty, if you won't cooperate, we'll have—"

"I'LL RIP OUT YOUR RIBS ONE AT A TIME! I'LL—"

This time, Mercy cut *him* off.

By leaping across the room and seizing him by the jaw. Her hand covered in a crystalline purple gauntlet, she squeezed across the muzzle on his face, slowly lifting him one-handed until his eyes were even with hers.

The chain binding him to the floor went taut, pulling his arms back by their manacles until his shoulders looked like they were ready to dislocate, but Mercy was filled with incandescent violet rage.

"Shut *up. SHUT UP!*" Her breathing was wild, her madra growing erratic, and shadows danced all around the room. "What do you think is going to happen? That I'm going to punish you and let your son free? What about your kingdom? You think if you take the blame, everyone else goes home?"

He tried to speak, but she shook him violently with one hand. "I *want* you to go home! You understand me? *That's what I want.* I am not here for *anyone* who doesn't deserve it. Not even you."

His muzzle blazed purple again and she shoved him back down, moving to the third Seishen sacred artist in line. Mercy tucked her hands behind her back, and Lindon knew they were shaking.

His heart ached for her. She must hate this.

Ordinarily, Lindon would feel the same way.

But under the circumstances, he could pass judgment on Daji with an ice-cold heart.

"Seishen Daji," Mercy said, "swear on your soul to tell me the truth."

"I swear," Daji said. He licked his lips but gave her a bold stare, as though trying to cover up fear with bravado.

Mercy drew herself up, and the pressure of her Overlord spirit built like a thunderhead. "Say the rest."

"I swear to tell you the truth."

Lindon felt the oath snap into place between the two of them, and he couldn't deny surprise. He had expected Daji to dodge the promise like his father had done.

Mercy brought out the spatial anchor. "What is this?"

"I don't know," Daji said easily.

So easily, and the oath didn't stop him.

Was it true?

Mercy's eyebrows twitched, but she went on. "A reliable witness saw you plant this, and then our Archlords stopped you from activating a gatestone. Where would the stone have taken you?"

The fear was leaking out of Daji, leaving confidence. "Home. I feared that a rival of mine would use underhanded tactics to get revenge on me." He gave an overt glance in Lindon's direction.

Lindon sensed the bond that stretched between Daji's soul and Mercy's. It didn't tremble.

What's going on? Lindon asked Dross.

Dross returned an image of himself with both boneless arms spread in a shrug. [Reigan Shen?]

It hadn't taken a genius to deduce who was behind the attack. The assassins had been openly wearing Shen's colors.

Still, no matter how certain they were, Malice was the only one who could push a grudge against a Monarch. Malice, and now Fury.

Until he ascended.

It had to have been Reigan Shen that allowed Daji to lie under oath. Not that Lindon had any idea how that would be possible.

But the Akura family hadn't blindly trusted Lindon because of his long association with Mercy. They'd taken his sworn statement and even read his memory of the event... though as far as they knew, that last part could have been fabricated by Dross.

Not to mention that Lindon hadn't been the only one on that rooftop. Four others had glimpsed Daji in the vicinity, or seen something thrown to the floor before the group vanished. Everyone here knew who the guilty party was.

Even so, this was only the first stage of the Akura clan's investigation. It would be long and, no doubt, exhaustive.

Daji's spine straightened, and he spoke with more confidence. "I know of no plot against the Akura clan, and neither does my father. We are loyal, and we do not deserve this treatment." He glared at Lindon openly now. "I only know of a plot against *us*."

Lindon's disgust ignited into hot, clean anger.

Mercy's hand trembled on the anchor. Next to her, Charity's face was a mask. King Dakata was panting, looking to his son with new hope, as though he hadn't dared to believe Daji might be innocent. Meira simply looked confused. Confused and tired.

The other Akura around the room glanced to Lindon, and he felt their attention on him. His nerves crawled, and in lesser company, he would have felt their suspicion.

But they hadn't earned their way into this room on combat strength alone. One by one they surveyed him, then returned their attention to Daji.

Who was trying his hardest to look innocent and hurt.

"If this is about my attack on *you*," Daji said to Mercy, "I can only beg your forgiveness. It was so long ago, and I pray to the heavens that you'll find the...*mercy*...to forgive me."

Silence rolled over the room like a boulder.

[Was that...was he making a joke?]

Mercy's expression twisted in disgust. "So then, you swear to me on your soul that this is nothing more than a personal grudge between you and the witness who reported you?"

"That is the only explanation that would satisfy me."

"You believe he has accused you falsely?"

"*Yes,*" Daji spat, but then he wrestled his anger under control again. "I mean, that's the only explanation I can think of. My loyalty is, and always has been, to the Akura clan."

Daji turned to shoot another look at Lindon, only to see—too late—King Dakata frantically shaking his head.

Mercy looked to Lindon with sadness in her eyes, but Lindon gave her a grim nod. He saw where this was going.

She regretted the necessity, but *he* didn't.

He slowly pushed past some members of the Akura family, limbering up his madra.

"Very well then," Mercy pronounced. "In the lack of further evidence, this must be nothing more than a personal grudge between Wei Shi Lindon Arelius and Seishen Daji of the Seishen Kingdom."

As Lindon's eyes darkened, Daji's skin paled.

Mercy continued as King Dakata started screaming into his muzzle again. "The investigation into the Seishen Kingdom will continue, but first let this personal grudge between accuser and accused be settled."

"Seishen Daji," Lindon said quietly, "I challenge you to a duel."

The other two prisoners were being hauled away—Meira quietly and Dakata struggling every inch of the way. An Underlady in Akura colors but with no purple eyes waved her hands over Daji, and a complex waterfall of emerald life madra cascaded down over him.

"No!" Daji shouted as his injuries knit together. "Why should I fight him? This isn't fair!"

Mercy sounded regretful, but she still spoke clearly. "What could be more fair? You're both Underlords. He has accused you of a terrible crime, for which he has provided evidence, but you insist he is only smearing your good name. Very well. Defend your honor."

"I don't have—"

"The Akura clan will uphold the results of the duel," Mercy interrupted.

Next to her, Charity nodded once.

Daji licked his lips, his eyes flitting around. "I...if I win, I'll go free?"

"If you win, we will continue our investigation as though Lindon accused you out of a personal grudge, which has been resolved," Mercy said. Which didn't quite answer the question.

Daji, though, grasped at the thin lifeline he had been offered. "Give me back my swords. And my armor."

"Your armor was damaged in your apprehension, and we found no swords on you."

Lindon's void key slipped open, the closet-sized door hanging in the air to his right. He sent his spiritual sense inside, summoning a pair of swords, which leaped to him with a quick application of force aura.

"I happen to have found these lying on the ground recently," Lindon said. "Do they suit you?"

They were, of course, Daji's.

He tossed them to Daji, who seized one thin sword in each hand. The Seishen Underlord hurled the sheaths off so they clattered to the ground. The Striker bindings in each blade kindled to life, and sparks ran up and down the metal.

"He has accepted his weapons," Mercy said. "Lindon, you may use weapons of your own."

Lindon folded his arms in front of him. "Gratitude, but I am as armed as I need to be."

The lithe, wolf-like Seishen Underlord leaned forward, shifting his weight from one foot to the other, swords held low. He radiated fear, anger. Hunger.

Lindon knew the feeling.

He remembered Akura Grace's cold, lifeless eyes. Courage's body. Douji's. Pride's bloody, beaten form as he swayed on his feet.

Daji had caused all that. If Lindon couldn't leave for Sacred Valley until the morning, at least this was worth some time.

"Begin," Mercy said.

A bolt of lightning madra coursed over Lindon's shoulder, but his fist had already smashed into Daji's nose.

The Seishen prince blasted backwards, his spine slamming into an old man in the audience.

Akura Justice was an ancient Archlord. Daji bounced off his palm as though he'd run into a brick wall.

Daji's face was a bloody mess, his nose shattered, and Lindon's next punch broke his ribs and lifted him into the air.

Outclassed he may have been, but Daji's body had still been remade in soulfire. He twisted in midair and his sword expanded to massive size with Forged madra. He slashed at Lindon, beneath him, with a blade the size of his entire body.

Lindon's eyes cooled as they turned to crystalline blue, and blue-white pure madra erupted into a dome all around him. He controlled the expansion of the Hollow Domain so he wouldn't catch any of the Akura clan in it, but Daji's technique slid through the dome.

It dissolved like dust in water.

Lindon let the cloud of harmless essence pass over him as Daji fell into the field and his Enforcer technique failed him. The prince twisted to land with his legs beneath him, but Lindon grabbed his ankle.

Daji caught himself with his hands, rather than crashing face-first into the ground, but that wasn't the result Lindon wanted.

So he lifted Daji one-handed and slammed the Underlord back into the ground.

At first, Daji twisted to kick Lindon's head with his free leg, but the power Lindon had drained from Crusher still flowed through him. The kick landed like a dragonfly smashing into a window.

Lindon smashed him into the ground again.

Daji kept trying to pull his madra together, but under the influence of the Hollow Domain and the trauma of the beating, he couldn't form a technique.

And Lindon was holding Daji's ankle with his right hand.

Whenever it looked like the prince was about to finish a technique, Lindon bled the madra away with the Consume technique and vented it into Daji's back. The force and earth madra came out like a fistful of bricks.

All the while, Lindon hammered him against the floor over and over.

It didn't resemble anything like an honorable sacred artist's duel. There was no dignity and no possibility of escape. Only when Daji was bloody, broken, and whimpering did Lindon let the Hollow Domain die and drop the prince one final time.

Everyone watched Daji land on the ground with a smack, where he curled in on himself with a sound like a cross between a scream and a groan.

Lindon knelt beside him, speaking quietly. "I tried to leave you alone."

Almost gently, he pulled the prince up from the ground by his collar. Daji sputtered and spat out blood.

"I know this was just you. Meira and your father...they're smarter than this. I don't think a Monarch would have approached them. Am I right?"

Daji burbled incoherently, his eyes spinning in their sockets to come to rest on Lindon. They were surprisingly lucid.

"You deserve to die. You know that. But *they* don't, do they?"

For a moment, the anger and the pain cleared from Daji's eyes. For the first time, Lindon saw something human in them.

Very slightly, the prince of the Seishen Kingdom shook

his head.

Lindon rose to his feet as Mercy, rather unnecessarily, announced victory. Seishen Daji was dragged off into the shadows, and Lindon remembered Orthos' words from long ago: *"The Akura do not kill honorably. They take prisoners."*

"I believe him," Lindon said to Mercy.

"Y-yeah..." Mercy said. She sounded like she was trying to encourage him.

"I know his confession won't make a difference." It wasn't as though a single shake of the head after a brutal beating counted as proof. Even the 'duel' had just been another way of punishing Daji within the Akura clan's rules, not a way of obtaining evidence.

But Lindon did believe him.

"I'll ask them to take it easy," Mercy promised.

Charity slipped up beside them. "We will take it easy on everyone but Daji. Unless we find evidence of collusion. How did you feel about your arbitration, Mercy?"

"Terrible."

Lindon gave her a comforting pat on the shoulder, but he was already turning to leave. "I have to prepare. I'll see you tonight."

"Where are you...no, it doesn't matter. I have to stay with Pride. I'll see you tonight!"

Charity's eyes narrowed on him. "You know not to leave the city, don't you?"

"Of course, Charity. Thank you for your concern."

It felt almost painful to call a Sage by her given name, but she only nodded before vanishing with Mercy.

Lindon rubbed at the blood on his fist as he walked through the artificial veil of shadow. Dross projected images of what the room had looked like before, so he strode through like the darkness was only a thin mist. His mental map would be accurate, assuming no furniture had been added that Dross didn't know about.

[Not to cast doubt on my own predictions, but I thought you were going to kill him.]

I wanted to, Lindon admitted. It had been a struggle to hold himself back from crushing Daji into a ball. He wasn't proud of that, but he couldn't pretend that Daji hadn't earned it.

[Why...ah, if you don't mind me asking, why didn't you?]

Lindon stretched out his newfound Sage's senses, feeling the tear in space where the Akura servants had slipped through a temporary portal. They had dragged the prisoners somewhere immediately, possibly Moongrave, where no one could interrupt them. Where Seishen Daji couldn't be saved, even by Reigan Shen.

Lindon responded silently to Dross.

My name isn't Mercy.

Uncle Fury's ascension ceremony should have been held in the main house, in a hall dedicated for that purpose. Mercy had heard of several family members who had ascended, but never in her lifetime. As far as she knew.

But most of the important members of the Akura clan had come here to Ninecloud City for the Uncrowned King tournament, and it would cost far too much to send everyone to Moongrave. Perhaps her mother could have done it, but she hadn't shown herself since the Monarch-level battle that had devastated the surrounding countryside.

Not even for her own son leaving the world.

Mercy had to admit that she couldn't know what kind of contact Uncle Fury and her mother had shared after his ascension to Monarch. Maybe they had enjoyed a heartfelt mother-and-son moment that she wasn't privy to.

It wasn't likely, but she could dream.

All the most critical members of the Akura clan gathered in a wide basement beneath their amethyst tower. The gathering had the atmosphere of a party, with the members who were leaving alongside Fury mingling and saying their good-byes while servants drifted around with trays of drinks and snacks.

Uncle Fury, his wife Naria, and many of their children would be leaving together. Their youngest were eight and twelve years old, while their oldest were white-haired and bent. Many of their children were staying; some were too critical to the function of the clan, like Aunt Charity, while others simply didn't want to leave.

A few of Fury's descendants had ascended already, many years before, though of course none had done so by reaching Monarch.

In addition to immediate relatives, several distant families under Fury's branch were coming along with him, as well as a retinue of servants and attendants. All told, about two hundred people were joining the newest Monarch in his ascension.

Some of them had not been here from the Uncrowned King tournament, but had been summoned by Aunt Charity and Uncle Fury at great expense.

Mercy milled around herself, saying good-byes and shedding her share of tears. She hadn't been especially close to any of those leaving except Aunt Naria, but these were still people she knew. Her family.

In a way, it was like they were dying.

She swiped her eyes as she emerged from a gaggle of her nieces and nephews—many of whom were decades older than she was—to see Lindon and Yerin arrive.

They were immediately mobbed by her relatives.

The sight warmed her heart. It hadn't been long since the Akura clan had looked down on Lindon and Yerin, and would have approached them only out of necessity or as part of a scheme.

Now, they were tripping over themselves to make a good impression.

Her friends had shown their worth. To everyone.

Lindon loomed over everyone else, and the look of discomfort on his face made him look more like he had before his advancement to Underlord: as though he was searching for something to punch. Unfortunately for him, as a Lord he was handsome enough to take the edge off, so his new admirers would take his expression to be stern and regal.

Yerin looked more at ease than Lindon, shoving through her much-larger crowd and cornering a servant holding a tray of tiny dumplings. She seized a pair for herself, then—when she saw that Lindon was still pinned by Akura clan members—reached in and pulled him out by the hand.

After he let himself be hauled to freedom, he didn't release her hand right away.

That sight made Mercy slow for a moment. She couldn't put a name to what she felt. It wasn't jealousy, exactly. At least, she didn't think so. Maybe envy.

She had never had many friends in the Akura clan. She considered herself a friend to almost everyone, but very few felt that way about her. From the moment she was chosen by the Book of Eternal Night, she was apart from the rest of them. Separate. A target of alliance for the ambitious, or a rival to be overcome, or perhaps even someone to be feared.

Despite only having known them a couple of years, she thought of Lindon and Yerin as her closest friends. And they were getting closer to each other, one step at a time.

Leaving her alone.

Yerin saw Mercy and brightened. It was still a shock to see Yerin with eyes that resembled Uncle Fury's, but Mercy waved cheerily. Yerin came over to meet her in a moment, still holding Lindon's hand.

The surrounding Akuras backed off to give them some space.

"Your family's a touch friendlier than before," Yerin remarked, popping a miniature dumpling into her mouth whole. "Wonder why."

Lindon finally slipped his hand from Yerin's, sliding it into the pocket of his outer robe instead. "I know why they want to talk to *you,* but I'm not sure what they want from *me.*"

"You did fantastic in the tournament!" Mercy assured him. But because she knew what he meant, she continued. "Some of them know about your performance in Sky's Edge, and the smarter ones *may* have heard about what...showed up in the sky."

Mercy couldn't believe it herself, though she had seen Lindon toy with Sophara, and she'd even witnessed the black hole that covered the clouds. Charity had explained it to her. A little.

Lindon was a Sage now.

Mercy still wasn't quite sure how that was possible.

Lindon looked relieved. "Gratitude. I was worried it was something...else."

Mercy wracked her brain, but couldn't imagine what he was talking about. "What else could it possibly be?"

"Apologies, I don't mean to speak ill of your family. I thought perhaps they were using me to get closer to Yerin, or trying to get revenge because I overshadowed them, or they wanted to blackmail me to force me to fight for them."

"Of course not!" Mercy exclaimed. Did her family really have that bad of a reputation in Lindon's eyes?

Yerin and Lindon looked at each other, exchanging a look between them that once again made Mercy feel left out.

"Truly, I do apologize, but...they've done all of those things."

Mercy shut her mouth. They were right. Now that she thought of it, she didn't know why she'd bothered to defend her relatives in the first place.

She had never liked the way her family handled things. They twisted themselves in knots to appease those stronger, and expected the same from those beneath them. They never associated with the weak unless they stood to gain something.

It wasn't as though she really thought her family was better than that, she just...wanted them to be.

"Yeah," she said quietly. "I'm sorry."

The emotions she'd been feeling before—sorrow at the loss of her family members—came back in full force and blended with her guilt. With Uncle Fury and his immediate family leaving, there were even fewer good people left in the Akura clan.

Not that Fury didn't have his share of issues. The legends of certain cultures regarded him as a monster.

Maybe there *were* no good people in her family.

The air around her began to literally darken as her shadow madra leaked out, reflecting her gloom.

Yerin rapped her on the top of the head with one knuckle.

She hadn't struck particularly hard, and Mercy's Overlord-level body was resilient. Even so, the impact *hurt.*

Mercy clapped one black-clad hand to the injury, but Yerin didn't look the least bit sympathetic. "You can cut that off right now. You know we're not putting anything they did on your account."

Mercy blinked rapidly and took deep breaths to get ahold of herself. It had been a *long* few days.

Before she could thank Yerin, Uncle Fury emerged from the crowd, looming over most everyone—though not Lindon—and beaming ear to ear.

He strode confidently up to Yerin, and to Mercy's horror, he had his right hand cocked back and gathering madra. It looked like he was about to *attack.*

Yerin pushed past Mercy, her own right hand drawn back.

Mercy's horror choked her, but disbelief prevented her from moving. Someone should stop this. *She* should stop this. What was—

The palms of the Herald and the Monarch cracked together in an explosion that left some of the nearby crowd stumbling back. The wind snatched at formal robes and shoved snacks off platters.

Yerin and Uncle Fury clasped hands, Fury grinning and Yerin wearing a similar expression.

"I'm so *jealous,*" Fury said. "What did it feel like, killing a Monarch?"

Yerin snorted. "Didn't get him in a fight, did I? About like swatting a fly."

Uncle Fury closed his eyes and breathed in slowly through the nose as though savoring a scent. "Like swatting a fly...oh, it's beautiful. It's better than I ever imagined. The King of

Dragons, swatted by a child. Like a fly."

He took another deep breath. "Perfect."

"Half-certain *I'm* the one who's meant to be jealous." After a deliberate pause, she added, "Monarch."

"You kidding me? Who am I going to get to fight me now?"

Lindon answered that one. "Heavenly warriors, I would guess."

Red eyes lit up, and Fury released Yerin's hand at last. "That's the idea!" He put fists on his hips, facing Lindon. "I've had somebody take care of your points. The rest of your team got to make their own choices from what we had left. I'd give you something myself, but I hear Charity's taking care of it."

Lindon forced a smile in return. "Gratitude. What about the ones we lost?"

That was enough to darken Mercy's mood again. She had seen Grace die, and Douji as well. She hadn't personally witnessed Courage fall, but she felt it.

"They were all clan members, and we take care of—Oh, hey, look at that!" He raised a hand and beckoned to someone in the crowd.

A moment later, a purple-eyed man and woman emerged. They looked to be in their mid-forties, but their faces were weathered and haggard as though they hadn't slept in days.

Mercy's throat tightened.

"Akura Earnest and Kiya," Uncle Fury said. "Grace's parents. They're coming with me tonight, but they wanted to meet you first."

Akura Grace had been the pride of her immediate family, skilled as she was among her generation. She was supposed to raise her parents up to further prestige within the clan.

Now she was gone.

Mercy hadn't seen Earnest or Kiya since their daughter's death. She'd been with Pride, and there had been too much going on.

Lindon looked like he wanted to bolt. He bowed as deeply to them as he had to Aunt Charity earlier. "This one cannot express his regret. Please accept my deepest apologies."

Grace's mother laid a hand on Lindon's arm. "For what?"
He straightened cautiously.

"You avenged our daughter," Earnest said. He bowed at
the waist. "She was a warrior, and an Underlady, and prepared to die. Still...please accept our thanks."

He pressed a purse into Lindon's hands.

The pouch of scripted purple cloth wasn't nearly as
high-quality of an item as a void key, but it was still made
by Charity to compress Forged madra. Indeed, Mercy could
sense the power of at least a dozen types of scales coming
from within.

They were leaving this world behind, and they had no other
children, so Mercy wouldn't be surprised if they had left their
entire fortune in that purse. They would have wracked their
brains for a gift worthy of Lindon. It wouldn't be unheard-of, to
leave such a reward to someone who had avenged a loved one.

Mercy knew Lindon well enough to see that he was struggling with himself. He looked as though he wanted to turn
this down, because he thought he didn't deserve it.

But his hands moved without him, and he tucked the
pouch into his pocket before they could change their minds
and take it back.

"Gratitude," Lindon said, dipping his head over a salute. "I
don't know how to properly express my condolences, other
than to wish you well as you journey onward."

Fury clapped Earnest on the shoulder. "Take it easy if you
need to. I'll join you in a minute."

Grace's parents saluted Lindon in return, bowed to Fury,
and then drifted away.

Once they had left, Uncle Fury watched their backs and
spoke with unusual gentleness. "Time doesn't heal everything, but it does help. Never gets easy, though."

Yerin looked up at him. "Is it good for them, going with
you? Could be like losing everybody at the same time."

Fury shrugged. "I think it'll help. They'll have a new
purpose, and a lot of their closer relatives are coming too.
But they wanted to come, and I'm not telling them no." He

turned back to Lindon and Yerin. "It's too bad you're not coming up yet. Never did get a chance to fight you."

"Apologies, but I don't think we would make worthy opponents."

"Well, yeah. Otherwise I'd be fighting you right now. But hey, I can wait a few years." He gave them a cheery wave and started to walk backwards into the crowd. "See you on the other side, you two! Mercy, you want to give me a hand?"

Uncle Fury didn't need her help. He just wanted to talk.

"Just a second," she said to Lindon and Yerin, and then she hurried after her uncle. Well, her half-brother.

He spun around, walking forward with both hands laced behind his neck. People to either side had to duck his outstretched elbows, but most of the attendees here were advanced sacred artists. They managed.

"Thought we ought to talk about you before I'm out of here. The three stars of the clan are down to two, now. I suspect we'll end up stronger than ever in the long run, now that the snake isn't around anymore, but that doesn't mean we won't have a weak point for a couple years."

Mercy straightened as she walked. "I'm ready to accept my responsibility."

"...yeah, I thought so. The family will expect a lot from you when I'm gone. They want you to fulfill your duty to the family, and they all have their own ideas for what that looks like."

This was strange. Uncle Fury was known for shirking any duty he could if it didn't involve advancement or combat.

"It's all a trap," he continued. "Don't get caught in it."

That sounded a lot more like Fury.

"At some point, you have to start leading." He grinned down on her and ruffled her hair. "Good luck."

She had thought of many things to say, but in the end, only one mattered: "Good-bye, Uncle Fury."

He threw his long arms around her in a hug, and she buried herself in his chest.

For a moment. Then he swept back into the party, leaving her to collect herself.

It was another hour before Fury was ready to depart. Mercy stuck with Lindon and Yerin as much as she could, helping to fend off those who wanted a moment alone with the stars of the Uncrowned King tournament.

Finally, after a long exchange with Charity that no one else could hear, Uncle Fury raised his voice.

"Looks like it's time to go!"

The words boomed through the enclosed basement. One of the less-advanced servants fell to his knees.

"I think I'm supposed to talk about how I'm sad to be leaving you all behind, but I really can't wait to go," he continued. "If you've got what it takes, catch up." He looked to someone at the front of the crowd and winked.

Mercy couldn't see, but she was certain he was looking at his daughter, the Sage.

"Anyway, that's enough from me. Later, everybody!"

And that was the end of a fairly typical Akura Fury speech.

As soon as the last word was out of his mouth, the room began to...stretch. It wasn't anything Mercy could put a name to precisely, but it looked as though the room was being pulled like taffy until it stretched into a long hallway.

The end of the basement, where Fury and those accompanying him stood in a large group, was now much longer than it had been before. It looked like a mirage, a trick of the eye, but she felt no madra gathered there.

Only something else.

An *absence* of madra, maybe. Fury was at the center of it, pushing—or perhaps pulling—on something deeper than vital aura. Something she didn't have the senses or the experience to name.

A blue light sparked in front of his outstretched hands.

It swelled as he concentrated, expanding to a ball that hovered in front of him. Unlike madra, this blue substance didn't look like it was made of light, but rather like a patchwork of every shade of blue that existed. It looked almost material, but it couldn't have been physical, and her eye couldn't exactly trace its edges or layers.

The blue ball expanded into a circle big enough to fill the basement from floor to ceiling...and then it was no longer a ball, but a circular doorway, the blue stretching on infinitely in the distance.

Mercy thought that whatever technique Uncle Fury was using had been completed, but he braced his hands as though getting a grip on empty air.

Then he pushed.

The blue power snapped into a wide ring. A ring that led into another world.

In the distance, silver towers stretched into the sky. Boxes of rough metal the size of buildings floated in the air, and the sky was surrounded by bars of impossible size, as though the entire world had been caught in a cage.

Immediately in front of the portal, it was a different story. They looked out onto an empty plaza of white stone, crystals the size of a human body hovering a few feet over the ground and shining blue.

Two figures flanked the portal on either side, each dressed in seamless eggshell-white armor. Abidan, like the one who had hijacked the Uncrowned King tournament. They stood under banners that depicted a stylized fox wrapped in its own tail, and as Lindon watched, the fox on the banner curled up tight. As though the ink was alive and the noise had interrupted its sleep.

"Welcome to Threshold, adept," a dark-skinned woman announced. Though she didn't sound like she'd raised her voice, her words echoed through the room. "You take your first steps into the world beyond."

"Thanks!" Uncle Fury said brightly. "Let's go, everybody!"

The group filed through side-by-side, some excited and others terrified. Lindon and Yerin stared hungrily through the portal.

Mercy tried not to feel like she was losing family.

But she did wonder what was so great about that other world that it was worth losing this one.

In a matter of moments, and to the cheers of the remaining Akura clan, Fury and his branch passed safely through. The portal collapsed in on itself, folding until it vanished.

Leaving the mortals behind.

第三章

CHAPTER THREE

Lindon stood with Yerin on the second floor of their cloud fortress, looking out through the wide windows to see Charity preparing their exit.

The Sage stood over one of the empty doorframes that had been a portal to Sky's Edge, weaving space and shadow so that darkness leaked from the edges like a gas. A dark haze was beginning to form so that it blocked out the light of the rising sun, and Lindon could feel the sensation of a door creaking open.

She was expanding the already-existing gate, since she wasn't strong or skilled enough on her own to create a portal leading so far away that could transfer so many people. He couldn't follow most of what she was doing, but he could *feel* it, and he tried to remember that sensation.

Not that he could concentrate well.

Yerin leaned against him as he stood over the cloud fortress' control panel, a warm and soft presence at his side, leaving him with a moment of indecision.

He could put his arm around her. He should, right? They had passed that point already.

But she was on his right side. Putting his Remnant arm around her struck him as a bit like throwing a corpse over her to protect her from the cold.

She glanced up at him and took his Remnant hand in hers. He could feel her, but distantly compared to his arm of flesh, as though he were imagining the sensation instead of physically feeling it.

Yerin laced her fingers with his. "You'd contend they'll listen to you?"

He didn't need to ask what she was talking about. She knew what was on his mind.

Would Sacred Valley listen to him?

His family was in greater danger every moment, but no amount of hurrying on his part would make things happen any faster. He felt like an axe was poised over Sacred Valley, and he was leisurely watching it happen.

He had gotten no sleep at all last night, cramming every minute with preparation.

"They will," he said. "If not to me, then to the army of Golds we're bringing to their door. I can't imagine we'll have to prove *something's* coming."

They had both lived through the rampage of the Bleeding Phoenix, and in their experience, Dreadgods were only slightly less subtle than the heavens collapsing.

"Plenty of room in here for your family," Yerin pointed out. "Even if they each bring a friend and their biggest dog."

Lindon looked to the illusory display rising from a script-circle, where an image of a purple cloudship floated. One of Charity's evacuation fleet.

As promised, there were two dozen ships lined up behind him. In one night. Even after a battle between Monarchs.

The Sage of the Silver Heart kept her word.

"If anyone will listen to us, we'll save them." There would always be a number of people who would stay in their homes no matter what he said, and presumably others who would try to escape on their own.

Outside of the clans and schools, there were a few isolated communities that lived in the wilderness at the heart of Sacred Valley. He planned to look for them, but if they really couldn't fly cloudships into the valley, it might be impossible to get everyone.

But he would do it.

This was what his power was meant for.

Lindon hesitated before squeezing back. Usually, when he tightened his grip on someone with his Remnant hand, it was because he was draining their soul.

She didn't react in disgust or try to pull away, which relieved him. Both for the obvious reason and because if she pulled away, she might forget her strength and pull his arm completely off.

"I plan to give Heaven's Glory a chance," he warned her.

Yerin didn't look at him, but she struggled with her response for a moment. "Some people, when they're drowning, you don't toss them a rope," she said at last. "They'll just pull you in with them."

"We don't need to take them with us," Lindon suggested. "We can give them a warning and then leave them to find their own way. It's no less than they deserve."

Lindon didn't actually expect resistance from Heaven's Glory, or much from anyone. With their current powers, Lindon would be surprised if they weren't *worshiped* in Sacred Valley.

But Yerin had her own reasons. If Heaven's Glory had cost him someone who had raised him like a father, he wouldn't feel particularly generous toward them either.

After hearing from Charity about the suppression field around the valley, he and Dross had done some research overnight.

He had to admit, he was a little bitter that the reason Sacred Valley had remained so weak was because of an external force. He had assumed it was a matter of isolation and poor education. Now that he knew there was a ceiling keeping his people from growing beyond Jade, he had to fight back some anger.

Partly at whoever had built the field in the first place, and partly at the Akura clan.

Was it their responsibility to relocate this one group of people in a distant corner of their empire? Not necessarily, but he still blamed them for not trying.

Then again, at least they were helping now.

The reports he and Dross had found disagreed about how intense the effects of the suppression were, but from Lindon's own experience, he suspected it would lower them down to Jade. Whether that process took hours, days, or even weeks was a matter he supposed they'd learn later.

But even if they were pushed down to Jade the second they stepped across the boundary, they would still fight like monsters compared to the natives.

Yerin watched his thoughts cross his face, radiating obvious concern. "I don't want to..." She trailed off and started again. "I'm not one to..."

She threw up her free hand in frustration. "Bleed me dry, I'm just going to say it. Don't kill a bunch of Jades."

Little Blue, curled up sleeping on the console, lifted her head and gave Yerin a wide-eyed stare.

Lindon felt much the same.

He leaned back so he could study her face more clearly. "Apologies, but I thought that was a talk I'd have to have with *you*."

She avoided his gaze. "Can't imagine what you mean," she muttered.

Little Blue let out the ringing of a bell, and through their newfound bond, Lindon felt her astonishment.

"You don't use a Monarch sword to swat flies," Yerin continued. "Not even when they bite you."

She stared off into the distance, and her hand gripped his so tight that he could feel the weight of her strength warping reality ever so subtly.

He matched it, mentally thanking Crusher for the donation.

"Are you sure?" he asked quietly.

"I hate them," Yerin whispered, and there were tears in her eyes. "He never touched them. Never cut them with so much as a word, but they hated him so much. They threw their own bodies at him. Didn't care if they lived, so long as he died. And there wasn't...I couldn't..."

She breathed deeply and wiped her eyes with a thumb. "But they're not worth half a glance from me, and I'll be dead and buried before I give them more than they deserve."

He had thought much the same about killing Jades, but it warmed him to hear that coming from Yerin. She had been thinking ahead, and had decided to treat the weak with compassion. Even considering what they'd done to her.

Lindon wasn't sure he'd be able to do the same.

It wasn't as though he had any attachment to the Heaven's Glory School himself, but he still put his free hand around her, pulling her close. "Thank you," he whispered into the top of her head.

She tilted her head up to him, cheeks tinged pink.

"He's watching," Lindon said.

"We'll be old and gray before he stops."

Lindon kissed her.

From the corner of the room, where they had both sensed him, Eithan sighed. "It was more fun when I could sneak up on you. I'll have to step up my veils."

Lindon separated from Yerin, focusing on his breathing technique to slow his heartbeat. "Have you heard from Ziel?"

Ziel owned the cloud fortress next to theirs, a blocky castle sitting on a plain blue cloud. He was supposedly traveling with them, but Lindon had heard nothing from him in the day since he'd joined them.

"He's fine." Eithan buffed his fingernails on the hem of his pink-and-purple outer robe. "You may have noticed, but I significantly helped his spiritual recovery. It cost me quite a bit, you know. Time. Materials. Expertise. *When* did I perform this costly task, you ask?"

"Stone-certain we didn't," Yerin said.

"To begin this story, we have to go all the way back to Tiberian Arelius' creation of—" Eithan's head snapped to the front, where a ship on a deep purple cloud was slowly looping around to join the procession behind them.

Eithan pointed. "That ship! Watch that ship."

Alerted by his tone, Lindon and Yerin both focused on the

cloudship. Yerin extended her perception, which crashed over her target like a storm-tossed wave. He doubted there was any spiritual power that could escape her notice.

By contrast, Lindon's own perception was a trickling creek. His perception was better-trained than the average Underlord, but it wasn't necessarily any more powerful.

However, he could sense things she couldn't.

He did not feel the strong will from the ship that suggested a Sage or Herald was involved. Instead, he felt the faint, flickering willpower of the ordinary Golds crewing the cloudship. Their will was diffuse, unfocused, barely there.

Between Yerin's overwhelming scan and his own, which could see into a different spectrum, he doubted they missed anything. They still couldn't sense the physical, only the spiritual, but something that had no power of madra or will wouldn't be a threat.

"Harder," Eithan insisted. "Look harder."

Lindon did, trying to pierce a veil he had missed the first time. Yerin pushed down with her scan so much that the Golds stopped in place, cycling their madra in resistance, spirits filling with fear.

A scan could be uncomfortable, but it wasn't threatening. But Yerin's power was an entire dimension higher than a normal Lord's, much less these Golds.

Only when he was sure there was nothing on the ship did Lindon become certain that Eithan was just distracting them.

"What happened to no secrets?" Lindon asked in a dry tone.

Eithan gave him a white, beaming smile. "A *surprise,* Lindon. A surprise. I assure you, you'll be glad I distracted you very soon."

Yerin started to extend her perception to the rest of their own cloudship, to find whatever Eithan had tried to hide from them, but Eithan leaped in front of her. "Don't you want your surprise?"

Yerin slowly let her scan fade. "...I do," she admitted, in a tone of heavy reluctance. "Got a creeping fear you're about to teach us a lesson."

"In a sense, can't you learn a lesson from anything?"

Lindon reached out with his own perception.

"It's not a lesson!" Eithan hurriedly added. "This is a *fun* surprise. Just relax, all right? Be casual."

In Lindon's mind, Dross began to whistle.

Lindon returned his attention to Charity, who had expanded the Sky's Edge gate into a broad screen of darkness. He didn't fully understand the impressions he was getting from his new senses, but the portal *felt* like it was almost complete.

"We can still make it, right?" Lindon asked.

For the sixth time since Fury's ascension ceremony the night before.

Eithan patted him on the shoulder. "The Wandering Titan is known for its inevitability. Not its speed."

Out the front windows, Charity lowered her hands.

Shadows covered the doorway to Sky's Edge, stretching up through the clouds in a pillar of darkness. It was a miniature version of the column that had taken them from the Blackflame Empire to the Night Wheel Valley.

The portal to Sky's Edge was complete.

Charity lifted from the cloudship dock, hovering in the air. She reached into another pool of shadow on her left: her void key.

A weapon flew out, slapping into her open hand. It looked like a short one-handed sword with a curving blade, but a closer inspection showed that it was a silver sickle. It buzzed and blurred to both Lindon's eyes and senses. This weapon operated on many levels, its powers interacting in a complex web that he couldn't begin to unravel.

Charity gestured to their ship, and Lindon activated a script-circle that lifted some of their protections.

A purple-and-silver owl appeared on the scripted wooden panels in front of Lindon.

Little Blue gave a loud peep and scurried up Lindon's arm.

"This portal cannot convey the Titan," Charity's voice said from the owl. "I will travel through first. If I do not return or contact you in five minutes, this way is closed to you."

A steel shield drifted out from her void key, and she snagged it from the air with her left hand. The shield was a heavy slab of metal half the size of her body, worked into the image of a twisted, grinning, monstrous face. The steel face twisted in place, alive and snarling.

Charity hefted the shield as though it were hollow, holding it to her left and her sickle to her right. "When I give the all-clear, you may follow me. Only fly where I direct you, but accelerate as quickly as you can. The Titan has more tempting targets, but if he does notice you, I will send you back through the portal immediately."

Lindon braced himself, cycling pure madra and controlling his breathing. Here they were, ready to return to Sacred Valley. The time had come.

Nothing between him and his family except a Dreadgod.

[Could be worse!] Dross pointed out. [There could be *two* Dreadgods.]

A ribbon seemingly made of liquid steel flowed out of Charity's void key, tying her hair into a short tail. That was a sacred instrument of concealment and banishment, with powers of stealth and space.

Now that Lindon could feel concepts like that, he had to wonder what his new perception could do for his Soulsmithing.

But that was an idea he could save for later.

"Prepare yourselves," Charity said. She raised her weapons, cycling her madra through her three sacred instruments, and Lindon felt the intimidating will of the Heart Sage equipped for war.

Then she flew through her column of darkness and vanished.

[Our escorts are ready. Or at least they *say* they are. Could be lying.]

Lindon steadied himself, running his madra through the cloudship. It had its own stored power, and was fueled partially by ambient vital aura, but he primed everything and powered as much of it himself as he could.

Propulsion constructs warmed up, the cloud beneath them bobbed a bit in the air, and scripts flared to life all over their portable island.

Only seconds after Charity had vanished into the darkness, her owl spoke again. "Clear!"

The fortress rocketed forward.

Shadow swallowed Lindon. As he'd experienced before, his senses vanished as though he no longer had them. He and Dross were left completely alone, floating in a sea of soundless, lightless black.

Only this time, the oblivion wasn't quite so absolute.

[Is this what spatial travel feels like?] Dross asked in awe. [It feels...twisty.]

Now that Lindon could feel the distortions in space, moving through a portal like this gave him a new perspective on transportation. Even when he'd pushed his way through space himself, he hadn't felt the substance he was working with so clearly.

Inside the darkness, it felt as though he was traveling through a tunnel. Someone had bored a hole, and they were in the middle of sliding through.

As Dross had mentioned, it felt almost like the tunnel was spinning around them, like they were being *twisted* somehow.

One impression was clear to Lindon: Charity hadn't done this herself. She had taken an existing route and widened it, but she couldn't create something on this scale on her own.

Akura Malice must have made the original doorway, leaving Charity to expand and direct it. He suspected she'd done the same thing all the way back in the Night Wheel Valley.

The realization encouraged him. He was starting to feel the edges of a Sage's power.

He would have plenty of time to experiment with his own powers, once Sacred Valley was safe. Once everything was over, and he had the rest of his life to explore...whatever he wanted.

The world faded in, and every protective script in the

fortress blazed against his spirit. They were holding against crushing spiritual pressure.

And the sky was dyed gold.

They were emerging above the fortress that the Seishen Kingdom had raised at the border of the seaside town called Sky's Edge. At least, they were supposed to. There was very little left to recognize.

The town was gone.

Most of the landscape was unrecognizable after the battle between Heralds, with chunks blown from the surrounding mountains and ravines carved in the ground.

Only a few features remained to remind Lindon of the town he'd left so recently, including the tower-sized sword of Frozen Blade madra plunging into the ground.

And the Dreadgod that cast its shadow over everything.

Though they had left the Ninecloud Court in the morning, the sun hung low over the western sea, behind the Titan. And as drastically as the surroundings had changed, they were hardly worth noticing next to the Wandering Titan itself.

The humanoid giant of dark stone knelt at the edge of the ocean, its feet still partially submerged in water. Its shoulders scraped the clouds, a turtle's shell rising behind it like a shield strapped to its back.

It was a titanic statue come to life, a walking mountain. Its face looked like a man's, but expressionless, as though it had indeed been carved. Stone eyes glowed slightly, dull yellow.

Just by its presence, it dominated the earth aura for many miles. Dozens. Maybe hundreds.

Lindon wasn't about to extend his perception to check.

Its control of earth aura was so intense that it stained the sky gold, as the Bleeding Phoenix had once enhanced blood aura until the sky blazed red. All around, mountains buzzed as though quivering in anticipation.

The Titan's arm was plunged into the earth up to the elbow, and it knelt almost motionless as it fed.

Power moved up its arm slowly but steadily, like sap in a tree. A hunger technique. Intense aura flowed into the

Dreadgod, but not just aura. Lindon couldn't be certain without a direct scan, but it felt like even physical materials were consumed by that hunger.

He had sensed the Wandering Titan directly before, perhaps closer than anyone other than a Monarch. He didn't want to try it again.

Stone and dirt slowly collapsed around the Titan's arm, falling inward like a sinkhole.

Lindon's right arm quivered, its madra resonating with the presence of the Dreadgod, but his will was stronger. The limb never left his control.

The Titan appeared almost motionless, except for its tail. It resembled a monkey's tail that stretched out into the ocean perhaps half the length of the Dreadgod's body, and it lashed back and forth like an impatient snake.

With every motion, it carved waves from the sea, sending walls of water splashing up to the sky.

Lindon put the Dreadgod to their backs and directed all his power to propulsion.

Their fortress shot forward.

Scripts inside manipulated aura to control air and gravity, preventing the inhabitants from pitching over at the sudden acceleration. He followed one of Charity's owls due east, chasing silver-purple tailfeathers.

He felt like he'd bared the back of his neck to a hungry tiger. It could strike at any second.

Sweat trickled down his back and his forehead, and he kept his eyes flicking between the window to the front and the projection of the Titan behind them. It didn't seem to be bothered by their presence, maintaining its hunger technique, but they wouldn't be out of danger until they were many miles away.

Charity stayed behind, next to the portal, as purple cloudships emerged one at a time and streaked after Lindon.

The Heart Sage floated in place with her shield raised, vigilantly watching the Dreadgod. It wasn't long before half the cloudships had emerged from the portal, trailing behind them like ducklings.

Lindon's fear started to fade into exhilaration. They'd made it. They were okay.

Then, in an inexorable tectonic shift, the Wandering Titan stood up.

Madra cycled through the Dreadgod's body, and in the same instant, their cloud fortress was buffeted in midair. The protective scripts screamed as they resisted an invisible assault, the projection construct fuzzing into chaos so that Lindon could no longer see what was behind them.

They were under attack.

It took all of Lindon's spirit to steady their flight and recover their path. He couldn't believe they'd survived one hit, but that certainly wasn't all the Dreadgod could do. That must have been only a glancing blow.

When the projection construct recovered, it showed them the Wandering Titan again.

It had turned a bit to its right, taking one long, slow stride that crossed the entire space where Sky's Edge had once stood.

Lindon's breath came in tight gasps.

The Dreadgod hadn't noticed them at all.

Shields of purple-and-silver madra faded from where Charity had protected the string of ships behind them, but for one cloudship, even her power hadn't been enough. It was a pile of smoking rubble on the ground below as though the Titan had swatted it out of the sky.

But the Wandering Titan had done no such thing. It had only cycled its madra for a brief instant. That was no more threatening than taking a breath.

They had taken casualties from the Dreadgod doing *nothing.*

Lindon felt the lost lives of the unknown Akura Golds settle on his conscience like a lead weight. He hadn't known anyone on the cloudship's crew, but they wouldn't have been here if not for him.

As they flew into the distance, leaving Charity watching the colossal monster behind them, the tension slowly deflated. In its place was only cold dread.

No one spoke.
There was really nothing to say.

第四章

CHAPTER FOUR

Miles of countryside slid by beneath their fortress, but not fast enough for Lindon.

If he took Eithan's cloudship, he could reach Sacred Valley much faster, and he'd considered it. But that would mean abandoning the Akura cloudships to defend themselves.

While he and Eithan and Yerin could handle anything they might run into on the way, the Golds might be in trouble without their help. They were under his protection, so he wouldn't leave them.

No matter how much he wanted to run ahead.

It was possible he could prepare the people of Sacred Valley for the arrival of the cloudships if he arrived first, but it was equally possible they wouldn't listen to him on his own. There was little he could actually do to help without the fleet of Akura cloudships.

Home seemed to linger in Lindon's head, as though he could feel Sacred Valley burning like a signal-flare in the distance. He even felt Orthos' presence more strongly than usual, so the turtle must be in the western Blackflame Empire somewhere.

Orthos' spirit only made Lindon's impatience worse. Was Orthos all right? Was he in the path of the Dreadgod? Would he be able to make it away in time?

Lindon had very little need to direct the fortress once their course was set—they were simply making a beeline for Sacred Valley. But he still left Dross at the controls just in case.

[I will take this responsibility as an honor and a privilege. Don't worry about anything! Think about it as if you yourself were still...oh hey, I don't know that mountain. Should we stop for a minute and check it out? Just a second, honestly.]

"Stick to the course."

[Right, yes, of course. Sticking to the course. Unless there's a *really* good reason not to.]

Lindon almost took over the panel again.

He needed something to distract him, so he turned to Yerin. "I haven't had a chance to take a tour of the fortress yet. How about you?"

"Sensed it, haven't seen it. Let's walk it out."

That brightened Lindon's mood. He wasn't certain he would be able to enjoy himself with the destruction of Sacred Valley looming over him, but at least a tour with Yerin was something to look forward to.

He felt Eithan's presence before the door to the second floor swung open, and Yerin was already yelling. "Not a candle's chance in a rainstorm."

Eithan slowly edged around the door, so they could see one eye and half his grin. "We could say that I'm taking my own tour. Separately, just...right behind you."

"Do you really need a tour?" Lindon asked. "Can't you see everything from here?"

"I can. Everything. Always. But the others aren't so lucky."

At first, Lindon assumed he meant Ziel. The word "others" only penetrated when Eithan let out a pulse of pure madra that was clearly a signal.

Shadow madra eased its way free as someone dropped a veil. "We made it!" Mercy cried from downstairs.

"Couldn't tell you why that needed to be a surprise," Yerin muttered.

Eithan beamed. "Isn't it more fun when you don't know?"

Mercy rushed up to the second story, immediately leaning on Suu to give them an apologetic bow. "I'm *so* sorry, I wanted to warn you, but Eithan's message said he wanted it to be a surprise..."

Lindon was more than happy to have Mercy along, but he remained a little puzzled. "Apologies, Mercy, but doesn't your family need you? Not that you aren't welcome aboard!"

"You can have Eithan's spot," Yerin agreed.

Mercy rubbed the back of her head and laughed awkwardly, in a manner that reminded Lindon vividly of Fury. "Yeah, well, Pride made it clear that he doesn't really need me around. With Uncle Fury gone, there's a lot to be done, but I just...I told Aunt Charity they'd have to get along without me for a few days. This might be my last chance to go out with you all, you know? I want to see it through to the end."

To the end.

At a certain point, Mercy was going to have to separate from the rest of them. She had responsibilities to her family that the rest of them didn't.

But he was still glad she'd delayed that moment again, so she could be with him when he put Suriel's vision of the future to rest. When he settled everything, once and for all.

He dipped his head in a silent apology, but next to him, Yerin snorted.

"Last chance? You think they'll haul you back from spending time with the youngest Sage and some kind of tiny Herald? Your mother's going to shove us down your throat until you're sick of us."

Mercy ran over to throw her arms around Yerin's neck, but Lindon's attention was grabbed by a bright ring. It didn't sound like a bell so much as the resonant sound of a script activating.

"I believe Ziel wants in," Eithan put in, though Lindon had already sensed the same thing.

Dross activated a projection construct, showing the image of Ziel slumped at their front door. A gray cloak hung from his shoulders, and he was leaning with his forehead against the doorframe, his emerald horns digging into the wood.

With a halfhearted shrug of his spirit, Ziel activated the alarm script again.

"You can let him in, Dross," Lindon said.

[I'm just savoring the moment. You know, if I didn't open the door, he couldn't get in? That means I, and I alone, have the power to determine his fate. It feels good. What do you call that?]

"Megalomania?" Eithan suggested.

[Oh, I like that word. Let's go with that.]

A ring echoed through the home again, and this time Lindon manually sent his own madra through the correct scripts.

Below, the door unlocked.

[Everything I do for fun, you just...crush it.]

"Since everyone's here, we might as well all go together," Lindon said. He had to admit, the presence of the others was keeping his mind off of Sacred Valley. They left together, meeting Ziel halfway up the stairs.

"...I could have waited for you outside," Ziel muttered.

A "cloud fortress" was just a type of cloudship designed for permanence rather than mobility. The Skysworn city of Stormrock was technically a cloud fortress, though on a much larger scale. Lindon thought of them as flying islands more than cloudships.

Though he had spent quite a bit of time negotiating extra speed for his. The basic navigation and propulsion systems came standard on all cloud fortresses produced by the Ninecloud Court, but Lindon had found that many of the exact features were up for negotiation. As long as you were willing to give up a few things.

No sooner had they left the house than Eithan asked, "So,

first things first: what did you decide to name this place?"

Yerin gestured to Lindon with open hands, offering him the chance to explain.

"Well, the only cloudships we've ever spent significant time on were Stormrock and your *Sky's Mercy*," Lindon said to Eithan. "But many of our memories on Stormrock were unpleasant, and we didn't want to presume to name the island after Mercy."

"Aw," Mercy said, disappointed.

"Ultimately, we felt that this place was a result of our good fortune," Lindon continued.

"And we'll take all the luck we can scrape up," Yerin added.

"So we decided to call this fortress *Windfall*."

It had taken hours of off-and-on discussion to land on that name, and Lindon was proud of it.

"Eh," Ziel said.

Mercy clapped her hands. "I like it! But are you sure you want to have 'fall' in the name? Seems like tempting fate, you know?"

"I'm just sad that I wasn't consulted," Eithan said with a sigh. "Since I own a third of the island, I think I should at least get a vote..."

Yerin's sword-arms bristled. "You take your third and walk it half a mile off the edge, and you can call it what you want."

"It's a good name," Lindon insisted.

Mercy nodded eagerly. "It is! I'm sorry I said anything, it's a good name."

"How about *Eithan's Rest*?" Eithan suggested.

Yerin jabbed at him with her sword.

He slipped to the side and regarded her oddly. "You *do* know I'm teasing you, right? You have to know that at this point. I find this violence disproportionate."

"Oh, I know," Yerin muttered. "It just scrapes me raw more than usual. Couldn't tell you why."

Eithan leaned in close to examine Yerin's eyes. "Ruby?" he asked.

"Her too."

She stabbed at him again, and he danced away.

Most of the open space on *Windfall* was rolling grassland. Lindon had initially tried to fill in the open space, but he needed the cycling mountain to be far enough away from the house that its aura wouldn't interfere with any scripts, and Lindon had been more concerned with the inner workings of the cloud fortress itself than the features on the surface.

Their first stop on the tour was the miniature mountain that would serve as their aura source. It resembled a rocky peak of dark stone, but only twice as wide as the house and half again as tall. The top belched smoke and flame, and if Lindon opened his aura sight, he could see the powers of fire and destruction braided together in coils of black and red.

Altogether, it resembled a smoldering volcano, though Lindon would eventually have to replace some of the natural treasures inside to keep the aura balanced.

There was a flat lip of stone beneath the peak, around which the Blackflame aura flowed. It would be the perfect place to sit and cycle, and if Lindon hadn't been dragging a party along with him, he would have tried it out immediately.

At the base of the mountain, an open cave yawned, filled with razor-sharp silvery protrusions like teeth. The air glistened with sword aura, but as Yerin saw it, her face fell.

"Bleed me, I'm going to need a source of blood aura now."

"We can find a natural treasure," Lindon assured her.

"Or just kill a man whenever you need to cycle," Eithan suggested.

Besides the fields of grass blowing in the wind of their passage, the second feature to catch the eye was a short purple-leafed tree with pale bark emerging from the plains.

"This is an orus tree," Lindon said when they reached it. "It's native to Sacred Valley. This one is three hundred and fifty years old, and it was raised in rich aura, so its spirit-fruits are stronger than usual. You'll get to try some for yourself once we..."

He trailed off as Ziel plucked the lowest-hanging fruit from the tree and took a bite. Lindon hadn't even tasted it yet.

But it wasn't as though he had asked them not to eat any fruit. He was the host here; it was his responsibility to see to the comfort of his guests.

"How is it?" Lindon asked.

Ziel shrugged.

As they passed another stretch of open grass, Eithan explained Lindon's plan to add a Soulsmith foundry to the space. Lindon couldn't recall ever having mentioned those plans aloud.

Then they came to a crystalline pool, shaded by broad-leafed bushes so tall they were almost like trees.

Little Blue splashed around in the pool, dipping beneath the surface to slide through the water like a fish. Faint blue spirits followed in her wake, spinning and swirling around after her.

She turned and gave a wave as she saw them approach.

"This is an area of balanced natural aura," Lindon said. "Sylvan Riverseeds are born in places like this, and they're said to be soothing for the soul." He could already feel a sort of invisible pressure lighten just by standing nearby, though he wasn't sure if that was relief from the constant presence of aura or if he was just starting to relax.

"Oh, you made her a little place to play!" Mercy said excitedly. "She's going to love this!"

Little Blue chirped agreement, but Lindon's cheeks grew hot.

"I mean, well, yes, but there are practical considerations too. Unintelligent Sylvan Riverseeds can be used in Soulsmithing, and there are certain plants that can only grow in a neutral aura environment."

Little Blue ran up a bush and leaped into the pool, landing with a tiny splash.

Half a dozen other splashes followed her a moment later, from the handful of pure scales that Eithan had just cast into the water. The lesser Riverseeds swarmed around them, eating the Forged madra one nibble at a time.

"Fatten, my little piglets!" Eithan cried. "Feed and grow strong!"

Popping her head out of the water, Little Blue gave a disapproving peep.

That brought them to Eithan's third of the island, which Lindon had been looking forward to. Eithan had a single tree and a hut of his own, but most of his territory was covered in cultivated rows of plants of all shapes and sizes. Lindon saw something that he even thought might be an artificial hive for bees.

"So this is where you got the herbs," Ziel said. "Squeezed them out of the Ninecloud Court."

Lindon was only too happy to learn more. "Your turn, Eithan. Can you tell us what these do? That one looks like a cloudbell bush."

"Ah, but who cares about my modest garden when we have yet to explore your luxurious home?"

"I do," Lindon said.

"Didn't you say you got the Ninecloud Court to install a redundant series of security scripts in your cloudbase? I would *love* to hear more about that."

Lindon wasn't fooled. Eithan just didn't want to talk about his plants. Either because he had some kind of plan in mind... or, equally likely, because he was feeling lazy and wanted to put Lindon on the spot.

Probably both.

On the other hand, Lindon would take any excuse to talk about the modifications the Court had made to the functions of his fortress. "We'll come back later, then. All fortresses come with a set of security circles to disperse hostile madra, but by giving up some features on the surface, I was able to get them to include a more thorough—"

Eithan threw up a hand. "Oh no! Danger! We'll have to pick this up some other time!"

Lindon extended his spiritual perception and soon found a flock of venomous presences approaching one of the Akura cloudships.

As Eithan and Mercy sprinted off, Lindon turned to Yerin. "I know he timed that."

"He can bleed and rot. Let him swat the birds down without us. You can tell *me* about the scripts. And the... constructs."

She was being completely sincere, but she didn't care about the way the fortress worked. He would be explaining for his own sake.

"No, let's go get some birds."

"You're stone-certain?" She'd stay if he wanted her to, and he knew that.

When he nodded, she shot off after the other two, stopping in midair to turn around and wave for him to follow.

Ziel stood motionless next to Lindon. The edges of his cloak fluttered in the wind. "I'd like to hear about the scripts," he said.

Lindon sighed. "Thanks."

The ships floating on their purple clouds stretched out behind Lindon and the others. He reached the edge of his own flying island in time to see a flock of beasts approach.

They were toxic green, leathery birds that trailed dull fog. The birds and the trails behind them gave off a powerful sensation of venom madra.

Mercy had already drawn her bow, shooting down the closest three birds before they could get even close to the cloudship they were targeting. Even so, the rest of the flock—several hundred strong, at least—didn't falter.

"I hope they're not intelligent," Mercy said.

Eithan put his hands on his hips. "If they are self-aware, and they're still attacking this convoy, they're certainly not very intelligent. In fact, how about a game?"

Yerin was about to race off and leap over to the next cloud, but Lindon saw her freeze at the suggestion.

"We've all advanced in some way recently," Eithan went on. "I'm sure I can't be the only one longing for a chance to stretch my muscles, spiritually speaking."

Mercy shot down another bird that was ahead of the group. "One technique apiece?"

"For educational purposes only! I wouldn't want to suffer the embarrassment of having all bets placed on me."

"And you're *sure* they aren't intelligent?"

"From their behavior, I would say no. Also from their spirits, the fact that they're screeching to one another instead of speaking, and from my extensive education. I'm familiar with this species, and they're slightly less intelligent than rats. Meaner, too."

"Then it sounds fun! I'll go!" Mercy seized the string of her bow in her black-gloved hands, pulling it back and Forging a dark arrow onto the string.

Her spirit surged, and the full power of an Overlady was focused onto the bow. Lindon felt the techniques layering onto the arrow one at a time, until the missile quivered with unreleased force. The dragon's head, now at the center of the bow, hissed angrily. Its eyes flashed violet.

Her will was clearly focused on the bow, but Lindon sensed something beyond that. Something he wouldn't have been able to put his finger on before, and that he still couldn't quite define. It felt as though her arrow was reaching a dimension beyond the physical. That was authority, he supposed, but only a whisper of it.

Mercy released the string.

The arrow whipped up a whirlwind, tearing up the grass as it blasted through the air. The sunlight flickered in its wake, as though the missile stained the air with darkness in its passing.

When the arrow impacted the flock, it tore a hole in the mass of birds.

Then it exploded into dark tendrils.

Strings of Shadow lashed out from where they'd been compressed into the arrow, snatching up nearby birds with oily arms and pulling them together. A mass of sealed, fused-together birds tumbled down through the sky.

Mercy held her hand over her eyes to peer down. "Thirty-four! I think I could get fifty next time."

The flock had noticed, and was wheeling around in the air to re-focus on Mercy's location.

"Looks like you'll get your chance to try," Eithan said, "but only on your next turn. Yerin, you must be dying to try out the extent of your powers."

"Like a starving dog," Yerin said fervently. Her hair blew over her shoulder as she stepped up, pulling a black-bladed sword from her new void key. Netherclaw had originally been chosen as the weapon of her Blood Shadow, but now it suited her madra better.

Now that she and Ruby had merged. Which still made Lindon feel...strange.

Yerin's gleaming scarlet sword-arms withdrew, sliding like liquid into her back. The lock of red in her hair shone slightly as she focused on the tip of her sword.

And if Mercy had added a touch of weight to her arrow with her will, this attack struck Lindon's new senses as though Yerin had strapped a boulder to the end of her weapon.

Silver-and-red light swirled around the blade, and Lindon recognized the technique she was forming: the Final Sword.

But it was rougher, less controlled than it had been before. Not only had they developed it as a pure sword technique, but she had lost the connection to the Sword Icon that had made the technique possible before.

Ruby had figured out a version of the Final Sword with her blood madra, but it had always been weaker than Yerin's. It looked like now, Yerin was compensating for her lack of experience in the aspect with pure, overwhelming power.

In fact...

Just from standing next to Yerin, Lindon was buffeted with force beyond the physical. Ziel had planted his feet, Mercy held a hand across her eyes, and Eithan cleared his throat.

"Yerin, perhaps we might reconsider—"

She unleashed the technique.

A beam of gleaming red-chrome energy shot forward from Yerin. It was rough like a river, not as smooth as black dragon's breath or sword-shaped like the former version of the Final Sword. It sounded like a long, ongoing explosion. Like a roar.

And it was wider than Yerin's entire body.

Where the passage of Mercy's technique had uprooted some grass, this one tore up a large trench of soil. The flock of venomous birds was aimed at their fortress, and the Final Sword speared through the center of them all.

Those in the middle were wiped out, of course, but power flickered out from the edges of the technique, whipping nearby birds from the air like lashes of liquid lightning.

After only a few seconds, the technique faded.

There was only one bird left, a straggler that had flapped heavily beneath the rest of its brethren. It let out a loud squawk and hauled itself in the other direction.

Yerin gave a long, low whistle as she limbered up her shoulder. "Now *that* fits like a good sheath."

Eithan ran a comb through his messy hair. "That, ladies and gentlemen, illustrates the strength of Heralds. While Sages focus their willpower outside of themselves, to make changes to the world directly, Heralds focus it inwardly. They enhance their own power beyond all limitations."

Lindon was already thinking about how he might do something similar. "And that involves fusing with your own Remnant?"

"Might be my ears are still tickling, but it *sounds* like you're thinking about trying it," Yerin said.

"Are you trying to be the world's first Underlord Monarch, Lindon?" Eithan asked curiously. "You know, if you tried that, I'm fairly certain you would fail *before* your spirit and body collapsed in on themselves like a burning house. But I've been wrong before. Maybe you'd make it all the way to the collapse."

Mercy gestured with Suu, which was now back in staff form. "That brings up another good point. Why are you still an Underlord, Lindon?"

In fact, Lindon had almost advanced the night before.

When he had found out they were supposed to stay in the Ninecloud Court one night longer than he wanted to, he had planned to immediately advance. He was sure he had his revelation figured out, and if not...well, the insight required to touch the Void Icon *had* to be harder than the one to reach Overlord.

But he and Dross had done some research.

"We looked up what Charity told us," he said. "If we're heading into the suppression field around Sacred Valley, it's more of an advantage *not* to advance. The more advanced you are, the more it takes from you."

"I will expect you all to carry me like a rescued princess," Eithan declared.

Mercy gave Lindon a sympathetic look. "Was it hard for you?"

"Had to take his void key," Yerin said. "Starting out, he told me not to let him advance, but he kept talking excuses. 'What if I don't get another chance?' 'I just want to see if I have the revelation right.'"

"I wasn't lying," Lindon protested.

Dross' voice came into their heads, muffled slightly by distance. [Yes, he was.]

"Lindon's cruel deceptions aside, it looks like we're out of targets," Eithan said. "The rest of us will have to wait for another chance."

Some of the targeted cloudships had strayed from the line, scared off either by the birds or by the massive technique Yerin had used to defend them.

Mercy moved to the edge of the cloud and straddled her staff. "I'm going to go check on the ships."

"I'll come," Yerin said, shoving her black-bladed sword back into her void key. "Have to show them I don't have claws. And I want to see if I can make the next ship in one jump."

"You definitely can," Mercy began, but Yerin had already leaped with enough force that she kicked up dirt behind her.

Mercy followed after, flying on Suu, leaving Lindon alone with Eithan.

Ziel had wandered off to lie down by the pond, and it looked like he had fallen asleep instantly. The Sylvan Riverseeds were dancing on his face.

Eithan was waiting expectantly, so Lindon continued as he would have if Eithan hadn't been present. He focused on a nearby clump of grass, steadying his breathing, gathering not madra or soulfire but his will.

"Hold," Lindon ordered.

The blades of grass froze, locking in place as the others bent and bobbed in the wind.

Lindon maintained his concentration, but the working of will released before he was ready, his clump of grass joining those around it once again.

"I don't know how to practice," Lindon admitted. "Dross has explained everything he knows about Sages, but it isn't much."

Most of the more useful works about Sages were either restricted or too strange for him to understand. Sages didn't usually write about their own powers to other Sages, after all.

There had been old attempts by Sages to pass down their powers to disciples, but they had never worked, and Lindon hadn't been able to find any of those attempts in his brief search of the Ninecloud library the night before.

Eithan stroked his chin. "Picture, if you will, a building with many floors. Each floor is higher than the last, and each supports the one above it. These floors are the laws that govern our existence. At the bottom, the foundation, are the physical laws."

He clapped his hands together. "It's no less complex than the other systems, and it forms the basis for all of them, but it is superseded by the level above it." He spread his palms apart slightly to reveal the blue-white coin he'd Forged. "Madra."

A snap, and the madra disappeared. "With madra, we can break and bend and overrule the physical laws that would have bound us otherwise. Within certain rules and limits, of course. If we continue this analogy, soulfire is the staircase between the madra system and the next level up. At which we exert our wills to control the world directly."

He gestured to the clump of grass that had once been frozen. "That is the level on which you and Yerin now operate. While she has enhanced her ability to add willpower to her own actions, you can take actions that you previously could not."

Most of that, Lindon had already figured out to one degree or another, but he peered into the Archlord's face for a long time, looking for...something.

After facing Eithan's pleasant smile for too long, Lindon finally asked the question that was on his mind. "How do you know? How do you know any of this?"

Though Eithan had promised to stop keeping secrets, Lindon still expected an evasion, but Eithan squinted up into the sky and spoke.

"I was an advisor to the Monarch Tiberian Arelius."

Lindon wondered if the "deflection" had been nothing more than a simple lie. "You were an Underlord."

"I didn't advise him on advancement, obviously. But I have always had an...instinctive grasp of the underlying theory behind the sacred arts, you might say. They found early on that I could handle dream tablets far beyond my age or advancement level, and that I could draw from them more insight than anyone else."

Eithan swept blowing hair out of his face and gave Lindon a serious look. "You can call me what you like. Genius. Savant. Prodigy. Virtuoso. Once-in-a-lifetime intellect. I've always preferred that people look *beyond* who I am on the inside and really appreciate my gorgeous exterior."

For a moment, Lindon was overwhelmed by the knowledge that Eithan had been advisor to a Monarch. He'd been trained by someone who had studied at the highest levels. Lindon wished he'd known earlier; he had missed *so* many chances to exploit Eithan's knowledge.

Then again...

Eithan had always *acted* like he knew everything. And he had been careful about doling out knowledge a little at a time.

Maybe this wasn't so much of a surprise.

Lindon pressed his fists together and bowed lightly. "Gratitude for your instruction."

"I would appreciate it if you would keep that between you and the others, by the way," Eithan said. "Most of my kinsmen don't even know."

"Pardon, but why not?"

"You know me, Lindon. I love nothing more than keeping a low profile."

第五章

CHAPTER FIVE

[INFORMATION REQUESTED: BIRTH OF THE MAD KING.]

BEGINNING REPORT...

King Daruman the First was not only the ruler who united his Iteration, but who ushered it into an unprecedented golden age.

As a warrior, he was unparalleled, bringing his sword against the planet-eaters that plagued his people.

As a king, he was known both for his wisdom and his character. Even his rivals found no blemish on his integrity, and his people were fed, happy, and educated. *"To seek the knowledge of Daruman"* became a common saying meaning "to seek absolute truth."

He ruled for three hundred years, until he felt the realm was stable enough to pass on to a successor. Not to a child of his, but to a candidate that proved themselves before the realm.

After watching over the second generation of his unified world, he ascended to seek more worlds to save.

The Abidan considered him perfect. Even as they delved into his mind, they found a humble hero, a ruler who wanted nothing more than to improve the world.

So they gave him worlds to improve.

Daruman was chosen by the second Court of Seven to be among the first of what they were to call their Executors. He was an agent of the Abidan, but un-bound to the Eledari Pact, so he was not prevented from interfering in Fate.

He and his four peers were sent to dying worlds, to defeat the threat from the inside and prolong the existence of the Iterations as long as possible.

At first, the experiment was declared a success.

None of those first-generation Executors were less than perfect, world-level combatants with sharp minds and resolute hearts. They saved world after world, allowing the Abidan to expand their Sectors and add more and more Iterations to their protection.

Daruman was not the first of those Executors to go rogue.

In fact, he was the last.

Though each Executor was mentally evaluated upon their return from a mission, their futures could not be read. By the nature of their work, they diverged from Fate regularly, so they became a blank spot for the Hounds.

When the first Executor fled Abidan control and took over a distant Iteration, the Hounds were shocked.

When the second gave up and lay down her weapon with no warning, they became alarmed. They enacted new restrictions on their remaining three Executors, as well as more extensive screening.

But by nature of their role, Executors were beyond Abidan monitoring while on assignment. The third Executor burned to the ground the world he was meant to save, insisting there was no other way to be rid of corruption.

Daruman chased down that peer himself, performing the execution with his own sword.

The fourth Executor attacked the Abidan. She tried to bring them down for reasons that were never clear, falling at the hands of Razael.

By this point, trust in the Executors was nonexistent. A second generation had already been appointed, but these had been raised from birth by the Abidan themselves, designed to be perfectly competent and loyal. Daruman was already considered a relic of an embarrassing past.

But he continued his role, finding satisfaction in saving world after world.

Until he found a world he couldn't save.

Oth'kimeth, the Conqueror, had been considered a Class Two Fiend when it broke through Sector Control to invade an Iteration. As it began to feed, its designation was raised to Class One, and Daruman himself went to stop it.

He spent fourteen years in that Iteration. Due to the influence of chaos, records of that time are spotty, but it is generally agreed that he found Oth'kimeth to be a much greater opponent than expected.

Finally, he determined that the only way to truly remove Oth'kimeth was to seal the Fiend inside a vessel capable of resisting its temptation: himself.

Daruman returned to Sanctum and reported to the Judges the successful completion of his mission. He invited them to inspect him for any signs of chaotic control. He was still in command of himself, and he could turn the powers of a Class One Fiend to good.

The Court of Seven, unable to read his fate, nevertheless knew that no one could resist the machinations of a Class One Fiend forever. They weren't even certain that he hadn't *already* been corrupted.

They imprisoned him in the depths of Haven.

There he languished for centuries, in the heart of the Abidan prison-world. Just him and Oth'kimeth.

Four hundred and nineteen years after his imprisonment, he escaped. It was a feat never equaled before or since in the history of the Abidan.

Daruman was pursued by the second Makiel, who chased him into the depths of the void. To the horror of the Court, Makiel was defeated, suffering damage to the origin of his existence that would eventually cause him to pass on his mantle.

In a message broadcast to all of Sanctum and several others of the Abidan core worlds, Daruman declared the Abidan tyrants and swore himself to their destruction. He gathered up his original Iteration, forging it into the great fortress Tal'gullour, and moved to another world.

The people were all that mattered to the Way, he said, not the Iterations themselves. The Abidan were nothing more than jailers, and he would gather power until he brought them down.

It was determined by the Court that his will had been corrupted by Oth'kimeth, and he was given his new title: the Mad King.

SUGGESTED TOPIC: THE FALL OF THE SECOND-GENERATION EXECUTORS. CONTINUE?

DENIED, REPORT COMPLETE.

Mount Samara's ring was beginning to fade when they arrived at the eastern entrance to Sacred Valley.

The white halo around the snow-peaked mountain was dimming with the approach of sunlight in the pre-dawn twilight, and Lindon found his eyes growing wet.

Every night of his life for fifteen years, he'd slept under the light of this mountain. Now, it filled the windows of his own personal cloud fortress as he returned.

Lindon blinked his vision clear. He'd been preparing for this moment since the day he'd left.

So he couldn't mess it up.

Tell the ships to land and power down, Lindon ordered Dross. *Send as many Golds after us as they can spare. We expect to return within three days.*

Dross obeyed, though he added his own commentary on the likelihood that they would *actually* be back within three days.

The Akura ships set down at the border of the blackened forest that represented the Desolate Wilds, but Lindon and the others flew closer to Mount Samara.

They couldn't get any closer than the smaller mountains and hills surrounding Sacred Valley, as the aura was starting to fade already. Lindon's spiritual sense couldn't penetrate far beyond this point, and he was having to spend more and more energy to keep their cloud base afloat.

Next to him, Eithan shuddered. "It's like diving face-first into a bucket of ink. I'm afraid my bloodline legacy won't be of much use to you from here on, although I myself will be the same emotional asset and source of courage as always."

Ziel slumped against the wall, his horns glowing slightly green as he regarded the view in front of them. "It'll be more uncomfortable than you think."

As Lindon landed on a snowy mountainside within sight of Mount Samara, he risked a moment of inattention to glance back at Ziel. He hadn't considered what entering a power-dampening boundary formation would feel like to Ziel. It could dredge up years of painful memories.

Then again, he hadn't considered Ziel much at all. Eithan was the one who had recruited the man, not Lindon. Ziel had linked his cloud fortress to theirs as they approached, so it would land as they did.

"If you would like to stay here, I would be grateful to have someone reliable protecting our base," Lindon suggested.

"I'm used to having my power suppressed. But if you want me to stay here, I'll stay here."

Lindon doubted he was just being polite. As usual, he sounded as though he wouldn't care if the ship exploded around him.

Mercy was standing right up against the window, staring at Samara's ring. "It's beautiful! I can't wait to see it from up close!"

"Only get that view if we stay at Heaven's Glory for the night," Yerin pointed out. "Which I'm not panting and begging to do."

From Lindon's shoulder, Little Blue gave a ringing agreement.

Lindon found it hard to pry his view away from the shining loop of light, but he forced himself to move. He ran his spiritual sense through the beautiful, roomy void key now hanging from his neck. His wintersteel badge hung on the outside, a lump of cold power that resonated as his attention moved over it.

Dross was ready. Little Blue was ready. Orthos was an indistinct lump in the back of his mind, a comforting heat. Lindon hoped for the chance to track him down after this was over.

"Let's go."

Lindon led the way out of the fortress.

Mount Samara was the highest, most visible mountain around them, but that didn't mean the surrounding peaks were small. This distance had taken them days for Lindon and Yerin to travel, even with the help of a Thousand-Mile Cloud, though they had been injured and weak at the time.

Now, they all had Thousand-Mile Clouds except Mercy, who followed them on her staff. Yerin pulled one from her own void key, which Lindon still wasn't used to. She had gone without a void key for so long, but neither the Winter Sage nor the Akura clan would have let the victor of the Uncrowned King tournament go without.

It would be a few minutes before the Golds were organized enough to catch up, but some had already begun gathering up on their own clouds. It seemed like they would be accompanied by about a dozen Golds from each of the remaining twenty-three ships, and Lindon was filled with gratitude at the sight. He would have to thank Charity when they returned.

He had plenty of time to think, because their Thousand-Mile Clouds moved at barely a crawl.

Their clouds couldn't reach anything close to full speed out here. This was within a few miles of the spot where Lindon had opened his Copper sight for the first time, and he remembered how vivid the colors had seemed. They had been almost blinding.

When Lindon opened that sight now, the colors were muted and washed out. Barely there. As though the vital aura had been squeezed dry.

Is this the Titan? Lindon asked Dross in alarm. The only bright colors came from the veins of yellow earth aura beneath their feet, which were clearly affected by the approach of the Dreadgod. Had he somehow used hunger madra to drain all the other types of aura into the ground?

Dross coughed politely. [The veins of earth aura staying bright are an effect of proximity to the Dreadgod, yes, I'm sure that's true. But everything else...uh, I think it's just like that here. Not that it isn't beautiful!]

Weak.

This place was so weak.

Their Thousand-Mile Clouds functioned, but they were built for areas with much higher concentration of aura. It might actually be faster to run.

Even so, these clouds were incomparably faster than the one that had originally taken Lindon and Yerin the other direction. This time, they covered that distance in under an hour.

When they arrived, Lindon withdrew his cloud into his void key and landed in the snow. He could feel the boundary in front of him. The border of Sacred Valley.

The vital aura was weak for miles around, certainly. When he crossed that line, it wouldn't be any weaker. But *he* would be.

There was an emptiness past this point. A vampiric power. A hunger.

Eithan put his hands on his hips and looked all the way up, as though regarding an invisible wall. "Well, isn't this unpleasant?"

"I'd rather walk headfirst into a sewer," Ziel said as he plunged into the field without hesitation. He didn't change visibly as he passed the barrier, trudging through the snow at the same rate.

Mercy leaned close to the invisible force, sticking her arm

in and shuddering, pulling it out. "How long before it affects us, you think?"

"Sooner we're in, sooner we're out," Ziel called back.

Eithan tucked his hands in his pockets and strolled across. "Since I can't watch everyone, I expect all of you to describe your actions in detail at all times. Start now."

[I'm looking through Lindon's memories for the path in,] Dross reported. [Looks like it's a straight line.]

"Excellent work, Dross."

Lindon didn't remember pulling out Suriel's marble, but he ran the warm glass through the fingers of his left hand. As usual, its steady blue light was a comfort.

Yerin had stayed back with him, and now she brushed the red streak of hair out of her eye and looked up at him in concern. "Won't blame you if your steps aren't steady."

"This route will take us past the Ancestor's Tomb," Lindon said quietly.

Yerin darkened. "Yeah." She gripped the hilt of the sword at her waist.

The one she'd pulled out of the Tomb.

She carried her other blade, Netherclaw, in her void key now. This one, she always strapped to her belt.

Side-by-side, they crossed the boundary into Sacred Valley.

Despite Lindon's expectation, it wasn't much different on the other side. He could feel something tugging on his power, as though his spirit had sprung a leak, and at the same time his senses were smothered by a blanket.

But neither were as uncomfortable as he'd imagined. At this rate, it would take days to weaken his spirit enough to make a difference. He might evacuate his family before he fell to the level of a Jade.

Yerin swayed in mid-step, and he reached out a hand.

He barely caught her before she collapsed.

In less than the blink of an eye, he had dashed out of the boundary formation, landing in a spray of snow. Yerin gasped as though she had emerged from deep water, her red eyes wide.

Lindon still clutched her in both hands. "What happened?"

"Too much," she said, still breathing heavily. "It took too much."

Only a few yards away, Eithan looked down at himself. "Hm...I see. The boundary siphons strength away rather than suppressing it as a veil would. I suspect I have only... let's say six or seven hours before I'm down to the level of a Jade. That will be a novel experience."

Lindon thought he saw the problem. Since she merged with her Blood Shadow, Yerin's body had partially fused with her spirit. Draining her madra would affect her physically even more than the rest of them.

"You can stay on *Windfall*," Lindon suggested. It would be better anyway, he realized. She wouldn't have to relive the trauma of losing her master by revisiting the site of his death, and she would still get to meet his family when he brought them out.

It made sense, but leaving her behind felt wrong. She had started this journey with him, and she should be with him to see it end.

He didn't expect her to agree. In fact, he expected her to leap out of his grasp and plunge straight into the Valley, heedless of the consequences.

Instead, she stayed where she was and turned to Eithan. "Am I going to fall apart if I head back in there?"

It was Ziel who answered. "Do Remnants form in there?"

"They do," Lindon confirmed.

"Then you'll survive. No matter how close to a spirit you are, you'll still be more solid than a Remnant." He pointed to Little Blue, who was leaning over Lindon's shoulder to regard Yerin with concern. "If *she* doesn't fall apart, you definitely won't. But..."

He let the silence stretch out until Lindon wondered whether he was thinking of the right words to say or if he was waiting for someone to ask a question.

"...a stable Herald wouldn't be affected as much as you are. Don't know if it's because you didn't hit Archlord first, or..."

He slumped in place, as though speaking so much had exhausted him. Eithan swept a hand toward him. "I concur with the champion of the Wastelands. This suppression field has revealed an imbalance in your body and spirit. I could speculate as to why, but it hardly matters now."

"So I'm *not* falling apart," Yerin said.

"You will not. In fact, I suspect you won't get any worse than you are now. Barring grievous injury, of course."

Yerin met Lindon's gaze. "My master dove into this with eyes open."

Lindon nodded and started to carry her back in. The second she weakened too much, he would leap free of the field again.

She cleared her throat. "Still got two feet."

Reluctantly, he lowered her down, although he supposed there wasn't much risk in her walking under her own power. Even an ordinary Overlady wouldn't be killed by falling flat on her face.

She squared herself and clutched her sword as she crossed the boundary, and her stride faltered almost immediately. Lindon reached for her, but she stopped him, taking a few deeper breaths to steady her spirit.

"Shaky as a two-day calf," she reported, "but on the sunny side, at least it won't get worse."

If Lindon's spirit felt as though it had sprung a leak, hers lost power like a shattered wine bottle. In less than a minute, she felt as weak to his perception as a Lowgold.

Lindon couldn't make himself comfortable with that.

"If we end up in a fight..." He trailed off. He didn't want to remind Yerin of her master's death, but on the other hand, the Sword Sage must have knowingly weakened himself by walking into this boundary field. He had risked his life and died for it.

And now they were repeating the same mistake.

Yerin raised her voice, addressing everyone. "I'll break easier than a glass egg in there. I'm aiming to head in anyway, but I know that's a rotten deal for you. Anybody wants me to stay here, I'll do it."

She sounded completely sincere, which once again surprised him a little. Part of him had expected her to insist that she could protect herself, no matter how weakened she became.

But that's what she would have done when she was here before. It had been a long time since then. She had seen and done more in the last few years than many sacred artists did in their entire lifetimes. She had grown.

Like he had.

"Of course we'll take care of you!" Mercy exclaimed. She sounded slightly offended.

Eithan beamed. "I have been covering for you all this time. The only difference now is that you're aware of it."

Ziel shrugged and kept walking farther in.

Even Little Blue gave an encouraging peep.

"You know I—" Lindon began, but she cut him off.

"I know," she said. "Sun's moving."

Together, they moved toward the Heaven's Glory School. Two or three hundred Akura Golds had massed behind them, but still hadn't quite caught up yet. Dross reported that they were passing out communication constructs.

Before Lindon had gone far, they came upon a simple gate. It was only a six-foot-high wall of bricks, enough that any sacred artist could clear it easily, but a squat tower rose behind it.

There were no constructs anywhere that Lindon could feel, but a few basic scripts could repel madra and keep out Remnants when activated.

Each of them hopped over the wall with ease, even Yerin.

[This is perfect! There's no one here. Maybe they'll just let us walk on through.]

Lindon knew that he and Yerin had only escaped so easily the first time because her rampage had already drawn most of the combat-capable Heaven's Glory members back to the school. This post should have been manned.

What had drawn them away this time?

They saw nothing and no one else remarkable until they

reached a massive block building standing proudly in the snow. It was covered with scars where it had been glued back together, piece by piece. Scars marred a mural of the four Dreadgods that hung over the entrance, wiping out the top halves of the Wandering Titan and Weeping Dragon.

The last time Lindon had seen this place, it had been a pile of rubble. The Heaven's Glory School must have spent a fortune in repairs. All things considered, they had done a good job.

The entire building had been fenced off and surrounded by boundary flags that would activate security measures if anyone broke the perimeter. The fence was just some wire stretched between wooden posts; a symbolic barrier to alert people to the presence of the script more than any real obstacle.

And to Lindon, that fence was the most substantial part of their defenses.

He walked up, gathering pure madra in his finger.

He flicked out the smallest amount of madra he could gather. It was no more a true technique than a mouthful of grass was a meal.

The script protecting the Ancestor's Tomb shone too bright and then flickered out, overloaded by his power so that the runes tore apart the flags into which they were woven. Sparks of essence rose from some buried constructs that had burst under the influx of power.

"Do you draw satisfaction from kicking over the sandcastles of children?" Eithan asked.

Lindon ignored him, looking to Yerin, whose gaze was locked on the Tomb. She adjusted the position of her sword-belt too many times.

"Do you want to go in?" Lindon asked.

She shook her head. "Can't stray off the trail. Once there's no Dreadgod about to fall on us, *then* we can track my master's footsteps."

"Ah. I retract my objection," Eithan said. "Kick as many sandcastles as you wish."

A stranger stumbled out from behind a nearby tree, golden technique forming.

[Heaven's Glory!] Dross shouted. [Get him, Lindon!]

The young man who faced them with a technique glowing in his outstretched palm wore an iron badge etched with an arrow. An Iron Striker. He wore a white and gold outer robe with a red sash; the uniform of a Heaven's Glory disciple.

Lindon felt a strange fondness when he saw that outfit. It really *had* been a long time.

"They're back!" the Iron shouted. He released a line of scorching golden light at Ziel.

The former Archlord kept on trudging through the snow.

Heaven's Glory madra splattered against him like spit against a boulder. His clothes weren't singed.

Ziel didn't even glance at the man.

Lindon was frozen in shock by the Iron's words. They had *recognized* him? How?

He had been gone for more than three years. He wore completely different clothes, had advanced seven times, and even lost an arm. In the first place, he had never known many people in the Heaven's Glory School. Odds were, he had never met this man.

[Maybe it's the badge?] Dross suggested.

While he *was* wearing the badge of an Unsouled, it was made from wintersteel, not wood. Had that one symbol really been enough to alert this lone Iron? Was Heaven's Glory that vigilant against his return?

Yerin, who had physically changed at least as much as he had, shouted to the Iron who was staggering back from Ziel in shock and fear. "Oi!" she called. "How do you know us?"

The Iron turned to run, but *turning* was as far as he got.

Eithan was already behind him, standing out from the white surroundings in his stylish cyan silk. He smiled and seized the Heaven's Glory disciple by the upper arms. "Relax, new friend!"

The stranger made a whimper like an animal with its leg caught in a trap.

Yerin strode over to him and snapped her fingers to get his attention. "Hey. Do you know my face? Did you draw swords on me before?"

There was anger in her voice, but Lindon was certain she wouldn't hurt him, no matter how he answered. The Iron was only sixteen or seventeen, and he paled and shifted as though looking around for help. "This one didn't see you! This one only happened to witness your friends."

"More of them in the trees," Ziel reported, as he continued to walk toward the sparse forest.

The hostage's eyes lit up. "This one would be honored to take you to the school's Elders. If you cooperate, this one is certain we could come to an understanding."

For the first time, Lindon witnessed what it was like to hear someone weaker than him speaking too humbly. It was painful.

He felt a moment of shame for his past self.

"You mentioned that you saw our friends," Eithan said casually. "Which ones? We're very friendly people, you see."

Lindon wondered if some of the Akura Golds had somehow managed to make it into the valley ahead of them.

"From...from last time," the Iron said. He spoke uncertainly, as though he hadn't understood the question. "The rest of you. Apologies, this one doesn't know which ones, he saw only techniques of light and fire."

"Who do you think we are?" Mercy asked curiously.

"You're...aren't you...exiles from the Wei clan?"

In the woods, techniques flashed as the other Heaven's Glory sentinels attacked Ziel.

Lindon grabbed the front of the boy's outer robe and forced him to meet his eyes. "You were attacked by exiles from the Wei clan?"

He waited for the boy's furious, desperate nod.

"When?"

"Two...no, three? Three days ago!"

An old man's commanding voice split the air. "Release him!"

Lindon looked up to see Elder Rahm, keeper of the Heaven's Glory School's Lesser Treasure Hall, facing them with his chin raised and his back straight. He stood with the vitality of a younger man, though he had to be at least eighty.

Four oblong security constructs floated behind him, a pair over each shoulder. Their tips shone with gold as they kindled their Striker techniques.

A jade badge hung on his chest, showing off a scepter emblem. A Ruler.

Lindon glanced behind the Elder to see Ziel's increasingly distant figure shrugging off a barrage of Iron-level techniques.

Lindon released the Iron disciple, taking a few steps closer to the Heaven's Glory Elder. He pushed his fists together, white knuckles against those of flesh, and dipped his head.

"Greetings, Elder Rahm," Lindon said. "It has been too long."

Rahm's eyes crawled from Lindon's face down to his badge before realization dawned on him. It quickly turned to disgust.

"Unsouled. I would take your hand for robbing me, but it looks like someone stole that pleasure from me."

Lindon wanted to be offended by that, but he probably deserved it. While the Heaven's Glory School had worked against him, Rahm had not started as an enemy himself. But Lindon and Yerin had robbed him anyway.

"How did you contact the other exiles?" Rahm continued, the constructs behind him growing hotter. "Or do they give you your orders?"

"I understand you've suffered from an attack, but we're not here to hurt you. We've actually come to help."

Elder Rahm's jaw slowly dropped. He looked as though he had just heard the most stupid statement he could possibly imagine.

"I was too lenient on you before, Unsouled. I've since learned better than to expect honor from a Wei."

He triggered all four of the launcher constructs. They

began gathering light and heat into points as the Striker bindings within them cycled power. There was a delay of only about a quarter second between Rahm triggering the constructs and their techniques activating.

In that gap, a finger-thin bar of Blackflame sliced all four of the weapons into pieces.

Four explosions echoed behind Elder Rahm before his eyes had a chance to widen.

Lindon closed the distance between them in a blink. He didn't use the Burning Cloak. He didn't need it.

"Tell me about the Wei clan exiles." Lindon said. He kept his voice quiet and firm, but he didn't want to sound too threatening.

The threat was already clear.

Elder Rahm's eyes moved to the others behind Lindon. "Did you really come from outside without knowing anything?"

"Apologies, Elder," Lindon said, "but answer my question."

Rahm's wrinkled face melted slightly, into an expression that was one degree below a smile. "The heavens hate you. Perhaps I was right all along to pity you."

"Clearly we're wasting our time," Eithan said with a sigh. "He has a soul of steel. We will never get any information out of him. We'll have to search for clues on our own."

There came a squawk and a handful of screams as Ziel pushed over a tree with one hand, sending the Irons hiding in its branches falling to the ground like overripe fruit.

Elder Rahm stiffened and gave Lindon a hateful glare. "Kill me. My Remnant will—"

"Oh, what great fortune!" Eithan cried. "A clue!" He was peering into the trees, shading his eyes with one hand. He leaped away, trusting the others to follow.

Mercy and Lindon both turned back to Yerin, who looked from one to the other. "Not at my peak, but I'm not *really* made of glass."

[Hey Mercy, why don't you keep her company?] Dross suggested, without letting Yerin in on the conversation.

[Lindon can carry the old man. Oh no, wait, I'm sorry he'd rather carry Yerin. Of course, that was stupid of me. *You* take the wrinkly one.]

"I'll take him," Lindon hurriedly insisted, tossing Elder Rahm over one shoulder. Rahm struggled and protested, but he was a Jade. He'd be fine.

"Then I'll—" Mercy began.

Yerin vanished in a flash of white light.

Her Moonlight Bridge could take her almost anywhere, but Lindon sensed her only a little ahead. She'd used it to catch up with Ziel.

"I really want one of those," Mercy sighed.

They caught up in seconds. Once they did, Eithan and Ziel stopped holding back and picked up their speed toward the Heaven's Glory School.

In only a few more minutes, they arrived. Yerin appeared in their midst at the center of a bright white light. She was breathing heavily, but using that Divine Treasure to transport shouldn't have been so tiring. There could be restrictions to using it while in Sacred Valley, but Lindon moved that question to the back of his mind.

Elder Rahm had shouted almost the entire time as they moved at speeds greater than he'd ever imagined, but now that they had come to a stop, he was quiet.

Lindon remembered the Heaven's Glory School—at least the part he'd seen—as a collection of smooth rainstone buildings that always glistened as though slick with water. Each living area was next to a small garden with a tree and a few colorful plants.

All of that...*had* been here, once.

Someone had treated the Heaven's Glory School like the Dreadgod had treated Sky's Edge. Buildings were sheared in half as though by massive swords, rubble was scattered around by explosions, and great gashes had been torn in the ground. Lindon didn't see a single garden that hadn't either been burned completely away or at least scorched.

Heaven's Glory apprentices with copper, iron, or even

wooden badges scurried everywhere, in the middle of construction projects. Some stood on ladders to repair rooftops, others filled in holes with dirt, still others patched up windows or carted away debris or re-planted trees.

And every one of them froze as Lindon and the others emerged abruptly from the woods.

One long pause later, they all screamed and ran, scurrying every direction and shouting for fighters to protect them.

Eithan walked casually up to the street that ran through the center of the school, gesturing to the debris around him. "Lindon, what's your take on this?"

Lindon unceremoniously dumped Elder Rahm from his shoulder. The old Jade twisted and landed in a crouch. He tried to dash away but ran straight into Yerin's outstretched hand.

Weakened she may have been, but Rahm was still no match for her. Her fist tightened on his outer robe, but she remained stone-faced. As he recalled, she didn't have the same grudge against Rahm that she had against the other Jades.

What do you think, Dross? Lindon asked.

In Lindon's vision, piles of debris and some of the streaks on the ground glowed purple. It took him a moment to sort all the information Dross was sending him, but once he did, Lindon began to speak.

"Heaven's Glory was pushed back to this point. Their barrier was halfway made of Forged madra, and not all of it has been reduced to essence yet." He gestured to a pile of what looked like golden glass shards. "The rest was stacks of wood, half of which was cleared away, but the rest is over there." A pile of charred wood rested against a building to their right.

Lindon pointed down the street, to a building that was completely ruined. "The attackers got whatever was in there, then tried to force their way through this direction, but were forced back by Heaven's Glory defenders."

That story was told by the angle of the scorch marks and

the damage on the buildings behind them. Lindon didn't even need Dross to tell that someone had been using some serious Striker techniques, firing in this direction. They had sliced straight through stone.

"Did you see this from up there?" Lindon asked.

"I assure you, my abilities are significantly reduced compared to normal. You'll have to take my word for it. Now, what's your conclusion?"

"Please correct me if I'm mistaken, but it seems to me that someone raided the School from deeper in the valley, stole whatever was in that building, and was discovered either when they were inside the building or shortly outside. Then they pushed their way in this direction in an attempt to escape."

The attackers had tried to leave Sacred Valley. Interesting that, after getting what they wanted from Heaven's Glory, they had wanted to escape the valley completely instead of returning home.

"That would be my guess as well," Eithan agreed. "However, it *is* a guess. Deduction is not an exact science. It could be that these attackers became enraged and wished to inflict damage on the rest of Heaven's Glory, not trying to escape."

"Pardon, but then I would expect more damage to the buildings." Most were broken in some way, true, but the enemy techniques had clearly been focused onto the barricade. If the attackers had been interested only in inflicting as much pain as possible, they could have launched these destructive techniques in every direction.

Eithan waved a hand. "Certainly. I just think we ought to remember that there are many things we can't know."

An alarm horn blared in the distance, and shouts showed that Heaven's Glory warriors were on their way.

"Now, I wonder..." Eithan began, and Lindon didn't need him to finish.

Both dashed over to the rubble of the most thoroughly destroyed building visible.

It was actually one house back from the street, and whatever battle had leveled the rainstone had carved visible chunks out of the surrounding homes. This building had been larger than the others, similar to the size Lindon remembered of the Lesser Treasure Hall, but otherwise Lindon could glean almost nothing from its remains.

At this point, it was basically a rectangular pit filled with fragments of a diced building.

"If you already know what's down there, I would appreciate it if you would tell me," Lindon said.

Eithan grimaced. "Lots of grimy blankets, some destroyed tools, and a shallow sewer of human waste. I would call it a prison, but those aren't usually kept twenty feet from the main thoroughfare."

People. People had been stored here.

Lindon didn't like the picture that was forming. Someone had attacked Heaven's Glory from within the valley, taking *someone* from this prison and leaving the building in ruins, and had then tried to leave. But they'd been forced to retreat.

And it seemed like this person was an exile of the Wei clan. Lindon was beginning to feel sick, and he couldn't tell if it was his imagination or a premonition.

A Striker technique lanced toward Eithan's back, a streaking line of golden madra.

Lindon reached out and caught it on his right hand, absorbing the power into his hunger arm. He vented what he couldn't process, but it was pathetically little.

Eithan dipped his head slightly. "Thank you."

"Name yourselves!" A furious woman's shout came from behind them.

Lindon turned to see an old woman with a jade badge leading a contingent of about ten Irons.

[Twelve,] Dross corrected.

Lindon held both his hands over his head. "I apologize for our haste, honored Elder, but we come in peace."

"Liar!" Elder Rahm shouted from where he stood behind Yerin. "These are enemies of the School!"

"Strikers!" the new Elder commanded.

Five more streaks of light flashed out, all aimed at Yerin.

Lindon felt a spike of alarm and anger. Mercy instantly moved to cover Yerin, and the knot in his heart loosened, but they had still attacked instantly. As far as he knew, they could have killed her.

In a flash, Yerin vanished.

She reappeared next to the Jade woman, blade drawn, its white edge pressed against the elder's throat.

The Irons behind panicked, staggering back and preparing weapons...but none of them attacked, clearly unwilling to risk the Jade's life.

Yerin spoke while panting. "Now...would you bet we're here to talk, or draw blood?"

After another moment, in which she met the eyes of all the Irons, Yerin slid her sword away and back into its sheath.

The elder raised two fingers to her throat, felt no blood, and then lowered her trembling hand. "Guests don't usually sneak in to capture one of our Jades."

Lindon took over. "We came to warn you. There is a great disaster on its way. You may have already felt it: earthquakes, spiritual pressure, earth aura behaving strangely."

The elder gave one cautious nod.

"It is coming to destroy Sacred Valley. We can take you to safety, but you have to leave with us."

Her eyes narrowed. "What reason do I have to think this isn't a plot to destroy us?"

"Because we don't need to plot to destroy you," Lindon said simply. He kept his spirit wide open, his madra cycling slowly.

After a moment, her spiritual perception extended from her and ran through him in a soul-shivering scan. He allowed it.

Her sense was vague and weak, but she shook when she was finished. He almost didn't hear her whisper "*Gold?* All of you?"

Lindon hesitated.

"Sure," Mercy allowed.

Yerin gave a dry laugh. "You're short by a long mile."

"We're far beyond Golds!" Eithan declared.

Ziel just shook his head.

The Elder looked to all of them in clear confusion, returning to Lindon. He simply said, "Yes."

Rahm scanned them all, and each time, the shock in his expression grew.

"Forgiveness," the Jade woman said with a bow. "I was disrespectful. We should find a place to talk where we won't be on display to every peeping Copper in the school."

There was indeed a significant crowd staring at them, some close and some far away, with varying degrees of anger or fear.

As he looked around, Lindon caught note of a building he recognized. He pointed. "We can speak in the Lesser Treasure Hall."

The female elder's face twisted in confusion. "Forgiveness, but the Treasure Hall is crowded. And I'm sure nothing in there would catch the eye of a Gold."

"I would feel more comfortable if we were in Elder Rahm's home," Lindon explained.

"Elder Rahm oversees all three of our Treasure Halls. At least let me guide you to the Elder Treasure Hall, where we are better equipped to host honored guests such as yourselves."

Lindon realized he was pinching his void key and lowered his hand. "Let's start with the Lesser Hall," he said. "One step at a time."

第六章

CHAPTER SIX

Lindon remembered the Lesser Treasure Hall of Heaven's Glory as a wide hall packed with pedestals. Sitting on each pedestal, covered in transparent panes of glass-like Forged madra, were *treasures*.

As he entered now, years later, the first thing he noticed was how small the place was.

Yerin glanced around at the floor and ceiling. "Got the place all swept and shiny new." There was no trace of her battle with Rahm, which had destroyed much of the interior before.

Elder Rahm gave a harsh laugh as she dragged him along behind. "Such little damage was simple to repair."

His colleague entered after the rest of them, following inside only after Mercy, Ziel, and Eithan had joined them. She didn't bring any guards along with her, though she did position herself near the exit.

When they had all entered, the old woman bowed. "Apologies for the late introduction. I am Grand Elder Emara. I have not held the position for long, so please forgive me if my knowledge is lacking."

"You're forgiven," Eithan intoned.

Lindon glanced at a wooden card sitting next to a case carrying a scripted sword. *Flying Sword,* it said. *When powered by Iron-quality madra, this weapon is capable of levitating through vital aura and striking with the force of a real sword.*

He remembered it, though he wasn't sure if this was the same weapon. When he was here before, he had ached at having to leave this behind. It had no aspect requirement, so he'd wanted to keep it for later in his advancement.

Next to it was a dormant construct, a tiny humanoid puppet of wood and bronze with arms curled around its knees. *Guardian Puppet. Requires a constant infusion of madra, but can be controlled directly in combat.*

Aspect requirement: earth preferred.

Lindon didn't remember seeing this one here before. Would he have taken it, if it had been? How would that have changed his first battles?

On his shoulder, Little Blue peeped curiously. He wondered if she remembered starting her life here.

Down the row, he spotted a shining Starlotus bud. The spirit-fruit that had started him to Copper. There were scripted boundary flags, various weapons, one construct he suspected was a drudge, even two Thousand-Mile Clouds.

Looking out over it all, Lindon found it hard to remember what he'd seen before.

"Some of these are the products of our craftsmen," Grand Elder Emara explained. "Others we have commissioned or captured. They might not meet your standards, but these can become valuable to the development of our young Coppers and Irons. Elder Rahm can explain further."

"I gave them a tour once," Rahm said stiffly. "I won't be repeating that mistake."

With a smile plastered on her face, Emara sidled up to Rahm to whisper into his ear.

Eithan held up a hand. "I'm sorry to order you about in your own home, but why don't you speak so we can all hear? We wouldn't want any collusion against us, would we?"

They all could have heard the two elders whispering from next door, especially Eithan, so Lindon wondered why he would prevent the Jades from talking. If they thought they were speaking privately, they might reveal something valuable.

But the elders were only getting part of his attention. Most of Lindon's focus went to the Lesser Treasure Hall.

Ziel strolled back down an aisle. When he reached Lindon, he spoke under his breath. "This is junk."

That summarized Lindon's thoughts rather succinctly.

The flying sword had been made from cheap iron. Its edges were brittle, its script clumsily carved. Just by etching the runes more precisely, they could have improved the efficiency by half. And the script was so long and poorly designed that it would interfere with any other scripts added to the weapon; if they had chosen their runes better, they could have added two, maybe three more modifications to the sword.

The Guardian Puppet would shatter like dry twigs in front of the first real attack. And it couldn't function autonomously *at all*, so what good was it? If you were pouring your madra into something, you might as well just swing a hammer.

Even the Starlotus bud, toward which Lindon still felt some affection, now struck him as pathetic. Compared to a real spirit-fruit, it was like a drop of dew next to a glass of wine.

"At least there's some halfsilver," Lindon whispered back to Ziel, who dipped his head in concession.

Of everything in the hall, the only things worth Lindon's attention were the weapons of halfsilver and goldsteel. And even then, only for their raw materials.

In an afternoon of work, Lindon could fill this hall with more powerful treasures. Using only local Remnants and scrap metal.

He shouldn't have been disappointed, but he was.

If he got the chance, he still wanted to check out the Elder Treasure Hall, but he was much less eager to do so. He now suspected there was nothing of value in this entire school.

"...would like to hear more about this threat," Emara was

saying to Eithan. "If you have come here in the hopes of conquering territory, I can assure you, the Heaven's Glory School is more than willing to negotiate."

"Ah, but *we* are not the threat. How could we be? Look at our charming faces! No, the threat comes from the west." Eithan tapped the ground with the point of his shoe. "Surely you've noticed."

Emara and Rahm exchanged glances, and this time even Rahm looked worried. The earth trembled beneath them at that moment. It was almost gentle, but some of the objects rattled against their cases.

"We have spoken with the other schools about these signs," the Grand Elder allowed. "Our final decision has been delayed due to a cowardly attack by our enemies."

Rahm shifted to whisper into Emara's ear, but he was stopped by a sharp smile from Eithan. The Jade woman continued without seeming to notice. "Please, allow us the time to consult with the other elders when they return."

"And where are they?" Eithan asked.

"They have gone to punish our attackers. We needed every Jade we could spare to deal with their—"

"Wait!" Rahm shouted, but he was too late to stop her.

"—giant turtle," she finished. Then she turned a frown on Rahm.

Lindon's breath left him.

He'd felt Orthos' presence as they approached. Those Striker techniques that had cut rainstone buildings to pieces: black dragon's breath.

Orthos had come here. To his home. He'd attacked the Heaven's Glory School to get something.

Someone.

He had tried to escape...and failed.

Three days ago.

Yerin seized the woman by the front of her outer robe. "Where?" Yerin demanded.

"The...the camp at the base of the Fallen Leaf—"

"*Point!*"

The Jade extended a shaky finger pointing deeper into the valley.

Eithan closed his eyes, and Lindon felt his perception extend. He even caught the hair-thin strands of madra from his Arelius bloodline power, so subtle that ordinarily no one could detect them.

"I see where they passed through, but I can't..." He gave a frustrated grunt and opened his eyes again. "...I can't see them. I'm sorry."

"But you can confirm their direction?" Lindon asked.

Eithan nodded.

Lindon slipped Little Blue into his void key, opening it for only an instant. Then he took off running.

He shot away from the Heaven's Glory School with the full speed of the Soul Cloak, pure madra flowing around him in waves of blue and white.

There were other routes out of the School. Heaven's Glory covered more of the mountain than he had ever seen, but he only knew one way in and out. Fortunately, it was the route just ahead of him.

A soft pink glow came from the edge of the cliff he was sprinting towards. But it wasn't a cliff; the road headed straight for it.

It was the top of a staircase.

Lindon plunged into the cloud of dream madra without hesitation.

When he was here last, the Heaven's Glory School had called the process of climbing these stairs the Trial of Glorious Ascension. Those students who could make it up within a time limit were rewarded beyond those who could not.

To the mortal eye, it looked like a cloud of pink mist with hazy silhouettes flickering through. Sounds, strange and intimidating, drifted away from its heart.

To the spiritual senses, it felt like a concentration of emotions and dreams, a nexus of spiritual pressure and illusions. It was haunted by Remnants and natural spirits, either grown in this unique environment or cultivated by the Heaven's Glory School. As soon as he crossed the barrier, they turned hungry eyes to him.

Then they bolted.

As Lindon sprinted down the vast staircase, he felt dream Remnants fleeing from him in all directions.

The illusions generated by dream aura, both naturally and as part of the Trial's intentionally designed mechanisms, didn't fool him for an instant. He ran through a paper-thin image of a bloody warrior with axe raised, and didn't flinch at the sound of his mother crying for his help.

He had dissected his share of dream Remnants. They hunted with their spiritual perception as well as some purely mental senses that didn't translate particularly well to living humans.

Whether they sensed his thoughts or his spirit or his will, they wanted only to avoid his notice.

Dross had been quiet for a while, but he was roused by the lesser spirits around him. [You know, I've always wondered what it was like to have someone cower before me. I like it. It's a lot more fun than being the one cowering.]

The staircase switched directions a few times, but for the most part was a straight shot down the mountain.

Lindon cleared it in minutes, leaping some of the longer sections. He emerged from the fog of pink aura, turning and sighting on the location of the Wei clan. It was close, nestled roughly to the northeast of the valley.

Eithan emerged from the Trial an instant behind him, and Lindon slowed to allow him to catch up.

The Arelius pointed one finger in the direction of Yoma Mountain. "That's where they headed, but they could have changed course."

If they really were heading to the base of the Fallen Leaf School, their route would take them *past* the Wei clan, not through it. Then again, the Heaven's Glory members hadn't said they were after the Wei clan, but rather Wei exiles.

Lindon flared the Soul Cloak and pushed his speed.

To his surprise, he quickly left Eithan behind.

Eithan's Path didn't have a full-body Enforcer technique, though he had never known Eithan to need one. This was the effect of Sacred Valley's suppression field.

He was starting to feel some effects himself, but as an Underlord, he would be drained far more slowly than Eithan the Archlord. To his spiritual sense, Eithan already felt more like a Truegold.

Which, he realized, was the weakest he'd ever sensed Eithan.

Lindon cut his speed. He wouldn't be any good without a guide, though it grated on him to slow at all.

Eithan grimaced. "I'm not used to people slowing down to let me catch up."

"I don't prefer it either. Have you found them yet?"

Mercy reached them, flying on her staff, though she lurched and bobbed unsteadily in midair, the aura too thin to support a smooth flight. "Do you know where we're going?"

Eithan ducked a tree branch that extended over the path. "They passed through here, but it won't be long before you'll be able to see farther than I can."

Lindon had extended his own spiritual perception before Eithan had said anything. Since leaving, he'd kept his spirit wide open.

Orthos' presence smoldered in the back of his mind.

The turtle didn't feel any closer now than he had before. Lindon was getting no direction, no clear emotion. It still felt like Orthos was a hundred miles away.

Were they going the wrong direction?

He had to trust in whatever Eithan saw, but he hated how little they knew. What if the Heaven's Glory Elders had misled them? What if the giant turtle who had fought them wasn't actually Orthos?

If everything was as it seemed, and a group of Heaven's Glory fighters had gone after Orthos, then Orthos would be in battle soon. He would give some signal, and Lindon would feel it.

Unless the curse of Sacred Valley interfered with their contract more than he suspected. Maybe Orthos was fighting *now*, and this was all Lindon could feel.

Dross tried to reassure him. They were doing the best they could with the information they had. But nothing helped his worries.

Until he felt what he was looking for.

Orthos' presence went from a smoldering coal to a dark, blazing torch. Hot anger covered a layer of cold fear, and it was all suffused with grim determination.

Lindon felt the moment when Orthos sensed his presence too.

Relief. Urgency. Pure joy.

Lindon couldn't tell where Orthos' feelings ended and his own began.

And now he had a direction.

"Follow me," Lindon ordered.

He filled himself with the Path of Black Flame, and the Burning Cloak blasted him onward.

Wei Shi Kelsa had failed everyone.

Heaven's Glory burned tents and sliced open boxes as they cut their way across what had once been the camp of the exiles that had sheltered her. There were hundreds of them, along with at least a dozen Jades, and they cut down stragglers and those too old or sick or injured to run. There was no mercy, only a burning, golden advance.

This was her fault.

It was her failing that had led her to be captured in Heaven's Glory. If she had been more skilled in the Path of the White Fox, they would never have been caught. If she were stronger, as strong as Orthos, then they could have won the fight. If she were smarter, she would have stopped them from tracking her back here.

She looked down over the camp as Heaven's Glory marched onward. Most of the exiles had escaped into the hills at the base of Yoma Mountain. Her father was among them. And her mother.

But they were caught between a tiger and a pack of wolves. The Fallen Leaf School wouldn't protect them, and this mountain was their home. The best they would do would be to hand the exiles back to Heaven's Glory.

Her father was with those fleeing up the mountain, but she had stayed back on this hill to watch the attack.

Her three allies—maybe the three most powerful people in Sacred Valley—stood with her. And none of them could do a thing.

Orthos grunted and hauled himself to his feet. The huge turtle's leathery black skin was wet with his blood. His left eye was swollen shut, he favored his left foreleg, and his spirit was weak. He was running on his last drops of madra, after having practically dragged her back here.

"Go," the turtle said, his voice like a gentle earthquake. "Hide with the others. I will thin their ranks."

Jai Chen stepped up on his other side, and her eyes were full of tears. She was a small woman, at least compared to Kelsa and her family, and she looked...soft. In every sense of the word. Eyes, skin, hair, hands, demeanor. Soft.

But she had fought at Kelsa's side, and soft didn't always mean weak.

She raised a trembling hand to place on Orthos, but his shell was radiating heat, and she couldn't touch him.

Her brother spoke softly to Kelsa from within the scripted red bandages that covered his head. "We should head up the mountain to the Fallen Leaf pass. All of us."

Kelsa grabbed his outer robe and bowed her head. She couldn't see his face even if she looked up, but she was about to make a shameless request, and she didn't want to see disgust in his eyes.

"Please, stay and fight. This one begs you."

Over the last week, she'd seen him in battle. If he and his

sister and Orthos chose to fight with her, maybe they could resist even these overwhelming numbers. They could hold a pass, or strike at them and retreat, or...something.

She was already in their debt. They had risked their safety for her, a stranger, and she couldn't repay them. Now, they weren't strangers any longer, but she hated to ask for any more.

Jai Long's voice sounded awkward when it wasn't cold and distant. "Kelsa, this is...hopeless. Come with us. I promise you, I can get your parents out."

"...I can't."

Kelsa released him and took a deep breath, squaring herself. She looked him evenly in the eyes. "This is my fault." Behind her, she felt the heat of Heaven's Glory madra like a wildfire. "I will pay the cost of my choices, but I would be grateful if you would look out for my parents as you leave."

"Fine." Jai Long's icy tone was back. He turned to Orthos. "And you?"

Orthos nudged Jai Chen with his head, sending her stumbling closer to her brother. "Go. They have no dragons fighting for them, so I say they're outnumbered." The blood running down his leg turned the dirt to mud.

"Very well, then. Die with honor, turtle."

"You as well, human."

They traded nods before Jai Long left, pulling Jai Chen behind him. She mouthed an apology to Orthos, and the pink serpentine dragon-spirit floating over her shoulder gave a long, mournful flute note.

But they both left.

Kelsa didn't blame them.

They had done more for her than they needed to. They weren't family. She had been embarrassed to ask for their help in the first place, and they were well within their rights to refuse.

She rose to her feet as gold light speared down from the heavens and incinerated the tree stump her father had used as a table for his game board.

"Okay. How can we do the most damage?" she asked.

Orthos looked at her with his one good eye and started to chuckle. "I don't need a Jade standing beside me."

"You're Jade too, for now," she pointed out. "And this is my mess. It's only fair that I clean it up."

The turtle squared himself on all four feet, including the injured one. Red light and black smoke rose from his shell. "What makes you think there will be any left for you?"

He unveiled his spirit.

And immediately froze.

Kelsa knew something was wrong, but she couldn't figure out what it was. She cycled her madra and extended her perception, trying to figure out if he was under attack or if he'd seen something else coming.

He began to laugh.

Not the grim chuckle of a moment before, but full-bellied, joyous laughter.

He had gone insane.

"He's here," Orthos said.

Kelsa was not following this at all, but Heaven's Glory had spotted them. Already hands and weapons were launching techniques in their direction, and she had to shelter behind a nearby tree. "Who?" she called.

The turtle didn't answer her, as chuckles shook his body. "Hold on for a little longer, girl. This battle is almost won."

No matter how Kelsa turned it in her mind, she didn't understand his confidence. No matter who came for them, they would be reduced to Jade, just like him.

But she held on to that tiny, flickering hope for all she was worth.

On the slopes of the mountain above them, green light flared. Sacred artists in the uniforms of the Fallen Leaf School shoved at the wave of fleeing people. Trees and vines came to life, pushing them back, trapping them.

At least the school hadn't started slaughtering the exiles, but it was the next best thing. Fallen Leaf had denied them shelter, leaving them to die.

Despair choked her, but it was nothing compared to the terror she felt when she turned back.

Heaven's Glory was already upon them.

Four Jades had abandoned their meticulous march, dashing out ahead of their fellows to focus on Orthos.

The man at their vanguard was in his forties, with silver-winged hair and a stern expression. He gestured one arm that had been scarred and mangled, and a scripted sword flew at them with the speed of an arrow.

Orthos breathed black-and-red fire at it, but a pane of golden glass appeared in front of his Striker technique. The Forged Heaven's Glory madra was destroyed, but it slowed the dragon's breath enough to allow the sword to follow its course.

Kelsa was ready to launch the Fox Dream, her Ruler technique, when she realized the weapon had changed direction.

It was coming for *her.*

Her technique scattered, and she dove away, using the tree as cover.

The sword broke the trunk in a spray of splinters. It crashed through and rushed at her, and she raised her hands to try and knock it aside. She knew it would be futile.

Orthos arrived like a dark wind.

Red-and-black light surrounded him in a blaze of fire and destruction, and she had to lean back from the heat even as he intercepted the sword on his shell.

He moved his head to swat it aside, but the sword changed direction again.

It plunged directly into Orthos' side.

He screamed in pain, letting out a rush of black dragon's breath.

All his time in Sacred Valley, Orthos had held back from killing as much as possible. She had seen it. He didn't want to make a habit out of killing the weak, he said. You couldn't always avoid it in a fight, but when he *could* spare someone, he did.

This time, his dragon's breath made a man vanish from the waist up.

Unfortunately, it wasn't the Elder who controlled the sword. That one gestured with his scarred hand again, and his flying sword pulled back and looped around.

Orthos dodged to one side, but his movements were heavy and his spirit was almost empty. Kelsa knew the feeling. She gathered more madra to work them into a technique, and it was like trying to mold handfuls of soft mud.

She was exhausted.

And then the other two Jades joined the battle.

Golden walls of transparent Forged madra grew around them, and constructs drifted over their heads. A man with a jade Enforcer badge ran in, carrying a two-handed hammer.

It crashed down on Orthos' shell, but it was only a glancing blow. Orthos' returning blast of dragon's breath was thin and insubstantial, and it splashed against a halfsilver-laced shield that the man raised.

Kelsa caught the Forger in a Fox Dream, and he staggered down the hill a few steps, but she couldn't do anything about the Enforcer or the flying sword.

Orthos bled from even fresher wounds, and he was still moving with more agility than she thought should be possible from a turtle.

He spun, flipping around the sword, and lashed his tail against the hammer-wielding Enforcer in midair.

The instant he landed, Orthos said, "Yield."

Neither men acknowledged him.

The third Jade, the woman Forger, shook off Kelsa's Fox Dream and re-focused on her with a look of irritation. She glared up the hill, gathering power.

"We have reinforcements coming," Orthos said again. "We will accept your surrender."

The Elder with the scarred arm gestured, and the flying sword flew back to his hand. It gathered power, then shot toward Orthos with greater power than ever before.

Orthos stood his ground, the last of his Blackflame madra gathering in his jaws.

The sword stopped.

It took Kelsa a moment to realize that someone was holding it.

A stranger had appeared out of *nowhere,* a blur of motion that Kelsa had barely registered before he arrived, and he held the flying sword by the hilt in the grip of a pale right hand.

She didn't recognize the huge man with the Remnant arm. He glared with eyes like Orthos', and he was covered by a translucent blaze of black and red. She sensed fiery destruction from him on a level greater even than the turtle.

He had run up *behind* the sword. Overtaking it and seizing it in mid-flight.

The sword shivered in his grip, trying to escape, but his fingers might as well have been cast from steel.

The stranger's red-and-black eyes stopped on Orthos before passing over her, and with the surge she felt from his spirit, she was sure he was about to kill her in rage.

He wore robes of black, white, and purple, and around his neck hung a shadesilk ribbon carrying a badge. Not a hammer, a shield, a scepter, or an arrow. One symbol in the old language was carved into that white metal.

Unsouled.

Suddenly, the image of this stranger congealed with the descriptions Orthos had given her. Even so, she couldn't bring herself to believe it.

How could this be her little brother?

"Lindon?"

Lindon spun and hurled the sword back at the Heaven's Glory Elder.

Flying swords were controlled by scripts. When activated by a specific wielder's madra, their script guided wind aura that allowed the weapon to fly.

You could never use a flying sword against its owner. It was keyed to their spirit. Throwing it back at them would only free up their weapon.

Unless, it seemed, you threw it with overwhelming strength.

The sword blasted straight through the center of the Elder, leaving a bloody hole in his middle and a crater in the earth behind him.

The man looked down at himself. His jade badge was gone.

He collapsed in a heap.

The Enforcer landed a hit, his two-handed hammer crashing into the side of Lindon's head. It had slightly less effect than a spoon tapping the side of a teacup.

A white hand closed around the neck of the Heaven's Glory Enforcer.

Gold walls were already going up around the rest of the area, and Kelsa knew from experience that, when broken, those panes of Forged madra burned like live coals.

Lindon gripped the Enforcer by the neck, then looked down the hill at the Forger who was raising her own defense.

He threw the full-grown Jade in his hand at the Forger in an overhand pitch.

The man blasted through three layers of Forged Heaven's Glory madra, and his clothes were burning with natural fire when he collided with the other Elder.

"Collided" was actually too polite a word. Together, they smashed against the bottom of the hill with a sickening crunch.

White light swelled into a bubble next to Kelsa, and she dodged backwards. She didn't sense Heaven's Glory madra from the light, but she knew it had to be an attack of theirs. Kelsa immediately wove her madra into Foxfire. She was draining her spirit dry, but she extended her perception to find the one who had cast the technique.

In the center of the white light, a girl appeared.

Shorter than Kelsa, she was compact, with flowing black hair interrupted by a streak of blood-red. Six arms of metallic crimson metal extended from her back, their ends sharpened and hammered flat like sword blades.

Hurriedly, Kelsa redirected her Foxfire and hurled it into the newcomer.

One of those sword-arms flicked the Striker technique out of the air. The scarlet girl turned, steadily getting her ragged breathing under control.

She didn't *seem* to move quickly, but before Kelsa knew what was happening, a hand grasped her by the throat.

Kelsa looked into red eyes and prepared to die.

"Hey, give me your name."

Kelsa found she had no trouble speaking. The young woman's grip was loose.

"You first," Kelsa said.

A faint smile pulled up the corner of the new girl's mouth. She let Kelsa go and turned to Orthos, taking in a sharp breath. "You look about five miles past dead."

He rumbled agreement. "Something stranger has happened to you."

"Can't argue with that." She placed a hand on Orthos' head, though even standing close to him must have been agonizing in the heat. "Wish you'd been with us."

She was Orthos' friend?

That meant...she didn't exactly match the description, but she must be Yerin. The girl who had taken Lindon away from Sacred Valley.

But Kelsa couldn't think about that now. There was still a battle going on.

Before Kelsa even looked back down the hill, she knew it had gotten worse. The heat had grown stifling, red fire aura rising by the second. The Heaven's Glory School must be gathering their Ruler techniques...

It took her a few seconds to put the scene together.

Lindon stood in the center of the burning wreckage that had once been the camp. Shattered Heaven's Glory Forger techniques surrounded him, licking his feet with flames, but even his shoes weren't burned.

Heaven's Glory Enforcers crawled away from him. As she watched, he caught one of their Striker techniques. The beam of golden light sank into his Remnant hand, and after only an instant he sent it back. It was tinged slightly darker than before.

But most of the enemies were fleeing. Maybe a hundred, maybe more, including some she recognized as Jades.

They fled because the sky had turned dark.

Hundreds of feet over Lindon's head, black and red aura swirled so intensely that they had become visible as a dense, spinning cloud of dark fire.

She spent several breaths fumbling with her new Jade senses, trying to unravel how Heaven's Glory had used such a Ruler technique and how Lindon had gained control of it.

Finally, she came to the inevitable conclusion: he had generated this all by himself.

"You should stop him," Orthos said. "He'll regret this."

Yerin patted him on the head. "You've been gone an age and a half. It's your turn."

Orthos lifted his wounded leg. "I'm not running anywhere."

Yerin lifted her hand from him and vanished in an implosion of light. She reappeared at the same instant next to Lindon, panting.

He turned immediately, focusing on her instead of Heaven's Glory, reaching out to steady her. She didn't need his help, but rested a hand on his left arm anyway.

Interesting.

They exchanged words, Lindon gesturing angrily to Heaven's Glory, but Yerin pointed back toward where Orthos stood.

The turtle inclined his head once.

Again, Lindon moved with speed Kelsa couldn't track, but this time she could at least see a blur like a flying arrow as he ran up the hill and came to a stop next to the turtle.

"Forgiveness," Lindon said. "I lost my focus."

When the dark fire and red circles bled from his eyes, leaving them human black, he looked to Kelsa with apology in his eyes.

That was the first time she really recognized her brother.

He gave her a gesture of acknowledgement, but first he turned to Orthos and threw his arms around the turtle's neck.

The sacred beast closed his good eye and rumbled deep in his chest.

They didn't say anything, but when Lindon separated, his eyes were wet. Only then did he return to Kelsa.

When he did, he bowed deeply over fists pressed together. "Forgiveness. I left without telling you. I...I had no idea you were...I didn't know things were this bad. My deepest apologies."

At the moment, Kelsa didn't understand her own feelings.

She was glad her brother wasn't the type of person to completely butcher a retreating enemy...but she had wanted him to do it.

He could never have known what Heaven's Glory had done in his absence...but part of her still blamed him for it.

For years, she had believed that he was dead, and was glad to see him alive...but he frightened her.

Orthos had told her stories about sacred artists outside, and about Lindon in particular, but her imagination had not been enough. She felt like she was within arm's reach of a wild tiger.

He was still bowing to her, and he would stay that way until she responded.

He had always been like that.

Kelsa's eyes filled, and she took in a rough breath. "You took too long," she said in a broken voice.

Lindon straightened, now even taller than she was, and she wrapped him up in a hug before she wept. From the shaking of his chest, she knew he was crying too.

第七章

CHAPTER SEVEN

Lindon watched Eithan spread his arms wide as if to embrace the crowd before him, his smile gentle. "Brothers and sisters of the Fallen Leaf School, I am humbled and grateful by this overwhelming show of hospitality."

All thirty-two Jades of the Fallen Leaf School knelt on the ground in front of him, their foreheads pressed to the dirt.

They had seen Lindon face Heaven's Glory, and that had been enough to stop them from pushing the exiles back. It hadn't made them open their doors.

That had taken the arrival of the Akura Golds.

If Eithan's power and skill hadn't intimidated them, the arrival of over two hundred and fifty new Jades—as the Sacred Valley inhabitants would see them—had certainly done the trick.

Lindon had seen only glimpses of the process. He'd been catching up with Orthos and waiting for Kelsa to find their parents; it was only at his sister's insistence that he hadn't gone to find them immediately.

In the few fragments he'd seen of Eithan's negotiation, the Fallen Leaf School representatives had gone from wary to goggle-eyed to tripping all over themselves to agree as more and more Golds in black and purple descended from the skies.

Lindon was fairly certain that they would have promised anything to get these outsiders to *leave.* They would marry off their children to the exiles if it would get these powerful outsiders to leave them alone.

He guessed it would only be a matter of minutes before the first members of the School approached them privately, trying to get a hint about how to grow stronger.

But that had little to do with Lindon.

The Fallen Leaf School looked more like a farming community than an organization dedicated to the sacred arts, with barns and tilled fields separated by grassy plains. He and Orthos stood in the shade of a tall, purple-leafed orus tree as Little Blue sat on the turtle's head, recounting their adventures to him in a series of chirps and ringing tones that sounded something like a bell tumbling down a flight of stairs.

Listening to Little Blue calmed him.

And the quiet gave him time to wrestle with his anger.

[Everyone's alive,] Dross pointed out. [Everyone you cared about, that is. *Some* people are dead. So it could be worse! They could have been killed while you were gone, when you would never have known.]

Orthos hadn't told him the details of what Heaven's Glory had done to his family, but he couldn't gloss over the core details.

The Heaven's Glory School had hunted Lindon's family down and punished them because of what Lindon had done. The Wei clan had given them up. They had suffered for over three years, living like scavengers in the wilderness.

And Lindon had held back his Void Dragon's Dance. He could have wiped them all out in one stroke.

He preferred the anger to the guilt. Picturing what he could do to the Heaven's Glory School kept him from thinking about what he should have done differently.

The sooner he punished them, the better. Both for his own satisfaction and because he was getting weaker.

He cycled Blackflame, and the madra felt fainter than it had in years. He hadn't recovered from his expense yesterday, and it seemed that while he was here, he wouldn't fully regain what he'd lost. The more power he spent, the weaker he would become, until he was truly fighting like a Jade.

But he had another core.

Even his pure madra was weaker than usual, but his second core gave him an advantage over the others. He could retain his power longer than anyone else. He would slowly lose it, just like everyone, but he could hold on to his original strength the longest.

Although he could bring ruin to Heaven's Glory even if he had to do it as a Jade.

Kelsa emerged from the other side of a tiny cabin. She looked leaner now than he remembered her, harder edged. The deprivation had left its mark.

[Hey, there's another bright side! As long as she's with you, she won't have to worry about food anymore!]

"No, she will not," Lindon said aloud.

Kelsa looked grave as she met his eyes. "Mother's only been back for a few days. She's still not quite herself, yet. She and Father haven't had much time to catch up. Did Orthos prepare you?"

Lindon found it hard to speak through the tightness in his throat. "Not...not really."

Kelsa's style had always been to deliver painful truth bluntly. A fast cut was cleaner.

"Father's eyes were burned," she said, and the words struck Lindon strangely. They should have meaning, but that meaning didn't quite sink in like it should. "He can see basic shapes and can tell the difference between light and dark, but he gets by mostly with his ears and his cane."

[There's a bright side to that too!] Dross was starting to sound a little desperate. [Human eyes aren't so great. With Remnant eyes, he'll be able to see brand-new colors he never even imagined!]

"He's been living this way for years now," Kelsa said. "It isn't so bad. To tell you the truth, he's still more upset about his leg."

That brought a faint smile from Lindon. As far back as he could remember, his father had been bitter about a leg injury he'd gotten as a young man. He blamed the wound for his failure to reach Jade.

"Mother has been held by Heaven's Glory. They needed her to work for them, so they didn't treat her too roughly, but she has been a prisoner for a long time. She hasn't slept in days, and she's still convinced that she will be captured again."

Lindon was more prepared for that. While Orthos had said little about his father, suggesting that it was Kelsa's place to tell him, the turtle couldn't avoid telling Lindon about his mother.

She was the one that Orthos and Kelsa had gone to rescue from Heaven's Glory.

Lindon had assumed that she'd been captured recently. He hadn't imagined that Seisha had been a prisoner for so *long.*

The guilt for that settled on him like a pile of bricks. It was yet another way that his family had paid the price for vengeance directed at him.

There's a bright side for you, Dross, Lindon said silently. *I'm done thinking about what I'm going to do to Heaven's Glory.*

There was no point wasting his thoughts on the dead.

[...I'm not sure how bright that side is.]

"And you?" Lindon asked Kelsa. "You can't have escaped unharmed."

She looked at him like he was crazy. "*They* were the ones who suffered. I was the lucky one."

Lindon had already heard from Orthos what she'd been through. He knew already.

His sister had lain motionless in the cold, waiting for sentries to pass, trying not to shiver in case they heard the motion. She'd stolen scraps of food, gotten caught, taken beatings, and gone back the next night because if she failed, their father wouldn't be able to eat. After a day of scavenging whatever she could, of taking care of exiles that weren't even part of her clan, she had spent nights studying her Path manual and working on the one technique she'd ever learned.

When Orthos arrived, she'd spent every spare moment training and re-training, un-learning the habits that Sacred Valley had ingrained into her. She had reversed her Iron body, a process that sounded agonizing, and gained another one so her foundation would be solid.

On the day she reached Jade, under Orthos' instruction, she had started working to free her mother.

Orthos said he saw Lindon in her, but Lindon didn't agree.

He had been shown a world beyond this one. When he pushed for improvement, it was because he knew improvement was possible.

She had fought for a victory that she must have believed impossible. Every day. For three years.

But she wouldn't have to anymore.

"I'm ready," Lindon said.

Kelsa didn't question that or prepare him any further. She didn't give him any more advice. She only walked through the cabin's door, leaving it open for him to follow.

Lindon ducked through the doorway and entered.

The interior of the cabin was simple: wooden walls and wooden floors, covered by a rough-woven rug. A one-person bed had been pushed against the back wall, and his parents sat at a tiny table in chairs that looked like they had been hand-carved by the cabin's owner.

These people *looked* like his parents, so familiar he could never mistake them. At the same time, they looked like strangers.

They were both tall, broad people, built for the battlefield. His father had more gray in his hair and had lost some of his muscle, his shoulders more rounded and his middle a little softer, but he was still unmistakably Wei Shi Jaran. His bad leg was stretched out on a chair, his cane held loosely across his lap.

Wei Shi Seisha had gray in her hair too, which he didn't remember, but hers was still a deep brown like no one else in the clan. She looked healthier than Jaran or Kelsa, and she had the same drudge floating over her shoulder: a brown segmented fish made of dead matter that reminded Lindon of petrified wood.

But even as his stomach made an eager leap at the sight of his mother and father, it sank as he saw the things that were different.

Seisha's head had shot up at the sound of the door opening, though Kelsa's return couldn't have come as a surprise. She held a book on which she could take notes, but instead of paying more attention to it than her surroundings, she clutched it like a child clenching a blanket to ward off nightmares.

Jaran's eyes were clouded over, and he stared slightly over the doorway. Kelsa announced herself as she entered, and Lindon realized she must have developed that habit for their father's sake. "It's me, and I brought Lindon."

Seisha's eyes grew wide as she saw him. "Lindon." She took a deep breath and said it again. "Lindon. You look... well."

The badge she wore was still iron. She couldn't sense him.

"I am."

There should be something better to say, but he couldn't find it.

Jaran smacked his cane on the ground. "Why didn't you come back?" he demanded.

Lindon wished his father had stabbed him instead.

"Not right now!" Kelsa snapped. "He's alive, and he's Gold now. He's going to take us away from here. Won't you, Lindon?"

"Yes," Lindon said, but the word came out as more of a whisper. "You can come live with me, and nobody will... nobody can...what I mean is, you'll be safe."

Neither of his parents said anything to that for a long time. Too long.

"So you're Gold?" his mother asked at last. She glanced down to his badge, which clearly wasn't made of gold.

"Something like that." That sounded like he was *weaker* than Gold, so he clarified. "I'm strong. More than any of us ever imagined, and the friends I brought are even stronger."

Seisha nodded and pointed her finger at the sky in a gesture so familiar it clenched a fist around his heart. That was what she did when she finally understood the truth of a problem.

"Ah, I see. So they lent you their power."

Jaran leaned forward. "Can they give it to us too? At least Kelsa, she's young. Orthos has trained her well."

Lindon looked to the floor.

Even now, his parents didn't believe that he could have earned power on his own. He must have borrowed someone else's.

Then again, they were somewhat right.

Yerin had protected him, pushed him, and fought for him when he was too weak to do it for himself. Eithan had given him his Iron body, his Blackflame Path, his Jade cycling technique, his contract with Orthos...almost everything. And what Eithan hadn't given him, Mercy's clan had.

The only one whose power he hadn't borrowed was Ziel.

Kelsa made a dismissive sound. "Stop it. I know you know about the fire in the sky that drove away Heaven's Glory. That was Lindon."

Jaran made an expression of clear doubt. "I heard that was Orthos."

"It was Lindon. Alone. If I had to bet on a fight between Lindon and the whole Heaven's Glory School, I'd put all my money on Lindon."

She glanced at Lindon quickly, and he suspected she wanted him to confirm that she was right. He gave her a tiny nod.

Jaran blew air out of his cheeks. "The heavens have blessed you enough for a lifetime, boy."

"They have."

That had been true before he'd even left Sacred Valley. If life was fair, Suriel descending from heaven to bring him back from death would have been the only miracle he ever received.

Seisha's hand tightened on her notebook. *"Are* you going to fight Heaven's Glory? You and your friends, I mean." She gave Kelsa a faint smile. "Orthos has already done more than we could expect, but if you and the others are really all Gold..."

"I'm sure we will." Lindon had been on fire to do that very thing before he'd walked into this room. Now, the cabin felt claustrophobic, and he wanted nothing more than to leave.

His mother's grip tightened further, to the point that the wooden backing of the notebook splintered slightly. "Do you have to? Can't we all go now?"

"I won't leave until we've made Heaven's Glory pay in blood!" Jaran announced.

"And what are *you* going to do?" Seisha shot back. "What can any of us do? They only came for us today because we fought them." She softened as she looked back to Kelsa. "Not that it's your fault. You were very brave."

"I don't think you understand how much stronger they are than the Jades," Kelsa said. "I'm not sure *I* understand."

Seisha carefully set her strained notebook down on the table. "No one is invincible. Orthos is stronger than they are, and look what happened to him."

"Now we have *hundreds* like Orthos," Jaran insisted. "We can take the fight to their gates!"

"I can't imagine they're all like Orthos. And how do we know what secrets the Schools have hidden up their sleeves?"

Lindon fumbled behind him for the door. He was afraid he was going to throw up.

This had been a mistake.

He should have saved his family without meeting them. What had he expected?

His family argued with each other as though he wasn't present. If he opened the door to leave, Kelsa would notice and include him in the conversation. His parents would halfheartedly loop him in, but they would continue making decisions without him.

It was as though he'd never left.

As he was about to turn, his vision filled with purple.

Dross, in physical form, drifted ahead of him. Seisha jerked back with a gasp while Kelsa gathered White Fox madra.

One boneless purple arm raised in greeting. [Hello! Don't be alarmed! I am Dross, the spirit that lives inside your son's brain.]

Jaran inclined his head in the entirely wrong direction. Dross' voice was inside his head, so it didn't give any clues to his location. "Greetings, Dross. I am Wei Shi Jaran. Thank you for protecting my son."

[Ah, yes, I *thought* you were making that mistake. It's not easy for me to admit this, but it's actually the other way around. Without him, I'd still be rusting at the bottom of a well. Oh no, wait, I'd have been torn apart by collapsing space. That's even worse than I thought.]

"You can stop, Dross," Lindon said quietly.

[I could show you some of your son's memories, or maybe all of them? No, he doesn't like that idea. So I guess that means he's going to share his thoughts with you the boring way: with his mouth. Now take it away, Lindon!] Dross drifted to the side, gesturing to Lindon with both arms wide.

The three members of Lindon's family waited.

"I don't want to do this," Lindon muttered.

[Oh, this is embarrassing. This is one of those things where he *says* one thing, but he actually means another, because he does have something he wants to say. Quite a lot, actually.]

Lindon looked back to his family and, after another moment where he desperately wished to leave, he allowed the words to spill out.

"I'm not a Gold. I'm a Lord. It's an entire realm beyond." His parents wrinkled their brows in confusion, but Kelsa nodded sharply.

"Even at that level, I'm..." He tried to think of a way to say it that didn't sound too proud, but he was too tired for that. "...I'm very good. One of the best. If you took away my advancement, I'd still be a better fighter than you or anyone you've ever met. Did Orthos tell you why I left?"

It didn't matter if he had or not, so Lindon just kept talking. "I saw the future. You were all going to die. Here. In this Dreadgod attack."

Or maybe another one. The attack Suriel had seen was supposed to happen in thirty years, not three, but he didn't think that was relevant enough to mention.

"If I got strong enough, I could stop it," he continued. "I left so I could grow. I left for *this*."

Lindon turned to his father. "You asked me why I didn't come back. Why *would* I come back?"

No one responded.

Dross gestured for him to keep going.

"I'm only here now because you're in danger. If I hadn't come back, you would have all died without knowing anything. Stick with me, and I'll protect you, because I *can*. While you're with me, you'll never have to worry about anything ever again."

He turned his back to them and grabbed the door handle. "But first, I'm taking you away from Sacred Valley whether you like it or not. After that, if you want to crawl back here and die, you can do it on your own."

Distracted, he pulled the door instead of pushing.

Lindon pulled the handle out with a snap. The entire door cracked down the side, and even the doorframe bent inward.

He almost apologized. Instead, he tapped into his soulfire and just blew the remaining door off its hinges.

Before the splinters had fallen to the ground, he was gone.

He didn't realize where he was going until he found Yerin sitting with Mercy and Orthos, a spoon halfway to her mouth.

Dross may have said something to her without informing Lindon, or maybe she just read it on his face. She dropped her bowl, following him to a lonely corner just outside the Fallen Leaf School.

When he was sure they were alone, Lindon broke down and wept.

CHAPTER EIGHT

Tal'gullour, Fortress of the Mad King

Daruman clenched his Scythe and focused his authority, preparing to re-enter the Way.

He had to be careful. He couldn't bring his fortress with him, and without Tal'gullour to contain his power, the entire Way would sense his movement. When he entered an Iteration, the very stars trembled.

With every step he took, the eyes of the Abidan would be upon him.

He could warp Fate by nature of his authority over chaos, and thus dodge the noses of the Hounds. If he could move without the Spiders detecting him immediately, he would have brought the Abidan system down before.

A dark voice laughed, unrestrained, in the depths of his soul. A voice so familiar that it was almost indistinguishable from his own.

You tried, once, the Conqueror reminded him.

Unbidden, the Fiend Oth'kimeth summoned up the memory of Daruman's most painful defeat.

He had spent centuries gathering the right ingredients. He personally retrieved the Mask of the Unweaver from an Assassin Idol's Temple in the fragment of a dead world. He traded with the Angler for an invisibility cloak she had woven with her own hands when she was a mortal. A world he conquered brought him tribute of the greatest artifacts ever forged in their Iteration, including a conceptual spirit of stealth who could hide from Fate itself.

And, in one of his greatest triumphs, he had raided the personal collection of the Third Judge of the Abidan Court: Darandiel, the Ghost. He had taken from her a band of silver bound with living runes, designed to allow even a Judge to veil their power.

His greatest craftsman, gathered from dozens of dead worlds, labored for years to break these items down to their conceptual essence and combine them together.

After thirty years, they forged his four priceless treasures into a device that would hide the very origin of his existence. It resembled a living, shifting thread made from smoke and shadow, which swirled around him in a twisting cocoon.

As they looked upon him, even his closest advisors could not recognize him. He was as a void in reality itself.

With his Origin Shroud upon him, he took a step into reality.

Into Iteration 216. The world called Limit.

Even two hundred standard years later, the memory frustrated him. Limit should have been the perfect world to experiment with. It was doomed to fall soon, its population devastated by a mystical plague and the rise of new insectoid monsters. The ecosystem was close to collapsing, and the decline of human lives had already led to steady breakdowns in local physics.

There was no reason for an Abidan to be there. In fact, he arrived over a churning sea without Sector Control contacting a Judge, and he knew he had won.

Oth'kimeth gleefully reminded him of the triumph he had felt in that moment. He had seen himself striding into Haven or Cradle or even Sanctum itself unnoticed, wreaking such devastation before the Judges were recalled that the Abidan would begin to crumble.

It was while he was lost in his own victory that he had felt another presence. A rock-solid presence of order buried beneath the ocean. An Abidan in Limit.

The timing, he felt, was perfect.

His enemy had not noticed him, and he could be upon them with lethal force in an instant. A shark taking a swimmer.

His will bent and tore reality—one more wound among many in the dying world—and he stepped through a hole in space. He found himself in an underground chamber that sheltered millions of local lives.

And he was standing face-to-face with Ozriel.

It was only afterwards that Oth'kimeth, acting in conjunction with his Presence, had reconstructed the image of the Abidan standing there in his black armor, white hair falling around his shoulders, ice-cold look on his face. The Mad King hadn't seen that at the time.

He had seen only the Scythe.

The first strike of the weapon blasted his mortal form to messy pieces, splattering him across the far wall in one blow.

He had re-formed in an instant, miles overhead, and begun to open a hole into the Void. His Origin Shroud was still intact, as Ozriel hadn't unleashed the full force of his Scythe.

Ozriel was hiding too. That was his only saving grace.

If he removed his Shroud and released his full power, so would Ozriel, and the remaining Judges would be on him in moments.

How had Ozriel known?

Even two hundred years later, Daruman couldn't figure it out. Had he really seen so far, through chaos-corrupted Fate?

At the time, he had been convinced that there had been some flaw in his Origin Shroud. If he could get away and fix it, he could try again.

But Ozriel had followed him.

They had traded blows in the sky, enough to tear space and strain the already-weak fabric of the Iteration, but neither at their full power.

Otherwise, their first exchange would have torn the planet in half.

Daruman had finally managed to keep his void portal open long enough to escape, but then Ozriel had spoken to him.

Oth'kimeth made sure he remembered the statement in Ozriel's own smug and icy tones.

"I can let you run...but I can't let you keep that."

The authority of Ozriel's Scythe focused on Daruman's Origin Shroud, and there was nothing he could do. The spinning thread of shadows and smoke was torn from him, its pieces drifting back into Limit as he himself fell into the Void.

So he couldn't even forge it again.

Oth'kimeth had been laughing at him about it for two hundred years.

You had to wait until Ozriel was gone. You creep around like a mouse because you cannot stride like a lion.

I can now, Daruman countered.

And he tore his way from the Void into a world. The Abidan called it Iteration One Twenty-nine: Oasis.

Reality screamed around him. Distant stars shook. Prophets and oracles fainted or died where they stood, sensing his presence.

And the fourteen Abidan stationed on this world instantly sent out desperate calls for aid. He couldn't stop them, but he didn't need to.

The Mad King had come. He wore his armor carved from the bones of Oth'kimeth's physical body, and in his right hand he clutched a Scythe of his own.

He no longer had any use for stealth. Let them see him coming.

He would crush them and their defenses together.

Daruman raised his Scythe and reaped Abidan lives.

⬡

Jai Long spoke coldly to the guardians of the Fallen Leaf School. "Let me out."

There was a living barrier between him and the northern exit from Sacred Valley. It was a nest of thorns thicker than his thumb, with a flock of sacred vultures flying overhead and cawing warnings down to him.

Three guards, a Jade and two Irons, stood in his way and prevented him from carving his way out. He could feel life madra from them, as he could from their entire School, but they were still Jades at best.

He could cut them apart as easily as the thorns, but his sister was with him, looking to him with concern. That, and he had killed those who were helpless to stop him before. He hadn't liked it.

Which annoyed him. A conscience wasn't something a sacred artist could afford, if he wished to keep climbing the ladder.

But then, Jai Long had come here specifically to *escape* that climb. In a sense, he wasn't even a sacred artist anymore.

Though he was still more of one than any five natives of Sacred Valley put together. Even if you set aside the curse, he had been thoroughly unimpressed with the attitudes of the people here. They spent all their time using the sacred arts to jockey for position instead of actually pursuing excellence.

Except Kelsa. He had grown to believe that she and her brother were unique among their kin.

She would do well no matter where she ended up, and her parents were safe now. Jai Long had no more reason to stay.

The Fallen Leaf Jade, a woman with gray in her hair, held up a staff. It was a sacred instrument designed to channel her life madra, and he could feel the connection it held to the thorns behind her. "You have been granted permission to stay among us, but not to use our gateway to the outside."

Jai Long gripped his spear and steadied himself. He knew that he was perhaps the most suspicious-looking person alive. As much with the script covering his head as without it.

But he was showing great restraint by talking to this person at all. He could defeat all three of them without killing them. Probably.

A white snake of madra curled around Jai Long's weapon. "I can leave whether you permit it or not. I am asking you to stand aside out of courtesy and a concern for your well-being."

The Irons, two boys that he suspected were brothers, paled and readied shining green light. They had brown hair and wore badges big enough to be half breastplates, covering most of their chests.

"If you can," the Jade said, "then do it."

A new voice rang out before the battle could begin: "Apologies!"

Jai Long kept a wary eye and his spiritual perception on the Jade guard, but he paced several steps to the side so he could catch a glimpse of the man who had spoken.

It was exactly who he had expected.

Wei Shi Lindon Arelius walked up in the clothes of the Akura clan, wearing his own badge, though his had the symbol for "Empty" in the old language. Its white material matched his new arm, which looked advanced for a Remnant prosthetic. Perhaps Jai Long had done him a favor by removing it.

Jai Chen bowed when she saw Lindon, but Jai Long had stayed on his guard. He had expected to run into Lindon at some point, but had hoped to escape before that.

When an old enemy showed up with an army at his back, it was wise to leave.

As far as Jai Long was concerned, accounts between the two of them had been balanced. But you could never tell who would hold a grudge.

This meant he had four people to disable without killing. Lindon was a real sacred artist, and therefore the most threatening among Jai Long's opponents, but that was like being the fattest mosquito in the swarm.

One swat would be good enough.

Lindon faced Jai Long, and his expression was difficult

to read. "Pardon, but you don't want to walk. The outside world is...inhospitable right now."

"We'll take our chances."

A blue spirit, like a tiny woman in a flowing dress, peeped and waved her hand at Jai Chen. Her eyes lit up in recognition; this must be the spirit who had helped restore the damage to her soul.

Jai Chen's dragon-spirit floated warily over to Lindon, giving him and the female spirit a curious inspection.

"What's wrong out there?" Jai Chen asked.

"There's a Dreadgod coming."

She gasped, and Jai Long suspected he had made a similar sound himself. They had sensed disturbances in the aura recently coming from the west, and everyone felt the tremors in the earth, but Dreadgods were several levels beyond what he had expected. At worst, he had thought it was Heralds coming to blows.

"The Wandering Titan?" he guessed, and Lindon nodded.

"The Akura clan has provided a fleet of cloudships for evacuation, and they're waiting at the eastern entrance."

"What is a Dreadgod?" the Fallen Leaf Jade asked sharply.

Lindon looked surprised, but he bowed to her over fists pressed together. "Forgiveness, please. I assumed the other elders had warned you. My friends and I have come to warn you of a monster of unimaginable strength making its way to Sacred Valley. Think of it as an insane sacred beast as tall as a mountain. We have plenty of room for you and your whole School to evacuate before its coming."

She did not look like someone who had just heard that her home was going to be destroyed. She wore an expression of deep skepticism. "Have the elders decided to flee before this threat?"

Lindon sighed. "They are still making their decision."

He turned back to the Jai siblings and dipped his head. "Apologies."

"I hope you can save your home," Jai Chen said.

"So do I." He gave her a sad half-smile. "I wish you could

stay here in peace. When the threat of the Dreadgod has passed, perhaps you can return."

"Thank you for the warning," Jai Long said, "but I'm not foolish enough to ignore an open door now for the promise of one later." He lifted his spear. "If there is a Dreadgod out there, all the more reason to leave as soon as we can."

It wasn't as though the Wandering Titan was crouched on the other side of this pass with its mouth open. It must be hundreds of miles away, and far to the west. They had witnessed the Bleeding Phoenix back in the Blackflame Empire, and Dreadgods were hard to miss.

They could leave through this entrance to the north, and then—if it turned out Lindon was telling the truth—they could take a cloudship anywhere they wanted.

Besides, he wouldn't trust a ship given to him by someone whose limb he had chopped off.

Life madra flowed out from the Fallen Leaf Jade, and thorns came to life behind her. Vines slithered over the ground even as his own white madra came to life in the form of serpents, hissing at their opponent.

"Please don't do that," Lindon said quietly.

Jai Long moved for one of the Irons first. Take out the weakest, reduce the numbers on the enemy side.

His Striker technique, in the form of a white snake, blasted out to protect him from the thorns as he lunged for the Iron.

He aimed for a shallow cut on the boy's calf. He would probably have to slap the Iron around a few times to get him to give up, but this would at least keep him out of the fight for a moment.

A blue-and-white figure stood between them.

It was Lindon, his eyes made of blue crystal with white circles for irises. He held Jai Long's spear in his hand of flesh and a sword in his right. The Iron had swung a blade to try and intercept Jai Long, and though the blow would never have landed, Lindon gripped the weapon by its blade with no apparent discomfort.

Thorns wrapped around his leg, but he ignored them,

turning his disquieting gaze on Jai Long. "We're trying to negotiate with the Fallen Leaf School. Please don't kill them."

Jai Long filled himself with his Flowing Starlight technique, which Enforced his entire body. White madra filled his limbs, standing out on his skin like shining serpentine tattoos.

With all the strength he could muster—what was left to him in this cursed valley—he pulled at his spear. Lindon didn't budge.

For the first time, Jai Long scanned Lindon.

And his heart ran cold.

He released his spear, staggering backward. He pushed his sister away. "Run!" he shouted.

She was the picture of confusion. Even her dragon flew in aimless loops in midair. More importantly, she *didn't* run.

"*Underlord!*" Jai Long screamed.

It was the worst-case scenario. One of their enemies had tracked them down from the world beyond, and had found them before the curse drained their power.

Lindon only gave off the spiritual strength of a Truegold, but Jai Long didn't know what kind of advantages a Lord's body would retain in this place.

Even if he was down to Lowgold, he had more strength left than Jai Long could call up. And he had a personal grudge. Lindon wouldn't give up until they were both dead.

Jai Chen looked from side to side. "I know."

Madra still ran through Jai Long's limbs, and he pushed his Enforcer technique as far as it would go, ready to intercept Lindon. Would he be fast enough?

But Lindon didn't move. He looked vaguely uncomfortable.

Only then did his sister's words make it into Jai Long's ears. "You know?"

"I scanned him when he walked up. I don't think he's going to attack us."

Lindon scratched the side of his head. "I'm not. If you don't want to come with us, you're welcome to go your own way. I just...don't recommend it."

Jai Chen walked up to look at the blue spirit on Lindon's shoulder. She extended a hand. "May I?"

The spirit chimed and stepped lightly onto her hand, scurrying up to her shoulder and chattering into her ear.

By this time, the Jade's thorns had wrapped all the way up Lindon's thigh. He glanced down. "Do you mind if I remove these? They're starting to get...uncomfortable."

"Not until you explain yourself," the Jade said firmly. "What is an Underlord? How do you know about this... Dread God?"

Lindon switched to his Blackflame core, controlled aura for just a blink, and the entire vine burned to ash. "Apologies, but that was making me nervous."

Jai Long found himself still in a fighting crouch, madra flowing through him, as Jai Chen chatted merrily to Lindon's Riverseed and Lindon himself reassured a Jade that he meant no harm.

At that moment, he was glad for the strips of cloth covering his face. He didn't want anyone seeing his face turn bright red.

"I feel like you're about to dump me into a pot and boil me," Orthos rumbled.

Lindon felt the turtle's emotions, and he wasn't as irritated as he pretended. He sat in front of a fireplace in a lodge of the Fallen Leaf School, taking up most of the living room. Orthos felt relaxed, as though he were with family for the first time in years.

Lindon only wished he felt the same with his own family.

The sacred turtle was covered in bandages. Eithan stood over him, one eye closed, examining him like a painter looking for the perfect spot to place a brush. With one swipe of his finger, he spread green goop over Orthos' injuries.

The room was already filled with the scent of mint and flowers, created by this powerful healing salve. The wound closed up instantly, but Eithan clicked his tongue and shook his head.

"Not enough. With only this much, I'm afraid the flavor won't set in."

Orthos flicked his tail. "Some Archlords do eat intelligent sacred beasts."

"There's one such Archlord before you now. Be silent and marinate."

Lindon returned his attention to the map spread out before him. He'd studied maps of Sacred Valley as a child working in their clan's library, and little had changed since then, but it was still better to refresh himself.

"We can reach the Wei clan well before sunrise," Lindon said. "But we can't go together. We don't—"

He was cut off by the ground quaking, rattling mugs on shelves and causing sparks to fly from the fire. Earth aura surged beneath his feet, accompanied by a fleeting sense of deep hunger.

"...we need to split everyone up," he continued. "We have almost three hundred Golds, and we need to put them to use."

He didn't need to say the rest. The Dreadgod was coming.

They were almost out of time.

Orthos snorted out smoke. A bandage covered one eye, though Lindon was sure that Eithan had already healed that eye with a pill, and his other eye swiveled to Lindon.

"Do you want to set the Wei clan aflame yourself?"

Lindon sighed. "No, I'm going to save them."

They may have exiled his family, which had led to his parents' suffering, but he didn't see what other choice the clan elders had. The Heaven's Glory School was both more powerful and more influential than the Wei clan.

Orthos made a sound like another earthquake. "Your sister isn't as inclined to forgiveness as you are."

"If I had been here, I might not be able to forgive them either." If he had *watched* the clan turn his family over, maybe he would leave them here to die, but he had enough distance that he was sure he could handle it.

Dross popped out over his right shoulder. [Don't worry! Lindon has me to restrain his murderous impulses. And I've seen his memories of this place; his clan leaders are reasonable people. We can talk it out, I'm certain.]

Lindon wondered if he and Dross had watched the same memories.

Eithan leaned over at a new angle, judging distance with his thumb, and then swiped another slash of green salve onto Orthos. Lindon didn't even think there was a wound there.

"Yerin and I can go to the Wei clan," Lindon said as he rolled up the map. "We still need people to visit the Holy Wind School, the Golden Sword School, the Li clan, and the Kazan clan. Eithan, why don't you assign people to those?"

"Hmmmmm...I don't know, I might just want to lounge here in the very lap of luxury." He poked a thin cushion with one hand, shuddered, and remained standing. "I don't see why I should bow to your authority."

Lindon suppressed his irritation. He didn't want to waste time dealing with Eithan's sense of humor, but at the same time, he *did* need Eithan's help.

He pressed his fists together. "Apologies. It was only a request, not a command."

"Ah, that's disappointing. Yes sir, I would certainly be more motivated if I knew that you were backing me with your *authority*. You don't need to be a *Sage* to see—"

Lindon held up a hand. "I understand." He didn't know if Eithan wanted to see how far Lindon had come or if he just wanted Lindon to dance to his tune, but he clearly wanted a demonstration of Sage powers.

Lindon had been looking for an excuse to practice anyway.

He focused his attention on one of the empty mugs on the shelf, gathering his concentration until only the mug existed. Finally, when it felt like he was pushing through a screen to something deeper than reality, he commanded the mug.

"Move."

The mug disappeared from the shelf and appeared on the table in front of him.

He sank down into his chair, taking a deep breath. Exercising his willpower like that didn't leave him physically exhausted exactly, but rather mentally drained. It took intense concentration, and tired him accordingly.

"And hence he earned his title," Eithan said gravely. "To this day, legends speak of the Cup Sage."

Orthos only had to stretch out his head to reach the table, and he examined the mug curiously. "So this is the power of a Sage. What else can you do?"

"I'm not sure yet. I plan on doing thorough research after we leave."

Eithan pulled a watch from his outer pocket and checked it. "The ladies have yet to return, so it seems that we have a few minutes free."

Lindon *wanted* to test out the scope of his authority, but this felt like a waste of time. Surely there was something else he could be doing to work toward the evacuation of Sacred Valley. Then again, if he could figure out how to open portals or other equally miraculous Sage abilities, that might be its own solution.

He moved his eyes to Dross. The spirit nodded eagerly.

"Just a little," Lindon allowed.

He focused on the mug again, finding it slightly easier the second time. This time, he wanted to transform the mug into something else. Not anything too complicated, like a living thing, but something similar enough that it might actually work. Maybe a bowl.

He pictured the mug flattening out, widening, taking the new shape in his mind. His will tightened.

"**Change**," Lindon ordered.

The mug rattled slightly.

Eithan, Dross, and Orthos all leaned closer and examined it.

"I see," Eithan said. "You have *changed* it to a different mug that is identical in appearance. Clever."

Lindon squeezed his eyes shut, waiting for the sense of exhaustion to pass. "That one doesn't work, Dross."

[I'll check it off the list. We *can't* change its shape. Boom, there it goes. Gone from the list. Now how about color, can you change the color?]

Lindon started to focus again, but Eithan waved a hand in front of his eyes to stop him. "I've heard it said that all Sages can accomplish with their authority whatever they could accomplish *without* it."

[Oh, that's clever!] Dross said. [Very memorable saying, very snappy. Too bad it's, you know, wrong.]

"I can't re-open a portal with my madra," Lindon pointed out.

"Ah, yes, let me clarify. There are things that *any* Sage can do, and then there are things that only *you* can do, with your Icon and your unique relationship to that Icon. I thought it might be prudent to start with the things that any Sage could do."

Lindon watched the mug as though committing it to memory might help him somehow. "Pardon, but I couldn't transport the mug directly from the shelf to the table without my authority."

"I can," Eithan said, rolling up his sleeves. "Let me show you."

His smile dropped and his eyes sharpened. He held out his hands, focusing his will.

Then he grabbed the mug, lifted it, and placed it on the other end of the table. "Behold!" he cried. "I have transported the cup!"

Dross applauded furiously.

Lindon spoke his own thoughts aloud. "So I get the same end result, but skip the process."

"That's *exactly* right." Eithan sounded somewhat surprised.

That was an intuitive connection, but it felt right. There was something missing, though. Charity had opened portals and brought techniques to life. Northstrider had brought back the dead. Those weren't things he was capable of doing without authority.

One step at a time, he reminded himself.

There was a large jug of clean water by the door, where

a Fallen Leaf Copper had left it for them. "With my hands, I could fill that cup," Lindon said.

Eithan gestured for him to go ahead. Orthos craned his neck to get a better look.

Lindon concentrated. This seemed to take more of his willpower than before, encompassing both the mug and the jar of water. Finally, when he could clearly picture water filling the cup, he spoke.

"**Fill.**"

Water appeared in the mug.

Lindon's vision faded.

He found himself lying on his back only seconds later, staring up at the wooden beams on the inside of the ceiling. Orthos radiated concern, and Dross curiosity.

Eithan was taking a sip of water.

"That obviously took more out of you," Eithan observed. "Do you—ah, this is crisp. Very refreshing. Do you know why?"

Lindon struggled to stand up, and he felt like he was speaking through a mouthful of cotton. "It's refreshing because it's still cold."

The water was most likely melted snow, and there were scripts around the jar that blocked heat.

"Ah, no, I meant 'Do you know why you struggled more with that working?'"

"I had to split my focus." He was working largely from instinct, but his will had encompassed both the mug and the water. That had made it more than twice as hard.

"Correct, but there are other factors at play as well." Eithan took another sip of water and then placed the mug back down. "Try emptying the mug."

Lindon shook his head. "Apologies, I'm too weak. I'll try again tomorrow."

"I highly doubt you will find this so exhausting."

Eithan must have a point. He always did. And despite feeling like he had just completed a hundred complex mathematical equations while performing a delicate Soulsmithing operation, Lindon was still ecstatic about getting some kind of grasp on his Sage abilities.

He could try a *little* more.

He gathered his focus and spoke the order: "**Empty.**"

The water vanished from the mug.

Lindon braced himself to fall again, but he felt nothing. He had ordered the water as easily as he might order a pet. Concentrating to gather his willpower was still a bit tiring, but the actual command had taken almost nothing out of him.

He understood why immediately, and it was like a light dawning in his mind, revealing an entirely new world of possibility.

"It's in line with my Icon."

"*And* it's something you were capable of doing on your own," Eithan pointed out. "Emptying a vessel is well within the concept of the Void, and pouring water out of a cup is simple for anyone. Also, you in particular could have burned that water away with Blackflame. Therefore, very easy."

Lindon peered into the jug. "Did the water return?"

"What do you think?"

"I suspect it did, because when I thought of emptying the cup, I thought of pouring it back into the jug. But that means all I *really* did was move water from one place to another. So why was that easier than moving the mug?"

Eithan waved a hand. "You're thinking about it like it's a sacred arts technique. You're working on a conceptual level now. Don't cling to literal definitions."

"If it's all a matter of perspective, then I can do anything," Lindon continued, letting his thoughts guide his words. "I could move the mug by *emptying* the shelf of the mug. Could I heal someone by *emptying* them of injuries?"

That sounded ridiculous, but maybe that was how Sages worked.

"That sounds ridiculous," Eithan said, and once again Lindon wondered if the man was reading his mind. "Some of those actions may be in line with your Icon, and some of them certainly are not, but you'll have to feel that out for yourself."

Lindon scooped up another glass of water, by hand this time, and concentrated, ready to try again. This time, he wanted to vanish the water entirely.

"**Empty**," he said.

The mug stayed full. Something had stopped him.

Someone.

He had felt the will working against his, and he recognized it. Lindon looked up to Eithan, who was giving a broad, innocent smile. "How did you do that?"

"If your will is the only one working on an object, you have complete authority over it. If someone else wants to do something with that object, you must overcome their will first." He took the mug from Lindon by hand and drank from it.

"As I am not yet a Sage, I can't do what you can do. But I can stop *you.*"

Lindon had hundreds of questions, most of which could only be answered through practice.

"Dross, can you model this?"

[Can I? Of course I can! Accurately? No. I don't *really* understand the limitations. We've seen enough Sages and Monarchs working, but I don't know what Icons they have connections to, and you weren't advanced enough to sense what wills might have been working against them at the time, and also being here in this valley tires me out, and I'd kind of like to start fresh in the morning. Maybe several mornings from now.]

Lindon couldn't wait. The sooner he could get a grasp on his abilities, the sooner he could begin thinking of new applications. Maybe new solutions.

He swept the table clear, moving his rolled-up map of Sacred Valley carefully to the side in case he spilled some water...and then he stopped with the map in his hand.

The ground shook beneath his feet.

"A few mornings from now," Lindon agreed. "That should be plenty."

Orthos glanced nervously at the earth aura beneath his feet.

Eithan cheerily raised his mug. "Plenty of time! I can't think of a single reason why we might need a Sage in the next few days."

Lindon snatched the mug back.

When everyone had returned and gathered around the table, Dross materialized in front of Lindon. He clapped his boneless arms together, projecting a deafening clapping noise into everyone's mind.

[We're going to make this quick, all right? Just listen to me, I'll give you your assignments, and everything will go smoothly. Focus...actually, that's too much, that's embarrassing. Everyone looking at me. Give me about eighty percent of your attention, that should be plenty.]

Little Blue, seated on the table, turned slightly so that she was only halfway looking at Dross.

[That's perfect, keep that ratio exactly.] He gestured, and a purple light shone over the map of Sacred Valley spread across the table. It lit up Mount Venture, the sacred peak to the west.

[There are four schools here, one on each mountain, and three clans splitting the valley part of the...valley. The school over here, to the west, is the Golden Sword School.]

He gestured again, and the purple light indicating the Golden Sword School was crossed out by a red slash. [They're gone! They're out. Vanished. Complete ghost town over there.]

The Fallen Leaf School had several methods of contacting the other schools, and some of the Akura Golds had techniques or constructs intended to spy on far-off locations. They were often slow or blurry because of the suppression field, but they all indicated the same thing: the Golden Sword School had left days ago, if not weeks.

"Where did they go?" Mercy asked, concerned.

Ziel sighed. "Anywhere's better than here."

"Yeah, but can a school full of Jades make it in the real world on their own?"

"They're going to have to," Lindon pointed out.

[Forget them, they're already dead. Probably. But who cares, really?] Dross waved again, and this time a light shone over the mountain to the south. The Greatfather.

[Holy Wind School, not gone yet, but going. At least there are *some* smart people in Sacred Valley.] A few images floated in the air, showing the mass exodus of the Holy Wind School. Most of them were carried on the back of a huge floating raft, not a cloudship, that inched its way south.

"They've been trapped here for generations," Orthos rumbled. "That doesn't make them idiots."

Lindon felt a surprising amount of irritation from Orthos on behalf of the inhabitants of Sacred Valley, which was touching. Lindon rested a hand on the back of the turtle's head and just enjoyed having him back.

[Oh, of course, yes. Not idiots. There are two more schools of non-idiots: here at the Fallen Leaf School—] A light shone on the north mountain. [—and the Heaven's Glory School. The most...wisdom-challenged...of them all. Then, of course, we have the three clans.]

Three more lights shone in the center of the valley. The Kazan clan to the west, the Li clan to the south, and the Wei clan to the northeast.

[We need somebody on each of these lights, not counting me, because I'm trapped inside a living skull.]

Yerin leaned against Lindon's side like he was a doorpost, arms crossed and Goldsigns fortunately retracted. "Don't think I'm jumping anybody to say we're going to the Wei clan. Can't head anywhere on my own, because I'm two seconds from falling on my face, and Lindon's been talking about going home since the day we left."

Lindon nodded silently. That was the most obvious assignment.

The violet light over the Wei clan turned into a little picture of Yerin. And Dross.

[All right, that's one taken care of. Good pace. Someone will have to stay here—]

"Apologies, but are you planning on leaving me behind?"

Dross gave an annoyed sigh. [Anywhere I go, you go. It's implied. But if it bothers you that much, I can soothe your ego.]

A tiny model of Lindon hovered next to Yerin. And over them both, like a fat moon, hung an image of Dross. He was much more detailed than they were, too.

[Now, who wants to make sure the Fallen Leaf School makes it out the eastern exit?]

"I will," Orthos said. "The exiles are here, and they know me."

And, Lindon knew, the other options required much more flying.

Little Blue piped up, standing up to her full foot of height and sticking her hand in the air. Lindon was shocked. She had never volunteered to be apart from him before.

She turned to look at Lindon, whistling a question, and he nodded. If she wanted to stay with Orthos, there was nothing wrong with that. And Orthos could protect her.

Then again, she had grown alongside Lindon for a long time now. Maybe *she* would be the one protecting *him*.

[Okay, Orthos and Blue here at Fallen Leaf.] Dross waved his hand and the northern mountain light changed to a model of Blue sitting on Orthos' shell. [Heaven's Glory, anyone? Yerin, how about you? You don't *need* to go with Lindon, and we didn't do a headcount of whatever Jades they have left. We probably wouldn't notice if one or two went missing...]

He let that temptation hang there in the air, but Eithan had already raised his hand.

"I would be delighted to secure Heaven's Glory myself. It's very important that we hold that exit and soothe relations between the school and the Golds, and you know what they say: if you want something done right, get Eithan to do it."

[Done!] The purple light shifted into an image of Eithan

sweeping something into a pile. It looked suspiciously like a pile of bodies. [That leaves the Li and Kazan clans for Ziel and Mercy. Who wants which one?]

"The Li clan!" Mercy said brightly. "I like their name!"

[Which leaves the Kazan for you, Ziel. You think you can handle it?]

"I know literally nothing about either of them. Just tell me where to go."

[I like you, Ziel,] Dross said. [You're so...compliant.]

第九章

CHAPTER NINE

Ziel took his host of Golds and marched for the Kazan clan territory.

Well, *they* took *him*.

He didn't mind his role here. He was saving people from a Dreadgod attack. That was worth his time and attention, so he was more than willing to do it. It's just that there wasn't much he could do that his bunch of Akura Golds couldn't handle on their own.

That suited him just fine. He would throw his weight around if necessary, but he didn't need to do much other than *be* there.

Ziel drifted along on a borrowed Thousand-Mile Cloud, letting the Truegold woman in charge of his retinue drag him after them.

The Kazan clan had a solid series of walls around their territory, large bricks mortared by layers of old scripts. Their gates were hammered bronze, lined here and there with half-silver or goldsteel to disperse attacks.

Ziel's Golds declared themselves to the sentries, negotiated their way inside, and arranged a meeting with the leaders of the Kazan clan while Ziel laid back on his cloud, half-asleep.

The people here seemed...sturdy. That was the best way to put it. They were generally stocky, looked as though they were no strangers to a hard day's work, and the badges on their chests were almost the size of breastplates.

Most of the homes here were made of stone and rough-hewn logs, and were built to last. He got the impression of a clan of people who valued diligence and practicality, with few frills or decorations to speak of. He approved. Sacred artists should be hard workers.

He was fully aware of his own position, lying on a cloud and drinking elixir straight from a bottle that he'd stored in his void key.

But his spirit hadn't settled yet. Eithan had completed the Pure Storm Baptism before leaving—otherwise, Ziel wouldn't have come along.

It would be some time before his madra system stabilized fully. Until then, he wasn't supposed to strain himself.

While he was reduced to the strength of a Jade, there wasn't much he *could* do to strain his madra channels. Jade madra shouldn't hurt him even if he tried to attack himself from the inside out.

Even so, it would be best to take it easy.

Ziel took another swig from the bottle. Technically it *was* an elixir, as it had beneficial effects on the spirit, but you could also accurately call it wine.

He laid back and threw his arm over his eyes to block out the sun.

They drifted through the Kazan clan for a while, his assistant explaining several times that they were Golds from outside of the valley, they represented the Akura clan and the Sage of Twin Stars, and they were here to warn the clan leaders of incoming danger.

At some point, they passed inside, and Ziel could stop protecting his eyes. It was cooler out of the sun, and a brief glimpse showed him that they were drifting through polished stone hallways with decorations of worked metal. He felt earth aura all around him, which would ordinarily feel soothing.

Now, it felt like he was inside a nervously beating heart.

The Dreadgod's influence was powerful here. The veins of aura throughout the stone quivered with chaos as the Wandering Titan grew closer.

They entered a bright room, and the murmur of people grew quiet. Ziel's cloud came to a halt.

"Patriarch of the Kazan clan," the Truegold woman announced, "I present to you Ziel of the Wastelands, chosen of Northstrider, Uncrowned of the Uncrowned King tournament, former leader of the Dawnwing Sect, and representative of the Akura clan and the Sage of Twin Stars. Let his words be as the voice of heaven to you."

Ziel groaned as he realized she was going to make him speak. He was not needed for this. She could tell them all about the Dreadgod, and only if they resisted would he need to strongarm them into listening.

But he was here now. He might as well do what he could.

Slowly, Ziel sat up and opened his eyes to see what he was dealing with.

The Kazan Patriarch was a stocky, black-bearded man clad in chainmail. His jade badge was roughly carved with a shield, and he wore a bear's pelt across his shoulders. He sat not at a desk, but on a log bench at the far end of a long table.

Ziel was certain there had been more people in the room before, as this seemed to be some kind of dining hall filled with empty tables, but apparently they had filtered out while his eyes were shut. He swept his spiritual perception out and found them clustered on the other sides of the oaken doors.

The only people in the large room with him were his Truegold assistant, the Patriarch, and a woman he assumed to be the Patriarch's wife. She stood behind him with a worried expression and a hand on his shoulder.

Her badge was made of iron, and she wore it literally as a breastplate, strapped to her as armor. There was no way this Patriarch would allow people he assumed to be Jade or higher to be alone with him and his Iron wife without some level of protection.

Instead of saying anything, Ziel leaned down to peer under the table, where he saw a dimly lit script around the two of them. He traced that script back to constructs all around the room.

With enough attention, he could figure out what they did, but that would take more attention than he was willing to spare.

By this point, he had been silent for a long time. He tapped the right side of his own breast.

"You have something in your pocket," Ziel said. "Take it out."

The Patriarch's wife frowned more deeply, but the Jade himself only reached with two fingers into a breast pocket behind his badge and pulled out a pair of halfsilver bracelets. He placed them down on the table without explanation.

Ziel held out both his wrists. "Go ahead."

The Akura Truegold threw out her hand to stop him. "I can't allow that, sir. We can't guarantee your safety with your spirit restricted."

"Your job isn't to protect me," Ziel said. "It's to protect them." He kept his arms out.

The Patriarch must have been confused, but he kept his expression blank as he slid the halfsilver rings over Ziel's wrists.

Ziel grunted in discomfort as the scripts in the rings activated, restricting his madra.

They weren't cuffs. He could throw them off if he wanted. They were surely designed to be tied in place somehow, but the gesture was what was important, not the actual effect on his spirit.

"This is not necessary," the Kazan Patriarch said. "I intend to hear you out in good faith."

"Yeah, well, I skipped a step. We're not here to hurt you or take anything. I'm going to lay out the situation for you, and if you don't like what I have to say, we'll turn around and leave."

The Patriarch's eyes flicked to the Akura Truegold, who

looked like she was having trouble keeping her hand away from the long knife at her belt. "Your people said you came to warn us."

Ziel jerked his head toward the stone wall. "You can feel it yourself. There's a monster coming." These people were earth artists; they would have sensed the Titan coming, even if they didn't know what caused it.

"It's called a Dreadgod, and we expect it to arrive in a matter of days. When it gets here, everybody in the valley is dead. We have cloudships to take you all to safety, but if you want to take your chances, that's up to you."

Ziel stopped to take another swig from his bottle. "That's it. If you don't trust us, you should still leave on your own."

He sensed another presence coming closer, creeping along the edges of the wall. It was only at the Foundation stage, so he ignored it.

"Our defenses are strong," the Kazan Patriarch said, and he didn't sound overly proud. He was simply stating a fact. "We had planned to retreat into our strongholds and withstand the coming storm."

"These strongholds. They're underground, aren't they?"

The Patriarch didn't say anything, but his wife twitched.

"This Dreadgod can eat entire mountains," Ziel said. "Hope you've got some good scripts."

With that, he looked down to his side, where the Foundation presence had reappeared. Dark, glittering eyes regarded his cloud in awe.

It was a child. A little boy.

The Patriarch's wife took in a breath. "Maret! Forgiveness, please, I'll take him!"

She rushed over as the boy grabbed onto Ziel's Thousand-Mile Cloud, pulling his tiny body up. Ziel dismissed him.

"He's fine. He won't hurt himself."

The boy's mother froze. She seemed to be holding herself back from snatching up her son. Ziel understood that; you never knew what would set off strange, possibly hostile sacred artists. If she expressed a lack of trust in him, then as far as she knew, he might become enraged at the disrespect and attack.

He let out a sigh. "I would never lower myself to harm a child. But if it would put you at ease, by all means take him."

The cloud bobbed beneath him as Maret jumped up and down, giggling at the springy cloud madra.

She looked somewhat relieved and bowed. "This one is... certain that he can come to no harm under your watch, so long as he is not giving offense."

Ziel had actually been hoping she *would* take the child back, but it was too much effort to clarify. He just pretended not to notice the boy jumping up and down behind him.

The Patriarch cleared his throat. "Pardon us. Our littlest one is a...curious child. I should have scanned for him when the others left the room."

Judging by the clumsiness Ziel had seen from the Jades here, his scan would have been slightly less useful than just glancing around with his eyes.

Tiny fists grabbed handfuls of Ziel's hair, but it would take hundreds of pounds more weight to free even one of Ziel's hairs. He pushed the boy to the back of his mind and continued.

"If you come with us, we can help you evacuate. We hope that you will be able to return soon, and that your homes will be intact. But if not...well, there is no replacing human lives."

"Forgiveness, but if you don't know how much destruction this Dreadgod will cause, then how much danger are we in?"

That slipped in through the cracks in Ziel's heart, finding an unexpectedly tender place.

He had spoken those words, or ones very similar, years ago upon finding out that the Weeping Dragon was approaching. He'd known all about the Dreadgods, of course, but their sect was ancient. Well-defended. Protected by scripts and constructs.

How much danger could they be in?

As it turned out, they had survived the Dreadgod itself. But not the scavengers that fed in its wake.

When Ziel spoke, his voice was dead. "I used to lead a sect of my own. We decided that we could survive a Dreadgod. I decided. First, we felt the aura tremble, like footsteps shaking the ground. What you're feeling now."

He nodded to the walls. "Next, the sky changed color. It's a change that accompanies each of the Dreadgods, as their power overwhelms all aspects of vital aura. We hunkered down inside defenses, layers of scripts that had stood for centuries."

Ziel trailed off for a moment as he remembered the sky, raining lightning.

No one else spoke.

"One by one, it stripped away our defenses. Tore off the roof. Toppled buildings. Our techniques were only food for it. And the Dreadgod never stopped, it never saw us, it simply flew on by. We were stripped to the bone by its footsteps, by the wind from its passage. To it, we were only ants."

Silence still reigned in the room.

Until Ziel felt a child giggle.

He realized that there was a weight on his head, and craned his eyes upward. While he'd been speaking, Maret had climbed up his hair and come to rest on top of his skull, and was now holding onto his horns, rocking back and forth as though riding a bull.

The horrified looks on the faces of the boy's parents now took on a whole new dimension.

The Patriarch tore his gaze down and cleared his throat. "My sympathies. If your home was destroyed by this Dreadgod as well, then you above all have reason to warn us."

"Not this Dreadgod," Ziel said. He reached up and peeled away the child from his head, holding him out to his mother.

She was only too glad to take him.

"There are three others," Ziel continued. "And what we survived was merely its passing. In front of an attack, there is no survival. There is escape, or there is death."

Slowly, with no sudden movements that might signal an attack, Ziel pulled off the halfsilver rings restricting his madra and placed them onto the table.

"It is your decision to make. But I wish I had taken this chance myself."

He turned and urged his Thousand-Mile Cloud to slide toward the door.

"We need time," the Patriarch called.

"You don't have it," Ziel responded.

"It will take at least a day for the clan to respond to our emergency beacon!" the Patriarch's wife protested.

Ziel stopped and slowly turned around. "You're going to call your clan to evacuate?"

The Patriarch nodded. "As soon as we leave this room. But our territory is large. One day is already the fastest we can gather, and that's if we use all our alarms of war and our swiftest riders."

"I thought you needed time to *decide*," Ziel said.

"Everything you've said lines up with the reports of our scouts and scholars. And I believe you." The Kazan Patriarch inclined his head. "We entrust ourselves to your honor."

"Oh. Well...good."

Ziel became acutely aware of the weight of command settling onto his shoulders. He realized he had just taken responsibility for another clan of people.

What a stupid decision.

He should have let the Golds handle it.

The wall surrounding the Li clan was a work of art, a smooth expanse of pale, polished wood decorated by a functional script in a way that evoked the image of a slithering serpent. Treetops rose from behind it, and the sky was filled with birds of every description.

Mercy was impressed. Their commitment to aesthetics was all the more commendable considering their lack of resources. She could only imagine the effort it would take to build something so expansive and delicate with a workforce of Irons.

She only wished she had seen more of the Li clan than the outside.

"The Matriarch has arrived," one of the guards announced from the top of the wall, and Mercy let out a relieved breath. She had spent most of the afternoon negotiating with underlings, trying to get a word with the clan leader.

Her Golds were behind her. She didn't want to overwhelm the Jades.

Now, at last, she'd finally gotten somewhere.

A gray-haired woman stepped up to the edge of the wall. She was tall, thin, and dignified, with an emerald-set silver tiara in her hair and rings on each finger. A snake rested on her shoulders, and even it was decorated with gold and jewels.

Mercy dipped her head. "Humble greetings, honored Matriarch. I am Akura Mercy, and I have come to offer the assistance of the Akura clan in the face of the incoming threat."

The Matriarch lifted one eyebrow. "And what threat is that?"

They knew exactly what the threat was. Even if they were blind to the increasing earthquakes and the bizarre behavior of the aura all around them, Mercy had explained the situation half a dozen times already.

But she gave no hint of impatience as she responded, "The Dreadgod, honored Matriarch. You can feel its footsteps in the earth. My mother is the guardian of the lands all around Sacred Valley, and I come as her representative to shelter you until the danger is passed."

"And what proof do you bring that this danger is real?"

"I would be happy to leave a dream tablet for you, or to swear an oath on my soul, if that would convince you."

The Matriarch waved a hand. "That isn't necessary yet. Assuming I believe you, what would you have us do?"

"We have a fleet of cloudships ready to evacuate your clan outside the eastern passage to the valley. I urge you to let us help evacuate you and your families, so that we can fly you to safety."

"Hmmm. Well, thank you for bringing this to my attention. I will consult with the clan elders and let you know our decision soon."

She began to turn away, but Mercy cut in desperately. "I apologize for pressing you for details, but how soon?"

"Soon."

"We expect the Wandering Titan to arrive in only a week, honored Matriarch. Once it begins its attack, it will be too late to escape."

"I'm beginning to find your insistence *rude*, Akura Mercy," the Matriarch said. She folded her arms and looked down on Mercy sternly. "If you really were the daughter of a ruler, you would know better than to show such...desperation. It is enough to make me wonder what you have to gain by rushing us into a decision. Perhaps you hope we will make ourselves vulnerable in our haste."

Frustration tightened its grip on Mercy's heart, but she threw herself to her knees. "I swear on my soul that every word I have said is true to the best of my knowledge," she called.

Her spirit tightened slightly. A one-sided oath wasn't as binding as an agreement with another soul, but it was still foolish to break.

"Then you are a very earnest messenger," the Matriarch said, "but still perhaps an enemy. Enough. I have heard everything I need to hear, and I will make my own decision."

With that, the leader of the Li clan strode away.

Mercy knelt in the dirt, frustration and helplessness twisting inside her.

She felt a building tide of madra, and looked to the side to see Kashi, the Truegold commander of her Akura troops. He was a conscript from Akura lands, not a member of the clan, and he wasganglier and more awkward than a stork.

He had drawn a pair of swords, which crackled with silver madra, and there was deadly ice in his eyes as he looked on the enemy wall.

"With your permission, Overlady, I can have her on her knees before you in ten breaths or less."

"No, that would send entirely the wrong message. We're here to help them."

"Then let's help them," Kashi said. "Whether they want us to or not."

Mercy pushed herself to her feet, brushing off her knees. "They've seen the signs of the Dreadgod's coming. They'll leave."

"Forgive me, Overlady, but we can't wait for them to come to a decision. If we can't start evacuating them now, then we won't have enough time to get them out."

"But she was right that we can't push her into a decision. We can afford to wait until tomorrow."

Tomorrow the Matriarch would see reason, Mercy told herself. Rushing would only ruin negotiations. The Titan was more than a day away; they would see it coming long before they ran out of time.

She kept telling herself that instead of chewing the Goldsign from her hand in frustration.

Jai Long sat with Jai Chen in the corner of a tiny cloud-ship. It was hard to call it a proper cloudship at all, actually; it was more of a raft on the back of a Thousand-Mile Cloud.

They were part of a small fleet of these...cloud-rafts, some of which had been brought by the Akura Golds, though most had been confiscated from the Fallen Leaf School. They were designed to work in this low-aura environment, and as such were painfully slow. Jai Long often considered leaping down to the ground and running.

But down there, he would run into trouble. Up here, at least he had an escort.

They were returning to the Heaven's Glory School—and the eastern exit from Sacred Valley—with a team of forty Akura Golds, a few dozen old or wounded exiles from the Wei clan...and Eithan Arelius.

Who would not leave them alone.

He drifted at their side on a dark blue one-person cloud that he had surely brought himself, and no matter how Jai Long steered his own raft, he couldn't escape.

Jai Long had managed to dodge or bluntly ignore all the Underlord's questions up until now, but Jai Chen wasn't helping. She chatted with him easily, she and her dragon spirit.

"You've cared for your bonded spirit well," Eithan observed. "Have you named it?"

"We call him Fingerling," Jai Chen said, looking a little sheepish. "He started off the size of a finger, and he loves eating small fish. It started as a nickname, but then it just...stuck."

The pink, serpentine dragon trilled proudly at the sound of his name. It undulated through the wind on Jai Chen's shoulder and gave Eithan a haughty look.

"I quite understand. In the original language of my homeland, 'Eithan' also means 'tiny fish.'"

She leaned forward. "Really?"

"No. It means 'embodiment of impossible perfection.'"

Jai Long didn't believe that either.

"Speaking of my homeland, I seem to recall that you were able to use a version of my bloodline power. Can you still see things through strands of madra around you?"

Jai Long shifted, trying to get his sister's attention to signal her not to answer the question. Eithan was pushing them, questing for their weaknesses. The less she told these strangers, the better.

"Only if I concentrate," Jai Chen said happily, and Jai Long cursed his own failure. He had raised her to be too trusting.

She gestured to her dragon. "He's better at it. If he really tries, he can see things over a mile away."

"Then he is *very* talented," Eithan said, and the sincerity in his voice convinced Jai Long that he must be lying. Of course, Jai Long thought the same about every word from Eithan's mouth.

The Underlord inclined his head to the pink dragon, and Fingerling preened under the attention.

"And how about you, Jai Long?" Eithan asked. "I hear you've been having quite the adventures here in Sacred Valley."

Jai Long had known this was coming, and he had an iron-clad defense ready.

"Not by choice. I have nothing left to do with the sacred arts. I'm done."

If he made a vague statement, the Arelius Patriarch would interpret it however he wanted. Jai Long would leave no doubt: he wanted nothing to do with the world of sacred artists anymore.

Eithan nodded along as though he understood. "A wise decision. Who needs to sprint from advancement to advancement? Stay as an Underlord, I say."

Jai Long had to keep himself from snorting in disdain. Eithan had made it to Underlord young enough that he would almost certainly reach Overlord one day, especially considering how strong he was and how many resources he had access to. There was no way he would be content as an Underlord.

Eithan snapped his fingers. "You're not an Underlord yet, are you? But you made it *so* close. Surely you'd want to stay somewhere with stronger aura for a while, just to see if you could take that last step."

"I would not dare to take the leap to Underlord so lightly, Patriarch Arelius." He hoped his tone would shut Eithan up, but if it didn't, he could stonewall the conversation all day.

In fact, he *had* been tempted to go stay outside Sacred Valley for a few months, to test himself and see if he could reach Underlord.

But that temptation was nothing weighed against safety. And Sacred Valley, while not exactly welcoming, was at least filled with weaklings.

"Patriarch Arelius?" Eithan repeated. "We're old friends at this point, Jai Long. By all means, relax."

"If you insist." It would be wiser to keep his mouth shut, but Jai Long saw the opportunity to strike back. "You must be proud to have trained another Underlord so young. Perhaps he'll even reach Overlord soon. Isn't the dream of every master to be surpassed by their student?"

Jai Long had known enough Underlords. They all said they wanted their disciples to surpass them, but every time someone showed greater talent than theirs, they erupted out of wounded pride.

That should be enough of a jab that he would get to enjoy some discomfort on Eithan's face, but not enough that he'd display open anger in front of all these Akura Golds.

Instead, Eithan's eyebrows shot up.

"Underlord? Haven't you heard? Lindon's a Sage."

This time, Jai Long *did* snort in disbelief. He didn't say anything, but his contempt should be clear. Joking around was one thing, but Eithan would have to make his lies more believable if he wanted to deceive Jai Long.

But Jai Long didn't like the look of the smile that slowly widened on Eithan's face. "Waaaaait a moment. Have you not scanned Yerin?"

He hadn't, but only because he'd been trying to stay away from Yerin as much as possible. Even if Lindon didn't hold a grudge—which Jai Long still doubted—the Sword Sage's apprentice certainly would.

"I did," Jai Chen put in. "I don't mean to be rude, but is there something wrong with her? Her spirit was...strange."

"How so?" Eithan asked, in the tone of a man who already knew the exact answer to his question.

"It felt like her spirit was all tangled up with her body. Like her madra channels had melted into her, if that makes sense." Jai Chen lowered her voice. "Was she injured? Is that why she's so weak now?"

"That is not why," Eithan said. "Young lady, you have done well to keep your eyes open. Your brother is...woefully uninformed."

Eithan was clearly implying something, but if he expected

Jai Long to display any curiosity whatsoever, then he was hoping in vain. This would all end with the Underlord trying to get something out of them, he was sure, and Jai Long wasn't about to fall for it.

Eithan waved a hand, and a Truegold in Akura colors quickly sped up to catch up with him. "Yes, Eithan?"

"Ikari, if you don't mind, would you address me by title? Just once."

"Of course, Archlord. In fact, I would be happy to continue—"

"You can go back to before, thank you, Ikari."

The Truegold woman gave a bow and fell back among her fellows, but Jai Long was staring at Eithan.

Archlord.

There was no way it was true.

Jai Long hadn't thoroughly scanned Eithan, that being a good way to start a fight, but he had been close enough to the man to get a good sense of his power. He was still an Underlord, Jai Long was sure.

Even accounting for the curse of Sacred Valley, which left them all little better than Jades, he was certain that Eithan hadn't grown any stronger than before.

He was...*almost* certain.

Eithan spread his arms wide. "By all means, Jai Long, I invite you to scan me and confirm for yourself."

With the feeling that he was falling for some kind of trap, Jai Long extended his spiritual perception.

He wasn't sure what he was looking for, exactly. He had never had the chance to personally sense an Overlord, much less an Archlord. If he could feel the full force of Eithan's spirit, he could be certain, but everyone was suppressed here.

Certainly, Eithan's body had been thoroughly reforged in soulfire. It felt like a perfect conduit for energy, even more so than the Underlords Jai Long had sensed before. But did that mean he had advanced, or just that he was above average in this one aspect?

Jai Long couldn't tell if the man was truly an Archlord or

simply a peak Underlord, and was about to say so.

"Ah, excuse me, I forgot a veil."

Then a dim part of Eithan's spirit became clear, and Jai Long felt the pool of soulfire at the center of his spirit. A dense flame of reflective chrome, like quicksilver imitating fire.

Archlord soulfire. It had to be.

Jai Long had never seen it before, but it was unmistakable. This was *at least* two grades higher than the soulfire he held in his own spirit.

He withdrew his perception as though the silver flame had burned him and fell to one knee. He was breathing unnaturally quickly, but he couldn't keep it under control.

This was what Eithan had been after. He'd been toying with them all along, just to see their reactions.

The difference between Underlord and Archlord was like the distance between the lowest valley and the highest stars. There was no Archlord in all the Blackflame Empire.

Even in Sacred Valley, where Eithan would be closer to mortal than anywhere else, Jai Long couldn't antagonize him any further. Who knew what an Archlord could do?

"Archlord, I apologize for any disrespect. I was ignorant and unaware."

"Aren't we all?" Eithan didn't seem to have reacted much to Jai Long's panic, though even Jai Chen had curled up and was holding Fingerling protectively in her hands.

He gave her a reassuring smile. "I have nothing but fondness for the both of you, don't worry. However, if it's not too much to ask, I would love to know one thing: after you leave the valley, where are you headed?"

This time, Jai Chen was the one to answer.

"We're not sure, Archlord."

"As a mighty Archlord, I command you to call me Eithan. Titles change too often."

"I still have contacts in the Desolate Wilds," Jai Long said, as much to take his attention away from Jai Chen as to demonstrate compliance. "They will shelter us for a time, but after that...wherever the heavens lead us."

He felt it was wise to give Eithan a vague answer, but it was also the truth. Their immediate plans were simply to get away from the Dreadgod.

"If by whatever twist of fate you find yourselves without a roof over your heads, I'm certain we can find space for you. We're quite in favor at the moment."

"Lindon already invited us," Jai Chen said. "But we can't commit to anyone with our futures so uncertain." She dipped her head, but Eithan looked surprised.

"Lindon invited you? Good for him! But I hate that I didn't know that already. I'm used to eavesdropping on him all the time, you see."

Jai Long felt an unexpected pang of sympathy for Lindon.

"Well, if either or both of you change your mind, I'm certain you can find a way to contact us. We'd be happy to have you."

The conversation ended there, which left Jai Long wondering...

Why?

Why had Lindon and Eithan both independently decided to recruit them? If Eithan was an Archlord, Lindon a Sage—which Jai Long still didn't believe—and Yerin a...whatever... then someone who hadn't even reached Underlord would be far beneath them.

They wouldn't be impressed by his advancement, so what was it? Jai Chen's bonded spirit and unique madra? Was this some kind of elaborate revenge, like taking a trophy?

By the time the fleet of clouds landed in the Heaven's Glory School, Jai Long still hadn't decided.

While the Akura clan unloaded refugees and Eithan established his leadership of Heaven's Glory, Jai Long and Jai Chen left.

They marched straight east, out of Sacred Valley the same way they came in. At first, he was certain that the dirty looks from Heaven's Glory would result in drawn weapons, but the presence of the Akura servants meant they didn't have to deal with anything more than glares.

Finally, more easily than he had ever imagined possible,

they stood in the passage leading out of Sacred Valley.

As the ring of light glared down on him from overhead, he stared at the forest beneath and the mountains ahead. Beyond them lay the Desolate Wilds, and even further, the Blackflame Empire.

Their past.

Jai Chen hitched a pack on her back, Fingerling trilled excitement, and she gave him a wide smile. "It's been a while since we've made a camp!"

He waited too long, lost in thought. When he realized she was waiting on a response, he grunted agreement.

They had spent the better part of two years here. Now, it was like that time had never happened.

In the end, there had been no point to anything they'd done. The long journey to get here, the home they'd built. The people they'd traded with.

Fighting side-by-side with Orthos and Wei Shi Kelsa. Learning to work with them. Rescuing Kelsa's mother. All the lives they'd taken from Heaven's Glory.

It all felt like such a waste.

They could have just stayed in hiding, then left when the Dreadgod grew close. Kelsa would have found another way to rescue her mother, with Orthos' help. She hadn't *really* needed his power in the first place.

Jai Chen leaned in, watching his face.

"They still need help with the evacuation," she pointed out.

Jai Long shook himself out of his own thoughts. "They can handle it. We need to put distance between us and the Titan."

He still wasn't sure if the Desolate Wilds would be far enough away to escape a Dreadgod, and the sooner they left, the safer they'd be.

"We'd make it a lot further on a cloudship," she pointed out.

Jai Long looked over all the large, passenger cloudships perched everywhere in view. They had been sent here for the mass exodus from Sacred Valley.

But they'd been sent by the Akura clan, which Jai Long only knew as a dark, distant force. He couldn't trust them.

"I don't want to take chances on strangers with a Dreadgod coming," he said.

"What chance? It's better to wait for the ships to leave than to walk. And in the meantime, we can help other people get out."

"That's true..." he murmured.

While he was still thinking, his sister led him back inside.

第十章

CHAPTER TEN

The walls of the Wei clan had seemed taller when Lindon was younger.

In his mind's eye, he saw the gates into the main clan territory as an ancient edifice that scraped the sky. He remembered when they had changed out the doors for freshly carved and decorated ones, in honor of the last Seven-Year Festival. But now, as an Underlord, he saw the plain wood used to make them. The peeling paint. And the walls were only about thirty feet tall.

He could leap over them with a flat-footed jump.

At least Elder Whisper's tower was as tall as he remembered it. It stood out like a spear from behind the wall. He wondered what the snowfox would say about Lindon's advancement.

He took another breath, more nervous than he should have been. He couldn't put a name to his mix of feelings.

Yerin took his left hand in hers. "Try your hardest not to burn the whole place down."

The Iron guard took a tight grip on his spear. "What?"

"Wouldn't judge if you had to kill one or two."

Foxfire gathered on the end of the Iron's weapon. He levered it at Yerin, but addressed Lindon. "Give me your name, Unsouled."

Lindon had not missed that title. But he couldn't blame the Iron for being on edge; there were forty Akura clan Golds behind them, after all, each hovering a foot or two off the ground on the back of a Thousand-Mile Cloud or other floating construct.

A Truegold man with gray in his hair stepped forward before Lindon could say anything. "The Akura clan presents the Sage of Twin Stars and the reigning champion of the Uncrowned King tournament. Present the leader of your clan or we will find them ourselves."

Lindon dipped his head. "Apologies, older brother. We intended no threats. My name is Wei Shi Lindon, and I am here to see the First Elder about the recent earthquakes."

The ground was steadily buzzing now, a low-pitched thrum beneath Lindon's feet that never went away. The veins of earth aura pulsed as though they ran with lightning.

The Iron looked up at the people spread out before him and set his jaw. He had no spiritual sense to speak of, but he had the confidence of a man with an entire clan at his back.

"You forget yourself, Unsouled." The Foxfire at the tip of his weapon disappeared, but the guard reversed his spear. "Whoever your masters are now, *you* should speak to me with respect."

He brandished the butt of his spear, cocking it back in a silent threat.

Lindon held up a hand before the Truegold to his left annihilated this Iron. "You see all these people behind me, don't you?"

"Word has already been sent to the Jades. They will decide what to do with our guests." The guard's chin tilted up. "In the meantime, I was told to expect outsiders at our gates. And to show them the strength and dignity of the Wei clan."

Lindon understood now. This guard thought they were inhabitants of Sacred Valley, but not one of the clans. He assumed they belonged to the collection of exiles and wild families that provided for themselves in the wilderness.

Even without his spiritual perception, he should have

seen better than that. They were far too well-equipped, and the Golds all wore a uniform.

But the Iron had made up his mind, and he stood proudly. "Hit me," Lindon said.

The guard frowned. "What did you say?"

"You suggested you were going to hit me with your spear. Do it. I want to show you something."

The Iron's frown took on an edge of disgust, and he drew himself up straighter. "I'm not giving you the excuse."

"Then I'm heading in." Lindon started to walk for the gate, with Yerin at his side. He expected her to be laughing to herself.

She wasn't. She scowled like she couldn't wait to punch a hole in this man's chest.

Sacred Valley really did not agree with her.

Finally, something in the Iron snapped. "Don't blame me for this!" he shouted to the Akura Golds.

The Truegold at the front rolled his eyes.

The Iron guard hauled back his spear and smacked Lindon's cheek with the butt end.

Wood cracked.

It wasn't a full-force blow, but the Iron hadn't exactly held back either. If Lindon really had been an Unsouled, he would have faced a broken jaw at least.

Old anger leaked out, but Lindon pushed it away. He couldn't hurl an Iron into the sky for doing as he'd asked.

He did, however, seize the spear. When the guard tried to pull it back with all his strength, Lindon's hand didn't budge an inch.

With one thumb, Lindon snapped off one third of the spear's shaft.

wThe guard abandoned his spear and ran through the half-open gates into the Wei clan, screaming for backup.

Yerin thumped Lindon's chest with the back of her fist. "Not certain I can take this. I was about to split him in half the long way."

"You were the one who told me to hold back."

"Easier to say it than do it."

Lindon stopped the Golds before they followed him through. "Stand by for now. We've made our show, so I want to meet with the elders first. I'll call you when we need you."

The Truegold looked displeased, but bowed in acceptance nonetheless.

When Lindon and Yerin walked through the gate, one of his suspicions was confirmed: the guard hadn't sent word to the First Elder. He'd gathered the other guards, half a dozen Irons who surrounded them with weapons drawn. A security script in the street just inside the gate lit up, trapping Lindon and Yerin inside.

Lindon felt crystal flasks in the ground drained of madra to power the script. From a quick glance at the runes, he felt certain it would block them from throwing any techniques out of the circle.

At least, it was supposed to.

The guards were shouting demands, but Lindon spoke quietly to Yerin. "We'll have to show off some more."

He expected a rejoinder from her, but he heard only harsh breathing.

When he looked to her, she was half bent over, her metallic crimson Goldsigns extended and sagging. She gripped her stomach with one hand as though her core was paining her, breathing harshly. It seemed like she was barely on her feet.

He instantly abandoned his previous plan.

Lindon drove his foot down and through the stone of the street, breaking the runes and the circle. The glowing script fuzzed and died, sending essence flying into the air like sparks.

The Fox Dream Ruler technique settled onto the both of them, intending to disrupt the dream aura in their minds.

[Wrong!] Dross shouted.

The Irons all flinched back. One fell onto his backside.

[I don't want to judge you based on your treatment of dream madra, I really don't, but if I *did,* I'd say you're like monkeys doing carpentry. That is to say, you're clumsy and very stupid.]

The Wei clan Irons were familiar with spirits advanced enough to talk, but they had probably never seen one speak into their minds before. Lindon left Dross to it; he could subdue this entire crowd alone if they caused a problem.

He was focused entirely on Yerin.

Fortunately, the second the script broke, Yerin had taken a deep breath and straightened. "Whew. Wouldn't try that again, if I get a wish."

"You can go back and rest, if you need to," Lindon said.

Yerin stretched her arms and Goldsigns. "Not sure I see what's so shiny and bright about being a Herald. These days, it's a bumpy path full of sharp rocks."

"Your madra was having enough trouble supporting your body in Sacred Valley at all."

Outside of Sacred Valley, she would have shrugged this off. It may have weakened her, if it had been powered by more than Iron-level madra, but it certainly wouldn't have crippled her.

Still, this was *far* more severe than it should have been. Lindon couldn't imagine Fury unable to breathe because of a simple script.

This was Lindon's fault. He had been careless.

He dipped his head. "Apolo—"

"Nope," she interrupted. "None of that. Time to get back to the job, true?"

The ground still vibrated beneath them while Dross kept the guards distracted with insults. One of the Irons, a blocky red-faced man with an Enforcer badge, looked at Lindon strangely.

"Shi Lindon?" he asked.

Lindon had given his name at the gate, but there was recognition in the man's voice. He looked closer at the face.

He thought he saw traces of a boy from years ago. They came with several unpleasant memories.

"Mon Teris?"

As a boy, Lindon had found himself on the receiving end

of Wei Mon Teris' temper several times. Including the memorable occasion when Teris had abandoned him to fight the Remnant of an ancestral tree, which had ended with Lindon taking down Teris' father with the Empty Palm.

Lindon hadn't thought of the Mon family in years.

Teris' expression was hard, but he looked from Lindon to the hole Lindon's foot had made in the stone. "I'll bring you to the First Elder. Come."

Lindon hesitated. The Mon family had never had any goodwill toward him, and the situation wouldn't be improved now that he had returned from the dead more than three years later.

Yerin nudged him with her elbow. "What's to worry about?"

[You should worry that he's *not* about to lead you into a trap. Hey, if he does betray you, do you think you could slam him through a tree?]

They had a point. Yerin did, at least. There was no point in doubting Wei Mon Teris.

What could Teris do?

What if there are more scripts like the last one? Lindon thought. He'd have to keep an eye out.

"Lead the way, cousin," Lindon said. He even attempted a smile, though it made Teris' scowl deepen.

Teris led Lindon down the main thoroughfare, the same street the Kazan and Li clans had marched through during the Seven-Year Festival so long ago. This time, the road trembled, and he saw very few people out and about.

Those he did see scurried from place to place, many keeping their eyes on the aura beneath their feet. He sensed most people huddled inside.

Everyone here was scared and on edge. He had to take that into account when they treated him like an enemy.

But he could save them. The thought straightened his spine. He could protect them all.

Teris turned off a smaller side street, and Lindon stopped. "Are we not going to the Hall of Elders?"

"The First Elder isn't there today. He's consulting with the Eighth Elder about the earth aura."

Lindon brightened at that. If the clan still had the same Eighth Elder as before, he had watched over Lindon in the clan archive. Lindon looked forward to seeing him again. He suspected Eithan and the Eighth Elder would get along well.

Teris marched on with no further explanation, but the tension was uncomfortable. When they left the main thoroughfare behind, they mostly passed isolated home complexes, most family homes surrounded by walls.

Families in the Wei clan had lots of space, and Lindon found himself staring into the patches of long grass and purple-leafed orus trees between the compounds and feeling pangs of nostalgia as he recognized certain sights. Or failed to recognize others.

Somewhere in this area was the Mon family home, and the thought gave Lindon an idea of how to push through the awkwardness. "Is your family well, cousin Teris?"

Teris shot a glance back at him. "Eri was accepted into the Holy Wind School. They say she'll be Jade one day."

He said it with a somewhat challenging tone, but Lindon was strangely happy to hear it. Eri had disturbed him, but he was glad to hear she was doing well.

Although the Holy Wind School was heading out of the valley already. Did Teris know that?

If he didn't, it wasn't really any of Lindon's business. At least Eri would be safer outside Sacred Valley than in it.

"And your father?" Lindon asked. There were more members of the Mon family, but he didn't know them well.

"Fine."

[I'm sure he's had a wonderful career as a warrior as long as he got over the humiliation of being defeated by a child.]

Dross had fortunately spoken only to Lindon.

They turned a corner to see a long grass path up a hill, to a walled compound that Lindon didn't remember. Teris held out a hand toward it.

"Is this the Eighth Elder's home?" Lindon asked.

"Did you forget?"

Lindon had. He was sure he must have seen the Eighth Elder's house as a child at some point, but he mostly saw the man at the library.

Do you remember? Lindon asked Dross.

[If you don't remember, I don't. Except for all the things I know that you don't. And all my secret plans.]

Lindon nodded, bracing himself, and walked toward the hill.

White Fox madra lit up behind him, and he closed his eyes. So Teris was betraying him after all.

He scanned thoroughly for scripts. There had to be more to this trap.

"Who are you?" Teris demanded. "Did you teach him that Enforcer technique?"

Slowly, Lindon turned around to see Teris holding a knife in front of Yerin.

For about half a second.

Then he was on the ground, his knife spinning off into the air, Yerin's foot pushing his face into the grassy earth.

Lindon understood his line of logic, if it could be called logic.

From Teris' perspective, Lindon was just Unsouled, so Yerin had to be the one in charge. And she had faltered in the script-circle earlier, so obviously something had weakened her. She must have been the one who had kept Lindon alive and taught him powerful new sacred arts, and now she was vulnerable.

An easy target.

Yerin's foot pressed down on the back of Teris' skull. "You're a spineless pack of rotten rat leavings, aren't you?"

Teris thrashed, trying to free himself.

[Can he breathe?] Dross wondered. [It doesn't *look* like he can breathe.]

Lindon crouched next to the Iron, speaking into his ear. "Do you feel the ground shaking?"

The Iron's scream was muffled by dirt.

"That means we don't have much time," Lindon went on. "I don't want to have to continually prove myself to everyone who sees my badge, so here's what I would prefer. Would you like to be my guide?"

Yerin eased up on his head, and Teris' muddy face came up into a gasp. "Yes! Yes! I'll do it!"

"Gratitude. I would be grateful if you could lead me to the First Elder, and if anyone else stops us, you can explain to them what a bad idea that would be. Do you agree?"

Teris nodded furiously.

"Perfect."

Yerin moved her foot off, and Lindon pulled him to his feet. He helped brush dirt from Teris' outer robe. "Now, where is the Elder?"

Teris shakily pointed up the hill to the house right in front of them.

"...really? He's really in there?"

"I told you, ah, this one told you, honored...guests. The First Elder is visiting the Eighth."

Yerin looked more offended now than when he'd pulled a weapon on her. "You pulled blades on us in bright sunlight ten steps from your clan elder's house?"

"Do not harm this one," Teris pleaded, bowing in half. "This one has a little girl."

Yerin turned to Lindon. "Did you get the only spine in your whole clan?"

Lindon wasn't listening.

"You have a daughter?" he asked.

Teris' eyes bounced around, but he answered warily, "This one is honored to have a daughter that will soon see her second year."

That was a bigger surprise to Lindon than when Teris had betrayed them. Teris was a year younger than Lindon himself.

A girl of eleven or twelve peeked her head out of the gate and saw them, shouting back inside that there was a fight going on outside. Yerin slapped Teris on the back.

"Your turn to guide."

Teris preceded them through the gate, and Lindon and

Yerin followed. As soon as they crossed through the compound wall, Lindon knew something was wrong.

The script around the outer wall had blocked his spiritual perception, which was already weaker here in Sacred Valley, so he hadn't sensed much. But the outer courtyard of the Eighth Elder's property was packed with people.

Wei clan members wearing iron or copper badges milled around in small groups, chatting nervously. They all turned to watch Lindon and Yerin enter, but they didn't seem too interested.

As an Underlord, Lindon's hearing was second only to Yerin's. He caught snatches of conversation without trying.

They were waiting for the decision of the elders.

If it was just the Eighth Elder meeting with the First, there wouldn't be so many people here. And they wouldn't expect a unified clan decision.

That was when Lindon recognized another familiar face.

Wei Jin Amon's hair was even longer and more luxurious than Lindon remembered. He stood proudly, a spear strapped to his back, and he reassured several Irons that his grandfather would sort things out.

Lindon extended his perception into the main house.

He didn't scan anyone specifically, but he still felt the presence of Jades. At least ten, probably twelve or thirteen, close together in the same room.

All the clan elders and the Patriarch were gathered together. Well, all the human elders. Elder Whisper was nowhere to be seen.

Teris was passionately explaining that Yerin must be a Jade with no badge, but he stiffened as Lindon rested a hand on his shoulder.

"Cousin Teris, did you know that all the elders were gathered?"

Teris didn't turn around, but he stammered an answer. "Th—this one didn't know for sure."

"That's perfect. Gratitude."

Lindon walked up to the outer house, where three guards

waited for him. One of them was a gray-haired man with a jade badge: the Tenth Elder, the youngest and least of the clan's ruling council.

Finally. A Jade, at least, would be able to sense his power.

Lindon pressed his fists together. "Honored Elder, my name is Wei Shi Lindon. I would like to address the elders about the shaking of the earth."

With that, he removed his veil.

The elder looked from Lindon to Yerin suspiciously, then reached out with his own spiritual sense. The touch of his perception was slow and clumsy, like a numb hand groping in the dark.

He held it on Lindon, scanning him for so long that the shivering sensation became somewhat uncomfortable, but his eyes widened with every second. He finally brushed it over Yerin, then bowed deeply over his fists pressed together.

"You have benefited greatly from surviving the outside, young Shi Lindon, to have reached Jade at such a young age."

Those close enough to hear exclaimed, and even Teris stiffened. Amon's head swiveled to stare at Lindon.

"May I ask, what news have you come to bring us?"

Lindon had prepared his words in advance. "The earthquakes are signs of a coming disaster. A mad beast powerful enough to destroy the entire valley. We bring help from outside, and a way to flee before the beast arrives."

Lindon couldn't name the expression on the Tenth Elder's face, but he bowed again. "That...is...difficult to hear, young Lindon. Come, present your case to the Patriarch."

As far as Lindon could recall, he'd never met the Tenth Elder. Elders tended to have better things to do than to meet with Unsouled. The First Elder was only an exception because he had taken something of a personal interest in Lindon from Lindon's first madra test.

The Tenth Elder led Lindon and Yerin past a network of hallways and a maze of curious, whispering people.

"You fast friends with these elders?" Yerin asked.

"There is one that I think will listen to me."

"If I had to take a blind stab, I'd say it's not your Patriarch."

"*He* probably hates me."

The Patriarch of the Wei clan had only taken special notice of Lindon once. It had been when Lindon defied him, then cheated his grandson Amon out of a coveted position in the Heaven's Glory School.

If the Patriarch remembered Lindon for anything else, it would be disappearing and bringing down Heaven's Glory on the Wei clan.

[It's too bad he doesn't remember getting his heart ripped out,] Dross mentioned. [Wait. That did happen, right?]

Yes, it did.

The invader from outside the world had killed the Patriarch shortly before he'd torn Lindon in half. Lindon remembered it clearly.

Dross gave a sigh of relief. [So that memory *is* real. I'd thought you said it was. Unless I remembered *that* wrong.]

Since they'd found out that some of Lindon's memories of Suriel had been protected, so Dross couldn't view them accurately, Lindon had gone over every inch and let Dross know what was accurate and what wasn't.

But Dross continued to doubt. The knowledge that some of his own memories couldn't be trusted had shaken him.

The Tenth Elder finally stopped and, without ceremony, threw open a perfectly ordinary door.

Lindon had somewhat expected to be beckoned into a great meeting hall, like the Hall of Elders where the Jades usually addressed the rest of the clan.

But this was just a family dining room.

Twelve men and women were inside the room. Eleven elders and the Patriarch. Most sat around a large dining table, though some sat on mismatched chairs or knelt on cushions around the walls.

The Patriarch, Wei Jin Sairus, paced in front of them all at the far end of the room with his hands clasped behind him. He had a mane like a gray lion, and Lindon remembered him as the picture of strength.

Though he'd never thought of it before, the Wei Patriarch of his memories gave him a similar impression to Reigan Shen. Powerful, regal, with the power and mane of a lion.

The Wei Jin Sairus of reality was...lacking.

His face was heavily creased, his build was flabbier than Lindon remembered, and the weakness of his spirit made him feel pathetic. He was considered perhaps the greatest fighter in the Wei clan, but from Lindon's perspective he was no better than the other Jades in the room.

The Patriarch was speaking as they entered. "...Kazan deception cannot be discounted. While I myself doubt that they can mobilize a boundary formation of this scale, we must be half trusting and twice cunning. We will seize one of their southern fields and test their reactions."

Some of the other elders had looked around at the opening door, but the Tenth Elder was clearly waiting for the Patriarch to finish speaking so he could introduce the visitors.

An ancient man with a white beard down to his waist examined them carefully. He stood in a corner, as though positioned to watch everyone else in the room, and he had turned his scrutiny to the newcomers.

Lindon didn't feel any spiritual sense on him, but his stomach churned nonetheless.

"...Lindon?" the First Elder asked.

The Patriarch stopped his speech to turn toward them. The Tenth Elder bowed. "This young clansman has returned from outside claiming to bring news of our current situation. If it pleases the Patriarch, allow me to introduce Wei Shi Lindon."

Several clumsy spiritual perceptions locked onto Lindon and began scanning his spirit, including the Patriarch's.

Yerin's red eyes remained on the Tenth Elder until it was clear he wasn't going to introduce her. "People from your homeland think asking my name's going to give them some nasty disease," she said to Lindon in a perfectly normal voice.

Several of the spiritual senses turned to her.

Lindon saluted the First Elder. "I have returned, honored Elder."

"Shi Lindon," the Patriarch said. "What entrance did you use to return to the Valley?"

Lindon knew what that question really meant. "I came through Heaven's Glory, Patriarch. And I brought allies with me."

No murmuring went up between the old men, but several exchanged meaningful gazes. Heaven's Glory had been after Lindon's blood, but he had come through them unharmed. With a large enough force to escort him through enemy territory.

This was the Wei clan. No one would take him at his word. They would investigate his claim, but that would take time.

Patriarch Sairus made a doubtful sound. "You must have mighty friends indeed, if Heaven's Glory respected them enough to allow you to pass."

Lindon met his eyes. "Yes, Patriarch, I do."

Before anyone could react to that statement, Lindon turned to the First Elder and dipped his head again. "A monster known as a Dreadgod comes for you. It is called the Wandering Titan, and the shaking in the earth you feel now is the least sign of its coming. If it passes through Sacred Valley, it will notice none of us, but its very footsteps will bury us all. You must leave."

The First Elder's white eyebrows climbed into his hair. "You have proof?"

"Dross," Lindon said aloud.

They had practiced this on the way.

On cue, Dross projected Lindon's memories into the minds of everyone in the room.

His first sight of the Wandering Titan sleeping face-down in the bay outside Sky's Edge, its black shell the size of an island. The close-up view of its hand, each finger like a collapsed tower, as Lindon reached out with his Remnant arm to touch its rocky skin.

The feeling of overwhelming strength as it woke, the

slashing of its tail kicking up waves, one cycle of its madra knocking a cloudship from the air.

With that, the memories cut off.

Every Elder exclaimed differently. Many of them had risen to their feet. Some demanded Lindon repeat his technique. Others were simply impressed, or in shock.

None looked more shocked than the First Elder. "Where did you train the Fox Dream?" he asked in disbelief. He glanced down at Lindon's badge. "We can find a Ruler badge for you."

That warmed Lindon more than he had expected. Even though *he* hadn't been the one to use the technique, and he had passed beyond the understanding of Sacred Valley's ranking system long ago.

Even so, this was the man who had once given him the badge declaring him Unsouled.

"You can't expect *us* to take an illusion as proof, no matter how carefully crafted," Patriarch Sairus said.

"Pardon, Patriarch," Lindon said, "but I didn't."

Then he unleashed the full might of his spirit.

He had been drained down to roughly Gold, but his pure core was mostly full, so it was stronger than his Blackflame madra. Exerting spiritual pressure on someone had better results the greater the power difference and the more sensitive the receiver's spiritual sense. It could be used on those under Jade, but its effects were blunted.

The senses of these Sacred Valley Jades were dull, but fortunately the gap in power was wide.

Everyone in the room collapsed to their knees, gasping for breath, as a great weight settled on them. Everyone *except* Lindon, Yerin, and the First Elder.

Lindon took it easy on him.

"I know more than most what power the words of the strong have over you," Lindon said. "Let this represent the weight of my words."

Patriarch Sairus struggled to speak, but Lindon continued. "I have strength beyond anyone and anything you have ever encountered." A moment later he added, "...in this life."

They had all seen Li Markuth and Suriel, though they had died for it.

"If I wanted you to suffer or die, I would not need to deceive you. I could have that now. If I wanted revenge, I could have it. I could have leveled the Heaven's Glory School, but I did not. I do not want your lives. I want you to *keep* your lives."

He released the spiritual pressure, and as they gasped and raised themselves, he bowed to the room in general. "Please, listen to me. We have vehicles prepared to take you to safety. Though I have not been here for several years, I do not want my own clan to fall."

The various elders all had their own opinions, from apologizing for treating him so rudely to demanding that *he* apologize for treating *them* so rudely, but he was listening only for the Patriarch's words.

"What would you have us do?" Patriarch Sairus finally asked. His voice was sore.

Lindon lifted himself from his bow. The Patriarch looked surly, but he should back down before superior power. At least when there was another way out that could benefit everyone.

"Contact everyone in the Wei clan, and anyone living in the wilds that you can. Bring everyone to the Heaven's Glory School. We will use their pathway to the outside."

"When?" the First Elder asked.

"Now. My allies are waiting just outside the walls to help."

The room was quiet. All of them felt the floor vibrating beneath them.

The Patriarch seemed to struggle with himself, but finally he turned to the First Elder. "Call them."

Relief flooded Lindon's chest. He had been afraid he would have to carry the Wei clan elders to Mount Samara on his back.

A grieved expression crossed the Elder's face, but he didn't protest what he must have heard as the order to leave the only home he'd ever known.

The First Elder nodded to the Patriarch and swept out of the room...but not before placing his hand on Lindon's shoulder.

"Welcome home, Lindon."

CHAPTER ELEVEN

It didn't take the Wei elders long to whip the entire clan into action.

The Path of the White Fox was excellent for sending messages, at least compared to the other Paths of Sacred Valley, and the commands of the Patriarch spread all over Wei territory over the course of the day. The Akura Golds spread out as well, shipping small families or individuals back to Heaven's Glory on personal clouds.

As the sun began to set and Samara's ring started to shine, families in white and purple flowed east in a river. They took hand-pulled carts, Remnant-led carriages, wardrobes floating on clouds...anything they could use to carry their belongings away from home.

Lindon could hardly believe it. From his Thousand-Mile Cloud floating high in the air, he watched people filter out from buildings and choke the road, but he couldn't convince himself that it had worked.

He was *sure* something would have gone wrong.

Have you heard from Eithan? Lindon asked Dross for the fifth time.

[I don't *remember* hearing from Eithan.]

Dross had sent a message to Eithan telling him to prepare

for the coming of the Wei clan, but they couldn't be sure their transmission had reached him. The first waves of the Akura clan hadn't returned yet either, so for the moment, they had to guess that Eithan had heard them.

They had also contacted Orthos at the Fallen Leaf School, but Lindon was certain that had worked. Orthos grew slightly closer by the minute.

Yerin braced herself on Lindon's shoulder to lean out and watch the people beneath them. "It's going to take them a year and a half to get out."

That was one of Lindon's concerns. Would the clan have enough time to escape before the Dreadgod arrived?

He opened his aura sight. Jagged veins of gold moving through the earth throbbed rapidly now, and the ground pulsed to the regular rhythm of a heartbeat.

While he couldn't feel the Dreadgod with his spiritual sense yet, it only took his eyes and ears to know the Wandering Titan was close.

They still had monumental work ahead of them if they wanted to evacuate everyone in Sacred Valley, but between the Wei clan sending out messages, the Akura Golds providing their assistance, and Mercy and Ziel visiting the other clans in person, it should be possible. They only needed a few more days. Surely they had that long.

Although Lindon was relieved that, even if they didn't manage to convince anyone else, at least he had helped his own clan.

He was somewhat ashamed of that thought. The other clans deserved to be saved just as much as his own, and he would still work to help them make it out, but the Wei clan just mattered more to him. Of course they did. They were his family.

[Should I start replaying the memories of all the horrible things they did to you, or do you not need my help with that?]

That didn't matter anymore. He had gotten them to listen, which felt in a strange way as though he had gotten some revenge. Like the rivers of white-and-purple marching beneath him proved his worth.

That was silly, but he felt pride in it anyway.

Yerin shaded her eyes with one hand and looked east, toward Mount Samara. "Well, bleed and bury me if that isn't a problem."

With so many weak presences beneath him, Lindon couldn't sense anything in that direction. At least not through the power of the Wandering Titan and the suppressive field of Sacred Valley.

But with Dross' help, he picked out figures moving through the woods on either side of the road.

Heaven's Glory. Armed and moving his direction.

[They really don't learn their lesson, do they?] Dross mused.

Lindon was more than capable of flying over and taking them out himself, but he was worried about Yerin and the Wei clan. It was hard to tell how weak Yerin might be, and if any of the enemies made it past him, the Wei clansmen would have no warning.

He tried to keep his irritation from rising into anger.

The Heaven's Glory School just *would not* leave them alone. He didn't know how they made it past Eithan, but he couldn't imagine they'd harmed him.

Then again, these were the very same people who had managed to kill the Sword Sage.

His frustration started to fade into worry as he landed next to the Patriarch. Wei Jin Sairus and a handful of Elders made a boulder in the flowing stream of the clan, and they stopped barking orders to turn to Lindon.

A couple of them saluted and bowed to him, and one elder Lindon didn't recognize beckoned to nearby servants, but Lindon kept his eyes on the Patriarch.

Sairus dipped his head slightly, but that was all.

"The Heaven's Glory School is coming," Lindon reported. "They'll reach our vanguard in minutes."

The Patriarch's gray eyebrows pinched together. "A battle group?"

"Weren't coming to scratch our backs," Yerin said.

"Then we should meet them ourselves." Sairus gestured, and the nearby servants—who had been rummaging in saddlebags—instead dashed off to prepare mounts for the elders.

"We'll meet you there," Lindon said.

Yerin had never stepped off the cloud. This time, she sat down, her legs dangling off the edge. "Not saving any for them," she muttered.

They arrived back at the forefront of the Wei clan evacuation as the people in purple-and-white were coming to a confused halt. Remnants pulled up short, carriages ground to a stop, and constructs settled to the ground.

Heaven's Glory stretched across the road, a dozen Irons led by half as many Jades. Including Grand Elder Emara.

What was Eithan doing?

The Grand Elder stepped forward...and bowed at the waist. "Wei Shi Lindon, I apologize if we frightened you. Your master, Eithan, sent us to help you."

Lindon felt like the world had flipped upside-down. He settled his cloud onto the ground as Thousand-Mile Clouds spread out behind the Heaven's Glory artists.

Yerin kept a hand on her sword as she hopped to the ground, clearly on edge against the Heaven's Glory Jades.

But the clan didn't stop just because they were blocking the road. Wei clansmen bustled around him, flowing along, intermittently cutting off his view of the Grand Elder as travelers passed between him and the old woman.

"I admit, I did not expect to hear from you yet, Elder," Lindon called over the din of the crowd. "If you could coordinate with the Wei elders, they will lead you to families that can use your help."

The Jade dipped her head again. "Our paths up the mountain are already crowded. We will carry some through the air, and others through side paths."

Heaven's Glory spread out even as the Tenth Wei Elder scurried to greet their leader.

[I don't like it here,] Dross muttered to Lindon. [There's

too many people around, and I can't sense anything.] Between the normal Sacred Valley restrictions and the presence of the Wandering Titan, Lindon's perception was restricted to the point that he felt as though he wore a wet sack over his head.

Keep an eye on them.

They had seen how strong Lindon was, and it seemed true that Eithan had sent them...but Lindon had killed several members of the Heaven's Glory School. He didn't trust them, and Yerin *certainly* didn't. He expected them to have some kind of plan.

Of course, no matter how a spider spun its web, it was useless against the tiger. Lindon would scatter Heaven's Glory one more time if it weren't for the Wei clan streaming between—

The second Lindon returned his attention to the Wei citizens in front of him, he and Dross realized the same thing at the same moment.

The drivers in their carriages, and the riders on the backs of their saddled Remnants, weren't casting nervous glances at Heaven's Glory.

They were looking fearfully at *Lindon.*

He had been betrayed.

Again.

A deep anger came up from where he'd buried it. He'd managed to fight it back ever since he'd arrived here, but now it bubbled up.

Into the Path of Black Flame.

His Blackflame madra was no better than a Jade's, but what more did he need? Threats would be worth more than truth, now, and intimidation better than actual power.

So Lindon drew inspiration from the person he knew who could best act like he was in charge even when surrounded by enemies, and he said what he thought Eithan would say.

"Gentlemen," Lindon said, "this is a mistake."

Each of the Wei clan surrounding them pumped madra

into lengths of cloth they revealed from their backpacks, saddlebags, from the sides of their carriages. Each was woven with scripts.

Boundary flags.

The boundary formation snapped into position immediately, locking the aura surrounding Lindon and Yerin and suppressing their power. Aura of light and dreams was agitated, casting phantom images and sounds all around them.

To Lindon, they were just noise and nonsense, but he put a hand on Yerin's shoulder. He needn't have bothered; she looked around with completely clear eyes and sneered.

"Heaven's truth, I was going to let them live," she muttered.

Dross, where are the Golds?

[Not too many around, and they can't see us. I can contact them, I think, but...] He hesitated. [Do we need them?]

Yerin might.

Dross sent out a call for help.

The Wei Patriarch arrived outside the circle, the First Elder at his side. "Stage two!" he shouted.

Wei clansmen ran forward, carrying a massive chain of scripted goldsteel and looping it around the outside of the boundary field.

Lindon's wariness spiked. A script in goldsteel would be significantly sturdier than boundary flags, so whatever it did, it might actually affect them.

If this went any further, he was going to have to burn his way out.

So he wouldn't let it go further.

He ignited the Burning Cloak and dashed in the direction of the Wei clan elders, who stood on a hill overlooking the road. He crashed into the side of a carriage, smashing the outside to splinters and sending it careening onto its side. The illusion field shattered.

Yerin followed up a second later, tapping one foot onto the upturned cart and leaping for the elders. Constructs erupted from the crowd all around.

Dozens.

Striker, Ruler, and Forger techniques shoved Yerin back with force, with wind, with water, with dreams, even with clouds.

She broke them all with a sweep of her sword, but they did push her back. Even Lindon felt like he had crashed into a soft cushion for a moment.

It was the clearest indication of how much advancement they'd lost. He should have waded through those techniques as though through still water.

In that second of distraction, the goldsteel chain finished wrapping around. The script-circle completed.

Instantly, bands wrapped around Lindon's spirit. It was nothing to him, only mildly unpleasant, but he recognized the feeling of the same script that had bound him at the entrance to the Wei clan.

He shot out to steady Yerin, who was having trouble even breathing and staying upright. Sweat began to bead on her forehead already, and her Goldsigns hung heavy.

Blackflame kindled in Lindon's outstretched hand. "Stop!" he demanded.

If he released, he was going to kill someone.

He turned to Heaven's Glory. "Help us!"

The Grand Elder folded her hands in front of her, staring blithely over his head. Lindon turned back to the Wei clan, and the Patriarch met his eyes with cold disdain. "Stage three!"

Fizzing bottles flew through the air and landed beside them. Some were refiner's work, elixirs that dispersed to gas immediately, but others were venom Ruler techniques. The air filled up with half a dozen types of poisonous gas.

Yerin flashed into white light. The Moonlight Bridge.

She reappeared two feet away, staggering and coughing.

She couldn't cross the goldsteel script.

The poison seeped into Lindon's lungs and crumbled before the might of his Bloodforged Iron body. His breathing would be more troubled by sitting too close to a campfire.

Dragon's breath blasted the goldsteel chain.

It grew red-hot, but that was all. The substance was naturally resistant to all kinds of madra, and the script weakened his techniques even further.

So he had to try something else.

But Yerin was coughing, and his solution would take a moment. With brief flicker of his madra, he opened an unsteady rift onto a luxurious house.

He had found this device in Sophara's void key, but he hadn't had a chance to test it yet. Normal void keys wouldn't close with a living being inside, but this was a home. It obeyed different rules. He hadn't wanted to rely on this until he tested it more thoroughly, but it was the quickest way he knew of to shelter Yerin if she couldn't leave.

Yerin stumbled through the gate, gasping in grateful lungfuls of air.

With a breath of relief, Lindon let the entrance close. Now he could gather his focus for a working. His authority as the Void Sage should be able to break—

The space spat Yerin back out.

She tumbled to the ground out of nowhere, and Lindon simply stared at her for a moment in disbelief. Why hadn't it worked?

He sensed a sort of instability from the space, as though it were barely holding together. It must have ejected her as a security measure.

But when he realized she was hacking and coughing with tears in her eyes, he grabbed her and pulled her to the edge of the circle, where the air was clearest.

He still wanted to try his Sage powers against the script, but they were untested. The sooner he got Yerin out of this, the better, so he leaned on the abilities he knew.

It felt like there was an invisible wall over the script, and Lindon ran his white hand down until he rested fingers on the goldsteel. He activated the binding in his arm, Consuming madra from the script.

[Behind!]

Lindon turned and slapped three halfsilver-tipped arrows

from the air.

A cloud of venom madra exploded at his feet, and Yerin shouted a warning.

The Wei Patriarch shouted again, and more arrows flew through the smoke. Lindon swatted them aside, but he felt so sluggish with his power restricted.

He missed one...and it stuck in his shoulder. The halfsilver penetrated only shallowly, but it disrupted his madra, stinging his body and spirit.

Through tear-stained eyes, Yerin saw him pull the halfsilver arrow from his arm.

She raised her sword. A distant bell rang, and was echoed by all the blades nearby. Sword aura erupted, tearing clothes and skin. It was enhanced by blood aura, so the cuts that bit flesh were deeper.

But the script had weakened her too much. One of the archers staggered back, but the others steadied bleeding hands and took aim.

At her, this time.

The world slowed and seemed to freeze.

Don't stop me, Dross, Lindon thought, and the world returned to normal speed as the spirit released his grip.

Just as Lindon released his own.

Dragon's breath obliterated one of the men standing over the goldsteel chain. The Striker technique burned arrows from the air, leaving sparkling bright arrowheads falling to the dirt.

With space cleared, Lindon fell down again, starting the Consume technique once more.

It was difficult to touch the chain directly, but that resistance was quickly overcome. Madra flooded into his white arm, most of it vented, but he cycled the Heart of Twin Stars and sorted it into its components.

There were a few different Paths used to fuel this barrier, but he kept only the madra from one of them. The most familiar.

Dross, Lindon thought.

[I'm not giving you a combat solution against a bunch of Irons.]

Break down the Path of the White Fox.

[Oh, that's easy. Done.]

More arrows and techniques poured in until the air was thick, but even unsteady on her feet and blind through tears, Yerin hacked them away herself. He was certain that the only thing keeping her from throwing herself at the enemy was his presence.

Finally, the script failed.

He pulled her in front of him, shielding her with his body, and whispered, "Head to the ships."

"Bury 'em," Yerin choked out.

In a flash of white, she vanished.

Leaving Lindon surrounded by enemies.

Lindon folded back into the poisonous smoke as techniques and arrows flew. When he was hidden, he Forged a disguise next to himself. It felt like molding a rough mannequin, but dream and light madra—guided by tweaks from Dross and Lindon's own instincts—filled in the details.

A perfect copy of Lindon stood next to him.

[They craft every detail themselves, so they can't get anything wrong. It's a lot better to stay loose.]

This was the Fox Mirror.

Lindon grabbed the aura around him with his White Fox madra, shaping it into a distraction. This time, he didn't have to fill in any of the details at all, other than ordering the illusion to make people look away from him. Their minds would fill in the details themselves.

He left the smoke, the Fox Dream hanging around him. The Irons who rushed in close, carrying weapons, were affected by the Dream and screamed or stared off in the distance or simply ignored him.

He walked through the crowd. This modification had been his own; he hadn't needed Dross' help with this one. He had worked enough with dream and light aura, and his own experience with shaping aura showed him that he could hold the Fox Dream as a continuous Ruler technique rather than a one-use ability that he simply cast on someone.

If anything, he was mimicking the same boundary field that the Wei clan had put up around him only a minute before.

The Patriarch and the Elder surrounding him were too far to be fooled by the Fox Dream, so they shouted orders.

Following their instructions, a steel-haired Jade with a pair of blades and a shield badge closed the distance with Lindon. One of the Elders, maybe the Seventh. Lindon didn't care.

A sword flashed at Lindon, but his *real* weapon went lower. This was the Foxtail, an Enforcer attack technique that bent light and perception to hide movement.

In a fight between equals, it was a huge advantage. Lindon had once been proud of the way other clans avoided duels with Wei Enforcers.

Lindon slid past the real strike, letting the illusion pass through him, and seized the man by the neck.

He Consumed enough White Fox madra to replenish the amount that already moved through his veins; he couldn't hold much without taking it into his core.

The man's madra was weak, diffuse, dirty, and he was using it wrong.

A wave of attacks had pierced the decoy Lindon behind him, and his Forged madra dissipated, but Heaven's Glory had gotten in on the action now. A wall of golden glass madra was Forged in front of him.

He conjured purple flickering Foxfire, and the Striker technique burned a doorway-shaped hole in the wall. They used their Striker technique only to inflict the illusion of pain, but it was a spiritual attack. It could fight against other spiritual energies, just like pure madra could.

Two Iron Enforcers waited for him on the other side, using the Foxtail, but he used the technique on his whole body at once.

His image lagged behind, and their real spears clashed in the middle of his afterimage. Lindon had never stopped walking up the hill where the elders stood.

Foxfire brought them both down.

He Forged a paper-thin illusion behind him according to the Fox Mirror. It was literally a huge blank wall. An Iron stumbled through it almost immediately, tearing the illusion apart.

But it did its job. It just needed to interrupt the view of the people behind him.

A pair of Akura Golds soared in on clouds, demanding to know what was happening, striking down a few who dared to launch techniques at them. They could handle themselves.

Lindon advanced on the two men who hadn't run.

The Patriarch and the First Elder.

The elder looked regretful, sighing into his long white beard. The Patriarch remained stone-faced.

"Why?" Lindon asked.

"You may have learned powerful sacred arts," the Patriarch said, "but you haven't learned how the world works. You do not have absolute power. You tire. You will run out of madra. You cannot take the Wei clan from us so easily."

In disbelief, Lindon turned to the First Elder. Was that *really* what they thought he was doing?

The First Elder regarded him with sad eyes. "Revenge does not become you, Lindon. If you had come to us with this talent, we would have welcomed you with open arms. But this...scheme..." He shook his head. "You never learned the real lessons you needed to."

"You..." Lindon didn't even know what to say. "...have you lied for so long that you are blind to the truth?"

The First Elder shook his sleeves out. "You may have great power, but we have honed our techniques over many years. You have never seen the true Path of the White Fox."

The aura in Lindon's mind was pinched with a deft touch. The First Elder was smoother, subtler, more skilled than any-one else Lindon had seen use the Fox Dream.

[He wants to distort our eyes so we see him to the right of where he actually is,] Dross reported. [Too bad his technique is...hm. Is it bad that I want to say "his technique is dross"?]

The Fox Dream technique itself was flawed. From the pathways the madra took through the First Elder's spirit to the way he moved the aura, every step was clunky and inefficient. He had developed great skill with the technique, but the tool itself was lacking.

He was a self-taught swordsman who didn't realize he was using a stick. No matter how skilled he became, he would never be as dangerous as someone with a real weapon.

At the same time, the First Elder Forged the image of a sword. He drew a three-foot blade from a sheath at his side, but the Forged image was a few inches shorter.

Between the Ruler technique and the Forger technique, anyone relying solely on their senses would be skewered before they realized what happened.

The elder twisted his sword through the air, lunging at Lindon in a practiced motion.

Lindon stepped to one side, seizing the First Elder's arm in his white hand.

"No," he said, "*this* is the Path of the White Fox. Pay attention."

Madra leaked into Lindon, refilling his channels again. The elder broke his grip, and Lindon allowed it.

He left an image of himself standing still while he ran invisibly toward the First Elder and cast the Fox Dream over the man's mind. The older man broke the Ruler technique, but Lindon had already caught him in the chest and shoved him back.

"One," Lindon said.

He threw a punch, and the Elder twisted to one side to avoid it, but Lindon had concealed his movements with the Foxtail technique. His real punch clipped the Elder on the chin.

Lindon held back so he didn't shatter the man's jaw. The Elder only missed a step.

"Two."

A sword came flashing in, but Lindon hurled a purple fireball and allowed the sword to land.

It stabbed into his shoulder...and stuck. With such little strength behind it, the blade couldn't penetrate his Underlord body any deeper than the skin.

The Elder dispersed the first ball of Foxfire, and the second, but then Lindon used the rest of his White Fox madra. A barrage of Striker techniques struck the Elder all over, sending him falling to his knees in a cry of pain.

The ground rumbled. Earth aura flashed.

"Three," Lindon announced. "I killed you three times."

With that, he returned his attention to the Patriarch. Wei Jin Sairus scowled at him. "You disrespect your elders, Shi Lindon."

His image stayed standing where it was. A Fox Mirror. But really, he crept invisibly to Lindon's other side, a dagger clutched in his hand.

Lindon had seen him use this technique in the same way before, but not so clearly. The Patriarch had done this against Li Markuth, the winged terror that Suriel had banished. Markuth had not been fooled either.

Lindon dipped his head to the Mirror. "Patriarch."

The Forger technique returned the gesture. Sairus really was skilled. "Unsouled," his illusion said.

Lindon turned his head to meet the eyes of the "invisible" Patriarch. "Not anymore."

As Sairus tried to plunge the dagger into Lindon's side, Lindon ducked and drove his palm into the Patriarch's core.

Pure madra flashed blue-white in a massive handprint that covered Sairus' entire midsection. The Empty Palm wiped out his madra, flooding his system...and the power of Lindon's spirit overwhelmed his.

Channels broke, his core cracked, and he convulsed with the pain in his soul. He made a choking sound and his eyes rolled up into his skull.

Without a word, the Patriarch fell to the ground as a spiritual cripple.

The First Elder straightened himself up in a display of dignity. "You will still not have your way. We will resist you to the death."

Lindon felt like his bones had turned to lead. The Heaven's Glory School had surrounded the hill. They were putting down more scripts. They *still* wouldn't listen. They wouldn't listen to reason, and they wouldn't listen to force.

He had accomplished nothing.

The ground was shaking constantly now, and he finally realized that the power of the earth aura had not subsided. Instead of ebbing and flowing, as it had been doing for days, it had grown and grown without cease.

He felt what was about to happen and looked up to the sky. Suriel had shown him how to prevent this from happening, but he had to wonder if she had foreseen this. Was this why she hadn't saved Sacred Valley herself? Because it was futile?

Why had she even saved Lindon?

One of the Akura clan shouted down to Lindon. "Honored Sage, we must leave! The Titan!"

Lindon nodded. Only a few more days, and they would have been able to evacuate everyone.

But what did it matter? These people didn't want help.

He seized the First Elder by the scruff of the neck, hauling him up bodily with one hand. He spun the old man around facing west and shook him.

"Look at the aura!" Lindon demanded. "Look at it!"

Around Mount Venture, the squat red-tinged peak to the west, the earth aura was growing brighter and brighter as the ground shook. So much that it began to bleed into visibility.

The elder squirmed in his grip. "How are you doing this? What are you showing me?"

Lindon shoved him forward, and the elder caught himself only a few steps away. He turned, but Lindon pointed a finger west.

"Walk. Take that with you." Lindon nudged the Patriarch with the tip of his toe. "You don't want me to save you? Maybe *he* will."

To the west, the Wandering Titan's power waxed like a rising sun. The Dreadgod was slow, making its way ponderously through the mountains, and its head wasn't visible yet.

But as the First Elder cast a nervous glance in that direction, the sky turned gold.

He opened his mouth, and Lindon didn't care to hear what he had to say. A thin bar of Blackflame scorched a line in the ground in front of the man's feet.

"I said **walk.**"

Lindon's vision swayed as the willpower flooded out of him. He had stretched himself too far with that working, and he wasn't even sure it would do what he wanted.

But, dragging the Patriarch behind him, the First Elder began to walk.

第十二章

CHAPTER TWELVE

Mercy was in the middle of negotiations when the sky changed color.

One moment, she was demanding to see the Matriarch of the Li clan again. The clan's Fourth Elder, manning the wall, repeatedly apologized and promised that the Matriarch would surely be on her way back soon. But they had been promising that for almost two days now.

When the sky turned gold, Mercy first felt panic. They were out of time. Even the smooth wooden walls of the Li clan shook with the quake that passed through Sacred Valley. Some of the guards lost their footing.

After the panic came relief. Now, surely, the Li clan would listen to her.

From her side, the Truegold Kashi fell to one knee to get her attention. "Please forgive me, Lady Mercy, but we must leave you now. Sage Charity's orders."

Some of the other Golds from the Akura clan had taken to their clouds, though none had left yet. They wouldn't want to flee without permission from a member of the head family.

Mercy's heart tightened. Without the support of the Golds, she wouldn't be able to save more than a handful of the Li clan.

She kept her voice even. "We're all leaving. Us, and as many of the Li clan as we can carry."

"Yes, of course, but I am afraid that we can't carry many of this clan if they fight us at every step."

The ground wasn't shaking anymore, which she prayed meant that the Dreadgod wasn't walking any closer. She hopped onto Suu, flying up above the walls.

Some of the guardian birds screeched a warning to her, but the sacred beasts were just as afraid of the Dreadgod as she was, and they left her alone.

When she rose high enough, she could see the situation inside the Li clan.

They were trying to escape.

A mass of people, hundreds if not a thousand, pushed against the main gate. They weren't exactly trampling each other yet, but they screamed for the door to open.

The Fourth Elder walked out on the wall, holding out his hands to calm them. "The Matriarch is on her way. When she arrives, she will guide us."

Mercy had spent enough time waiting on that woman. She extended her spiritual perception, hunting for the Jade.

The Matriarch, it turned out, wasn't far away. She stood on a roof, peering up at the sky and consulting with other elders.

Mercy kept her staff low, flying close enough to hear.

It didn't take long. As an Overlady, her hearing stretched further than the spiritual senses of any of these Jades.

"...activate the scripts," the Matriarch was saying. "Find the keys to the guardians, seal the gates, and inspect the boundary flags. If the heavens fall upon us, they will crack on our roof. Have we heard anything from the Kazan clan?"

An old man next to her, wearing an elaborate network of gold and jewels, shook his head. "We've heard they're on the move, but not for us. They seem to be headed east. This has the feel of one of their boundary fields, though; in this one's humble opinion, they have activated this formation to aid them in battle against the outsiders."

Sickness bubbled up from Mercy's stomach.

They hadn't been listening to her at all. The Matriarch had been stringing Mercy along, and now she was taking the signs of the Dreadgod's coming as evidence that there *was* no Dreadgod.

Mercy hovered there on her staff, cold wind whipping her hair, as she fought with her choices.

The Golds wanted to leave, and she couldn't blame them. While she still had them, they could tear the gates of the Li clan open and let the average citizens free.

She could grab the Matriarch herself and fly her up to where the Dreadgod was visible, but depending on the Titan's location, that could take hours.

And—as the Fourth Elder had reminded Mercy repeatedly over the last day—the Wei clan could craft convincing illusions. Just seeing with one's own eyes was not necessarily evidence.

There was no guarantee she could convince them, but if she just captured the clan and dragged them off, they would work against her.

She couldn't avoid the question that slipped out from the depths of her heart: *What would my mother do?*

Mercy knew exactly what Malice would do in this situation. Her exploits were practically myths in the Akura clan. Her approach would work, too.

Mercy just didn't want to do it.

But it would save lives...

With more time, she could come up with a better plan. If only she didn't need to act *now.*

With a sudden burst of speed, Mercy zipped up to the edge of the flat roof where the Matriarch was speaking. She was up and over as the first Jades were spinning at the feel of her spirit, pulling up their venomous techniques.

Mercy had already landed, staff whirling.

Two Jade elders went to the ground in the first instant, one clipped across the head and the other with her feet swept out from under her. An Iron Enforcer went over the edge of the roof, and she webbed a second guard to the floor with Strings of Shadow.

A Forged arrowhead of venomous madra crashed into her chest, shattering on her bloodline armor. She broke the wrist of the Jade who had used that technique and buckled the knees of another.

The Matriarch had begun a Ruler and Striker technique at the same time, venom aura condensing over her shoulder as green light twisted in her hand.

Mercy's staff came up as a bow, the violet-eyed dragon's head glaring at the Matriarch. Her arrow's point gleamed black.

"Drop your technique," Mercy commanded.

The Matriarch's eyes shifted as she took in the situation.

Mercy released her bowstring.

The arrow pinned the Jade's wrist to the wall behind her. She grunted in pain, and her two techniques puffed to nothing as her madra was overwhelmed by shadow.

When the arrow was removed, there would be no wound in the woman's flesh, but as long as it was embedded here, it would still hurt.

Mercy leaned closer, tapping into her bloodline legacy just enough to make sure her eyes were shining. "When I give you an instruction, you do not hesitate to obey. Do you understand?"

Behind her, one of the Jades started forming another technique.

She shot Strings of Shadow out blindly, and the technique stopped.

"Answer me."

"I understand," the Matriarch said quickly. "You have defeated me, but it will take more than you alone to conquer the Li clan."

"No, it won't." Mercy triggered a communication construct inside her pocket in a prearranged signal. "But why would I waste so much time?"

Only a second later, the first Akura rose into the sky outside the Li clan walls. The other fifty followed suit a moment afterwards, spreading out in the sky.

The Matriarch inclined her head. "You are very strong. But we in the Li clan are not without our own—"

Mercy used her communication construct again, and this time she spoke a command. "Unveil."

It took a moment for the message to reach the others, but when it did, the Akura Golds revealed the full extent of their power immediately.

The Li Jades gasped, and the Matriarch's eyes bulged in their sockets. "Jades? All of them?"

"Scan me," Mercy ordered.

When the Matriarch hesitated, Mercy lifted her bow again.

Immediately, a scan shivered through Mercy's spirit. This time, the older woman's breath caught. Color drained from her skin, and she dropped to her knees. Awkwardly, as her wrist was still pinned to the wall behind her. "Gold," she breathed.

The others on the roof were face-down in moments.

"No," Mercy corrected. "Gold is what *they* are."

"Forgiveness, please. This one has offended you. If only you had revealed yourselves, we would have given you our entire clan at a moment's notice."

"We're not here to take your clan. We're here to *save* your clan."

The Matriarch trembled. "Then...there's really..."

"I would not tarnish my own soul by lying to a Jade. Now, how fast can you evacuate your clan?"

"We can have nine out of ten at Heaven's Glory by the setting of the sun, honored...Sage." Mercy made a face at the title, but the Matriarch took it as displeasure and hurried on. "Apologies, but that is truly the fastest that our lacking abilities will allow."

"No, that is faster than I expected of you," Mercy allowed, still holding on to her impression of Malice. "Do not over-estimate your own abilities because you think it will please me. If you say you can reach Heaven's Glory by sunset, that is the standard to which I will hold you."

"It is the pride of the Li clan that we have the greatest number of clouds and flying chariots in Sacred Valley, outside the Holy Wind School. As we had been preparing for an attack since we first began feeling the unnatural earthquakes, we are ready to mobilize as soon as this one gives the signal. With your permission, of course."

Mercy reached out and touched the arrow, which dissolved into motes of black essence rising into the air. The others on the roof murmured when they saw that it had left no wound, which almost made Mercy roll her eyes. Even they had seen more impressive feats of sacred arts than this one, they were only trying to flatter her with a show of awe.

"You have more than my permission," Mercy said. "It is my command. My soldiers wear black and violet. Let those who cannot reach Heaven's Glory by sunset tonight report to them, and they will be carried. Everyone else is to travel for Heaven's Glory at all speed."

The Matriarch bowed deeply. "This one will comply. And this one thanks you once again for you—"

"Go. You all are no exceptions."

The roof cleared as though Mercy had pushed them. The old man covered in jewelry actually leaped down to the streets.

Only seconds later, a horn signaled all throughout the Li clan. A moment later, the Matriarch's words echoed out, repeating Mercy's orders.

Once Mercy was alone, she collapsed.

She leaned up against the low wall around the rooftop, pulling up her legs and hugging her knees to herself.

All along, she had known this would work. In most places in the world, sacred artists were used to taking orders from the stronger. Even those like the Matriarch who were accustomed to power had spent their Iron years bowing before Jades, and their Copper years bowing before Irons. It was behavior ingrained so deep that it was practically instinct.

Malice wielded that instinct like a club, which Mercy hated. She had always tried to avoid it, whenever she could.

But this time she couldn't. She'd had no choice, and this was for their own good.

Which was exactly what her mother always said.

When the sky turned gold, Ziel and the Kazan clan were caught off-guard. The change in color had been accompanied by one last, great heave of the earth, and their group had already been making their way across the uncertain footing of rocky foothills.

The Kazan clan stretched off in sinuous lines, and at the shaking of the earth, Ziel couldn't count the number of people who fell.

From carriages losing their grip on the edge of a gravel road to rocks falling out from under marching feet, people slipped or slid or tumbled in a dozen different ways.

Some of the Akura Golds reacted, diving on their clouds to catch those nearby, but none of them were faster than Ziel.

A ring of green runes appeared beneath the first carriage he saw, catching it on a gentle plane of force, but he was already throwing out another. And another.

He didn't have time to evaluate who was in the most danger, or even who was closer. He just Forged rings as fast as he could, straining himself to the limit in only a handful of seconds.

Then the quake was over. Anyone who was going to fall had already done so.

He hadn't caught everyone. He hadn't even been able to *see* everyone. But at least a dozen people were climbing out of his rings and back to safety.

"We don't have time for a head count," Ziel said, his eyes on the western sky. "Grab anyone who fell, but we have to keep moving." Some of those who'd fallen would be safe, thanks to an Iron body or simply the luck of the fall.

The Akura Truegold looked at him strangely. "Regrettably,

we have to leave. The Sage told us to prioritize our own lives at the first sign of the Titan's approach."

Some of the other Golds had already begun flying away, but she glanced to the Patriarch and his family. "We can take a handful with us," she said. "Including you, of course."

Ziel was already watching the nearby Patriarch and his family give orders and instruction. The column behind them stopped, as most people Ziel could see stared at the golden sky in horror, and their four children clustered around their mother's knees.

He could guarantee they, at least, were safe. But if everyone saw the Patriarch's family flying to safety, there would be even more panic.

"Make the offer," he said to her in a low voice. "And please, don't leave without taking some of them with you. Emphasize families with children."

The Truegold woman reached out to a construct strapped to her wrist. "I'll call them back. But once we fill our clouds, we're leaving."

"Good. Don't take chances with a Dreadgod."

Ziel settled wearily down on his own cloud, shutting his eyes so he wouldn't have to see the Titan's tinted sky.

"You can lead the way," she said. "We'll catch up to you."

"I'll stick with them a while longer. Don't know how far they'll make it without me around."

There was a long pause before she said, "Yes, Archlord."

"I'm not an Archlord," he said automatically.

Though, he realized, his channels hadn't felt like they were full of needles when he'd tossed out so many techniques in a handful of seconds. That wouldn't make him an Archlord, even outside—he'd settle for being as capable as an Underlord—but it was a cheering thought.

Or it *would* cheer him, once there wasn't a Dreadgod looming overhead.

"Of course, Archlord."

She was mocking him. He cracked one eye, where the Truegold woman took a moment from staring worriedly at the western horizon to give him a brief smile.

She was young, if she still had the spirit to needle him with the Wandering Titan bearing down on them. Although, now that he thought of it, she couldn't be more than five years younger than he was.

What a difference a life made.

"What's your name?" he asked, for the first time.

"Akura Shira, Archlord." So a close enough relative that she got the clan name, but not close to the head family. Otherwise she would have been named after one of their virtues, and she probably wouldn't be stuck at Truegold.

"We were introduced when I was assigned to you," she went on.

"Yeah, but I wasn't paying attention. Stop dragging your feet and get out of here, Shira."

Her brow creased in worry, and she looked from him to the clouds flying away, now with small Kazan families in tow. "If you don't leave now, you'll miss the cloudships."

"Don't worry, I know better than to stick around."

Surviving one Dreadgod attack was enough for a lifetime. The second he saw an inch of the Wandering Titan's tail, he was *gone*.

Until then, he could afford to wait for a little while.

Yerin reappeared a long way from where she meant to end up.

She generally recognized the spot. She was in between Mount Yoma to the north and Mount Somara to the east, in a grove of those purple-leafed orus trees. She wasn't too far away from Orthos as he led the natives from the Fallen Leaf School to Heaven's Glory, as she felt his presence. She'd be able to pinpoint him if she could focus her perception for a real scan.

The problem was, her Moonlight Bridge wasn't supposed to *miss*.

Every time she'd used it before, she had just imagined where she wanted to end up, and the Bridge had taken her there. This time, it was off. Why?

Might be because I'm falling to pieces.

She had arrived on hands and knees, heaving air into scorched lungs, every breath coming out with a cough. Her whole body felt weak, her spirit ached, and she saw the trees only through a haze of pain, tears, and fury.

The Moonlight Bridge hadn't worked quite right ever since they'd crossed the border to Sacred Valley. It took more out of her than it should.

Lindon had speculated that it was drawing on her will-power to make up for the authority that was being suppressed by Sacred Valley's script, but he was just guessing.

Didn't mean he was *wrong.* But it meant that she was lost and weak when she really didn't want to be.

She caught her breath, wiped her eyes clean, and felt the Moonlight Bridge to see how much longer it might need to recharge. Her lungs had already started to clear, and she didn't know if she had her almost-Herald body to thank for that or the weakness of the Wei clan poison.

That brought her thoughts back to Lindon, and her anger and fear came flooding back. By all rights, the Wei clan's betrayal shouldn't hurt anything more than his feelings. If he wanted, he could clean them up with no more madra than it took him to light a torch. Dross could probably do it without Lindon lifting a finger.

But her master had thought he was so far above that he was untouchable, and he had taken stupid risks.

Stupid risks like coming into this place.

This place that choked the sacred arts, the *life,* from your spirit. This place that bred treacherous idiots who would stab any hand extended to save them.

Images of Jades swarming over her master overlapped with Lindon, and she pushed herself to her feet. The Moonlight Bridge had recovered, and though she looked forward to using it again about as much as a Copper looked forward to carrying a boulder uphill, Lindon was in danger.

She'd have given up her sword to turn around and help, but she was a boulder tied to Lindon's ankle here. Orthos could help. Lindon just needed to hang on until he got there. He could do that.

As long as nothing else went wrong.

At the *exact* moment she thought as much, the ground trembled strongly enough to shake her balance. She looked down at the earth aura and saw it brighter than ever, bleeding up into the air. It overwhelmed all other aspects of aura until it was visible to the naked eye.

That was when the sky turned gold. It might have been an earthquake, but she could have sworn she heard a distant roar.

For just a moment, she stared blankly into the west, with one thought dominating her mind.

This place is cursed.

Then the panic overtook her and she walked through the Moonlight Bridge.

It was like sliding through a tunnel of white light, and this time it came out where she intended: next to Orthos.

The great black turtle was munching on a fallen log as he marched, surrounded by the Fallen Leaf School. Little Blue sat on his head, and both of them turned to Yerin in surprise as she appeared.

"Lindon..." she said between breaths. "...clan...betrayed..."

She bent over and rested hands on her knees, gulping down air. Heavens above, she hated being weak. She wished she could scream out her words.

Orthos exchanged glances with Little Blue. "He does not feel like he is in danger."

Blue chirped agreement.

Yerin's heart eased a little. She had worried that Orthos would tell her that Lindon was horribly injured. Yerin took that to mean that she had enough spare time to catch her breath before she responded. "What does he feel like?"

"Old anger," Orthos responded. "And deep sorrow."

Blue sang a long, sad note.

"Bleed and bury them." She was starting to think the Wei clan might be worth even less than the Heaven's Glory School, though she suspected there wasn't a rat hair's difference between them. "Go anyway. Scoop up Lindon, and let's fly 'til we run out of sky. Let this whole place burn."

Orthos' head tilted upward again. "We were just discussing the sky. From what Little Blue tells me, *that's* what we should be worried about."

The Riverseed spread her arms and gave a high chime, emphasizing the size of the Dreadgod.

"Can't contend she's wrong."

Yerin looked up to the rust-colored mountain, which had been stained with gold.

How much time did they have left? Two days? Three? Or would the Titan stop dragging its feet and just kill everyone already?

Yeah, it was time to leave. If anyone decided to stay after being warned and got crushed under a Dreadgod's heel, that was between them and the heavens.

Something moved in the horizon, and she realized one of the distant peaks past Mount Venture had crumbled. No surprise there. With the earth shaking like it—

Her thought cut off as the Wandering Titan crashed through the mountain.

It swept through the mountain like it was brushing aside tree branches. Its dark silhouette was distant, and clouds cut off its head.

It walked a few steps closer, but those steps must have eaten miles. Only then did it move to its knees, disappearing below the reddish mountain.

The sound of a crash hit her like thunder a moment later, but her heart was racing.

The Titan wasn't days away.

It was *here.*

It could make it to the Valley inside the hour, if it wanted. It was just taking its time.

Orthos took in a long breath. "The Wandering Titan...

never did I think I would see not one, but two Dreadgods. And only a few years apart."

"*Trapped,*" Yerin whispered.

They couldn't escape in time. It was too late. Ziel and Mercy were too far away, and she couldn't carry anyone in her Moonlight Bridge. She wasn't certain how many more times she could use it herself.

They needed more time.

They needed *help.*

Yerin limbered up her shoulders, stretching herself as madra ran through her channels. None of that helped the soul-deep fatigue that came from the Moonlight Bridge, but she still focused her will.

"Grab Lindon," she said. "I've got my own ditch to dig."

Little Blue gave a whistle of alarm, and Orthos looked as though he agreed with the Riverseed. "What are you doing, Yerin?"

"Somebody's got to slow that thing down. Heavens know I can't do it myself."

"You're not from the Kazan clan!" Elder Rahm shouted.

Eithan held a hand to his chest, feigning offense. "Am I not? How can you be sure? Perhaps we're very, very distant relatives."

Elder Rahm thrust a finger at the small crowd of people hurrying into a two-story house. "Then what do you care about them?"

Unlike most of the other buildings in Heaven's Glory, this house wasn't made of rainstone, but of pale orus wood.

It was actually quite beautiful. Eithan wondered how much it had cost to import the lumber up the mountain.

"I consider myself a great humanitarian. How could I watch prisoners suffer, even when they are taken from a clan other than my own?"

These twelve prisoners from the Kazan clan hadn't been abused as far as Eithan could tell, only confined. He suspected they were political hostages to keep the clan in line.

But the Heaven's Glory School had planned to keep them here.

And unfortunately, he had only found them after his team of Akura Golds had all abandoned him. Shame on them, prioritizing things like "their individual human lives."

The Heaven's Glory School hadn't listened at all when he told them about the doom that was coming, and indeed had ignored even his considerable charms.

Ordinarily, at this point, he would have resulted to threatening them until they were more frightened of him than of leaving their homes.

But he was already little better than a genuine Jade, and his bloodline senses were dull. He had to be careful...without *looking* like he was being careful.

He had given up on persuading the school, but he would take their prisoners with him. There were quite a few of those, it turned out. Several hundred scattered all over their territory. He had started with the Kazan hostages, but they needed somewhere to wait while the other prisoners were gathered.

So Eithan had co-opted Elder Rahm's beautiful orus-wood home.

The prisoners filed through the door, huddling together, and Eithan waved at them to encourage them to head into the house. "If you don't want to leave, I can't make you," Eithan said, though he regretted the truth of the statement. "But I would at least like to save those who are blameless."

Elder Rahm spat on the ground. "*Save.* We are not children, to be led into death by obvious lies."

"Let me ask: if I'm walking into certain death, why do you care if I take the prisoners with me?"

"They are not my enemies. They are the responsibility of Heaven's Glory. It is up to us to preserve, protect, or punish them as they deserve."

Eithan knew the real answer. Elder Rahm was stubbornly opposing anything Eithan wanted. He didn't need a reason for it other than his distrust of outsiders.

They had no time for this. The aura was already in chaos. If the Dreadgod was more than two days away, then he had lost his touch. If they delayed any longer, the Akura cloudships would leave.

Eithan spread his hands and gave a helpless smile. "If I cannot persuade you, then so be it. As long as you allow others to leave as they wish."

"You think too highly of yourself." The old man's glare was cutting. "It will be the ruin of you."

"So I've been told."

A shout for Elder Rahm came from behind Eithan, so he whirled around, striding across the street. "My apologies, but Elder Rahm is weary from diligent pursuit of his duties. How may I assist you?"

The Copper Heaven's Glory disciple looked very uncertain, glancing over Eithan's shoulder at Elder Rahm, but he quickly looked back to Eithan's face. "This one was coming to tell the Elder that our envoy departed on time."

With strands of his bloodline power, Eithan watched the Elder behind him. The old man stared furiously at Eithan's back, gathering aura of fire and light.

A Ruler attack was the correct tool to use against Eithan, but the Sacred Valley Jade didn't know that. Eithan raised his voice. "Don't make a mistake you'll regret, Elder Rahm."

Rahm froze in the middle of his Ruler technique, then stubbornly continued pulling it together.

Something the Copper had said caught Eithan's attention. "I'm sorry, young man. Your envoy to whom?"

"To...to the Wei clan."

Lindon and Yerin were at the Wei clan. Eithan had just received a garbled transmission in Dross' voice that he suspected meant the clan was on its way.

Heaven's Glory had found out first and enacted a plan. That was galling. Eithan preferred to be the better-informed one.

"You've done a bad thing, Elder Rahm," Eithan said as he slowly turned around.

"Not yet."

The Ruler technique snapped into place. It was crude, but as soon as it completed, Eithan felt a genuine spike of alarm.

It wasn't aimed at him.

A line of light focused on the wooden house.

Where the focused sunlight streamed down from heaven and touched the wood, flames leaped up as though the house had been soaked in lamp-oil.

Screams came from inside, but it would take a moment before the fire reached them. They could escape.

Eithan had already dashed back, seizing Rahm by the front of his robe. "What is this?" he asked quietly.

Elder Rahm's jaw remained stubbornly shut, but there was a gleam of hatred in his eyes.

Heaven's Glory members had filtered out from all over to watch. They muttered about the fire, but their attention was focused on Eithan.

He had come here prepared to be betrayed. If they all jumped him at once, he could still walk out with ease.

But now, he would have to abandon people under his protection.

A Kazan prisoner stumbled out of the door, but a line of Heaven's Glory madra streaked in front of him, burning through the doorframe and setting it on fire. The prisoner staggered back, then turned to find another exit. The fire hadn't spread fully yet. He could escape.

More Striker techniques poured in from the bystanders.

They couldn't fight him.

But they defied him now.

Eithan turned his attention back to Rahm. "You would rather die than let them leave?"

"Rather die than bow to you."

Eithan watched the old man's face, and it was as though he saw Rahm through a new lens. He looked alien, like he had transformed into something other than human.

But he hadn't changed. This was what people had always been like.

"Very well," Eithan said.

He shoved Rahm back two steps, where a star from the Hollow King's Crown hung in the air like a blue-white jewel. The Jade looked up.

The pure madra blasted down, spearing him through the soul.

His Remnant slowly split itself in half as it tried to rise, but Eithan had turned his attention to the rest of Heaven's Glory. They had piled Striker and Ruler techniques onto the house, openly defying him, and still none had dared to actually attack him.

With his powers restricted, their numbers mattered. They could overwhelm him if they figured out something that would penetrate his Archlord body. Once he ran out of his weak and limited madra, anyway.

He could still leave, regroup with Lindon and Yerin, and together they would plow through the Heaven's Glory School.

He would just have to leave twelve people in a burning building.

Eithan had made that choice long ago.

He stripped his turquoise outer robe, letting it fall to the snow. Before it landed, he'd reached an Iron Ruler holding sword and shield.

One twist, and the man's arm was broken, his sword falling. Eithan reversed it, shattering his shin with the hilt.

A Striker technique lanced through the air where Eithan's head had been a second ago. He stood in front of the Striker who'd launched it, breaking the woman's jaw with the flat of his new sword.

A trio of Enforcers approached together.

Seconds later, when he was done with them, he stood over their groaning, bleeding, but still-living forms with blood spattered all over his face.

"Anyone who comes into that building with me will be forgiven," Eithan said.

Several Heaven's Glory ran away. Most people peeked around corners, unwilling to get closer. The house was all but consumed by fire now.

Eithan turned to the home himself. The sleeves of his under-robe were too long, so he tore them off. "I will remember this."

Then he plunged into the flames.

Striker techniques followed him.

第十三章

CHAPTER THIRTEEN

Yerin wasn't really sure how her Moonlight Bridge worked.

When Ruby had stolen the Bridge to go to Lindon, she hadn't given the Bridge any directions, and hadn't known exactly where Lindon was. She had just willed the Divine Treasure to take her to Lindon, and it had done so.

Did the Bridge scan the whole world, find the person who matched her thoughts, and then take her there? Did it read her mind for some coordinates that even she wasn't aware of? If she told it to take her to her closest living relative, or to the person who hated her the most, would it be able to do that?

Lindon would have already tested it to find out. Eventually, she would too. If you relied on a weapon you didn't understand, you might find it turning in your hand.

But when she finally escaped the suppression field of Sacred Valley and willed the Moonlight Bridge to take her to Akura Malice, she was terrified.

What if the destination was off-track again? What if it stranded her far away, then took the full three days to recharge?

As it turned out, there was no need to brace herself. She

was washed away in white light, re-forming immediately on the outstretched branch of an enormous tree.

Just the branch was as wide as a road prepared for wagons, and it looked thin as a twig next to the trunk of the tree itself, which stood as tall and wide as one of Ninecloud City's towers. An icy wind blew leaves big enough to use as tents, and darkness covered the lands beneath her.

Shadow aura.

Akura Malice hovered above Yerin's tree, close enough that Yerin could have lobbed a pebble and hit the Monarch in the back of the purple silk dress. Spread out before them both was a broad valley, not too unlike Sacred Valley, filled with buildings that looked as though they had been stolen from all over the world. They resembled toys from this distance, but no two were alike.

Except in their condition. If they were toys, the child playing with them had gotten bored and smashed them, poking holes in them or tossing them here and there. Long holes were gouged into the earth, and there was a broad indent in the center of the valley in which several buildings had been crushed. Yerin was uncomfortably certain it was a footprint.

A bow appeared in Malice's hands, its shaft seemingly made of glacial ice that shimmered like moonbeams. Yerin's spiritual sense shivered as she felt it, and while she didn't examine it any closer, she tasted a confusing riot of impressions.

Malice lazily pulled back the string, and an arrow of the same material as the shaft appeared on the bow. She spent a moment taking aim, then loosed the arrow.

In the distance, a flock of silhouettes flapped furiously away. They were far enough away that they looked like a featureless cloud until Yerin focused on them.

That entire cloud dropped to the ground at the same instant Malice released her bowstring. Yerin tightened her gaze, finding her Herald body responding easily.

As she'd suspected, there was an iridescent blue-and-green arrow stuck in the body of each gold dragon.

"I'm so glad you decided to visit," Malice said warmly, though she didn't look down. She seemed to be tracking another target. "Would you like a turn?"

Yerin didn't want to openly express her disgust at the sight of a Monarch taking lesser lives out of petty revenge, and she was in a hurry. "Don't have so many seconds left that I can spare one."

"Quite understandable. Would it help you if you knew what they'd done?" She flicked a hand, and tendrils of shadow seized a gold dragon halfway across the valley. Yerin wasn't even sure how she'd understood where to look; maybe Malice was transmitting her intentions directly.

"He has power roughly equivalent to an Overlord, like yourself only recently, and he led many raids on human towns in the Wasteland. When he did, he would take living trophies. Once, he captured all of a town's children, then trapped them on a small island with one knife each and told them that the one survivor would be rewarded and released unharmed."

Yerin's stomach twisted. "Burn him, then. Monarch, I need your help to stop the Titan."

"Their desperation and lack of skill amused him," Malice went on. "He was true to his word, in the end. He patched up the winner's wounds, gave the boy food and water and a powerful sacred instrument, and released him. I was think-ing I might do something similar. Poetic justice, I suppose."

Malice drifted down to stand on the branch beside Yerin. "I could tell him I'll release him if he defeats you in a duel, how about that? Or we could gather up some survivors, seal off their sacred arts, and make them scratch and claw each other until we spare the victor. What do you think?"

"Don't want a turn of any game *he'd* play. If he deserves killing, kill him. Don't play toys with him. But there's a Dreadgod—"

"He *does* deserve it," Malice said. The shadow-arms reached up and swallowed the golden speck whole; Yerin could sense nothing of him anymore, and she couldn't be sure if Malice had erased the dragon or transported him somewhere else for capture.

"I respect your position," the Monarch went on. "The rule of humanity is civilization, and civilizations are based on laws. We should not lower ourselves to our base instincts, or we are no better than they."

Malice gave a cold smile. "And while I agree up to a point, there is something to be said for...proportional response."

Yerin surveyed the ravaged valley. "Looks to me like you've got your response."

"It is yet *far* from proportional." But Malice warmed once again as she faced Yerin. "But they can wait. They are bare of defense before me...thanks to *you*." She took Yerin's hand in both of hers. "How can I bless your life, Yerin?"

You could start by opening your ears, Yerin thought.

But the sudden change in attitude threw her off. She had expected a positive reception—she *had* killed Malice's biggest enemy, after all—but this was a little much.

Yerin met purple eyes that glistened in the picture of motherly affection. "What can you do about the Wandering Titan?"

"Oh my, you *do* think the world of me, don't you?" Malice brushed a strand of hair away from Yerin's eye. "You're close enough to a Herald now; you should have a more realistic view of a Monarch's limitations. I was able to keep the Bleeding Phoenix away from certain areas for a few days, but even so, I was not able to drive it off completely. And it had awakened early; it was not fighting at full strength. There's an argument to be made that it would have destroyed *less* property in total had I not matched it in battle."

Yerin appreciated the scale involved, but that didn't change what she needed. "It's about to trip over a boundary field that'll make it weaker, if that helps you. The script's supposed to work better and faster the stronger you are, and it's got me weaker than a day-old kitten."

"Is that so?" Malice murmured. "Poor thing. However, I'm afraid that there's more. Last time, my focus on the Bleeding

Phoenix and my subsequent recovery cost my people all over the world. We lost entire cities, alliances shifted, and territory changed hands while my eyes were turned."

Yerin straightened her back. "Came armed for that. If all the Monarchs are riding in one boat, you can't sink each other, true? Willing to make this my prize for the tournament."

The final prize of the tournament had hovered in the back of her mind since she'd won. She and Lindon had spent a while talking about it, and while he was full of ideas, even he wasn't sure what she should spend it on.

The obvious answer was "power," but there wasn't much more power the Monarchs could give her. And what else could they grant her that she couldn't earn on her own?

Malice put a hand to her lips in a show of surprise. "Are you now? Well, then, how can we waste time?"

She swirled her hand, and darkness swallowed everything but Yerin and Malice. They still stood on a solid surface, but the whole world was blacker than a nightmare.

Yerin found that she could understand what Malice was doing even though her spiritual perception was blacked out. They hadn't physically moved anywhere; this was just a way of communicating over great distances, like some kind of Monarch-level messenger construct.

She supposed she was sensing Malice's will through the working, which was a strange feeling. She needed to get used to that.

A call had gone out in many different directions, and while Yerin couldn't trace most of them, she knew one at least had gone out to Reigan Shen and his faction.

She knew that because the Blood Sage appeared before them almost instantly, the image of a roaring white lion announcing his presence.

The Sage of Red Faith was a tall, skeletal man with white hair all the way down to his knees and red lines tracing down from the corners of his eyes so that it always looked like he was weeping bloody tears. He was hunched forward like a scarecrow about to fall off its post, scanning the darkness.

When he saw Yerin, his eyes lit with a feverish light. He lunged forward, reaching for her, though his image didn't move through the darkness at all.

"My girl!" he whispered. "Dear, sweet, wise, *wonderful* girl. You did it, you did it, you *did it!* Truly, it is the master's joy to see his apprentice surpass him, but I would have never—"

"You're not my master," Yerin said, but he didn't pause for even an instant to listen.

"—thought that you would proceed from such a great state of instability. Give me your memory, let me see it, and that's the end. Our work will be complete. You and I will be responsible for the greatest revolution in the sacred arts since Emriss—no, we will be beyond even her; she can help us spread the word, others must know! Give me the dream tablet, make me a tablet, I want to see your memory, I want to *taste it.*"

"I don't recall inviting you, Red Faith." Malice sounded amused rather than disgusted, as Yerin had imagined she would be. "I'm surprised to see Shen trusted you with the authority to speak on his behalf."

"Shen? We don't *need* Shen anymore, don't you understand?" He was still fixated on Yerin. "You hate Redmoon Hall, I know you do. I'll tear it down with my own hands. Not a rat will remain alive. I'll give you their heads, or I'll deliver them to you alive, or I'll *pay* you, I can *pay you—*"

He kept ranting, waving his hands in demonstration, but he no longer made a sound.

Another woman sighed in relief, though Yerin hadn't seen her arrive. "Thank you, Malice. Our meetings are never productive with him around."

Her skin was a human shade of dark brown, but it had the texture of bark. A reminder of her original life as a tree, like her hair, which was made of glowing blue-green vines braided together. She tapped the invisible ground with her staff, which was topped with a diamond shaped like a blooming flower.

Emriss gave Yerin a kindly smile. "He is correct in one respect: there is much to be learned from your advancement. I hope you do indeed share your experiences, though...not necessarily with him."

Red Faith was biting at his fingernails as though to chew away the restriction of silence.

Yerin dipped her head to Emriss. "Thanks, Monarch. I know he's a cockroach walking like a man, but he *did* help me out of a tough spot."

Red Faith nodded furiously, pointing to Yerin. An indescribable, invisible ripple broke the darkness, and he pushed through Malice's command for silence.

"Don't be close-minded! She could share with *all* of us! This is the way forward! This is—"

His voice vanished again.

"Now, where did he find the authority for *that?*" Malice asked.

Emriss shook her head. "He is very old, and craftier than he appears. Who can say for certain what tricks he has in his pockets?"

Yerin couldn't signal the Sage of Red Faith. The two Monarchs could sense everything she did, even in a sealed space like this. Maybe especially here.

But she lingered on his eyes longer than she needed to, hoping he would notice.

He didn't stop chewing on his fingers, but she thought she saw his intelligence shine through for a moment. He gave her a brief, barely perceptible nod.

That's a start, she thought.

When the fight for Sacred Valley was over, she had a use for him. Long ago, Eithan had stolen one of this man's dream tablets for her. He'd given it to Yerin, which had helped her cultivate her Blood Shadow.

He'd gotten it from the labyrinth.

Where he had once performed experiments on the Bleeding Phoenix.

The dream tablet hadn't been thorough; it was more of a personal recollection on his understanding of Blood Shadows. She wasn't clear whether he'd had the entire Phoenix down there, or just pieces of it, or if the labyrinth was just where you went to hide if you wanted to do Dreadgod research.

But it was a firm connection between the Bleeding Phoenix and the labyrinth her master had been exploring before he died.

Now that she was back in Sacred Valley, it was time to track down some answers.

Or almost time. Once the *other* Dreadgod was taken care of.

While Yerin got the Sage's attention, another woman had appeared, beneath the shining image of a golden knight. She was dressed in intricate golden armor, but she had her helmet off, revealing messy blonde hair.

Larian of the Eight-Man Empire looked around the circle, stopping to glare at the Blood Sage. "Who invited Red Faith? I won't speak anywhere he does."

Red Faith shouted something, but it released no sound.

"...perfect," Larian finished.

A red dragon head with golden eyes snapped at the darkness, and Northstrider strode out from beneath that emblem. His hair was still trimmed and neat, his facial hair short, and he wore clean clothes. Similar to how he had appeared in the finals of the Uncrowned King tournament.

Yerin had expected him to go back to his homeless wanderer look by now.

"Has the time come for the champion to name her wish?" Northstrider asked.

He gave Yerin a...she couldn't call it a smile, but it was at least an approving look. "We should all be of one mind. Let her state her desire so that we may grant it in all haste. I, for one, do not wish to take my gaze from the Titan for longer than I must."

Yerin didn't know if they were waiting on anyone else—

had the Arelius family even been invited? What about the Ninecloud Court?—but she knew an opening when she saw one.

"You're cutting to the heart of it," Yerin said. "I want you to keep the Wandering Titan away from where it's going. Don't have to try and kill it, just push it away until we can get people out."

There was silence around the circle. Malice looked amused.

Northstrider folded black-scaled arms. "There are restrictions on what requests we fulfill and how we fulfill them. If there were not, the winner could wish for one of us as a slave, or for the death of an entire country. One of those restrictions is that we will not satisfy a request that endangers the life of a Monarch or the existence of their faction."

"Fighting a Dreadgod counts," Larian said.

"It's headed into a formation that keeps it tied up tight," Yerin insisted. "This might be your chance to bury it for good."

Emriss sighed. "That's what we thought before."

She leaned heavily on her flower-topped staff, and an image drifted up into the air ahead of her: a black-striped white tiger with an oversized white halo. It was big as an elephant, and Yerin recognized it from descriptions as the Silent King, though as a Dreadgod it was relatively tiny. It would have looked like a pet next to the Titan.

The only thing huge about it was the army of Remnants, sacred beasts, and blank-eyed sacred artists stretched out over the countryside behind it. And Yerin recognized that countryside.

Sacred Valley. It looked somewhat different—the mountains around it were shaped differently in ways she couldn't quite put her finger on—but it was clearly the same place.

"The suppression field over the labyrinth will indeed weaken Dreadgods," Emriss said. "Within minutes. It is designed to do precisely that. However..."

A flame kindled in the distance like an orange star, growing quickly as it approached until a fireball swallowed the entire horizon. It fell on Sacred Valley like the sun was collapsing.

"...it will do the same for us."

The fireball itself split up into a thousand sparks as it sank closer and closer to Sacred Valley. Flames rained down all over, catching trees alight, but they didn't even burn most of the sacred artists in the Silent King's horde. Much less the Dreadgod itself.

All the power had been stolen by the suppression field.

The vision winked out.

"The Silent King is theoretically the most vulnerable of the Dreadgods, yet we were no more successful in damaging it there than anywhere else." Emriss shook her head. "What we *did* learn is that the Dreadgods are unable to retrieve their prize, even without our intervention, and will soon forget its location and return to their random wandering. There are other entrances to the labyrinth, and they've never been successful in breaching those either."

Yerin paid close attention to the story, filing it away for later, but none of that solved her problems.

"If I pare it down to the bone," Yerin said, "you're saying you won't help."

Emriss moved her gaze to the Akura Monarch. "Any evacuation of the native population should fall to Malice."

Yerin didn't wait for Malice to respond. "And what if that was my wish? What if I'm asking you to make sure everybody in the land gets a safe place to go?"

"Nah." The blonde woman in the golden armor scratched vigorously at the back of her neck; uncomfortably so, as though she were trying to rid herself of a flea. "Can't let you waste your request. Doesn't look good for us if word gets out that we sent the best young Lady in the world away with a glass of water and a pat on the head, would it?"

Yerin was growing irritated by all these restrictions, so she fired back. "Glass of water's worth a long stretch more than what I've gotten from you so far."

The woman barked a chuckle, but still seemed more focused on scratching her elusive itch.

"Yerin," Malice said, "didn't you mention being uncomfortable in the valley? Why is that, do you think?"

Yerin saw through the tactic immediately. Malice was trying to steer her toward making some different wish.

Every second they wasted here was a second closer to Sacred Valley's death.

Holding up two fingers, Yerin addressed the room. "Don't have time to dance around, so there's two trails we can take here. One, help me with the Dreadgod, and we're all squared up. Two, I say you've all broken your promise to the Uncrowned. I'm making a wish inside your rules, and you're turning me down. Monarchs should keep their word."

Larian gave her a dangerous look, and Northstrider frowned. "Do not take advantage of your station to threaten us," he said. "You do not understand the scope of what is involved."

His tone rubbed Yerin the wrong way, but he wasn't *wrong,* so she only spoke irritably. "Fine. Make me an offer."

"I think I will," Malice said. "We can fix you."

"Your spirit and body merged, but they're not balanced yet," Larian said. She rapped her knuckles on her armor. "We see that from time to time. It can happen with new Heralds, and those who advance too fast. You're both."

Emriss picked up smoothly from where the Eight-Man Empire's representative had left off. "Your condition is unique, and it's possible that you would have reached equilibrium with enough time. However, being inside the suppression field so soon after your advancement has distorted you further."

Yerin's stomach twisted. "Feel fine when I'm not in the valley."

"Of course. You're still *more* than any other Overlord; your limitations will show only in conditions of extreme spiritual stress. Unfortunately, that includes any time you attempt to advance. The most likely scenario is that you spend the rest of your life as an incomplete pseudo-Herald."

The rest of her life.

It didn't hit Yerin as hard as she'd thought it would. She had been prepared for something like this when she'd advanced in the first place. At least she would keep the advancement she already had. As long as she stayed alive, there was a chance to find another solution.

And Emriss wouldn't have brought this up if she didn't have some kind of cure.

The Sage of Red Faith gestured furiously, and he looked like he was trying to catch Yerin's attention, but Emriss held up a hand to soothe him.

"As I said, this case is unique. There are possible solutions, and it could be that if you avoid further spiritual stress for long enough, your body will balance itself."

"Taking care of the Wandering Titan would save me worlds of stress."

Malice leaned around to peek at Yerin. "Of course...the *best* solution would be for us to stabilize this fusion for you. It would save you *years* of suffering and roadblocks."

"Agreed," Northstrider said. "It is the one change we can make that will simultaneously grant you great power and improve your day-to-day life."

Yerin looked from one Monarch to another, and they all seemed to have made up their minds. Even Red Faith was steadily nodding.

With a brief effort, Yerin tapped into the minor Divine Treasure resting in her soul, like a loop around her core. A black ring sprang into being over her head, distinct even from the darkness behind her.

"I'm not cracked in the head," Yerin said quietly, as her Broken Crown burned in the darkness over her. "You can snap me like an old bone anytime you want. Don't intend disrespect. But there's a Dreadgod breathing down my collar *right now.*"

She met the eyes of all the others one at a time. None looked away. "Came here for help, 'cause I'm at the end of my road, and fixing me doesn't fix *that*. It's a shiny prize, and I'd chew it over any other day. But today, I'm drowning, and you're throwing me a bottle of wine."

She let her Broken Crown vanish. "So you tell me what I'm supposed to make with that."

Malice's lips quirked up, and it might be Yerin's imagination, but she thought the Monarch looked a little impressed. "Would it ease your worry to know that the Wandering Titan has not entered the valley yet? It has settled down to feed, and will remain in place for at least a short while."

That was more than nothing, but it made Yerin even more eager to get this over with. If the Monarchs weren't going to help, she had to return and move everybody away. She had *some* time now, but that didn't mean she wanted to spend time polishing words.

Northstrider's face, as usual, was stone. "We are united in recommending that you correct the instability of your spirit, a problem for which there is no quick cure besides rewriting reality itself. If you would prefer us to evacuate this territory before the Wandering Titan arrives, we will do that instead."

Yerin breathed deeply. She hated feeling like she was cornered like this, and the fact that they had left her with no option other than to do as they wished made her want to refuse out of sheer brick-headed stubbornness.

But that would be stupid.

"This will help me work in Sacred Valley?" she asked.

"The suppression field will affect you no more than your peers," Emriss confirmed. "You won't be able to fully express the powers of a Herald until you reach the peak of Archlord no matter what we do, but this will remove the weaknesses and potential problems that might prevent you from getting there."

"And you're all telling me to do this?"

"You'd be stupid not to," Larian said bluntly. "You've got time to get anybody you *really* like to safety, and even if everybody else dies, you'll be able to save more later."

The Blood Sage nodded along, which almost made Yerin

change her mind.

"Right, then." She'd hoped to return to Sacred Valley with her chin up, proudly saying that she'd taken care of the Dreadgod. But if she couldn't do that, at least the suppression field wouldn't cut so many of her strings anymore.

So there wouldn't be any confusion, she continued. "As the Uncrowned King—Queen, whatever—I'm wishing for you to fix me up. Do what you can for me."

And, because she didn't want to leave *too* much of a bad impression on the collected Monarchs, she added, "Thank you."

Though this was the wish they had decided on her behalf, so her gratitude had definite limits.

A great pulse of will passed between all the Monarchs, and they nodded as one. Yerin got the impression that the wave of intentions and willpower had moved far beyond them, connecting to Reigan Shen and Sha Miara and maybe some others, wherever they were.

"As the arbiter of the Uncrowned King tournament and the representative of the Monarchs' collective decision, I agree to grant your request," Northstrider said formally. "Brace yourself, and receive your reward."

Suddenly the images of all the Monarchs flickered, and they were standing before her...but they were also standing thousands of miles away, and their wills reached out and held her, cupping her, surrounding her like an eggshell.

It was a disturbingly vulnerable feeling, as though they could flex their fist and crush her, but something else around her was unraveling. She couldn't even tell what. Her fate, maybe?

Many voices spoke in unison, and it was as though the world itself spoke.

"Be healed."

Yerin's senses blanked out.

She came to herself an unknown time later, standing on the bough of the giant tree, staring down into the ruined valley of the gold dragons. Smoke and clouds of dust still rose.

Malice stood at her side, wearing a mysterious smile. "How do you feel?"

"If I'm any sturdier than I was two seconds ago, I couldn't prove it." Yerin felt cheated. She had only the Monarchs' word for it that anything about her had changed at all.

"You will feel the effect of your request once you return to the boundary formation, but the true value you should hopefully never feel. We have removed problems that you *would* have faced, so if we have done our job, then you will never see them at all." She ran hands down her bowstring and looked into the distance. "Now, shall we go greet the Wandering Titan?"

Yerin had thought she was following along, but now her thoughts scraped to a halt.

"...you played me like a flute."

"The others will feel my power when I engage the Titan, but the more misinformation I spread about my intentions, the better." She shot Yerin a wink. "Also, you called me petty earlier, so I thought I would prove you right."

"Never said that."

"That's what you meant. Of course I was always going to help you. You killed Seshethkunaaz, may his name be forgotten by all who walk the earth. At the moment, you're my favorite."

Yerin was thoroughly sick of Monarchs. "What was all that about losing cities?"

Malice shrugged. "What's a city or two compared to the favor of the Uncrowned Queen?"

Reigan Shen emerged from a tear in the world, striding out onto the blighted rock of the Wastelands.

He had gone to absurd lengths to disguise his actions from the other Monarchs. Usually, they would be able to track him the moment he stepped through the Way. Especially if they were watching him, and Malice had kept purple eyes trained on him for days.

He couldn't imagine why.

Now, not only had he covered his tracks with false trails, dummy portals, and truly delicate manipulation of spatial authority, but Malice had finally taken her attention off him.

It would take her too long to realize her protections had been breached. By then, it would be too late.

Reigan Shen clasped hands behind his back and surveyed the round crimson shapes sticking onto the landscape. There were millions of them, like seed pods clutching anything they could reach all the way out to the horizon, each the size of his head. Some clung to crystal arches, others shone from within caves, and still others stuck to one another and hung from petrified trees like clusters of grapes.

Eggs of the Bleeding Phoenix.

When they felt the power in his blood, the eggs began to roll toward him or stretch out hair-thin feelers. He kept them away with an effortless use of aura.

The eggs couldn't be destroyed, not really. They could be broken apart, but they would only re-form. Any attack capable of removing them conceptually would prompt the Dreadgod to reintegrate. Or, as with a lethal attack on any Dreadgod, would awaken the other three of its kind.

The previous generation of Monarchs had learned that the hard way.

The only realistic way to slow the Bleeding Phoenix's recovery was to give its eggs nothing to feed on. Malice had quarantined this entire area, sealed it with scripts, troops, and constructs, and thereby kept as much prey away as possible.

Even so, every creature with blood running through its veins that had once lived in this section of the Wastelands was now part of the Dreadgod.

If someone else managed to break through the layers of security, they would only become Phoenix food. Even another Monarch wouldn't be able to do much except potentially antagonize a deadly foe.

They didn't have the key.

From one of his isolated pocket spaces, Reigan Shen pulled an oblong rectangular box. To the eye, it seemed to be made of seamless, unblemished steel polished to a mirror's shine.

No force in Cradle could break this container. It was an Abidan artifact, one of the few in Shen's possession.

It responded to his will as its rightful owner, unfolding like a flower into a square platter presenting its contents. The key to the western labyrinth, which Tiberian had once shown him.

A shriveled, mummified, chalk-white right hand.

Hunger of every kind passed through Shen. Hunger for food, yes, but also for recognition, for respect, for love, for attention, for success, for safety, for power. Greed flowed through him, and bloodlust, and plain old classic lust.

He relished the sensations as, around him, the stone shook. Pebbles lifted into the air, drifting closer to the hand as its hunger warped even gravity.

The Way stirred around him, affected by an artifact of such incredible significance. If he held the hand exposed long enough, it might manifest an Icon.

He wouldn't need that long.

With shocking speed, eggs tumbled into one another, sticking together, forming a shapeless clump. Soon, living creatures infested by the eggs would come running to donate themselves to the Dreadgod. Nine out of ten victims of these Phoenix fragments became mindless husks controlled by their parasite, and the tenth gained the dubious honor of a Blood Shadow.

The balls of blood and hunger madra began to melt like wax, taking on a more familiar form.

The Bleeding Phoenix congealed in front of him, its eyes blazing scarlet. It was small enough to fit in a barn, for now, but with every second more eggs hurled themselves into its body, adding to its mass.

Shen's heart pounded. He couldn't show weakness in

front of the greatest predator in this world, but even before it was fully formed, the Phoenix radiated a pressure that gripped his spirit painfully tight.

When it lowered its beak and let out a shrieking cry, it was all he could do not to retreat back through space.

Instead, with deliberately casual movements, he snapped off a fingertip of the mummified hand. The last joint of the pinky.

Then he flicked the treat to the Dreadgod.

A beak snapped, and the Phoenix swallowed the tiny piece of power whole.

Reigan Shen spoke as he tucked the rest of the hand back into the box. "That should be enough for you. Now you know the way home."

The Abidan container melded shut, cutting off all power from the hand. The Phoenix bobbed its head around him, trying to sense—or perhaps smell—any other trace.

The Emperor of the Rosegold continent very much *did not* sweat as the Dreadgod's beak brushed by his mane. He remained icy and cool, both mentally and physically, and he would annihilate anyone who implied otherwise.

He would be able to defend himself from a Phoenix of this level, of course. In a body this small, it posed only a little threat to him.

But it would re-form soon, and if it remembered him in its complete form, his life could be in danger.

Fortunately, the Phoenix's attention left him. It looked west.

Where it now knew its goal waited. The being that some called the fifth Dreadgod, and others called the father of the Dreadgods. Their progenitor, the original, from which they were all formed. Subject One.

The Bleeding Phoenix spread its wings, and Reigan Shen slipped off into another portal. He breathed a sigh of relief when it worked; the Dreadgod could have stopped him, had it wanted to.

His work here was done, but the next phase of his plan was even more dangerous.

Now, while the Dreadgod cleared his way, he had to follow it without anyone detecting him. Besides the danger, it was the stealth that really stuck in his craw.

Sneaking was for mice.

第十四章

CHAPTER FOURTEEN

Lindon drove an Empty Palm into the core of the Third Elder. The plump old man doubled over, wheezing, but Lindon hadn't used the force he'd unleashed on the Patriarch. The Third Elder would recover his madra in minutes.

Lindon leaned over to speak into the man's ear. "I cannot be surprised. I cannot be ambushed. My eye sees all."

Though Lindon didn't summon him, Dross popped out in front of the Third Elder, his purple eye wide open and menacing.

The elder shuddered, and Lindon played along. "Here it is now."

[I am the Great Eye,] Dross intoned. [My gaze pierces cloud, shadow, earth, and...what else? Metal. Leather. And cloth, it penetrates cloth.]

His gaze drifted down from the Third Elder's face, and the old Jade blushed and hurriedly clutched his outer robe closer.

The golden sky loomed over them, and the ground shook, so Lindon's fear shook him to action again. He pulled the elder to his feet with one hand, shoving him toward the buildings of the Wei clan. "You're on duty," Lindon ordered. "Search for stragglers. Get them running for Heaven's Glory by any means necessary."

With fists pressed together, the Third Elder started to bow to him, but Lindon shouted "Now! Go!"

Their trip to the east was a mad rush, and they weren't the only ones with the same idea. Streams of people trickled in from all over Sacred Valley, pushing for the exit farthest from the encroaching threat.

But none were as frightened as Lindon. He *knew* what was out there.

At least he could vaguely sense the Wandering Titan's location. While his spiritual perception was still restricted, the Titan was a big target. It hadn't moved all day, feeding on aura and physical materials from the earth.

That pause was just a temporary reprieve that could end at any time. Whenever the Dreadgod changed its mind, or drained that location dry, it would move east once more.

Only a few more of its strides would break through the mountain and set it loose on Sacred Valley.

So Lindon made sure the Wei clan flowed to the east, occasionally stopping to prevent some Iron from robbing a group of Coppers, or a family from dragging a massive bundle of what looked to be all their earthly belongings.

For the moment, the elders followed Lindon out of fear. Fear both of him and of the Dreadgod. But most of the clan had no idea who he was, and he couldn't keep demonstrating his strength to everyone he passed.

Fear of the Titan would have to be enough.

The Heaven's Glory artists and their Grand Patriarch were bound in scripted chains, struggling from the back of a wagon that Lindon kept a special eye on. He might need to use them as hostages when he reached their school.

But as the day crept along, the golden sky's shine fading to a duller hue, they finally came up to the foot of Mount Samara. Its ring hadn't started to form yet, and Lindon could already tell something had changed in Heaven's Glory.

The normal path up the mountain, with its wide road crawling upward in a series of switchbacks, was packed with people. That much, Lindon had expected.

To the side, however, the Trial of Glorious Ascension was gone. The bright pink haze that had once covered the long staircase was gone, leaving flights upon flights of bare stone steps. Some Remnants still wandered in confusion around the slopes, and a few of the scripts still flickered fitfully with dream madra, but it was mostly clear.

So the Heaven's Glory School had deactivated their formation to allow people to reach the top faster. Good for them. Eithan must have really taken over.

Which might explain the other difference he'd noticed: the column of smoke drifting up from the school proper.

Lindon rose on his Thousand-Mile Cloud, glancing over the Wei clan to make sure they would follow his instructions—although there wasn't much chance of the opposite, at this point. They were stuck in a thick tide of fleeing people, so there would be nothing to do but wait to move forward.

He flew toward Heaven's Glory, keeping his perception extended and scanning for Eithan. He'd expected the Archlord to have taken over one of the Jade Elders' houses, but he felt nothing from that direction.

In fact, as he gained altitude, he saw that one of those homes was the source of the smoke he'd noticed earlier.

When he didn't spot Eithan where he expected, he extended the radius of his search, sweeping the Heaven's Glory School.

Dross cleared his throat. [Don't be mad at me. It's a miracle I can see anything with your senses like this.]

What is it?

[There's a battle.]

Dross dragged Lindon's attention to the wild territory behind the Heaven's Glory School, where once Yerin had run from the school's pursuers. Those slopes were mostly snow and Remnants, with occasional sparse bushes or trees, but Lindon quickly sensed what Dross was talking about: flares of light and heat in his spiritual perception.

A fight.

Lindon flew over, but only when he came closer did he

feel Eithan's presence. Weak. Flickering. Low on madra. Heavily drained.

Dread made his heart pound, and he reached into his void key. Wavedancer flew sluggishly over to him; the aura was just barely thick enough to support a flying sword, but this one was used to richer environments. The artfully crafted weapon lurched like a graceful fish squirming through mud.

That didn't stop it working as a sword, though. Lindon clutched the weapon in his left hand as constructs took aim at him.

Heaven's Glory had protected themselves from the air.

An accelerated missile of Forged force madra shot for him, and if Lindon had been any more than a Jade, he would have just let it hit him.

Instead, he slapped it from the air with Wavedancer's blade. A gust of the Hollow Domain wiped out a Heaven's Glory Striker technique, and then he'd located all six flying constructs in the area.

He pointed and wiped them out one at a time with dragon's breath.

When Lindon hovered over Eithan's location, he stepped off the Cloud and fell through the trees. A few thin branches snapped beneath him on the way down, but as he landed, a pair of sacred artists aimed weapons at him.

One swung a hammer that gathered earth aura as she swung, and the other was simply planning to club him with a brick of brown Forged madra.

If their sacred arts hadn't clued him in, their massive badges—almost like breastplates—showed him their identity clearly. These were members of the Kazan clan. Had Ziel brought them here?

He slipped aside from the hammer, letting it crash into the trunk of a tree, and the brick he caught in his Remnant hand.

When he held both Iron sacred artists still, he spoke calmly. "Pardon, but I'm only here to help."

Eithan, who had been slumped at the base of the tree, sputtered and spat splintered bark out of his mouth. "Is there sap in my hair? You'd tell me if there was sap in my hair, wouldn't you?"

He looked like he'd just crawled out of a fire.

Half his hair was singed off, his left eye was matted shut with dried blood, and his turquoise robes were burned and shredded. His core was almost empty, and he looked like he had been soaked in blood.

This was the worst Lindon had seen Eithan except immediately after his fight with the Blood Sage, and concern for the man overwhelmed even his worry about the Dreadgod.

Briefly. Until he scanned Eithan and realized he wasn't wounded at all. He was just tired.

"Not my blood," said the red-soaked Archlord.

Lindon let out a breath of relief, but responded lightly. "Apologies. I'm afraid your hair is done for."

Eithan wilted against the tree. His eyes slowly closed.

"Put me out of my misery. Make it quick."

The Kazan clansmen were murmuring behind Lindon, but their mutters turned to shouts as Heaven's Glory techniques blasted through the trees.

Though it was a drain on his limited madra, Lindon projected the Hollow Domain around himself and the seven or eight Kazan members in range. There were a dozen nearby, and they began to crowd inside when they saw Heaven's Glory madra melting at the edge of his blue-white boundary.

"What happened?" Lindon quietly asked Eithan.

"Believe it or not, they took advantage of my compassionate nature. My reserves are finite, especially here."

"I can't believe *anyone* pushed you this far."

"Lost my Golds at the wrong moment. Hostages are as effective against me as against anyone, but...well, I'll put it to you this way: they're running drastically low on manpower."

Lindon dropped the Hollow Domain, which was tiring to keep up inside the suppression field, just as a trio of Iron Enforcers charged in.

Eithan jerked his head in their general direction without opening his eyes. "If you could clean up here, I'd appreciate it."

The three Enforcers were covered by three more Strikers, two Rulers, and a Forger. Constructs flanked them all, and they carried steel weapons banded with halfsilver. It was a charge worthy of attacking a Jade, and showed more tactical skill than Lindon had seen from Heaven's Glory thus far.

[Not bad, not bad,] Dross said. [I'm afraid to say you'll have to take a hit.]

Ten seconds later, Lindon was pinning the last standing Heaven's Glory member up against a tree with one hand. "Where are your Jades?"

He released his grip so that the man could answer. Nearby, one of the destroyed constructs finished falling through the air, exploding as it hit the ground.

"Gone, they're gone, they're...I don't know!" The Iron man's eyes were wild. "They're dead or crippled. He was going to kill us all!"

"I was not!" Eithan shouted. "I told you that!"

Lindon released the Heaven's Glory member to stand on his own. "I am Wei Shi Lindon, and I claim Heaven's Glory School in the absence of its Jades. If you find an elder, bring them to me. Otherwise, you're to help everyone leave the valley."

The man glanced down at Lindon's badge, but Lindon caught his eyes again. "Spread the word."

The man ran, leaving Lindon to repeat himself to all the other members of Heaven's Glory on the ground. He'd left them only lightly injured, and as a result he'd taken the cut that Dross had promised. A tiny slice across his left forearm.

It was already healing.

Lindon marched back to Eithan, but he started speaking early. Eithan would be able to hear him. "I can't imagine that would have been much threat to you."

"It's not the first twenty ambushes that get you," Eithan called.

When Lindon returned to Eithan, the crowd of Kazan members were huddled together, looking to him with awe and fear, as though he might decide to execute them at any second.

Lindon bowed to them. "Gratitude," he said. "My thanks for protecting my master in my absence."

At the word "master," their eyes widened.

"If you don't mind, you should leave as soon as possible. I can't be sure that Heaven's Glory will leave you alone, even now. We don't have much—"

[Oh no,] Dross whispered.

"What?" Eithan asked. "What is it? I can't see anything! I *hate* this place."

Lindon hopped on his Thousand-Mile Cloud without finishing his sentence, zooming up above the surrounding trees.

He looked over to the west. Something had changed with the Wandering Titan, but he couldn't identify exactly what.

Then he opened his aura sight.

It was like watching the opposite of an earthquake. Starting from Mount Venture to the west, the ground— which had been steadily shaking all day—stopped moving. Earth aura froze.

The wave of silence reached them, and the rumbling of the ground ceased. Only a few boulders tumbled down the nearby slopes.

There came one, loud crash. Then another. Footsteps.

A dark stone head appeared over the western peak, and the Wandering Titan let out a roar that shook the golden sky.

"Run!" Lindon shouted down. Eithan was already on his feet, shakily ushering the Kazan clansmen forward, but they would only slam into the wall of people trying to choke themselves through the narrow exit from Sacred Valley.

They were beginning to stampede, even trampling each other in their desperation to get away. A massive golden light shone behind Eithan, resolving into his cloudship: *The Bounding Gazelle.*

It would barely fly in aura this thin, if indeed it would fly at all, but Eithan was clearly willing to try. He ushered the Kazan sacred artists onboard, physically hurling one and carrying two children under his arms before leaping up to the control console.

Lindon began flying away, toward the exit. The Akura cloudships should be gone by now, but he was seeing Fallen Leaf uniforms, and he could feel Orthos around. At least they had made it.

Eithan's golden cloudship lurched along like a stone skipping across the surface of a lake, barely able to lift up before it had to sit back down, but it was still faster than dragging all the Kazan by hand.

Lindon left them behind, soaring over the line of people screaming and pushing to make it through the Heaven's Glory exit.

To his relief, he could see a ship on a purple cloud flying off with its deck packed with people. Not all the Akura cloudships had taken off after all. Another, resting on the ground, was steadily filling with people.

But as he looked back west, over Sacred Valley, despair choked him again. There were still uncountably many people left. He couldn't begin to see the end of the human line stretching off into the distant clan buildings and beyond.

Not everyone would make it.

But his family still could.

The skies were relatively clear, most ordinary citizens of Sacred Valley not having access to a flying vehicle, so Lindon soared easily over to where Orthos and Little Blue waited for him.

Kelsa paced next to the turtle, Jaran crouched on a stool and impatiently juggled his cane, while Seisha adjusted settings on her drudge. The hovering brown fish bristled with sensors and detectors; Lindon's mother was clearly trying to figure out more information about what was happening.

All four of them stood on *Windfall*'s blue cloud base, and Lindon immediately recognized why. They had been directed to the right place, but they couldn't open the door.

Lindon tried to reach out with his madra, but failed. Though he had left the suppression field, his spirit hadn't fully recovered yet, and his pure madra dissipated only a few feet from his body.

Orthos had been watching Lindon fly up, and at his words, Lindon's mother and sister looked up.

Lindon landed in front of them, his left hand resting on the door to his fortress. At the touch of his madra, the door slid soundlessly open.

The ramps to the nearby Akura ships were clogged, blocked by crowds of people trying to fight their way on, though the Akura Golds easily prevented any unwanted stowaways. A few of those waiting to board noticed Lindon's fortress opening, and some groups began to run for his wide blue cloud.

"Where were you?" Lindon's father demanded.

From her seat atop Orthos' head, Little Blue whistled concern for the others.

"Get inside," Lindon said, his voice low. He tried to give them a reassuring glance, but his eyes were locked on the golden horizon to the west. "Eithan will be joining us soon. Yerin got away on her own. Mercy and Ziel, I...I don't know."

"How are we going to carry everyone?" Kelsa asked. She had a huge backpack strapped on, but she was shifting from foot to foot, as though she longed to toss it aside and go find some people to save.

That first group of people had almost reached Lindon's fortress, running desperately as though they thought he might take off at any moment.

"I don't know," Lindon said again. "We need more time. Get inside."

His mother looked uneasily at the people clamoring to reach the fortress. "How much room do we have?"

"Enough for these, at least," Lindon said, and Kelsa let out a sigh of relief. Had she expected him to turn away people for no reason? "We don't have to carry them far."

A crash deafened the world, and screams rose from the nearby crowds. Rocks and ice tumbled down from Samara's peak. Lindon wondered if Mount Venture was still intact.

With a spiritual effort, Lindon commanded the fortress' cloud to lower, forming a ramp to allow the fleeing Sacred

Valley citizens access. The closest batch was from the Li clan, he noted, with their fancy badges and elaborate jewelry.

Not that clan distinctions mattered now, but that made him hopeful that Mercy was here somewhere.

Orthos led Lindon's family inside, with Little Blue giving directions. When the first family reached the top of the ramp, Lindon held out a hand to stop them.

They tried to barrel past him, but the gray-haired Iron Enforcer at the front crashed into Lindon's extended arm as though into a steel bar.

"No fighting while you're in my home," Lindon said quietly.

The Ruler behind the Enforcer bobbed her head while holding a green-wrapped infant girl on one hip. "Yes, yes, whatever you say."

She was echoed by all the fifteen or so members of the Li clan, who all cried either agreement or begged him to hurry.

[Eighteen,] Dross corrected. [You didn't count the baby ones.]

Lindon moved his arm and stood aside, letting them rush onboard, while he conversed with Dross. *How many can we hold?*

[Well, the aura is still thin here. It depends on how many belongings they have, and how much space they take up on average...]

More and more people had noticed that his fortress was wide and relatively open, so they had begun rushing for him.

[...at least two hundred, easily. No, a hundred and eighty. Say one seventy-five, to be safe.]

A roar sounded out, causing the Irons and Coppers and Jades to scream and clap hands to their ears. Lindon thought some of them might be deafened.

[I, uh, hate to waste calculations, but I don't think storage space will be our limiting factor.]

Time. They would have to take off before they were full. He looked at the mass of humanity pouring out of the Heaven's Glory passageway, knowing there were hundreds of thousands of people still inside.

Was the Titan in there already? Had he crushed the Wei clan to rubble?

"Prepare to leave," Lindon ordered, and Dross materialized, drifting off into the network of scripts and constructs that formed the organs of the cloud fortress.

Eithan's hopping golden cloudship came to a rest by Lindon, and a number of shelter-seeking families ran over to him as a ramp extended.

Lindon looked up to Mount Samara, where a white ring was forming. He didn't want to see the truth on the other side, but he had to know.

He called his Thousand-Mile Cloud again and launched himself into the air as fast as he could.

Mount Samara, seething with people desperately seeking safety, fell away beneath his feet. He shot up and up, past thin clouds, above the circle of light ringing the peak. Up close, Samara's ring was thicker than he had ever realized.

Finally, Lindon looked down upon Sacred Valley.

Mount Venture was gone.

Reddish rocks were scattered all over the center of the valley, crushing trees and buildings as far away as the Wei and Li territories. The Kazan clan was...buried.

A monster crouched on their former home. The Wandering Titan was hunched over once again, feeding, but this time it wasn't wrist-deep in the ground.

Mount Venture had been cracked open like a shell, revealing a golden treasure within.

A beacon of yellow light shone in a pillar up to the sky. Even suppressed by Sacred Valley's formation, it gave off a sense of power that felt completely out of place here.

The source of that light was covered in the Wandering Titan's hands, and it fed deeply, drawing with hunger madra. As he watched, Lindon was struck with how *similar* the two felt. It was like the Titan had been reunited with a piece of itself.

But second by second, the light began to flicker. Almost imperceptible at first, but it wouldn't be too long until the Titan was done feeding.

[It's not...it's not getting *stronger*, is it?] Dross asked nervously. He was still inside the fortress, but he could share Lindon's thoughts anyway.

Hard to tell. The Dreadgod gave off the impression of overwhelming power, but inside the suppression field, the Titan was certainly weaker than it was outside. Though Lindon thought perhaps it *did* feel a little stronger than before. Then again, he was having an easier time sensing everything in Sacred Valley. It must be an effect of leaving the formation behind himself, and having his former power slowly restored.

Dross' mental voice was high-pitched. [Ready, ah, ready to leave!]

Go! Now!

Under Dross' control, *Windfall* lifted off even as Lindon streaked down to meet them. One Li family was halfway on, and two members tumbled off the side.

He swooped down and caught them by the backs of their collars, hauling them up to the rest of their family.

He could do nothing for the others.

The ones left behind screamed and begged for him to return, but he had already landed on the house. There was a hatch on the roof, and he used his power as a key to prove his identity and slip inside.

Dross was launching the fortress now, but his madra wouldn't be enough to fuel it for long, with the aura here as thin as it was. Lindon took over as soon as he entered the control room, letting pure madra flood out to the scripts.

To his surprise, the control room was crowded. Orthos and his family sat off to the side, but so did many of the refugees from the Li, Kazan, and Wei clans, each keeping to their third of the room.

He had expected them to spread out across the fortress. He supposed they were seeking comfort in company.

The cloudship shot further into the air, but he activated another script, showing him Eithan's cloudship. It was still grounded.

Did Eithan even have the madra to take off?

He was about to go back and help when Eithan's ramp smoothly folded up, the ship lifting effortlessly from the ground. That was one problem solved.

Now he just had to pretend they weren't leaving thousands upon thousands of people to die.

The Akura cloudships had stopped taking passengers as well, though some were still empty. They rushed away ahead of him, moving away from the Dreadgod as fast as possible. He didn't blame them. They had stayed longer than he expected.

He tried to keep his thoughts focused, but somehow he had already activated a viewing construct to show him the scene behind him. The crowd of desperate people dashing down the slopes of Mount Samara was projected into the air. He couldn't tear his eyes away from it.

Maybe some of them would make it.

"You saved these lives," Orthos said gravely. "Focus on that."

Lindon tried.

"Needed more time," his father said. "With only another week, we could have gotten everyone."

Lindon had faced enough trouble trying to get people to listen to him even *with* the imminent threat of a Dreadgod looming over them. Would they have listened to him at all if the danger weren't at their heels?

Maybe. He could have tried.

[East!] Dross shouted suddenly. [East, east, east!]

The spirit's emotions were hard to untangle, but they were definitely urgent. Lindon activated the viewing construct directed to the east, but he saw only the Desolate Wilds and the purple Akura cloudships dashing away.

But he thought he felt something. And he saw a speck...

No sooner had he noticed than the speck rushed over their heads. It was a long shaft of Forged crystalline madra the size of a tower, and it sped overhead at impossible speeds, kicking up a snowstorm as it passed by Samara's peak.

The arrow struck with a deafening explosion, followed shortly by the roar of the Wandering Titan.

Then the golden sky darkened. Not with clouds, but with shadow madra.

With his delicate Sage senses, Lindon felt the fabric of the world ripple. A woman stepped from a tall column of darkness, a woman clad head-to-toe in armor of purple crystal and carrying a shimmering blue bow.

Akura Malice didn't stand as tall as when she'd faced the Bleeding Phoenix, but she still towered over his airborne cloudship. She nodded once to his fortress—to him—and then rose into the air.

She took aim with her bow again, and Lindon's heart lifted. They were saved.

But why had she stopped to see him?

A knock came from the door, and the feeling of a familiar presence soothed him. He released a heavy breath.

The hatch in the ceiling opened and Yerin dropped down. She landed easily, stretching her arms as though exhausted. "I'd contend I've done my part. How many Monarchs have *you* recruited today?"

Lindon commanded the cloudship to land.

第十五章

CHAPTER FIFTEEN

If Lindon had thought the ground was trembling *before,* it was nothing compared to what the battle between Monarch and Dreadgod did to the earth.

The Desolate Wilds quaked around him, black trees losing leaves by the bushel. The Purelake, the glistening pool of crystalline water that nourished most of the wilds, shook as though in a high storm.

Families rushed off of Lindon's fortress. They hadn't wanted to leave so relatively close to Sacred Valley, but there wasn't much choice.

He was going to fly back.

Ideally, they would take the people of Sacred Valley much further away, but this much of a head start was better than nothing. They needed to go back and give others the same chance.

The factions of the Desolate Wilds might not be welcoming to refugees, so Lindon left each family with a weapon, a handful of Underlord scales, and a wax seal stamped with the Arelius family crest.

That should be enough to get them started here, but if it failed...well, at least fellow sacred artists had more mercy than a Dreadgod.

Worse, *The Bounding Gazelle* had given up, and Eithan had withdrawn it.

"It's made for high performance," he'd said, "so it needs either richer aura or more madra. I'd prefer both."

There had been discussion of Lindon possibly taking over the faster cloudship and Yerin flying *Windfall*, but the discussion threatened to eat more time than it saved. Eithan was now asleep in his house on the island, and Lindon had to hope that he would recover enough madra by the time they arrived that he could power *The Bounding Gazelle* again.

While they flew, they all watched the battle.

Malice's massive form was visible in the sky, even hundreds of miles away, standing like a violet statue on a platform of air. She hovered just outside the boundary of Sacred Valley's suppression field, firing arrows into her enemy.

At first, Lindon had wondered why the Monarchs had never taken this opportunity to kill the Dreadgods here before. Just trap them inside the field and then bombard them with attacks from outside.

But each arrow dimmed and shrunk the second it crossed the border into Sacred Valley. The Monarch techniques lost their power in seconds, though they still contained a depth of complexity and reality-warping weight that he couldn't fully understand.

He knew they were making an impact because the Titan roared in response to each one. As Lindon turned the fortress to drift back to Sacred Valley, he felt the golden power of the Dreadgod flare...and then retreat.

Not far. The Titan was only lumbering back the other way. But as Malice flew around the edges of the circular suppression field, keeping up her barrage of attacks, Lindon's heart climbed.

She was doing it.

Lindon's mother wrote furiously on her notepad. "Do you gain in size as you advance? Or can you control your growth?"

"Sacred beasts can get bigger than a pregnant mountain,"

Yerin answered quickly. "People don't, at least not any I've clapped eyes on." She nodded to Malice. "That one's not much bigger than me. Shorter than you. It's the armor that grows, it's like a shell."

Yerin was standing stiffly, her back straight, deliberately looking in another direction to appear casual but flicking her gaze to Seisha with every word.

Lindon's mother brightened, her writing picking up speed. "*Really.* And you've met her?"

"Not to polish myself up, but I fought under her banner in the Uncr—uh, a tournament for the whole world." Yerin's Broken Crown bloomed over her head, a wide black halo. "Came in first, as it happens. Not that trophies matter."

Lindon had tried to leave his family behind as they had set down in the Desolate Wilds. He had been thoroughly outvoted.

Seisha made an appropriate sound of awe, and even Jaran grunted approvingly. Kelsa leaned forward. "Pardon if this is too much to ask, but can I see the trophy?"

Lindon thought Yerin was about to start sweating. "No, well, I was just talking out the side of my mouth. Didn't get a trophy. But I would have, if they...had one."

Without taking his attention from the controls, or the battle happening in the sky, Lindon gestured to the Broken Crown. "That's the trophy. It's a unique treasure that only the top eight of each tournament earn."

Kelsa reached out her hands as though to touch it, but pulled back before she did. Seisha's pen moved so that Lindon was sure she was sketching the Crown.

"Were you watching the tournament?" Jaran asked.

While Lindon was trying to think of the best way to dodge the question, Yerin popped in. "He fought himself. Top sixteen. There are recordings of his fights, or you can get a memory from the audience. Now I think of it, Dross could..."

She trailed off and looked at Lindon hopefully.

[I could give them Lindon's memories, but they might be too...ah, what's the word...*heavy* for them. The recordings released by the Ninecloud Court are appropriate for all advancement levels. I could try reproducing them myself, but it might be better to get one from the Court.]

Jaran grunted. "Sixteen. Out of how many?"

"It doesn't matter," Lindon said. "*Yerin* won, and the woman fighting up there is queen over most of the continent. She came here as a personal favor to Yerin."

Yerin's cheeks tinged red, but she glanced at Lindon's parents, clearly eager to see how they would take the news.

Lindon was hoping to keep the topic of conversation away from himself. He couldn't explain anything he'd done in simple enough terms to get his parents to understand it without looking like he was desperately bragging.

[Maybe I *could* do a better job than the Court,] Dross mused to no one in particular. [I could add my own special flair to it.]

"*You* brought her here?" Kelsa asked in awe. She could have watched the battle through the projection construct, but instead she was craning her neck to watch Malice out the windows with her own eyes.

Seisha dipped her head to Yerin. "This one thanks you for going to such lengths for our home."

Jaran inclined his head too, though he was looking slightly in the wrong direction. "Yes, we are honored to have you go so far for your student."

The console flared a little too brightly as Lindon's madra became disordered.

Yerin's mouth dropped open. "Yeah, student, not...I mean to say, uh, bleed me. Lindon, did you tell them—"

"No!" Lindon steadied his breathing. "I haven't spoken with them much at all. There's been no time. There isn't much time *now,* in fact. We should be arriving soon."

The colossal sounds of battle had grown distant, though the occasional flare of madra suggested that Malice was still fighting the Titan on the other side of the mountains.

Jaran frowned, but Kelsa and Seisha had caught the scent of blood.

Orthos chuckled and opened his mouth wide to take a bite out of a nearby chair, but he reluctantly closed his jaws again. "You don't have a snack, do you?"

Lindon quickly opened his void key, pulled out a bundle of firewood, and tossed it to the turtle, who snapped it out of the air.

Little Blue peeped up in agreement, and Lindon flipped her a scale of pure madra.

"So she's not your teacher," Kelsa went on. Her back was to the window now, and she settled into the chair that Orthos had been about to eat.

Lindon's mother smiled kindly. "Yerin, wasn't it? Why don't you come here so I can get a better look at you?"

Yerin breathed like she was facing down an executioner, but turned stiffly on her heel. Her six Goldsigns quivered behind her.

"Well, Lindon." Jaran's mood had markedly improved. "You must have grown into yourself since you left. Tall, strong, good shoulders. I bet you have my jawline, too. How's his chin?"

"We could be in for a rough landing," Lindon said anxiously. "We'll have to be ready to move quickly. Now would be a good time to get prepared."

Dross piped up. [Oh, right, you haven't seen him! Here, I can show you. Consider this a sample of what I can do with the memories of the tournament.]

A moment later, Jaran's eyebrows lifted. "Makes sense now. Advancement does the body good."

"She's a powerful sacred artist," Kelsa said. "She doesn't care about his jawline."

Seisha shrugged. "I'm sure it didn't hurt. So, Yerin, you must know Lindon well."

"Yes." Yerin's Goldsigns were trying to tie themselves in knots.

"We haven't gotten to know the new Lindon much ourselves. I'd be very grateful if you could fill us in on what we missed."

It was his mother's way of asking *"What do you see in him?"* without sounding rude, and Lindon was honestly relieved. Yerin wouldn't answer that question.

Either she would hear an implied insult to Lindon, in which case she would strike back, or she would be embarrassed by the question and dodge it.

[Oooohhh you should have asked me for a simulation on that one,] Dross said.

What do you mean?

[That's what Yerin *would* have done. Before.]

Lindon didn't figure out what Dross meant before Yerin responded. "Might be you know this already, but he doesn't give up. If you cut off two legs and an arm, he'd fight you with one hand and his teeth. If there's a way to win, he'll hunt it down or he'll die on the trail."

Lindon was too stunned to be flattered.

Yerin went on smoothly. "Haven't spent long in your valley, but everybody I met tripped all over each other to see who could stab me in the back first. Guess you taught him right, because he'd twist himself inside out before he turned on me. If my core popped tomorrow and I was no better than a Copper, he wouldn't leave me alone until he found a way to put me back together."

The room was very quiet except for Orthos munching on firewood.

"He could have set himself up like a king in some corner of the world. Could have scooped you three up, set fire to Heaven's Glory, and left. But he stuck around for people who treated him like their least-favorite whipping boy. Don't know who he was before, but that's who he is now."

Her Goldsigns twisted again, and she coughed. "That's what I contend, anyway. In my view. Might be I've polished him up too much."

Lindon finally understood what Dross meant. Not long ago, Yerin would have been too embarrassed to say any of that.

But Ruby wouldn't be.

Red eyes moved to his, and she gave him a shaky smile.

He couldn't return it. He stared into her, thinking about how she saw him. He wasn't as great as she described.

But he wanted to be.

She saw through him, and her smile became more genuine.

"Heavens above," Kelsa muttered. "I should have left too."

When they landed and left the cloud fortress, there were even more people flooding out of Sacred Valley. With the Akura cloudships gone, the number of people seeking refuge seemed endless.

Many of them had given up on the cloudships and now ran out into the world themselves, crossing the mountains and foothills east of Mount Samara on foot or in whatever vehicles they had brought with them.

Lindon wished them luck. There was no way he could go after them himself; he was going to have enough trouble with the people waiting for rides.

Hopefully, none of this would end up being necessary. Malice would drive off the Wandering Titan, and there would be no further damage to Sacred Valley or the other mountains.

If the only problem Lindon had to deal with in the aftermath of a Dreadgod attack was locating everyone who ran and bringing them home to rebuild, he would thank the heavens.

As their fortress began to fill up, he received another piece of good news: Mercy flew in unharmed, bobbing on her staff and waving eagerly to him.

When she reached him, she began to speak before she finished drifting to a halt. "So...who called my mother?"

"Don't know why I needed to," Yerin said. "I'd take it personal if a Dreadgod stomped around *my* back yard."

"At least she came! But don't be too grateful. She wouldn't have shown up here if there wasn't something in it for the family."

Mercy leaned against the base of their cloud fortress, which she sank into like a giant pillow. As she did, she surreptitiously pushed something into the ground with the heel of her foot.

Without Dross, Lindon might not have noticed. The object she'd buried wasn't easy to sense; it felt entirely mundane, with only lingering traces of spiritual power, so it was probably some scripted tool.

But around it, the world felt...thin. Like the invisible indentation Lindon had pressed on to create a portal.

"What was—" he began, but Mercy cut him off.

"The Li clan wasn't as bad as you said they'd be," she reported. "They wouldn't listen to me at first, but once I impressed them a little, they did whatever I said."

Dross materialized onto Lindon's shoulder, frowning at Mercy's foot. [You'll have to do better than that to hide something from me. If you're hiding something. If you're not, stop acting like you are.]

Lindon sent his thoughts silently to the spirit. *I don't think we're the ones she's hiding from. Stop drawing attention.*

Mercy gave him a wide-eyed plea, and Lindon nodded. He understood. Yerin looked between them, glanced at the ground, and then stretched out her arms. "Sounds like we've got more people to load. No time to stand around flapping our lips."

Dross was still staring obviously at the spot under Mercy's foot. His one eye couldn't be open any wider, and he was slowly drifting closer to the ground.

"Dross," Lindon said aloud.

[Yes?]

"We need to get back to work."

[Okay, yes, of course, let's go.]

He didn't hide his staring at all.

With his Remnant arm, Lindon seized the spirit and spun

him to face another direction. Dross' eye swiveled to stay where it was.

You've got to stop.

[To stifle my intellectual curiosity would be to deny who I am.]

I suspect we both know what it is.

[That's why I'm so curious! Are we right? Are you wrong? We must *confirm*.]

Get back in my head.

In a huff, Dross vanished.

Mercy was acting as casually as she could while kicking dirt over the spot where she'd just been standing. "Looks like you've got a full load here. I can stay here, keep the peace."

"I'd feel steadier if you rode with us," Yerin said. "If we have to bolt, we want to stay together."

That brought up something Lindon had wondered about for a while. "Speaking of which, have you seen Ziel?"

Mercy sighed and shook her head. "If anyone's heard from him, I thought it would be you and Dross. I could stay back and wait for him! It might be...inconvenient...having me aboard. Under these circumstances."

From the other side of Sacred Valley, a tongue of shadow madra leaped into the air like a burst of flame from a bonfire.

Lindon *had* wondered why Malice hadn't taken Mercy back already. Maybe she hadn't noticed her daughter's presence in Sacred Valley...or maybe she had been waiting for Mercy to leave on her own.

"We're more than happy to have you aboard," Lindon said, hopping onto the cloud himself. "I would feel better if you were with us too."

Mercy scratched her nose, glanced around as though looking for another opinion, then sighed and joined them.

They lifted off for the second time, Samara's ring now bright. The golden sky had dulled to bronze, and the Titan's influence had thinned so that stars even peeked through here and there.

As they drifted higher, past the curving light of Samara's

ring, they caught sight of the Monarch's fight once again.

Malice stood almost as tall as the Dreadgod now, though the Titan still loomed over her. Its back was to Sacred Valley, and thus to Lindon, and its tail flattened trees as it lashed back and forth.

The Monarch looked like a tamer working with a dangerous creature. She leaned close, provoking the Dreadgod to swipe at her, and then stepped backwards to loose an arrow of Forged blue madra.

Weakened by the field around Sacred Valley, the arrow only splashed against the Wandering Titan's rocky skin, but it still enraged the Dreadgod.

The creature roared, bringing its hands together. Loose stones rose from the earth for miles, gathering in the air between its palms. Golden light formed a ball around them, until the Titan held a sphere of deadly madra, aura, and actual physical stones in its hands.

Lindon had seen Abyssal Palace priests use a similar technique, though of course never on this scale. And the Titan was *still* within Sacred Valley's restrictions. How could it use sacred arts of that level with its advancement suppressed?

The technique blasted out, but Malice simply let it crash onto her breastplate. The amethyst armor stood firm, rocks and chunks of yellow madra spraying out over the landscape for miles behind her.

The Dreadgod gave one more frustrated roar, throwing its head back to scream into the sky...

...then it marched out of Sacred Valley.

Its black, serpentine tail carved a canyon in the soil as it followed Malice, furious. Lindon could feel its power recovering with every breath, and so of course could Malice; she created space by leaping backwards, readying an arrow on her bow.

She needed to keep the Titan on the hook, so she couldn't move too far away, lest it turn back again. At the same time, she didn't want to fully engage and risk starting a full-scale fight here.

Malice still needed to tease the enemy away, but as far as Lindon was concerned, she'd won. She had pulled the Dreadgod away from Sacred Valley.

Granted, the Valley wasn't in pristine shape anymore, but it was mostly intact. He could see Elder Whisper's tall tower from here, and the purple slopes of Yoma Mountain. They could rebuild.

Yerin gripped Lindon's forearm. "Lindon."

He leaned toward her, giving her some of his attention, but didn't take his eyes from the battle.

"*Lindon.*"

His bones were starting to hurt under her grip. He looked up to her...and her red eyes were shining. Literally. They lit up like scripts, and he could feel blood aura slowly strengthening all around her.

But not *just* around her.

Outside the windows, the burnished bronze of the sky began to swirl with another, brighter color. The moon, a dim secondary light to Samara's ring, slowly melted from a cool and soothing blue to a bright pink-tinged red.

[Uh, Lindon...]

No, Lindon prayed. *Please no.*

He held Suriel's marble in a tight fist. Maybe his wishes could reach Suriel, and she could turn back time or rewrite the truth. Anything to undo what he felt now.

One of the refugees in the room began to scream. She wore a stained bandage around one arm, and the blood had begun to writhe under the wrappings.

From beneath the red moon, there came the searing cry of a great phoenix.

第十六章

CHAPTER SIXTEEN

Northstrider drove his boot down on a skull bigger than he was. With the slightest flex of blood and force aura, the power carried throughout the creature's body.

Every bone in the dreadbeast shattered at once. Its heart burst.

The twisted, corrupted lizard—the size of a large house—had only been a Lord-level beast. But you never knew what abominations would crawl out of a Dreadgod's wake. It was always best to wipe pests out when you had the chance.

The important thing was that he stay where he was.

He stood in the center of a wide swath of devastation that the Wandering Titan had cut across the landscape as it marched eastward from Sky's Edge. It had ruined many of the squat towers that Abyssal Palace had left for it, but the cult wouldn't mind. The towers were meant to be destroyed.

The towers would collect the Dreadgod's power and store it in scripts in the foundation, waiting to be harvested by Abyssal Palace members later. It was one of the many ways in which the cultists benefited from the destruction the Dreadgod brought.

At least, they *would* benefit from it. If Northstrider weren't standing in their way.

Ordinarily, he wouldn't be able to block an entire Dreadgod cult like this. Abyssal Palace had enough experts, and enough high-grade weapons made from the Titan's madra, that they could be a threat even to him.

But the floating pyramid that was their headquarters, rolling on a cloud of hovering boulders, now listed to one side. A jagged hole had been torn into the Palace itself, and their Herald was recovering within.

They might have been able to push Northstrider aside...except they had just spent their resources on *another* Monarch. Akura Fury had cost the cults more than they ever expected to spend.

They had survived, though the other three fled. Northstrider knew from experience that it was hard to fully destroy such an ancient organization, even if they didn't have a Monarch backing them. Which they did.

But at the same time, unless one of them was carrying Reigan Shen in their pocket, there was nothing they could do to push past Northstrider.

So he had stayed here for days in a stalemate as they waited for him to leave. That was their miscalculation. He didn't hold many lands, as the other Monarchs did, so he had few vulnerabilities that could be exploited in his absence.

His research could be completed here almost as well as anywhere.

With a thought and a quick twist of aura, he drew streams of blood from the hundreds of dreadbeast corpses surrounding him. The liquid separated themselves into vials, which returned to his void key. At the same time, their hunger bindings ripped themselves free of flesh and separated into cases.

He had no use for such worthless power personally, but all dreadbeasts experienced changes in the presence of the Dreadgods. He understood the nature of hunger madra better than anyone else alive, but it was still valuable to study its effects on flesh, which could hopefully one day be controlled. Since he would never risk the inside of the labyrinth again, the wild dreadbeasts were the best source of information and materials.

This was just a side project for him, but side projects could sometimes lead to unexpected benefits.

At the same time, he kept his spiritual perception on the Titan. The main reason he had personally intervened with the Dreadgods this time was their strange behavior the past few years, starting with the early awakening of the Phoenix. Now, the Titan had fixated on one particular labyrinth entrance.

Were they learning?

It hardly took any concentration to feel the Titan. It was only a few hundred miles away, and Dreadgods were spiritually...loud.

It was impossible to miss one, but precisely because of that, they tended to deafen you to anything else happening around them.

The Bleeding Phoenix, for instance, had been scattered over miles of wilderness for two years, so it was a constant noise. It had been stirring all day, most likely in response to the proximity of its sibling.

He kept his attention primarily focused on the Titan, sparing only a thought for the Phoenix. Malice was steering her opponent away from the labyrinth entrance without fully engaging it, which was perfect. Northstrider stood in reserve, but he would prefer not to engage the Dreadgods himself. It was best to let them rampage for a while, tire themselves out, and then return to their rest.

His oracle codex shouted into his mind: [Warning! Threat approaching!]

It redirected his attention north, to the Phoenix.

Northstrider clenched his fists tight, and before he realized it, he was drifting upward. Abyssal Palace engaged its propulsion constructs and began to flee, but he had no attention to spare for them.

The Phoenix was moving. Fast.

It was heading for the Titan.

With a tight focus of will, Northstrider pushed through the Way. He was swallowed up in blue flows for a moment, taking him to his destination, but he had them spit him back into reality a few miles from his destination.

He needed to be close, but not *too* close. The Dreadgods had powerful wills, and he would be vulnerable coming out of the portal.

When he emerged again, he was hovering in the clouds over a mountain whose peak had been broken off long ago. It was covered in streams, one in particular forming a river that stretched down into a valley.

He looked to the east, where he heard a searing cry. The Phoenix swooped in, spraying condensed blood madra over the ground. From this distance, he couldn't tell if it was striking at a target or just expressing its wrath, but its deadly breath scorched the ground for miles.

If the beam of red light had been any aspect other than blood, it would have left the terrain devastated, but blood madra disproportionately affected flesh. Any animal in the path of that Striker technique was now dead.

And Malice was on the other side of the valley.

His codex sped up his thoughts, so it seemed time slowed down. Malice, with her armor the size of the Titan itself, was on the west side of the suppression field. The Titan had just emerged from the field itself, and it too was distracted by the arrival of its brother.

On the east side, the Phoenix was turning toward the valley. Refugees fled beneath it, but they were so weak as to be invisible to the Dreadgod. That didn't make them *safe*—on the contrary, they would be torn apart by the bloodspawn, not to mention the collateral damage from the Phoenix itself—but no one down there could attract the attention of a hungry Dreadgod.

Until his oracle codex drew his attention to his own spiritual perception, and he realized who he was feeling down there.

Then his irritation flared into true anger.

The most valuable young sacred artists on the continent were all down there, clustered together. With Dross, a powerful tool deserving of further study. They had deliberately placed themselves in the path of a Dreadgod.

And Malice had *allowed* this...idiocy.

Including a pseudo-Herald who had merged with her Blood Shadow. The power of the Phoenix itself.

The Dreadgod's scarlet eye swiveled to focus on a particular cloudship down there, and Northstrider unleashed his spirit.

Malice was going to owe him for this.

Ziel and the Kazan clan reached the base of Mount Samara, and the huge river of people pushing to get out.

It had been hard enough to march across the landscape with it constantly shaking under the footsteps of two giants. The most vulnerable members of the clan, and the families with small children—including the Patriarch's wife and children—had flown off long before, but the Kazan had no abundance of flying mounts or constructs.

Therefore, they had to make their painful way across a ground that tossed like a sea in storm as the Monarch clashed with the Dreadgod. Each arrow that crashed into the Titan's skin sounded like a collapsing tower, though Ziel recognized that the Monarch's might was suppressed by the field around Sacred Valley just like everyone else's.

Every step the clan took was shrouded in fear, because the very earth could betray them. A tree might fall, crushing someone, or a wagon would be swallowed up by a chasm.

Even Ziel cheered her on. In his own way. He nodded approvingly and grunted once or twice, at least.

He would rather lose someone here and there to accidents than everyone to a Dreadgod. At least in this scenario, when he was quick enough, he could save some.

And Akura Malice was pushing the Titan away. In only a few more steps, it would be drawn away from Sacred Valley entirely.

So when he and the Kazan clan did finally reach the mass of humanity pushing to leave through Heaven's Glory, Ziel's heart flooded with relief. He made the mistake of thinking, *We made it.*

Then the crystal song of a giant bird filled the air. Rather than peaceful, it sounded like a war cry, and the sky began to swirl with red.

Ziel had never heard that song before, but it didn't take a genius to figure out what it was.

He called his hammer from his soulspace. Not that he thought he could fight; he clutched it to stop his hands from trembling.

Around him, Kazan men and women mounted on their craghounds shifted and muttered uneasily. The Patriarch and several elders looked to Ziel. "Pardon, but what was that?"

Ziel's gaze was nailed to the east.

He remembered the storm rolling in, flashing blue and gold as living lightning slipped in and out like fish in the sea. The majestic roar, as the Weeping Dragon approached. He had watched the horizon then, awed by its majesty.

His mouth was too dry for the first word. He swallowed, cleared his throat, and tried again. "Run," Ziel whispered.

Around them, some of the other Kazan began to scream. They had traveled overland during a fight between the Wandering Titan and a Monarch; not one of them was free of scratches and bruises, even discounting the greater wounds.

Wherever blood dripped from the ground, separating itself from the body of the host, bloodspawn began to rise.

They were slow here. Weak. The blood aura was thin.

The Patriarch seized Ziel by the front of the outer robe. "What is happening?" he demanded.

"Go to the north," Ziel said. "Or the south. Anywhere... anywhere else."

A Dreadgod to the west, and a Dreadgod to the east.

What had he been thinking, staying with these people and taking his chances with the Titan? Then again, how could he have known they were only moving *toward* the Phoenix?

Effortlessly, he broke the Patriarch's hold on him and returned to the one remaining flying transport in the clan: his own Thousand-Mile Cloud.

He rose into the air even as the Bleeding Phoenix itself flew past Samara's ring. It seemed as big as a mountain, and it looked exactly as he'd always heard: smooth as a liquid, pure red, and somehow...revolting. Twisted. Wrong.

The Dreadgod gave another resonant, echoing cry, and spewed red light down on the land outside the valley.

Ziel flew resolutely away.

His hammer weighed down the Thousand-Mile Cloud, so he sucked the weapon back into his soulspace, but without anything to hold onto, his fingers kept shaking. He had to clasp them together.

He paid no attention to the screams from beneath him, because they were drowned out by other screams. Older screams.

The Weeping Dragon had brought with it lesser dragons, spirits of Stormcaller madra, which had been repelled by the Dawnwing sect's defenses. Until the Stormcallers themselves had torn those defenses down.

Then he'd seen hungry lightning tear men apart.

Ziel intentionally fixed his eyes on the sky so as not to see the bloodspawn, so it was with a strange sense of separation that he realized he was actually staring at the ground.

Bloodspawn, like little parodies of men constructed from blood madra and the will of the Phoenix. They were red puppets, some of them shifting to take on crude shapes of the madra of those they fed on. When they rose from the Kazan clan, they were mostly blocky clay men.

Here, a Kazan woman pushed her copy back and smashed its head open with a club. Some of his followers had resisted the dragons too.

There, a young man was beaten down by the hammer-like fists of a bloodspawn. He was lucky. The dragons had been even more brutal.

Directly beneath Ziel, a bloodspawn's head opened wide

to feast on a fallen man. This was the one common aspect between all the Dreadgods: hunger. Those of them that Forged these spirits did so to feed.

So he had seen this before. Over and over again. As the Sage of Calling Storms bound him in place and propped him up so he could see the rest of the sect being devoured.

At first, he had strained, trembling in helpless fury. Wishing he could tear free, his hammer in hand, and splatter the dragons into a red spray.

Wait.

The dragons were spirits of lightning madra. They had no blood. When they were destroyed, they splattered into blue essence and gold sparks.

So why was he covered in slowly dissolving blood madra?

The fallen man at his feet stirred, but Ziel had already swung into another of the spawn nearby. The feeling of it splattering was viscerally satisfying.

He focused on that with such intensity that he forgot his fear of the Dreadgods. Their situation faded into the back of his mind.

It was all about breaking bloodspawn.

He crushed a few more, but others already rose. If he really wanted to win this game, he would need his Path.

He poured himself into Forging a green rune, bigger than his chest, complex and intricate. He threw it hundreds of yards away, but it would only hover as long as he didn't quite complete the Forging. So he had to hold the technique as he Forged more and more.

As he did, the Kazan clan gathered around him. They fought the spawn of the Bleeding Phoenix, covering Ziel, apparently realizing that whatever he was doing, it would win them the day.

But the bloodspawn realized something too, pushing against the human barrier around Ziel. One of their necks stretched, carrying its featureless head close to Ziel. A mouth stretched across its blank crimson face, cracking into a maw full of teeth so it could take a bite out of Ziel's flesh. His body was stronger than the others here, richer in blood aura, so it was the most tempting treat.

Ziel didn't care.

He was solely focused on breaking as many of these spawn as possible. It was the only thought he still had room for.

The bloodspawn's jaws snapped down on him, its upper teeth scraping his horns.

Then he triggered his boundary field.

Every one of the bloodspawn exploded.

They sprayed liquid blood madra—and in some cases, actual blood—over everyone around. Ziel stood in the center of seven orbiting green runes, and the circle was perhaps three or four hundred yards wide. He had caught hundreds of spawn.

Or so his spiritual sense told him.

His face was covered in blood.

He wiped his eyes clean with his fingers and glanced around, finding the Kazan clan packing in close around him. A cheer rose from among them as though of its own accord.

The Patriarch slapped Ziel on the back. "Gratitude! But you should warn us next time. We thought you were leaving us."

The state of unnatural focus passed, but it didn't leave the fear in its wake. Instead, Ziel felt like himself again.

He sighed.

"What would be the point of that?" Ziel said. "Not like I have anywhere to go."

That wasn't true, and he knew it. Akura Malice was here, and she wouldn't let her daughter face down a Dreadgod without giving her a way out. If he could get to Mercy, he could still escape from this mess.

But that would mean leaving these people behind.

The one good thing about the arrival of the Bleeding Phoenix was that it had scared off the people trying to leave through Heaven's Glory. The crowd pushing their way up the side of Mount Samara had scattered, fleeing in every other direction.

Ziel pointed. "Hey, look at that. Line's shorter."

Lindon felt his eyes change to blue as pure madra flowed through him.

He grabbed Yerin's wrist, pulling her off-balance while he dropped low to drive his left palm at her core.

A Forged blue-white imprint of his palm covered her midsection as his Empty Palm landed, driving madra from her core.

But he didn't know how the Empty Palm would affect a Herald.

Combat report! Lindon called desperately.

[Call me naïve, but I think we should save that for an actual enemy.]

Yerin grunted when the technique landed, but she gave him a reproachful look afterwards. "Still me. Phoenix doesn't hold my leash."

"Apologies. I wasn't certain."

Yerin waved a hand casually behind her, and a pulse of blood and sword aura tore the half-formed bloodspawn to pieces as it tried to emerge from the girl's bandage.

The girl shrieked and tore off her wrappings, crawling as far away from them as possible. Lindon admired her appropriate reaction.

"More spawn rising," Yerin reported. "I'll take care of them. Just get us away."

Another cry came from the north, and this time Lindon could see something slowly flapping great wings. Something that covered the northern horizon like a bank of clouds.

Kelsa walked up behind him, her mouth open in horror. "Is that..."

"A second one," Lindon confirmed. His stomach churned.

"...what about the people who haven't made it out?"

That was what he wanted to know too.

"We've done everything we can," he said, voice tight. "We just have to hope the Phoenix leaves them alone."

[*And* doesn't follow us,] Dross put in.

Kelsa's face twisted in pain and concern, but she nodded. As Yerin made her way out the door to deal with bloodspawn, he focused entirely on pouring his spirit into the control console. There was no such thing as running too fast.

While he did, he glanced back at the projection that showed what was behind him. Shadow crawled over Malice, and she started to melt into the ground...only for the Wandering Titan to stomp its foot.

From miles away, Lindon felt her portal break.

The darkness shattered, and Malice stood exactly where she'd started, but she didn't hesitate. She hurled a glob of sticky shadow madra with one hand, and it exploded into a web. The Strings of Shadow tied the Titan down, while at the same time, heavy darkness rippled through the depths of her violet armor like a wave.

Her full-body Enforcer technique made her sink deeper into the ground, but Lindon could feel the weight as she speared the Titan in the chest with the butt of her bow.

A column of wind blasted over Sacred Valley, tearing up yet more trees. Mount Samara should be far enough away that the Irons and Coppers down there wouldn't be in too much danger, but Lindon worried for anyone left down in the valley itself.

The Titan staggered back a step, but its tail whipped up and struck Malice in the side. She was knocked off her feet, and Lindon thought she might stumble through a mountain...but, gracefully, she turned that fall into flight.

Wind aura cushioned her before she hit the ground, and in another great hurricane burst, she shot away.

Heading south.

Lindon was certain the Monarch was about to circle around the outside of the suppression field to meet the Phoenix, but he didn't see it happen. His attention was called away by a bright red light filtering through the windows.

The Phoenix's head swiveled to look at them.

Lindon was growing used to feeling the willpower of others. He had Consumed thoughts from the Titan itself, had withstood Fury's test of will, and he'd been sensing the weight of will behind Malice's attacks.

Only when he felt the Bleeding Phoenix focus on his cloudship did he realize how far he still had to go.

The weight of the Dreadgod's attention caused the blood aura in the area to flare in power. Lindon reacted immediately, flooding out the Hollow Domain and his own willpower to push against the pressure.

He defended his family and some of the others from Sacred Valley, but he couldn't cover everyone. He hadn't been out of Sacred Valley's suppression field for long, and hadn't regained his full strength.

One man from the Li clan keeled over, blood running from his eyes. Several others collapsed, their bodies twitching.

Bloodspawn didn't rise from them...at least not yet.

The cloud fortress had a script specifically to protect it from sudden destruction by Sages and Heralds. It protected them from the worst of the Phoenix's attention. So this could only get worse.

Lindon could feel the script, all around the ship. It blazed bright red, overloaded by the Phoenix's power. The protection was only meant to stop glancing blows, and wouldn't protect from an all-out attack. Or sustained pressure.

Beneath them, the scripts began to crack.

Under the Dreadgod's *stare.*

What can we do? Lindon demanded of Dross. He was already going over every weapon and ability he had. Sages were supposed to be able to help against Dreadgods.

[Lindon, I...] Dross was at a loss for words.

Yerin whimpered behind him. He spun to see her curled up in a ball in the corner. Her knees were drawn up, her six Goldsigns covering her in a cage. Her red eyes were filled with absolute terror.

"It wants me back," she whispered, and Lindon heard Ruby in those words.

A stone sank into Lindon's gut as he realized it was true. The Phoenix wasn't focused on the rest of them. It was looking for *Yerin.*

Lindon focused as he hadn't since pulling Dross back from Northstrider. He felt space bend and buckle beneath this will, desperately drawing his power together to get them *away* from here.

The Phoenix's willpower brushed his aside like a passing ship shoving past a fish.

It let out another cry, and Yerin staggered to her feet. White light gathered around her as she prepared to activate the Moonlight Bridge.

She was running. Trying to draw the Phoenix away.

Lindon lunged for her...but her Divine Treasure faded on its own. It hadn't recovered yet.

The scripts in the cloudship cracked further.

And suddenly, the pressure on them lifted.

The Dreadgod's great head snapped up, focusing on a new figure. A tiny dot in the distance, to Lindon's eyes, shrouded in a spiraling serpent of red light.

Northstrider slammed his fist into the head of the Dreadgod with an explosion of force. Trees far below were stripped of leaves. Even miles away, the broad windows on their cloudship cracked. The sound was deafening.

The Phoenix was hammered down from the sky, almost slamming into the earth before it caught itself on its massive wings and a cushion of wind aura.

Lindon took a deep breath. If it had crashed into the ground, the impact might have destroyed the entire Desolate Wilds.

He sent pure madra flooding into the controls so they drifted away from the fight as the Monarch of the Hungry Deep met the Bleeding Phoenix in battle.

Legions of spirits rose from the Phoenix, tiny versions of itself splitting off from its body. They looked like red raindrops rising upward from its body. Northstrider responded with another punch that launched a serpentine dragon of scarlet madra. The dragon devoured the cloud of phoenixes, roaring as it did.

That was the only exchange slow enough for Lindon to catch.

In the next second, the Dreadgod unleashed lightning, a wall of sword-madra slashes, a smaller cloud of bird-spirits, and a beam of concentrated destructive light from its beak. All of its techniques were tinged blood-red. It moved constantly as it fought, a blur of motion covering half the sky.

Northstrider conjured dragons, he struck with blows that split the clouds, he summoned planes of black force that shielded him, and he moved even faster than the Phoenix. They spiraled around one another so that even Dross couldn't track them perfectly.

But it was obvious, even to Lindon, that Northstrider was out of his depth.

The dragons he Forged were torn apart by the slightest brush of the Phoenix's talons. His walls of force—no doubt created by a sacred instrument of some kind—shattered before they could cover him. And the feeling of the Phoenix continued growing by the moment.

Even so, Northstrider wasn't overwhelmed. The battle was tilted against him, but not so terribly as Lindon had imagined.

He understood for the first time the dilemma the Monarchs faced with the Dreadgods. They could fight on an *almost* even level, but if the Monarchs pushed too hard, the Dreadgods would awaken and work together. And the Monarchs had people to protect, while the Dreadgods didn't.

But there was something to that explanation that didn't quite satisfy Lindon.

The Monarchs were *that* close in power to the Phoenix; Malice had fought it more or less to a standstill for three days the last time. And even if the Dreadgods joined forces, they were still outnumbered by Monarchs.

There had to be something else. Something...

A feeling of utter cold passed over *Windfall* like a glacier shooting through the sky. Lindon's body and spirit shivered together as it chilled him on a more-than-physical level, but it was past them in a second.

The Phoenix's head came up, and it snapped its beak onto one of Malice's glistening blue arrows. The missile shattered.

A purple-armored fist followed it an instant later as Malice punched the Dreadgod in the ribs.

This time, the impact *did* blow out Lindon's windows.

He was ready for it, pushing out with force and wind aura to blast the glass shards back before they slashed all the Sacred Valley refugees to ribbons. The crowd was screaming, but Lindon couldn't hear them.

Now darkness was interspersed with red light as the second Monarch joined the battle. If Lindon had thought it was hard to follow before, it was chaos now.

And devastating for the land beneath.

Malice strode through foothills, and they became a plain. The impact from one of Northstrider's strikes stripped a forest bare. One of the Phoenix's techniques was deflected, and bloody fire rained down.

There was only one saving grace: the Monarchs were pulling the battle away from Sacred Valley. Every second, they were further north.

Lindon's heart hammered, and he checked the viewing constructs in the fortress. Some of them had blown out, or the scripts that controlled them had, but some were still intact. An image floated over his console, flickering and indistinct because of the damage.

The eastern slopes of Mount Samara were covered in rubble. And filled with bodies.

As he watched, armies of bloodspawn rose like ants.

He quickly turned the projection to another direction, trying not to vomit all over the control panels. How many people who had left Sacred Valley on foot had survived? Had anyone?

His own spiritual sense told him that the suppression field had stopped the worst of it for the people inside, blunting even the physical force from the blows. Crowds still pushed their way out of Heaven's Glory...though the human tide slowed with reluctance as they saw the bodies piled on the eastern side.

Then he found the Titan.

It was standing just outside the ruins of Mount Venture, still except for its lashing tail, watching as the northern horizon was lit red by the battle. Lindon's heart tensed as he waited for it to go join the fight. If it did, would the Monarchs be overwhelmed? Or did they have some kind of plan? Maybe an ambush?

His first breath passed while the Wandering Titan stood still, except for its writhing tail. Then his second breath.

His third breath caught in his throat as the Titan turned. Slow, lumbering, the giant turned back toward Sacred Valley.

The yellow beacon that had once rested inside Mount Venture was still dim and flickering, but the Titan marched over in one stride, ignoring it. The Dreadgod took one purposeful step after another, marching across Sacred Valley.

And leaving it in ruins.

Its footsteps crushed trees like grass. Its tail lashed out behind it, knocking more chunks from the ruined Mount Venture...and as it continued walking, its tail cut into more and more.

Lindon felt like his heart had stopped beating.

From their vantage point, high above Samara's ring and moving south quickly, the high-quality viewing constructs from the Ninecloud Court picked up the destruction in great detail. Not all of them had been damaged, and *this* projection was crystal clear.

So Lindon missed nothing as the Dreadgod waded into the Wei clan.

The central avenue, the artery that supplied traffic for all the major businesses in the clan, vanished beneath its colossal foot.

Earth aura flashed out in a golden wave, and the earth rippled like water. Entire housing districts were torn apart by rolling earth, including the Shi family. Somewhere in that chaos of destroyed buildings and uprooted trees rested the remnants of Lindon's childhood home.

A black tail slashed through the middle of Elder Whisper's tower, and the top half toppled slowly to shatter on the ground.

If the elder hadn't escaped when he had the chance, then he was dead now.

The Titan didn't even notice as it kicked aside the arena where the last Seven-Year Festival had been fought. Where Lindon had met Suriel. Where he had first seen this vision of the Titan wading into Sacred Valley.

The vision he'd failed to stop.

With inexorable steps, the Titan was heading their direction. It seemed to be drawn to Samara's ring, but not in a particular hurry. To the Dreadgod, it was simply time for a stroll.

Mercy laid a hand on his shoulder. "You should turn that off," she said quietly.

Only then did Lindon remember that the construct was projecting this image into the air. If he could see it, so could everyone else.

His family, and several dozen other refugees from Sacred Valley, had just seen their home destroyed.

"Apologies," Lindon whispered.

The view cut off.

But he could still see it. He could feel it, his entire being focused on it.

Tears tracked down his sister's face as she approached him. "Is there...is there something we can do?"

Lindon barely saw her.

"Maybe we could go back? We can find more room. Even...even if we can save one more person..."

The Titan wasn't in a hurry, but Sacred Valley wasn't a long walk for it. If it continued walking in the same direction, it would reach Mount Samara in a matter of minutes.

Lindon stopped the cloud's propulsion. They could go

back. At the very least, they'd be able to pick up a few more people.

His spirit screamed a warning, and he looked up at the windows that were once full of glass. All he could see was a wall of purple crystal.

Mercy threw herself at it, leaping forward. "Stop!" she shouted.

Akura Malice's fist closed around the cloudship, and they were swallowed in shadow. For a few long heartbeats, Lindon was alone in the darkness.

He couldn't even feel his own body. All he could feel was the space twisting around him and the sinking numbness of failure.

[It...it wasn't a failure,] Dross said. [It wasn't! ...Lindon?]

The darkness fell away.

They floated over a dark city. Spires of smooth black stone reached to the violet-tinted sky, and the shadow aura was thick here. Luminous flowers shone white, pink, or blue from carefully cultivated public gardens, and Remnant horses pulled carriages through the sky on tracks of purple flame. All around the city, walls stretched up, black and imposing.

Some of the remaining Irons cried out, groping blindly as their senses weren't strong enough to penetrate the haze. Lindon had to steer the fortress away from a smaller cloudship before it crashed directly into them.

Far below, a scripted spire stood proudly from an open courtyard. A teleportation anchor.

Even for a Monarch, it would have been hard to send their entire cloudship through space in one trip. Malice had sent them to the one place she could reach easily.

Moongrave. Capital of the Akura clan.

The fight for Sacred Valley was over.

第十七章

CHAPTER SEVENTEEN

The cloudship was anything but quiet as they drifted in the wind over Moongrave.

While Lindon had been focusing on the battle with the Dreadgods, bloodspawn had risen all over the ship. Some of them had been destroyed, but others were still attacking, and it took him and Eithan a moment of concentration to destroy them.

In the meantime, virtually everyone was shouting *something*.

"What happened?" Lindon's father demanded. "We're not moving!"

His mother clung to Kelsa, holding a glowing blue-and-yellow sword in one hand and a matching shield in the other. Products of her Soulsmithing, which she must have been hiding somewhere. She looked to Lindon with terrified eyes. "Where are we?" she asked, and she probably meant to sound demanding, but it came out as a plea.

Kelsa pushed her way free of her mother, dashing aside to the open windows to peer down, getting a look around and shouting descriptions of their surroundings.

Orthos was a burning lump of shell in the corner, and his head snuck out of his shell. He let out a long breath of smoke. "Safe. We are safe."

Yerin wasn't shuddering in the corner anymore. She was slumped against the wall, her head hanging. "Useless," she mumbled.

For Lindon, every second crawled by as though Dross was speeding up his thoughts, but that one word from Yerin speared him through the heart.

He turned around and gathered her up. She let him, all eight arms hanging limply to her sides.

"Lost my spine. Almost buried you all."

No. She wasn't the one who had led them all to the edge of their deaths.

"I'm so sorry," Lindon whispered into her hair. "Yerin, I...I'm just...I'm *so sorry.*"

She gave a dry laugh. "Sorry for dragging us along?" Yerin tapped the side of her head. "Mostly, there's only one in here. For a blink there, we had two again. Both of us about to ruin our robes, and curled up like we're looking to die."

Lindon squeezed tighter. That wasn't what had scared him.

She *hadn't* frozen up. She'd tried to leave. He had seen the Moonlight Bridge begin to activate.

If she could have, she would have tossed herself to the Bleeding Phoenix.

A hand rested on Lindon's shoulder, and he turned to see Eithan looking serious. "Ziel isn't here," he said in a low voice. "Nor are Jai Long and Jai Chen. They're resourceful enough that they may survive, but in a battle like that, there are no guarantees."

Kelsa straightened up. "Jai Long? They left. They've been gone for...what, two days?"

Eithan gave her a sympathetic smile, but he didn't correct himself.

And Lindon knew just as well what Eithan *wasn't* saying.
Dross, what happens if the Wandering Titan keeps heading east?

[He might stop at the mountain. If one of them had a huge power source like that, best to guess that they all do. Then maybe he'll feed on that and go back to sleep!]

And if it doesn't?

[...there's no source of aura to interest him for who knows how many thousands of miles east. The Desolate Wilds and Blackflame Empire are too weak. He'll probably stop to feed on *something,* but more likely he just keeps wandering until he gets tired.]

And that was assuming the Titan didn't stop and turn Sacred Valley upside-down looking for whatever prize it wanted. Lindon had been assured several times that ancient security measures had stopped that from happening before, but there was no guarantee it would be the same result this time.

The *most* likely scenario was that it wandered east, wrecking the Desolate Wilds and the Blackflame Empire. The same way it had destroyed Sacred Valley.

Lindon pulled away from Yerin and removed Suriel's marble from his pocket. The candle-flame burned as steady and blue as ever, but its calming aura felt like a lie.

The vision of his own future had stopped when he died, so he hadn't seen what the Dreadgod had done after destroying Sacred Valley. Maybe in this reality, they had averted a worse future. Even if that were true, the fate had come a lot sooner.

And Lindon had failed to stop it.

[Ah, but look at it this way,] Dross said. [*Did* you fail?]

Dross drew his attention to the dozens of lives still remaining in the cloudship. They were battered and cut and bruised and in terrible shape, but they were alive.

Not to mention the hundreds—maybe thousands; Lindon couldn't be sure—who had made it out on the Akura ships before. Dross pulled up that memory and shoved it right into his mind's eye.

The spirit prodded him further. [What did you *really* set out to do?]

To save Sacred Valley.

That was the answer, and they were the words he'd always used to himself when he thought about his purpose for gaining strength.

But what did that mean, really?

Saving his family? They were safe. Here in Moongrave, with Mercy's endorsement, they could be as safe as anywhere. Once their cloud fortress was repaired, he could take them with him or even leave them here.

Lindon had always pictured himself saving his home, but deep down, he had wished for something else as well. He'd wanted to stride back into the Wei clan and show them his great power.

He mocked himself for that now. The people of Sacred Valley hadn't been impressed even when they *should* have been.

The best he'd accomplished was bullying them into obeying.

As a distant third, he'd wanted to preserve the place he'd grown up. He had been gone from Sacred Valley for a long time now, but it had been his home for longer. He had almost as many fond memories there as painful ones.

Now...it was too late for that. It was gone.

The images of the bodies, spilled all over the foothills of Mount Samara, cut him as though the memory was razor-edged. They had died outside Sacred Valley, just as they would have died if they had stayed home.

But some had made it.

And some were still trying to leave. Still trying to escape.

Even so, Lindon felt the burden on himself lighten. Akura Charity had been a Sage before he was born—before his father was born, probably—and even she couldn't have taken him across the continent in one trip. There was nothing he could do. The battle was over.

[Ooh, that's what I said! I said that! Focus on the victory and not, you know, the failure. All that failure.]

Lindon did, and he found the lack of responsibility a welcome relief. He would be wrestling with himself for the rest of his life, he knew, looking to find every little detail he should have done differently to save more lives.

But right now, he couldn't save more than he already had.

Only then did he notice Mercy, standing against the windows. She held her dragon-headed staff loosely in one hand, and the wind from outside stirred glass shards around her feet and whipped her ponytail into her face.

She had turned around, but otherwise stood exactly where she'd reached when she'd lunged for her mother's hand. Now she chewed on her lip so strongly that blood welled up.

As Lindon met her eyes, she spoke, as reluctantly as if he'd pulled the words out of her.

"Does anyone want to go back?"

A buzz passed through Lindon's body. At the same time, he and Dross remembered the item she'd left buried outside of Sacred Valley's suppression field.

I was right, Lindon thought, and he himself didn't know if the words were excited or hollow.

[I was *way* off,] Dross said.

From her void key, Mercy pulled out a stone carved with script. It looked as though she'd etched the scripts herself, and Lindon knew what it was even without inspecting it closely.

The stone itself wouldn't do anything. Neither did the script, when it was powered. It only linked to a teleportation anchor.

Like the one Mercy had taken from Daji. The one she'd left buried in Sacred Valley when she'd seen her mother show up.

She had known Malice might send her away, and had prepared herself a way back.

That same anchor had allowed the Blood Sage to transport a group of Overlords halfway across the world in one trip. Such small teleportation anchors were disposable—permanent ones were huge, like the tower beneath them that Malice had used to send them here to Moongrave—but this one had been made by Reigan Shen. It would last another trip.

"We'll need you to carry us there, if you can," Mercy went

on. They all knew it would be difficult for Lindon to move so many people, even if the anchor made it possible. "But... do we..."

She took a deep breath.

"It's not like there's much we can do. We can't bring anyone back."

That was a safe bet. Now that they were here, Lindon could carve a device with the corresponding script to the anchor beneath them, so they had a route back to Moongrave.

But he wasn't sure he could make it all the way to Sacred Valley, much less come back. And there was no *way* he could bring back more people than he started with.

Which meant there would be only one reason to go back.

To stall the Titan.

His mother was breathing heavily, a notepad clutched to her chest. "Going *back?*" A general stir of terrified confusion passed through the Sacred Valley residents in the room.

"Don't be stupid," Jaran said, rapping his cane on the floor.

Kelsa slumped into a chair. She looked exhausted, and tears had run tracks in the ash and dust caking her face, but her voice was firm. "It wouldn't be fair to you to go back. You owe them nothing. In fact, everyone who escaped owes you all their lives."

Lindon's sister turned to him, straightened her back in the chair, and dipped her head. "Gratitude."

Repeated bows and murmurs of "Gratitude" passed through the room.

They weren't bowing just to him, but to all the outsiders: Eithan, Mercy, Yerin, and Orthos. But those four looked to Lindon.

This was his home. They were only here because of him. And they would go back if he asked them to.

But what was he going to do? Fight a Dreadgod to buy time in the hopes that a few more people might get away? It might already be too late; the Titan may have crashed through Mount Samara and killed everyone by now.

Lindon could *theoretically* affect a Dreadgod, but *theoretically* a child with a sharpened stick could kill a tiger.

He had never stopped rolling Suriel's marble between his fingers, and now he held it up. All this power, he had gained to protect Sacred Valley.

Now, he didn't know what to do.

For the second time in a day, he gripped the marble and prayed.

I don't know what to do. Help me.

Unknown Location

The Way

[Report complete,] Suriel's Presence said.

As Suriel drifted along the blue rivers that made up the basis of all existence, she caught up on the diversion that she had allowed to distract her for the last few standard years: the journey of Wei Shi Lindon.

He had grown faster than she had expected. Faster than most models of him had predicted, though at the time, she hadn't realized how much Ozriel's meddling had changed things. Or how Makiel's alterations would speed Cradle's destiny.

By all odds, Lindon should have been dead by now, but here he was, debating whether to go back and face down a Dreadgod. She looked forward to his choice.

[The battle with the Vroshir might make it difficult to get further news from Cradle,] her Presence reminded her. [Probability of future delay is very high.]

She considered that. As always, her Presence didn't speak solely in words, but also in thoughts and impressions, meaning conveyed directly into her mind.

It was reminding her that, the next time she got news

from Cradle, there was every chance that Lindon would be dead.

Cradle would be protected even in the most extreme circumstances of the war, so she didn't fear for the world itself too much. The Vroshir would have to extend themselves on several fronts and sacrifice valuable worlds to penetrate Sector Eleven.

They didn't work that way. They were bandits, after as much bounty as they could with as little risk to themselves as possible.

The one exception was the Mad King, and Suriel went to face him now.

And she didn't need her Presence to remind her that it might not be Wei Shi Lindon who died first. Despite all odds and projections, it was a possibility that he might outlive her.

Do you have a suggestion? Suriel asked.

Her Presence had its personality tuned down—she liked conversation, and would have enjoyed a more expressive companion, but she found chatty Presences unprofessional. Still, that didn't mean the construct had nothing to say.

[Beacon located,] the Presence said, transmitting the image of the sealed marble containing Suriel's power. Lindon was currently rolling it in his hands, trying to make a decision. [Temporal synchronization possible. Communication possible. Expected delay to final destination: point-zero-four-three seconds.]

Suriel had given Lindon the marble so that she could find him again if and when he ascended. Or possibly when he faced the choice of whether or not to ascend. This was too early, and her Presence knew that.

Then again, that was only something she had decided herself. She hadn't spoken any sort of oath.

And Lindon had manifested an Icon, even brushing against the Way at a rudimentary level. Technically, he could ascend now, far ahead of schedule.

That should be rewarded.

Begin transmission, Suriel commanded.

[Excellent decision,] her Presence said.

Suriel began to wonder if its personality might be set too high after all.

As Lindon stared into the blue flame of Suriel's marble, Dross began to panic.

[What is this? What's happening? Hey, get out of here! Shoo! No, you can't kick me out! I live h—]

A cool, distant, female voice replaced his. One that Lindon recognized. [Prepare to receive transmission.]

Before Lindon could "prepare" anything, he found himself sitting in a simple, wooden room.

It was primitive, but comfortable. The ceiling, walls, and floor were all polished wood, and each seemed to be made of one piece rather than planks bound together. There were no windows, but a fire burned in a hearth, the smoke carried up the chimney. Even the hearth and the chimney looked like they had been grown out of the same wood that made up the rest of the room.

He sat in a smooth wooden chair, though it was darker than the walls, and faced a similar chair a few feet away from him. That one was empty.

Other than the fireplace, the only features of the room were trophies hanging on the wall. Bunches of herbs, with flowers that radiated life aura. A red potion spinning in a sealed bottle, sitting on a tiny shelf. A dagger with a long handle and tiny, razor-sharp blade was mounted on a ceramic plaque on the wall. That weapon felt *heavy* to his Sage senses, like the attacks he'd sensed from Malice.

A structure emerged from one wall like moss-colored antlers, though he was certain they had not been taken from any dead animal. They felt alive in their own right, even then. They hung next to a drifting oval of pure strands of light and a few tiny winged spirits in a glass cage.

Lindon took in all the objects with his eyes and perception in one brief moment, but none caught his attention fully.

He was focused on figuring out what this was.

He could still *use* his spiritual perception, which implied that his spirit was here, and his body felt physically present. He moved with no problems, and the room smelled of woodsmoke and flowers, so his senses were working.

But Dross was gone, and the voice had told him to prepare for transmission. Either he had been transmitted somewhere else, or someone was transmitting a message directly into his mind. Or some other, stranger method that he had no frame of reference to understand.

Still, he felt excitement rather than fear. His clothes had come with him, but not his void keys or his badge. The one object that had followed him was Suriel's marble, still burning steadily in his hand.

And he was certain he recognized that ghostly voice.

A moment later, he was proven right.

Suriel materialized in the far corner of the room, smiling gently.

She looked different than he remembered her, and he didn't know if his memory had faded with time or if she had dulled her appearance before. Rather than a deep, muddy green, her hair was now a bright and vivid emerald. Her eyes were purple, but brighter and less human than Mercy's, and symbols swirled in the iris.

His immediate instinct was to lean closer and try to figure out those runes, but it was a fleeting thought.

She wore seamless white armor, as she had before, which flowed like a liquid rather than having any sort of visible joints. Lines of gray smoke snaked up from her fingertips on one arm, terminating at the back of her skull.

And Suriel herself was flawless, like she had been perfected. She stood out in this wooden room like a shining jewel sitting on a dirty kitchen counter.

He hurriedly stood and bowed, but she strolled around to the second chair, pulling it back and sliding in. She sat comfortably, one leg crossed over the other, and spoke softly.

"Wei Shi Lindon. It's good to speak with you directly again."

"The honor and pleasure are mine. I had never thought that I would have the great fortune to meet you again until I left my world behind."

"I hadn't expected that either. There are circumstances in the greater realms of existence that have changed much of what we thought would come to pass." She waved a hand. "You can sit. This space is modeled on a house that I've always liked. My old home, back in my world."

As Lindon sat, Suriel chuckled. "The reality is much cozier than this. I have so many treasures and trophies that it can be difficult for visitors to walk."

Lindon glanced to the walls. "So, if you don't mind me asking, are these illusions? Or are they copies? They feel so real."

If they *were* copies, perhaps he could take one. Even the crude imitation of something that Suriel would collect might turn his situation entirely around.

"They are real, but they aren't precisely *here*. These are just the projections of those treasures I've collected that are so significant they intrude even on depictions of the place."

Lindon leaned forward, looking earnestly into her eyes.

If he paid close enough attention, he was certain he could draw some of those runes. They seemed to shift, as though multiple symbols occupied the same space at the same time.

"Gratitude. I need your help now more than ever. The Wandering Titan has come to Sacred Valley."

He wasn't sure if he would have to explain the situation further—honestly, he expected that she was more familiar with Cradle than he was—but she nodded along.

"I know. I've been keeping my eye on you."

That was comforting, on one level. He had always somewhat hoped that Suriel was watching over him from above.

But to be told that in person was unexpectedly embarrassing.

He was suddenly flooded with all the memories she might have seen. Had she seen him fail over and over again, learning Soulsmithing? Several of those constructs had blown up. Had she heard the awkward words he'd stumbled over as he tried to express his feelings to Yerin?

Heavens above, had she been reading his *thoughts?*

He had to put a stop to that before the shame overcame him, so he bowed his head. "Gratitude. I am...relieved to have such a reliable ally."

"I would have watched you die," Suriel said, in the same gentle, kindly tone as before. "I expected I would, more than once. It would sadden me, and I hoped for your success, but I could not guarantee it. As I told you before, we have rules restricting the degree to which we can interfere."

Lindon squeezed the marble in his hand. "I know," he said, "but please accept my gratitude regardless. You have helped me..."

He had been about to say *"You have helped me more than you know,"* but that surely wasn't true. And was probably insulting to someone who could read thoughts and the future.

"...more than I deserve," he finished. "But, if you'll forgive my curiosity, how are you able to contact me now? Is this not interference?"

Her expression grew more serious. "I spoke of dire circumstances before. We are fighting battles outside of your world, battles that shouldn't affect you...but they might anyway. Cradle may begin experiencing minor corruption. It's possible that those in your world may begin to encounter spaces or beings for whom the rules of reality no longer consistently apply. Strange apparitions, monsters, locations where nightmares crawl from your mind or the sacred arts no longer function.

"If you see these things, know that you will never be abandoned. My organization considers Cradle one of our core worlds, meaning that we will defend you to our last breath."

Lindon felt a chill.

If there was something going on outside Cradle that required so much attention from not just Suriel, but the others at her level, then how much danger were they in?

Lindon remembered the projection from Ozriel's marble, where he had seen the Abidan spread out in white-armored legions, each with abilities beyond the Monarchs. And Suriel had been among the seven—or eight; Lindon didn't understand exactly where Ozriel fit into the structure—at the forefront of them all.

Then again, if they were dealing with threats on that scope, surely one little Dreadgod would be nothing to her.

"There are very few advantages to such a situation," Suriel continued. "One is that I have some more leeway in how I am permitted to act. As they say: when your boat already has a hole in the bottom, no one cares if you chip the paint."

Lindon seized on that. "I know this is shameless for me to ask, when you've already done so much, but if you can intervene...please, save Sacred Valley."

Her smile returned. "I already did."

"Yes, I'm sorry, I know you've descended to save us once already. It's asking too much for you to—"

She looked nothing like his actual mother, but he felt motherly kindness radiating from her. "You are my solution. Fate has been accelerated so this day arrived sooner than it ever should have. But now it's here, and you are in position."

Lindon's stomach twisted as he realized she was relying on him to go back and face the Dreadgod...because she thought he could do something. Her estimation of him was too high.

"Apologies, but I'm afraid I might be weaker than you think." He was afraid to look her in the eyes. "I'm not...I don't mean to argue with you, but I am not ready."

He would do what he could, would strain himself to his limit, but he understood where his limits lay. He wasn't powerful enough to save everyone.

"Ready?" She leaned forward and tapped him on the forehead with two fingers.

Suddenly, he was seeing through someone else's eyes. Crouched, shivering, on the deck of a cloudship as men and women in Akura colors passed out hot food.

The deck wasn't full, but it was crowded. The people from Sacred Valley had divided themselves—clans and Schools sticking with their own kind—but there were at least a few dozen visible, and he saw a few heading downstairs, suggesting more on a lower deck.

Her fingers released, and the vision faded.

"Lindon, when I said I already saved them, I meant *I already did.*" She leaned back in her chair, satisfied. "Or should I say, *you* already did."

He remembered the sight of the crowds squeezing out of the exit on Mount Samara. "There are so many people still back there."

"You don't have to save everyone," Suriel said. "It's a lesson you learn and learn. I wasn't the one who told you to save Sacred Valley. You decided to do that, so you decide when you've succeeded."

She moved until her scripted eyes had his full attention. "And you decide who you're going to be after that."

Lindon knew what he was going to do afterwards. He was going to return to his advancement without so much pressure hanging over his head.

A faint smile crossed her lips again, and she gestured as though tapping him on the forehead one more time.

Suddenly, he was hovering over Sacred Valley, a Thousand-Mile Cloud beneath his feet. Yerin and Eithan floated to either side of him, and the Wandering Titan stared them down.

The three of them unloaded their most powerful attacks in coordination, and they struck a heavy blow against the Titan.

Until its tail caught Yerin unexpectedly. Lindon lunged out of position, and the hand of a Dreadgod closed over him.

Lindon died.

Then he was on *Windfall,* and he decided not to go back. The months sped by as they gathered the remainders of

Sacred Valley. There were more survivors than he expected; tens of thousands of them.

They re-settled Sacred Valley one restored building at a time. The suppression field was weakened, and somehow—the vision skipped over this part—he managed to deactivate it completely.

Lindon saw himself, looking virtually the same as he did now, tutoring his three black-haired children in the sacred arts with Yerin at his side. His future self reached out, scanning the children...and checking each of their twin cores.

The futures washed over Lindon, so he only got a glimpse of each.

There were futures where he and Yerin split up and went their own separate ways, futures where he had children, futures where he and Yerin ascended from Cradle in months, even futures where he married Mercy.

And there were futures where he killed the Dreadgods.

He saw himself years in the future, one arm white and one coated in what looked like black scales, his eyes black pools with white circles. He stood over the crumpled body of the Wandering Titan, cycling its power...and condensing the spare earth madra as he vented it, tucking it away for storage.

Northstrider loomed up opposite him, moving for the Titan, and Lindon appeared in his way. The clash of their wills warped space, and the vision changed.

Lindon saw himself with a giant white tiger—the Silent King—splayed open and hanging in the air in front of him. Blood spattered the room, and he sawed away with Wavedancer, carving out a beautiful binding like a smooth pearl.

Outside, the world trembled under the pressure of the three remaining Dreadgods, but he had his prize already. He could do what no one had ever been able to do: forge a weapon with the power of a Dreadgod.

The visions passed, leaving Lindon feeling out of breath. He sunk deeper into his chair, though surely he didn't have lungs here.

"That...those were...*possible* futures, right?"

"Strands of Fate. All possible, if some more likely than others. And that list was by no means exhaustive."

"My children..." It seemed like a silly detail to focus on, but his curiosity pushed him forward. "Did they practice the Heart of Twin Stars?"

"If things play out as they do in that strand, you'll leave behind a more powerful bloodline legacy than just split cores. Not to mention the gifts they receive from their mother."

Lindon's imagination spun ahead of him. How powerful *would* his children be? He might leave behind an ability that outshone even the Arelius detection web.

He noticed Suriel watching him, running armored fingertips over the smoky lines that drifted across the back of her arm. "You could leave behind a bloodline that has all the advantages you lacked. They would have a much easier start than you did. But how many people, from powerful families with unending resources, have made it as far as you have so quickly?"

The gray ghost of a woman appeared over her shoulder and began to speak, but Suriel stopped it with a gesture. "The legacy you inherit is nothing compared to the legacy you leave behind."

Suriel waved to her ghost, exchanging words with it that Lindon was not permitted to understand. That left him to his thoughts, chewing over her words.

When their incomprehensible conversation ended, Suriel sighed and turned back to Lindon. "Even here, we don't have unlimited time. But I hope this has helped you."

Lindon pressed his fists together and stood so he could bow deeply. "I cannot express my gratitude enough."

The Abidan continued softly. "I'm sure you remember what I said before. Any sage will tell you that every Path boils down to one: improve yourself. But you're a Sage yourself now. You should know the rest."

She stood from her own chair, lifting his face to meet

hers. "You improve yourself, but not for yourself alone. For a greater purpose."

"Apologies," Lindon said, "but this is my purpose."

"No, this was your goal. Not your purpose."

"So then...what is it?"

She rested her hand on his shoulder, and rather than a messenger of the distant heavens, he saw her as a friend lending him encouragement.

"You have the chance to show me that. Wei Shi Lindon... show me the future."

[—here! You're just a guest! You—Lindon! Where did you go? Wait, *are* you back? Is it really you? Say something that only the original you, and not an exact, perfect copy of yourself, would ever say.]

Lindon didn't say anything.

With a brief effort of will, he opened a void key. Not his. Sophara's.

Ekeri's armored Remnant growled at Lindon as he entered, but he wasn't here for her. At his intention, natural treasures began to rise from their sealed, scripted chests all around the room.

There were two here that were more powerful than the others: a source of water and fire aura. They were sealed off now, in scripted jars of their own, but he could still feel them.

For this, he didn't need them. He needed balance. He gathered up some of the weaker treasures, matching them effortlessly to one another and burning them for soulfire. He needed to top himself off for this, and he had used up some of his soulfire. More had leaked away under the influence of Sacred Valley's suppression field.

When he had replenished himself, he began to arrange stronger treasures in a circle around him.

[Advancing won't be an advantage inside the suppression field,] Dross pointed out. [We'll just lose power faster.]

But it will help against the Titan.

["Help" is such a strong word.]

Advancing to Overlord to fight a Dreadgod was like a child bringing *two* sharpened sticks to fight a tiger instead of one, but Lindon would take everything he could get.

Someone sidled up beside him, but Lindon had felt him on his way. "You should stand back," Lindon said. "If I make a mistake, you could be hurt."

"Don't make a mistake," Orthos said before crunching into an empty wooden chest that had recently contained a natural treasure.

Lindon nodded absently. He was already hesitant to waste time advancing when every second counted, but the better prepared he could be, the more people he could save.

When the treasures had been arranged neatly around him, Lindon felt the soulfire in his spirit begin to resonate. The aura that blew in from Moongrave, rich and thick compared to Sacred Valley, shook in harmony with his soul.

And Lindon prepared himself with the words he had figured out days before. The Underlord revelation was about what motivated you to begin, but the Overlord revelation was who you were now.

"I...advance," Lindon said.

He moved forward, onto the next challenge, no matter what stood in his way.

Even the Wandering Titan itself.

The aura shook around him, the treasures burned to colorless fire, and they swirled through him. Unlike his Underlord revelation, which felt like it had deconstructed and rebuilt him from head to toe, this advancement was a cleansing.

The soulfire passed through him in a hot wind, searing and comforting at once. His channels grew stronger, his cores flared brighter, and the lingering weakness from his time in the suppression field was washed away.

In seconds, Lindon walked away as an Overlord. He could have imagined it, but it seemed that Ekeri's Remnant nodded to him.

Orthos stayed where he was, watching the other natural treasures. "I would like to use these."

The turtle would need soulfire too, but Lindon didn't at the moment. All the other tools he required were in his personal key.

He took the golden ring on its cord off his neck, putting Sophara's void key around Orthos' head. Then he rested his hand on the turtle's shell.

"I'm glad we found you," Lindon said quietly.

"I was never lost."

Lindon walked back out of the void key, where of course everyone had felt his advancement. Yerin gave him a lopsided smile and gripped her sword, ready to fight. Mercy nodded, but she looked worried. Eithan stroked his chin thoughtfully.

Lindon held up one hand to Mercy, and she tossed him the scripted stone.

"Hold on a moment," Eithan said, but he was standing too far away.

Lindon caught the stone and focused his will. He met Yerin's red eyes. "I'll see you soon."

The horrified realization had only just appeared on her face when she lunged for him, but she couldn't stop him that way. She would have been better off standing in place and pitting her willpower against his.

"Return," Lindon commanded himself.

In a rush of blue, he vanished.

With every swing of his spear, Jai Long cursed himself. He was a fool.

They should have left the second they knew a Dreadgod

was involved. Why had they ever stayed to take their chances?

Now they were miles outside of Sacred Valley, but the world was still a nightmare battlefield. The forest around them—their leaves only slightly tinged black with the corruption of the Desolate Wilds—had been completely leveled. The battle between the Dreadgod and the giant had devastated the landscape for as far as he could see; footprints left lakes, and he could see straight through a hole in a far-off mountain.

Or he could, if he could spare the attention to look.

Each sweep of his spearhead traced white light behind it, and the Stellar Spear madra came alive with the will of the Remnant who had long ago infested him. The Striker technique became a snake that sought out enemies, drilling through their head or chest.

But there were always more bloodspawn.

Jai Chen directed Fingerling, who breathed his strange pink madra over a bloodspawn that looked like it had been made from scarlet scissors strapped together to walk like a man. Fingerling's breath didn't behave like fire, or even fire madra, but like a dense cloud that passed over the jagged spawn and dissolved it.

But as this bloodspawn fell, it stretched out its arms and slashed at the legs of a man who was trying to sprint passed it. The man screamed, but even the new hole in his leg didn't stop him from continuing to flee, hobbling and leaking a red trail with every step.

And from that trail, another bloodspawn rose.

Jai Long speared it as it formed, but they were surrounded by bodies, and either the Phoenix hadn't moved far enough away, or its influence lingered. Blood gathered up into these grotesque puppets of men and women.

He tried to use his techniques sparingly, but if *he* was growing exhausted, his sister could barely breathe.

Around him, he felt only chaos. Pressure from the Dreadgods, malicious hunger from the bloodspawn, and disordered madra of every aspect from the crowds of people fleeing Sacred Valley and spreading into the forest.

Jai Long looked east, and he saw a swath carved through the forest ahead of them. Black spots were dashing across that space, and only by focusing his spiritual perception did he realize those were dreadbeasts.

First a few, but that trickle almost immediately became a torrent. Dreadbeasts were famously enraged by the approach of Dreadgods, and the Desolate Wilds was home to more dreadbeasts than anywhere else he'd ever heard of.

Coldly, Jai Long realized that they were about to die.

He had known they might be killed by the Wandering Titan, but that was like being killed by a thunderbolt or torn apart by an aura-storm. It was a force of nature you could do nothing about, and at least it was over in a moment.

Now, the bloodspawn would wear them down. Even if they escaped, there were dreadbeasts ahead of them and the Wandering Titan behind.

With one surge of soulfire-enhanced madra, Jai Long whipped his spear in a circle. The force of his blow and the power of his serpents of living madra tore open a clear space around him. Bodies and bloodspawn were equally torn apart and shoved back, giving him enough space to work.

He leaped over to a log, dragging it closer. With a few quick stabs, he separated the fallen tree into segments, and dragged them into a circle around the edges of the empty space.

A bloodspawn clambered over the side, and he blocked its Striker technique before returning one of his own.

His core flickered, dim at the center of his spirit, but he focused on his task. Jai Chen had picked up on his project, and was helping him keep the circle clear. That took enough pressure off that he could begin carving symbols into the segments of log.

The work couldn't have taken more than two or three minutes, but it felt like hours before their crude script— stabbed into pieces of log arranged in a rough circle—activated with a flare of white light.

It would push spiritual powers away, repelling Remnants and bloodspawn. Even dreadbeasts, to a lesser extent.

But it couldn't stop them. Any script *that* solid would put too much strain on the material, and the first impact against it would send his logs tumbling.

Upon immediate activation, a bloodspawn with flourishing tree branches for limbs stumbled back, then shuffled around the edges of the script to look for prey elsewhere.

It would help...but it wouldn't stop everything.

Sure enough, a dense, more advanced bloodspawn shaped like a man with a sword in his hand shied back from the script, but he crawled over the log to get to them. Jai Long faced him with no techniques, but they had to exchange blows several times before he got the better of the spawn, sending a chunk of its madra fizzing away to essence.

Jai Chen had finished another on her side, but even Fingerling was growing tired, drifting lower in the air.

More bloodspawn flowed around them, but some still ignored the repulsion and climbed in.

They would still die now, only slower. This was nothing but a way to stall for a little more time.

But wasn't that every day?

A bear-like dreadbeast leaped over the back log, and Jai Long braced his spear against the ground. The rotting bear impaled its chest on the length of the spear, but didn't seem to care, rabidly snarling and swiping at Jai Long.

He left the spear and the bear, turning to stiffen his fingers and Enforce them like a weapon. The Star's Edge technique sharpened his hand with a point of bright white sword-and-light madra, and he drove his fingers through a bloodspawn's chest.

While the technique was still going, he spun and slashed open the bear's throat.

Jai Long was breathing hard, and his mask seemed to be getting in his way. Roughly, he tore off the bandages, baring his hideous fanged smile to the world.

The air wasn't fresh, it was filled with smoke and dust and

the stink of blood and rot, but he gulped down deep breaths anyway.

He seized his spear, kicked the dying bear dreadbeast off the end, and turned his weapon to work on a bloodspawn.

The last of his madra failed him, and soon he was fighting with nothing but the strength of his limbs. Even so, he swore an oath to the heavens.

If nothing else, he would die before his sister did.

One long second after vanishing from Moongrave, Lindon landed on his hands and knees in half-melted snow, surrounded by debris and wind-torn trees. People screamed around him as they fought featureless humanoids of red madra that rose from mere droplets of blood. To the east, Lindon felt hordes of dreadbeasts filtering out from the Desolate Wilds, driven mad by the presence of a Dreadgod.

As he recovered from the exhaustion of his working, Lindon felt nothing but relief. Mount Samara was still in one place. He'd made it.

The earth shook beneath his hands to a steady rhythm. Footsteps. Lindon heaved a breath and pushed himself to his feet.

He hadn't come here to rest.

The chaos around him resembled a battlefield. More and more people poured endlessly from the Heaven's Glory pass, stumbling over bodies, and Lindon couldn't tell if they had been destroyed by the powerful wind or the falling boulders or if they had simply been trampled alive.

Formerly bound Remnants ran wild, darting through the crowd. Children hunkered together behind a broken and overturned cart. And everywhere, people ran from or struggled with freshly risen bloodspawn.

All the while, the dreadbeasts were on their way.

Do we have enough launchers? Lindon asked Dross.

[We need to hurry.] The earthquakes now couldn't be compared to the ones from before; with each heavy pound of the Titan's footsteps on the earth, Lindon was lifted off his feet. [...but yeah, we have enough to eliminate a majority. The bloodspawn here are especially weak, thanks to the aura and the general flimsiness of the hosts.]

Lindon's void key opened, causing several people nearby to scream and flee. Launcher constructs, some complete and some half-formed, flew out on gusts of air. He had stocked up, in case he needed to make another cannon. Wavedancer followed, sluggish in this aura.

Take over.

[Yes, Captain!]

Lindon rose into the air on cushions of wind aura. Though the vital aura here was weak, he still had an easier time controlling it thanks to his Overlord spirit. He wouldn't be able to freely fly like this, but he could hover in the air, giving Dross a better vantage point. Now they could see far more targets.

Lindon controlled the aura and powered the constructs, but Dross handled targeting. The spirit's attention split thirty, forty, fifty ways.

[Aaaannnnd done!]

Lindon triggered all the launchers at once.

Striker techniques of every color and description lanced out, tracing a web all over the pandemonium of fleeing people. Bloodspawn splattered, melted, imploded, wilted, dissolved, collapsed, and deflated.

The second, third, fourth, and fifth shots came on the heels of the first. Some of the bindings and unfinished constructs broke after the first shot, some after the second, and a few more on the third.

In only a breath, over a hundred bloodspawn had been eliminated. Not a single bystander was scratched.

Lindon let the expended launchers fall to the ground, hissing essence of every color into the air, and returned the functional constructs to his void key. His eyes were on the sky.

The footsteps were growing heavier.

The entire process had taken only a breath, but it was still time they couldn't afford to lose. The constructs traded place with his Thousand-Mile Cloud, and he raced into the sky.

Jai Long had felt Lindon arrive.

Even exhausted and weak as his spirit was, he could sense the arrival of a spirit much stronger than anything in his immediate vicinity.

He didn't feel any hope. He was too tired for that. Even if Lindon had come to save him specifically, Jai Long couldn't spare any attention from the battle.

He climbed over dreadbeast corpses, hefting the halves of his broken spear in each hand. His sister screamed nonsense as she stabbed her dagger into a rabbit dreadbeast's eye, and he hurled his spearhead through a flying bloodspawn that had tried to take advantage of her distraction.

Then the sky lit up.

Pulses of light—Striker techniques—rushed out in every color. Dreadbeasts exploded into corrupted flesh. Bloodspawn were torn to essence.

Where monsters were, light followed.

Jai Long's weapons fell from numb, tingling fingers. He had seen sights like this before; when an entire sect of sacred artists unleashed a barrage of Striker techniques all at once.

He turned to the source.

Lindon hovered in the air, his back to Jai Long. He was surrounded by a halo of shining constructs, firing in every direction. A rainbow of colors streaked out from him, and just for that moment, he looked like he had sprouted a pair of wings made of light.

For a frozen moment he hung there, blazing like a many-colored phoenix.

Then the Striker techniques stopped. The world settled down.

Compared to the noise of battle before, the silence that settled over them in that moment felt unnatural. Jai Chen hobbled up to stand next to her brother, her mouth hanging open and an expression of awe on her blood-spattered face.

Sound returned with a deep rumble as the earth shook like a drum. A footstep of the Wandering Titan.

Lindon summoned a Thousand-Mile Cloud and flew off.

Sage of Twin Stars, Jai Long thought. He believed it now.

Then he collapsed.

第十八章

CHAPTER EIGHTEEN

Iteration 129: Oasis

Images, impressions, and desperate voices screamed through Suriel's head. From a hundred Iterations at once, Abidan begged for help.

The Vroshir had held nothing back. In one world, their war machines crashed through deserts, while in another their fleets blackened planets, and all across the cosmos their champions met Abidan guardians blade-to-blade.

They were defending only a pathetic number of worlds, and only the ones held by Judges had any guarantee of victory. Dozens of Iterations called for Suriel to defend them.

As she entered Oasis, she cut off their voices.

This world needed her more than any other.

The fabric of reality itself trembled, every particle quaking in fear. Oasis' central planet was a blue marble beneath Suriel's feet, and she could feel the sudden terror rising from the billions of lives down below.

All across the thousands of islands that made up Oasis' land, those sensitive to power collapsed under the weight of visions, or screamed at the feeling of a predator descended to take them all. She sent out her own influence to calm them, but there was only so much she could do.

She couldn't hide the power of the Mad King.

Her Presence showed him drifting on the other side of the planet, eyes blazing from beneath the shadow of his bone helmet, his yellowed armor and fur cloak shrouding his figure. He clutched Ozriel's Scythe in his right hand, and glared in her direction.

But not actually *at* her.

She floated next to Makiel, in his full battle gear. His seamless white armor covered him up to the neck, and he held the Sword of Makiel in both hands. The massive two-handed blade had once been used to pass capital punishment on the first generation of Abidan, and purple energy passed through its steel in complex veins.

Unlike the other Judges, he hadn't perfected his physical form. His dark skin was weathered by his mortal life, and his hair had been touched with gray for millennia. His weary face did not turn to her as he spoke. "You could save more lives elsewhere."

"Not yours."

She might really be able to save an entire Iteration of her own if she left, but Makiel would be much safer with her around. Perhaps together, they could drive the Mad King away.

Together, they looked into Fate.

The future crackled and twisted, each vision unfolding with slippery uncertainty as the King's chaotic presence warped Fate itself. But with the stabilizing presence of two Judges, and Makiel's skill and significance at her side, they could see victory.

With the two of them together, a chance had opened up.

Not of slaying the Mad King, of course. It would take at least one more Judge joining them to make that a possibility, and they couldn't abandon too many other worlds.

But she could see herself reverting a wave of devastating chaotic fire to nothing, giving Makiel the chance to strike a full-power blow and piercing the Mad King's armor.

The outcome was by no means certain, but they could do it. If they made the Mad King leave the field, they would free up the Judges. The entire battle, across all of creation, could turn here.

"'With our swords, we carve our place in destiny,'" Makiel recited.

"Don't quote yourself. It's not flattering."

Blue power vented behind him, taking on the image of sapphire wings. "I first heard that from *him.*"

From the other side of the planet, Daruman spoke, and they heard him. "If you're standing against me, you must believe you can win."

"We stand before you to save the lives of trillions," Suriel said coldly.

"And I am willing to spill that blood so that the survivors can live free. You have to know that you won't shake my resolve with a few words."

Makiel raised his sword, the purple lines shining. "Daruman, King of Madness, the Court of Seven sentences you to die."

"If you believe you have seen that, then the eye of the Hound has grown truly dim."

Suriel saw the attack a moment before it happened. A black slash, so vast that the concept of size no longer applied.

With one swing of the Scythe, the Mad King sliced the Iteration in half.

The entire universe split with the blue planet at the center, the two halves drifting apart, the Void stretching between them.

The Mantle of Suriel flared, and she channeled the Way, reversing the damage. Restoring order.

Makiel didn't wait for her to finish stitching reality together before returning a strike of his own.

The inexorable will of the Hound, focused by his blade, closed on the Mad King to tear him from existence. The Vroshir broke the working, but then Suriel had finished restoring the Iteration. Her Razor bloomed from a two-meter bar of blue steel into a multi-pronged weapon of shining blades, like a razor-sharp tree.

She thrust with the full force of her authority. The Razor was a tool for violently separating the diseased from the healthy, and the Mad King was a blight on reality, a cancer. She cut him free, the space around him glaring bright blue as she cut at the fact of his existence.

His armor anchored him, and he struck back, a wave of darkness and spinning multi-colored chaos.

Makiel had already predicted it and shunted it off to the side.

Thousands of stars vanished. Removed from reality.

Then the fight began in earnest.

Each of them watched the future, anticipating the enemy's move and countering it. They only took action when they could ensure an advantage or mitigate a disadvantage.

Makiel and the Mad King traded blows that destroyed both of their mortal forms, the force causing deadly earthquakes on the planet below. But Makiel spared no thought for his own defense; Suriel revived him a moment later, and he reincorporated already spearing Daruman with a dozen ghostly projections of Makiel's Sword.

The Mad King had to revive himself, and the more he was destroyed, the shakier his existence would become. In theory, they could kill him permanently that way.

In practice...

He gripped Suriel in one fist, though she was hundreds of thousands of kilometers away, and her Presence blared a warning as her armor began to buckle.

While she was focused on protecting herself, throwing up protective barriers of pure order, he struck with the combined authority of the Mad King who conquered worlds and the Scythe who destroyed them whole.

Makiel met the blow with the Sword of the First Judge, the weapon that had been the symbol of order since the ancient Abidan had risen from Cradle so long ago.

Reality itself screamed, existence warping all over the

world. Humans died en masse down on the central planet simply from the backlash, and the Iteration's connection to the Way grew thin.

Suriel stretched out her Mantle, her authority as the Phoenix, as the ultimate healer, and dragged the Way back.

The humans blinked back to life, the shredded atmosphere repaired, the laws returning. As order flooded back in, Makiel broke the Mad King's blow.

But the Vroshir had gained the momentum back.

They clashed again and again, fighting first in the future and then in the present, angling for advantage over the tiny blue gem at the center of this reality. A working of the Mad King's would cast Makiel through space, but Suriel would break it. Makiel would blast the Mad King out of the world, and Suriel would try to seal the breach and keep him out, but with the Scythe he could cut his way back in.

The longer the battle raged, the less stable the Iteration became.

Stars winked out from the distant stretches of the universe, galaxies collapsing and fading to nothing, crumbling into the Void. Gravity and reality held less sway, dreams became real, people vanished as though they never existed.

Suriel spent more and more of her power on keeping the world intact, but she was straining herself, straining her mantle, straining even the connection between this Iteration and the Way. She had to give ground, preserving and restoring only the most necessary.

But the Mad King had died many times.

All at once, a path shone in Fate, as though their persistence had opened a door. It was one road, shining and bright, leading to the vision they'd seen before.

As one, without discussion, the two Judges took it.

Makiel met a blow head-on that cast him into the Void, removing him from reality for but a moment. That left an opening that the Mad King exploited, and he swept one arm, casting a wave of chaotic many-colored fire that swept all the way across the planet.

Rather than protecting the world with a barrier, as the enemy would no doubt expect, Suriel did as she had seen her future self do.

With all the power of the Razor, the Mantle of Suriel, and her own will, she focused on the wave of chaos-fire. Though sparks of it fell in a deadly meteor rain onto the planet below, she was able to catch the existence of the attack almost in its entirety.

With the last of her energy, she reverted it to nothing.

The Mad King's will clashed with hers, fighting her authority, and the wave of fire faded in and out of existence for a moment.

As Makiel popped back into reality, physically only a meter away from the King. He swung his massive sword two-handed, the full weight of his will behind it.

They had seen this blow crack his armor, but in the microscopic instant that Makiel used to swing, Suriel saw her vision of the future warp and twist.

[WARNING: Deviation detected], her Presence warned.

The Sword of Makiel landed on the blade of the Scythe. The clash between the two weapons blasted a crater in the central planet of Oasis, and tens of millions died instantly.

Suriel left them to die.

She appeared next to Makiel, adding the defense of her Razor to his Sword. The Scythe still swept down, cracking both their armor.

With Makiel in her arms, Suriel wrenched open the Way. And fled.

Lindon rose up on his cloud until he was even with the halo of light around Mount Samara. He was still outside the suppression field, but only by a few feet. Any technique he threw into Sacred Valley would be weakened.

But his heart pounded and the skin all over his body

tightened as he looked inside and came face-to-face with the Wandering Titan.

In reality, they were still maybe a mile apart. But the Dreadgod was so huge that Lindon felt like it could lean forward and snap him up in its jaws.

Its eyes were swirling clouds of every shade of yellow, and it scanned Mount Samara up and down, as though looking for something.

Far down below, at its feet, the river of fleeing people on the mountain slopes had scattered like ants. Some of them continued running up the mountain to safety, but others scurried any direction that was away from the Titan's feet.

Even back into Sacred Valley, which had been...broken. Shattered. Churned beyond recognition, like meat in a grinder.

Only three of the four sacred peaks still stood, and the Titan was eyeing this one. Every second the Dreadgod delayed was more lives spared.

And there was only one person here whose techniques could affect a Dreadgod.

"Dross," Lindon said aloud, "I would be very grateful if you had a battle plan for me."

[Battle. A *battle* plan. I've got a wonderful strategic retreat plan.]

Lindon was already mentally exhausted just from bringing himself here, but as he understood it, willpower wasn't like madra. He didn't have a finite amount that could run out. As long as he could concentrate, he could keep fighting.

He trembled all over. Not only did he feel like a mouse staring up at a lion, but even his spirit shook before the irresistible pressure of the Dreadgod.

And the Titan was being suppressed while he wasn't.

Still, he drew up his focus. If the heavens were kind, the Titan would turn away and leave entirely. Maybe Lindon wouldn't have to do anything at all.

Why hasn't it left the valley already?

[I'll show you if you promise to take me far, far away from

here.] Despite his words, Dross pulled Lindon's attention to the north, where—even in the fractured mess that remained of Sacred Valley—Lindon could make out shapes. Footprints.

It had walked north, stopped at Mount Yoma, and then headed east again.

Why?

Now it was examining Mount Samara, and Lindon felt an inhalation filled with hunger madra. The Dreadgod was sniffing for something in the mountain.

That wasn't an attack, and the Titan was still trapped in the suppression field, but Lindon still hoped the act of breathing in wouldn't be enough to kill the people at the Dreadgod's feet.

He had the impression that the Titan had been at this for a while, and Lindon fervently hoped that it would continue for even longer. Maybe the bulk of the people beneath him would be able to flee before the Dreadgod had found whatever it was looking for. He might not have to do anything at all.

Slowly, like an old man reaching for his medication, the Titan reached up toward Lindon.

He panicked and shot backwards, but it was clear that the Titan had no interest in Lindon at all. It was grabbing for the circle of light around the peak.

Now was his chance. The collapse of the ring might send madra raining down on the people below...but more personally, Lindon couldn't bear the thought of the Dreadgod destroying Samara's ring.

There was too little of Sacred Valley left.

From watching Malice, he hadn't been able to tell if techniques were weaker if they originated from outside the script or from inside. He would try the former first.

With both hands in front of him, he opened his spirit wide, channeling Blackflame into dragon's breath. At the same time, he poured his Overlord soulfire into it, which was now a brighter and more vivid silver than the diffuse, colorless flame of an Underlord. On top of all that, he added his will.

Dragon's breath was a force of destruction. If he was the

Void Sage, he should have the authority for this.

A dark beam, thicker than his two arms, burst out from his palms. The technique reminded him of Yerin's Final Sword, and it carried weight far beyond the power of its madra.

It passed through the suppression field and...faded.

Instead of a liquid-smooth beam, the technique dispersed into a gaseous spray that resembled natural flame. The red streaks were more prominent than they had been, and the authority he'd managed to scrape up weakened to almost nothing.

Dragon's breath passed over the Titan's stone arm and washed over, harmless.

A dark fist closed over Samara's ring. The light was Forged madra, an ancient construct, and the Dreadgod tore away a chunk as though it were made of rotten wood. Bright white-and-gold essence drifted upwards like sparks of a campfire from the damaged construct.

The rest of the ring hung in the air, but the light over Sacred Valley darkened.

The Dreadgod lifted the Forged madra to its face, examining it, and then Lindon felt hunger grow. The chunk of construct disappeared completely, the motes disappearing into the Titan's body. The cracks of its shell, and the crags all over its body, shone briefly yellow.

When the Titan returned its attention to Mount Samara, its hunger was like a physical force. It didn't move immediately, but its tail lashed faster and faster behind it. Lindon knew it was about to move.

And hurling Striker techniques from outside the field had done nothing. He had to plunge inside.

Behind him, space cracked.

Dross gave a squeal, then covered it up with a cough. [I'm not relieved. But we *are* saved. But it's fine, I'm not excited. You're excited.]

Yerin dashed out of a blue-edged crack in space before the portal had finished forming, and she shot through the air to land on his cloud.

She caught the very edge of the Thousand-Mile Cloud, where the madra was thinner. She could catch herself with aura control or by summoning her own cloud, but he caught her arm and pulled her onto his anyway.

She grabbed edges of his outer robe in both fists, but didn't raise her head to look at him. "I know I'm cutting myself with my own knife saying this, but if you thought you could cross swords with a Dreadgod and leave me behind, you..." Her breath caught as she glanced to the side and looked into the Titan's face. Her whole body shivered. "... bleed and bury me."

Lindon spoke quietly. "I don't know if I can stop even one of its techniques. I couldn't ask you all to come protect *my* home when I'm not sure I can keep you safe."

She looked up at him, and rather than angry, she looked amused. "Didn't, did you? I'd contend you asked us to stay behind. But we're not exactly tripping over people who can tickle Dreadgods. My list ends with me and you."

A voice shouted distantly from beneath them, muffled and unintelligible.

Down on the ground, the spatial crack hadn't widened into a stable portal. Mercy had stumbled out of it, and she was pulling the last inch of Suu free, when Orthos shoved his way forward. His presence in Lindon's spirit was brighter than ever, stronger, more vivid. But to the naked eye, he looked no different.

Finally, Eithan strode out of the messy blue light.

He released a heavy breath, as though he'd been holding it, and wiped sweat from his brow as the crack in the world sealed itself behind him.

"I said 'put me on your list,'" Eithan called up. "You couldn't hear me, could you?" He sighed and began drifting up to join them.

Lindon and Yerin exchanged glances.

"Can you help?" Lindon asked. "Any of you?" He didn't raise his voice, though Eithan was still far away. Eithan would hear him.

He had meant that to include Mercy and Orthos as well, but as soon as they arrived, they took off east. In seconds, they were rounding up people, stopping fights, and pulling them out of overturned shelters.

They knew they couldn't touch a Dreadgod, but were still doing whatever they could to help.

Lindon wished they wouldn't. Now he had more to worry about.

"You don't think I'll be an asset?" Eithan asked as he finally reached their level.

Yerin's eyebrows lifted. "If I had to pick between you and a rusty spoon, I'd have to think about it first."

"Infusing techniques with willpower is not the exclusive domain of Sages and Heralds. They're just better at it." Eithan planted fists on his hips and glared at the Dreadgod. "I will defy this beast with all the power of a leaf drifting on the wind!"

[Oh, and you're not going to get in our way by making us cover for you? That's impressive.]

"I make no such promise," Eithan said. "But I can't let you stand up against a Dreadgod without me. It's a bit earlier than I planned, but who could object to one little life-threatening practice run?"

Yerin squeezed Lindon's ribs and then slipped away, stepping onto a purple Thousand-Mile Cloud of her own. "Have to say, I'm not looking for death here. If there's nothing we can do, we're leaving, even if I have to grab you both by the neck and drag you off."

The Titan still hadn't stirred. It remained searching for something. Or waiting.

But as Lindon looked at Yerin and Eithan on either side of him, mist formed in his eyes. They didn't need to be here. If he had full control over his abilities, he would have sent them back.

At the same time, he was glad they were there.

"Gratitude," Lindon said.

[Awww, that's sweet. Very sweet. But I'm going to need

you all to focus so that we don't die. First of all, none of us move until the Titan does, even if you stand still until your fleshy human feet decay.]

"We won't have to wait quite *that* long," Eithan said, spinning his black fabric scissors around his thumb. "The Titan is famous for its...lethargy...but when it is ready to move, it does so quickly."

[So, objective one: we're holding it back as long as we can. If we lose and it breaks through the mountain, we leave.]

Lindon wasn't happy about that, but he knew that if the Titan left the suppression field, their chance was up. If they couldn't match the Dreadgod *inside* the valley, they would have no chance outside.

[Objective two: don't die. Wait, how about we make that objective one?]

Almost casually, the Wandering Titan began drawing its hand back for a swipe. Wind swirled around them, snatching at their clothes and pulling their Clouds.

The fear and pressure returned. Eithan's smile dropped, and madra flowed through his black scissors. Yerin pulled a sword in each hand, one white and one black, her gleaming red Goldsigns extended.

Lindon focused all his panicked energy and his resolve on the Dreadgod's hand. Whatever technique it was about to use, he needed to be ready.

But it was no technique. The Titan swiped at Mount Samara like a child knocking over his own sandcastle.

Every fiber of Lindon drew to a point. He pushed past the rules of the world, substituting his own will.

"Stop!" Lindon shouted.

The Titan's hand slowed, as though it had been caught in an invisible net. Then Lindon felt an outside consciousness pushing against his own; a mind he'd felt before, when he had Consumed some of its thoughts.

But the Wandering Titan had been sleeping then.

This time, it turned its attention to the force restricting its hand in dull annoyance. Lindon's working tore like spiderwebs.

It was like a cat had clawed the inside of Lindon's head. His vision blanked out as madra streamed from both Yerin and Eithan.

An instant later, when he could see again, Lindon saw Eithan's Striker technique—the Hollow King's Spear—breaking on the boundary of the suppression field. It faded from a clear, defined spear to a diffuse stream of madra, though it still impacted the wrist of the Dreadgod where it landed.

It pushed the Titan's arm. Slightly. Like a gentle breeze.

Yerin's gleaming silver-red madra broke as it entered Sacred Valley too, but it rained down on the Titan in a thousand needles. The Dreadgod swatted at its own chest in irritation, then roared.

Lindon felt the sound in his bones.

He cycled madra to his ears to stop from going deaf, but even as the roar drowned out all sound, Dross spoke into their heads.

[As reluctant as I am to encourage this insanity, if we're going to do this, then it's time to go inside.]

While they would weaken steadily inside the field, they wouldn't be in there long enough to reduce to Jades. From within, they would be more effective. At least a little.

Together, they flew toward the Dreadgod.

From that moment, Lindon had no time to think.

A ball of stone and chaos formed in the Titan's hand, and a blue-white Spear of the Hollow King pierced it through. Now that the Spear didn't have to pass through the wall of the script-circle, the technique looked like a real spear, in full physical detail. However, it still wasn't nearly as powerful as an Archlord technique should have been.

At the same time, a wave of yellow earth madra pulsed out from the Titan's chest, and Lindon met it with a Hollow Domain and the full force of his will.

It still battered him back, smacking him like a fist across the whole body, but it created a weak point in the Dreadgod's technique.

Yerin rushed through, a shining meteor of silver and red.

She focused the Final Sword through her blade.

With Lindon and Eithan taking care of the Titan's techniques, hers landed. A lance of bright red madra pierced through the Dreadgod.

It streaked behind, stretching for miles.

Dreadgods had blood, Lindon knew. He had dissected enough dreadbeasts. As they were made of flesh, Yerin's madra should tear it apart.

But that little pinprick didn't even slow the Wandering Titan down. Its free hand came in as a fist, striking at Yerin.

She leaped off her Cloud, meeting it in midair with both her swords. She had nothing to push on but aura, so the strike should have sent her flying into the horizon.

But Lindon felt power beyond the physical, a weight of conceptual strength like he had once felt from Crusher. For just an instant, the Dreadgod's fist hit Yerin and *stopped.*

Together, Lindon and Eithan launched Striker techniques at the same time.

The Spear of the Hollow King and breath of a black dragon struck the Wandering Titan in the eye.

It blinked and flinched back like Lindon might have done at an unexpected flash of light.

Its knuckles, having stopped for an instant on Yerin's swords, pushed forward again. This time, she hurtled into the side of Mount Samara. The ground exploded into dust and snow, but he could feel her power was barely diminished.

Outside Sacred Valley, a direct hit like that would have killed her.

Lindon had already begun drawing up his will again, preparing to command the Dreadgod to stop. Or at least to try.

[We talked about this!] Dross said desperately.

He brought up Lindon's own memories. Neither Charity nor Malice had commanded Dreadgods directly. They had worked their Sage powers through their techniques.

Lindon opened his void key.

He wished he had kept Sophara's void key, since she had

a Heaven's Torch, the ultimate source of fire aura.

But his own fire treasures weren't too bad either.

Fire aura *gushed* out, far stronger than any other source of aura in Sacred Valley. As for destruction aura...that was all around them.

In moments, Lindon gathered black-and-red aura into a cloud swirling around him, but he wasn't forming a Void Dragon's Dance. He blended the Ruler technique with madra Forged into a dragon's claw, and fueled it with a focused application of the Burning Cloak.

Crystallized Blackflame madra covered his left hand, trailing black and red energy behind him as he shot toward the Titan.

Eithan was flying just beneath the cloud, Forging madra as he moved into huge stars the size of the Titan's eyes.

As the Dreadgod squared itself and roared, Lindon felt another source of aura: blood and sword madra gathering at its feet.

Lindon reached out for the Void Icon.

And together, the three of them all triggered their techniques.

A distant bell rang, and blood and flesh flew from the Titan's calves. Lines of blue-white light speared down from the Hollow Crown, tearing into the spirit that was entwined with its body. And Lindon slammed the Dragon Descends technique into the Dreadgod's chest.

It detonated in a black explosion, washing over the Titan in a tide of dark fire.

Not black-and-red fire. Pure black flame.

The power of the Void Icon was strong in that technique.

Lindon wanted to keep up the barrage, but he had wrung himself dry in body and mind. They had already unleashed power on a scale that Sacred Valley actively suppressed. If the heavens were kind, they would have at least gained the Titan's attention.

Dross spoke in a panic. [Oh yay, we did it!]

The Dreadgod's tail whipped out from the cloud of

destructive flame. Yerin rocketed up hundreds of feet to crash into the tail, blocking the strike, but a hand was coming Lindon's way again.

Without Dross, Lindon wouldn't have been fast enough to avoid it. The Soul Cloak sprang up around him, and he leaped and twisted in midair. Fingers the width of roads crashed into his Thousand-Mile Cloud, dispersing the construct. Lindon landed on the back of its wrist, clinging to stone-like skin for his life.

At the same time, the Titan opened its mouth and breathed out onto Eithan.

A stream of golden madra covered the Archlord whole, driving him backwards. Lindon didn't see him land, but the Striker technique in the Dreadgod's breath tore a chunk from the peak of Mount Samara.

Eithan was gone.

Lindon could feel his spirit, and the amount of pure madra that had gone into defending himself, but Eithan had to be out of the fight.

He couldn't even spare a thought for concern; the sky was falling.

The world slowed down as Dross accelerated his perception. The ceiling falling on him was the Dreadgod's tail, plunging onto his head to swat him like a fly.

He dashed out, running across the Titan's hand for the rapidly narrowing stretch of sky that meant freedom.

[Below!] Dross shouted.

But there was no dodging.

Earth aura reached out from the skin, pulling Lindon down. He stumbled, and it took the whole strength of his Soul Cloak to keep him standing upright.

The tail was coming down.

Lindon opened his void key.

He tumbled inside just as the Titan's tail and arm crashed together. It was like being in the middle of two islands collapsing, and the wind rushing in blasted everything in his void key to the other side of the room.

The hand of the Dreadgod passed over the doorway...but the willpower accompanying the blow did not.

Lindon felt it like a sudden weight dropping on the void key, and the opening back into the world began to stress and fracture. If he hadn't focused on it, reinforcing it with its authority, the void space opened by his key would have collapsed. Leaving him stranded.

The view returned in just a moment, giving Lindon clear line of sight as the hand lifted away. His storage space was still floating in midair, so he found himself around the height of the Titan's shoulder.

The Dreadgod turned, moving away from Mount Samara. Toward Yerin.

Dross, Lindon begged, *give me something.*

[I gave you all the advice you need: don't do this. We can get away!]

The Titan raising its foot seemed slow, but only because of Dross' acceleration.

What about Yerin?

[Well yes, of course, we're going to save Yerin. I'm not a monster. But then we can *leave.*]

I don't want to run, Dross. I want to win.

[Lindon, this...I...] Dross sounded less certain than ever. [...I don't want to do this. It's too much.]

Please, Lindon said.

[I don't have anything for you,] Dross said at last, and Lindon's heart clenched. [No, now, hold on. I don't have anything for *you.* Alone.]

Dross sounded like he was taking a deep breath. [Brace yourself.]

His thought carried the impression of great pain, so Lindon prepared himself. *I can handle pain.*

[Oh no, this is worse than just hurting you. It's about to hurt *me.*]

Ziel's Thousand-Mile Cloud carried him south, toward the mountain that looked like a broken bottle gushing water. The east exit was far too popular; he'd meet up with the rest again once he left the valley.

Except, considering the fact that they were fighting the Wandering Titan right now, he would probably never see them again because of their sheer stupidity.

The wind from the fight buffeted his cloud, and the aura here was thin anyway, so it was slow going. But every foot of progress was a foot away from the Dreadgod.

He had thought his progress was slow before, so he almost panicked when he stopped entirely. For a moment, he was certain the Dreadgod had caught him in some kind of Ruler technique.

When he realized the whole *world* had stopped, Dross popped into existence in front of him.

Lindon's spirit panted, though Ziel was certain he wouldn't need to breathe, and swiped one of his boneless arms across a forehead that was basically just his upper eyelid.

[Okay, I don't have much time, so just do what I tell you. Okay? We need your help against the Dreadgod. All you have to do—]

"No," Ziel said.

[Let me finish! Let me finish. I only need you to make a couple of platforms. Just put them where I tell you, when I tell you.]

"No."

[Don't—Look, Dreadgods don't fight to the death. If the prey takes too much energy to beat, they back off, and *everything* takes too much energy here. We're just...pushing it back a little, that's all. All we're doing. Not going in for the kill.]

Ziel tried to say no a third time, but he couldn't stop himself from imagining what it could have been like years ago. To watch the Weeping Dragon turn around and drift away, looking for easier prey.

"...fine," he said reluctantly.

[That's a promise! You've promised now, you can't break it! And that's perfect, because I was lying before, I need you to do more than just make platforms. I need you to make a *lot* of platforms.]

Mercy herded her crowd of Irons to the south. She had gathered up over two hundred of them, according to her Moon's Eye lens, and they were dragging even more wounded on litters.

It had taken her only minutes to draw so many people together. They had been several groups before, she had just flown over and stopped them from panicking so they could band together.

Under her guidance, they gathered as one. Her guidance and Jai Chen's, since the Jai girl had formed the largest group before Mercy's arrival, but Jai Chen was growing more and more concerned about her brother.

Mercy was surprised to find them out here; she had expected them to retreat long before this. She wished they had; she hated to see them so exhausted and soaked in blood. Of course, that described everyone out here except her.

They were about to enter a clutch of trees in which her Lens had spotted a pack of dreadbeasts. She could handle them all herself, but she couldn't watch every single falling tree and flying rock.

"Keep the wounded on the inside," Mercy called. "If you have a shield and you're in the outer ring, raise it up. I'll clear the trees of dreadbeasts, but cover your eyes and close your ears."

No one responded. They had all frozen in place.

[Mercy!] Dross shouted, appearing suddenly in front of her. [Sorry, that was loud, wasn't it? Anyway, we need you.]

Mercy tried to twist and see if she could spot Lindon, who must be in trouble if he was sending Dross, but she couldn't actually move her body. So Dross was projecting himself into her mind.

Her spiritual perception still worked, and she felt Lindon far behind her. It felt like he was a hundred miles away, but she recognized the dampening effect of the suppression field.

"Is Lindon okay? Did something happen?" When she spoke, she *felt* like she was moving her mouth, but she supposed she probably wasn't. It was a strange sensation.

[No, but it's about to,] Dross responded. [We need you. Against the Titan.]

"Got it." When time unfroze, Mercy would put Jai Chen in charge and fly back into Sacred Valley.

Dross waved his tendrils in the air as though trying to shoo something away. [I don't...ah, I don't exactly know how to say this, but you...oh, well, actually I know exactly how to say this. What I need you to do, it's going to hurt. A lot. Not permanently, I'm sure. Your family can fix you. They can fix you, right?]

"Yes, they can," Mercy said firmly.

No matter what Dross wanted her to do, it wouldn't hurt as badly as seeing Pride so badly hurt. She didn't want to go through that again, not so soon, and not with Lindon and Yerin.

"What do you need from me?"

[Your bloodline,] Dross said.

"What do you want from me now?" Orthos rumbled.

He didn't have the non-lethal abilities the others did, so he'd stuck to his strengths: running around and eliminating dreadbeasts, bloodspawn, and piles of debris that blocked the way of the humans fleeing down Mount Samara.

It had been surprisingly fun. And then Dross interrupted him.

[Normally, there's nothing an Underlord can do to a

Dreadgod. But since it's in Sacred Valley, it's a little more subject to physical laws—]

"Underlord? Who said I was an Underlord?"

[You...you know Lindon can feel you, right? If Lindon can feel it, I can feel it. He hasn't been thinking about it, but it's clear to *me* that you used the treasures inside Lindon's void key to advance. That wasn't supposed to be a surprise, was it?]

If Orthos could move his body, he would have turned away to chew on a nearby rock. Or some nice, soft wood.

[Even the others can sense you,] Dross went on, driving the knife deeper. [You had to know they would all recognize it immediately.]

"There is nothing wrong with a little celebration," Orthos said with great dignity.

[N-no! No, and in fact, I can make it even better than a surprise! A huge event! You'll really, ooohhh, you'll really show them. They'll say, 'Underlord Orthos is so great, I can't believe that we ever cared about him before. I really hate who he used to be. Compared to now, I mean. Just...just hate him.']

That was possibly the worst sales pitch Orthos had ever heard.

But he was still intrigued.

"I'm listening," he said.

Eithan's entire body was pain.

He lay in a pile of twisted limbs in the rubble that had once been the peak of Mount Samara, silently counting his broken bones. He had blocked the madra with his own, then cushioned the impact of his fall with aura while strengthening his Archlord body with soulfire.

Even so, he hadn't fully recovered his power since spending so long in Sacred Valley, and here he was back in it again.

Not to mention that he had taken a blow from the Titan head-on.

There were parts of the world where "hitting like a Dreadgod" was a common saying. It did not do the experience justice.

He realized immediately when Dross contacted him and accelerated his perception of time. It happened when he was in the middle of tenderly extending one thread of madra to activate his void key, hoping to pull out some more of his medical supplies. He'd drunk more medicine than water, these past few days; clearly he was off his game.

"How many ways have you split yourself, Dross?" Eithan asked, before the spirit had fully manifested to him.

[Six,] Dross panted. [It's...a lot, but I'm fine. Maybe. I'm probably fine.]

"Well, don't waste your valuable time on me," he said. "Just tell me my role." He admired how sprightly his voice still sounded, despite the state of his ribs. And every other part of his body.

[Perfect! The Titan is going to throw a Striker technique at Lindon, and I need you to stop it from hitting him.]

"Where? I'm not quite as ambulatory as usual."

[We'll get you down, don't worry. Just worry about stopping the technique. Please do worry about that.]

Eithan tried to make a gesture of agreement, but his hand was trapped beneath his body. And it pulsed with pain, except for his fingertips, which were completely numb.

That could be a problem, he thought.

"No problem!" he said.

Dross made a relieved sound and vanished, leaving Eithan alone to think. That was good, because he needed the time.

How was he supposed to block a Dreadgod's technique in this condition?

⬡

When time froze, the pressure on Yerin didn't let up. From her perspective, the sky was covered by the Wandering Titan's foot, and while it hadn't plunged down on her yet, it couldn't be far off.

The pressure she felt was from the Titan's spirit, pressing down on her almost as heavily as if the Dreadgod was already standing on her. She held her two swords above her, crossed white and black, and she had already begun filling them with madra and soulfire.

She didn't know how many of those stomps she could take, but she wouldn't be able to escape fast enough with its will weighing her down anyway. So she would weather the first one, then hope somebody else pulled the Titan off her before she was smeared to paste.

Yerin had prepared herself, so when Dross showed up, he was more of a distraction than anything.

"Spit it out," Yerin growled. She was still under the Dreadgod's spiritual pressure, and time not passing was only extending that agony.

Dross breathed harshly as he spoke. [Sorry...I'm...doing a lot...right now.]

Even in her situation, Yerin felt concern worry its way into her heart. She couldn't exactly move her eyes, but she focused on Dross. "You solid, Dross?"

He fixed her with a stare, pulling himself together. [Yeah, no problem, nothing to worry about. Listen, we need something from you, but it's going to be...it won't be much fun for you, I'll say that.]

"You see where I'm standing right now, true? Would you contend I'm on a holiday?"

[We need you to hold the Titan in place so Lindon can hit it. You'll need to use your sword.]

She shifted her attention to her master's blade. For the most part, she had avoided using its binding since advancing during the Uncrowned King tournament. "Madra's not like it used to be. Could use Netherclaw, if that'll work."

[It, uh, it won't.]

A queasy sense of nausea passed through her. "Sword will make it through, though, right?"

Dross hesitated.

"Dross?"

[I think this is one of those times where I'm *supposed* to lie, but I don't have a whole lot of time. You'll have to overload the sword. No way around it, unless you're ready to advance to Archlord. That would solve a lot of my problems today, actually.]

Even if she were, she couldn't do it here in Sacred Valley, and Dross knew that.

"Winter Sage. She can fix it, though, true?"

Dross bobbed upward in the air as he brightened. [Could be! That's certainly a real possibility!]

No sense hesitating. She had agreed to risk her life here, for people that Lindon didn't even really know. She'd be cracked in the head if she wasn't willing to risk one weapon.

"Got it. Grab my eye when you want me."

[I'll have to signal the others, but you...just do it when the foot comes down, all right?]

"Not likely to forget that one."

[You won't have to remember it for long, because I can't hold this anymore. You ready?]

She tried to nod. Dross must have gotten the picture, because the world came roaring back to normal speed.

The Titan's foot came down.

第十九章

CHAPTER NINETEEN

Lindon didn't hear what Dross said to the other five. He just felt the spirit splitting his attention so many different ways, and time stood still while Dross delivered his instructions.

When he finished, everything happened at once.

The Titan's foot came down. Yerin's madra flared beneath it, so powerful that it felt like she was pouring her entire spirit into one attack. But it wasn't an attack; white mist and points of ice-cold light burst into being around her, consuming the Titan up to the knee.

Its foot landed, but was frozen in place. Lindon was astonished at the power output of the weapon, but it was overshadowed by worry for Yerin.

Not that he had time to dwell on it. There was too much else going on.

Green rings had bloomed one after the other, stretching off to the south. Ziel flew through the air like an arrow, each ring of script hurling him into the next. Lindon wondered why Ziel hadn't used that technique to escape, but his question was answered by a quick scan of his spirit.

He was straining his channels and running out of madra. He couldn't keep this up for long.

As he flew in, another spiritual presence caught Lindon's attention. Mercy dashed in, covered in her Akura bloodline armor, and she wasn't flying. She was running.

She was already the size of a tall building, and she carried something tucked under her right arm.

No, Lindon realized what the object was as soon as he noticed it.

It was Orthos, all curled up in his shell.

Orthos, whose body was slowly filling with soulfire.

When the Titan found its leg stuck by Yerin's technique, it threw a punch at Mercy. A golden nimbus covered its fist: the original version of the Enforcer technique the Abyssal Palace cultists had used.

The wind from the punch was like the breath of a hurricane.

Mercy slipped under the punch. Her armor was still growing, and Lindon knew from his experience with Harmony— and his own research—how much of a burden the armor put on the spirit. The larger it was, the harder it was to control. But she moved with liquid grace as she ducked the punch.

Then she took a lightning-quick tail to the breastplate.

It cracked, and Lindon fully expected the armor to shatter. Instead, despite what must have been horrific spiritual pain, she braced her feet and stood her ground.

As she did, Mercy lobbed Orthos through the Dreadgod's legs.

And the turtle began to grow.

Soulfire burned away by the second as it expanded Orthos' body. He landed with legs the width of tree trunks, but they grew to cover houses in a moment. Soon, he was half the height of the Titan.

The Dreadgod turned over its shoulder, madra building between its jaws.

[That's your cue!] Dross shouted.

On his Thousand-Mile Cloud, Lindon shot forward.

No matter how much madra he poured into the cloud, it would be a few seconds before he reached the Titan. It would have shoved Mercy back and released its technique on Orthos by then. Dross had called him in too late.

Green light flared behind Lindon.

He couldn't spare the attention to turn and watch, but he wished he could. His spiritual senses treated him to the feeling of Eithan flying through the air like a thrown spear.

He was kept aloft by his own aura control, so Ziel's circle only added acceleration. As he flew closer, Lindon heard a voice, which started soft and steadily grew louder as its source approached.

"Jump!" Eithan called as he flew past Lindon's face.

Mercy endured another heavy blow, falling to one knee under the pressure. The Titan unleashed a stream of powerful earth madra with its breath. Orthos shoved himself into position, and—though he took a glancing blow on his shell that left cracks and a lancing pain that Lindon could feel through their bond—he and Mercy managed to wrestle the Dreadgod around to face Lindon.

It didn't cut off its Striker technique. As it braced itself on its tail, it refocused on the next target it saw: Eithan, whose madra was blazing like a beacon.

Lindon expected Eithan to take the hit on his Hollow Armor, but Lindon had been given his instructions. He jumped.

Eithan reversed direction in a burst of force aura, shoving himself down and to one side. The Titan's Striker technique streaked past in a thundering stream of bright golden light.

The river of madra passed over both Eithan and Lindon's heads.

It tapered out almost immediately as the Titan returned its attention to Mercy and Orthos, grabbing one in each hand.

Lindon dragged his Thousand-Mile Cloud down to him, and once again it caught him.

He saw what Eithan had done. If the Titan had noticed Lindon, that blast would have been on target, and it might have even moved its head to follow Lindon as he fell. Instead, Eithan had drawn its attention upward.

By falling suddenly, Lindon had ducked it.

Orthos roared, and now that he was empty of soulfire, he was truly gigantic. While not a match for the Dreadgod, he was at least the size of a large dog compared to the Titan.

But he was still just an Underlord.

No matter how weak the Wandering Titan had become, and no matter the equalizing effect of the suppression field, Orthos was no match for a Dreadgod under any conditions. His shell splintered as the Dreadgod's grip tightened, and Orthos would be torn apart in moments.

Lindon tried to send reassurance through their bond. Orthos didn't need to hold on for long.

Lindon was coming.

He landed a moment later on the back of the Titan's neck.

And with all his will, he began to Consume.

Lindon had fed on the thoughts and memories of the Wandering Titan before, so he knew what to expect this time. Even so, he was almost overwhelmed on every front.

The madra threatened to break his arm, and to be too much for his Heart of Twin Stars to process. The memories and impressions flooded Dross, poised to drown Lindon's identity. And the willpower, titanic and voracious, crashed into Lindon's like an avalanche.

Lindon was tossed in a whirlpool of the Wandering Titan's emotions, but they weren't the timeless fury that he had expected.

He felt frustration.

Irritation.

Dissatisfaction.

Exhaustion.

He had come here to satisfy its eternal hunger. He'd followed the scent of the one thing that could end its suffering, only to find that it wasn't here. The trail was cold. And now he was being kept awake by some annoying, buzzing flies when all he wanted to do was eat and then sleep.

No, *he* wasn't. *The Titan* was.

It was hard to tell the difference.

He broke contact with a gasp, his head pounding. The Titan rumbled beneath him, and this was as far as Dross had guided Lindon.

It's working too hard, Lindon reported to Dross. *I want to... it wants to leave. We can drive it out.*

The Dreadgod tossed Mercy down, and her armor shattered. Essence covered the valley in a luminous violet cloud.

It dragged a struggling Orthos in its left hand, like a forgotten toy.

Slowly, the Titan turned back to Mount Samara again, and this time Lindon knew why.

It wasn't focused on cracking open the mountain and getting to the treasure inside, though Lindon was certain there *was* another one in there. It didn't even care to eradicate the people trying to escape.

It just wanted out of the suppression field. And this mountain was in its way.

First, it had thought this mountain might be its ancient home, but a long inspection had determined that not to be the case. It simply felt wrong.

This was not home. Not quite.

The Titan lifted the giant Orthos, and Lindon's stomach twisted as he realized what it was about to do. It was about to hurl Orthos at the mountain.

[Deeper!] Dross shouted. [Dig deeper!]

This was the one chance Dross had seen of them driving off the Dreadgod.

The Titan abandoned targets that cost it too much energy. And Lindon could take that energy away directly, but he could only hold so much. His arm had limits, and so did he.

Though he hadn't rested enough, he returned his right hand to the stony skin and once again used Consume.

As the Titan's power crashed over him again, Lindon knew immediately that they weren't going to make it.

This amount of energy loss was nothing to the Titan. It was vaguely aware that there was some kind of flea draining its spirit, but it couldn't be bothered to deal with him yet.

Lindon could drain its power all day, and maybe *then* tire the Titan enough to make it a little sleepy. But before that happened, it would have long since swatted Lindon away.

And that was the Titan already weakened by the suppression field.

Dross groaned. [I was *really* hoping this would work. It's been in Sacred Valley a long time. There were good odds.]

Orthos was raised high over the Titan's head, ready to throw.

What do we do? Lindon begged.

Time slowed one more time. Distantly, Lindon was surprised that Dross still had enough power left to do this, but he didn't have time to worry.

[Hey, Lindon. You wouldn't...you wouldn't throw me away, would you?]

Dross sounded nervous all of a sudden, and Lindon's heart dropped as he wondered what the spirit was about to propose. *Am I not going to like this?*

[I just, well, I'm not exactly proud of this, but I've always been afraid of being thrown away. Please, just keep me around.]

Lindon couldn't understand why Dross was wasting madra for this conversation. *I'm not throwing you away, now please help!*

Dross let out a relieved breath. [Okay good, I just needed to hear it.]

Then dream aura *flooded* out of him. In a tide so expansive that Lindon wondered where it had all come from. How had Lindon not sensed vital aura this strong in Sacred Valley?

But he *had* sensed it, he realized. This was the power he'd drained from the Titan's thoughts. Lindon had left sorting those to Dross.

Now, the aura flowed out, but not in a disorganized mess. It was being woven into a technique. A technique Lindon recognized.

The Fox Dream.

Dross *blazed* with madra, so much that even Lindon was

surprised. The Titan paused, Orthos still struggling over-head, and Lindon added his contribution. Soulfire merged into the technique, and Lindon joined his will to Dross'.

Because of that link, he saw the vision Dross sent to the Titan.

It was nothing complicated. The Dreadgod saw eight fig-ures hovering over Mount Samara, all Monarchs. It felt their power.

And one more detail: the turtle in its hands had vanished.

The Titan felt no fear, only irritation and disappointment. It had thought it was about to find its ancient home, only to find a patch of nothing. *Well-defended* nothing, too. And there was nothing it hated more than wasting its effort.

With a slow, ponderous motion, the Titan turned.

And walked back the way it came.

It lowered its arms, absently dropping the giant Orthos to the ground. Orthos hit and roared again, which Lindon worried would break the illusion of the Fox Dream, but the Dreadgod kept walking unaffected. From the pain through their bond, Lindon knew the turtle was still alive.

And each earth-shaking footstep grew more and more distant.

Lindon fell back on his Thousand-Mile Cloud, sagging in relief.

"Dross...thank you. You saved us."

When no one responded, Lindon stretched his perception into his own spirit.

"Dross?"

第二十章

CHAPTER TWENTY

Iteration 001: Sanctum

In the center of an isolation chamber buried deep beneath the sprawling megacity of Sanctum, Suriel slowly restored Makiel.

His body drifted in the center of the empty gold-walled room, runes all around glowing blue to enhance the effect of the Way. His mind was awake and active, but he gazed into the future. Trying to find a way to preserve Fate.

She could have had him back on his feet in an instant, but his existence had been severely damaged. His power would suffer unless she healed him slowly and carefully.

In the meantime, she was given little choice but to contemplate the situation among the worlds.

A blooming map of existence spread out in front of her at her will, a twisting nest of blue light with bright lights hanging off it like berries on a bush. The branches were the Way, the spots of light the Iterations.

All of them should be bright blue with a core of white, but too many of them were gray. Far, far too many.

As she watched, one of the lights from the cluster labeled 'Sector 12' turned black and withered away. Iteration 129: Oasis.

The Mad King and his Scythe had finished their reaping.

Suriel continued focusing on Makiel's restoration. There was one more thing she could do for the good of all existence, but first she had to wait.

Finally, she felt the touch of Telariel, the Spider.

He rarely left Sanctum, but now even he was on the battlefield, retreating temporarily from a victory to connect her to all the other Judges. She caught brief glimpses of the remaining four, each engaged in battle, as Telariel wove his strands of authority to link them across time and space.

When all the Judges could hear her, Suriel spoke.

"Makiel is in recovery. We faced the Mad King and were defeated."

She felt the reactions of the various Judges as though they were her own. Gadrael, the Titan, was astonished that his sponsor could have failed. Razael, the Wolf, wanted to test her own sword against the Vroshir. Zerachiel, the Fox, immediately ran to an Iteration farther away from the Mad King.

"By Makiel's authorization and my own, I send the following command. All Judges, do not engage the Mad King. Abandon any world you cannot hold, and fortify those you can. The Vroshir will finish their raid, and many will die, but soon enough they will leave. We will retreat, and endure, and rebuild."

The Spider and the Fox immediately sent their agreement. They prioritized their own lives and those of the Abidan above all else.

The Titan was next. Any world he was in would be well-fortified indeed, and he would follow any instruction of Makiel's.

The Ghost sent no reply, but Suriel took that as agreement. The Wolf was the last to agree, frustrated that she couldn't vent her frustrations on the enemy, but she satisfied herself with the knowledge that they would strike back someday.

The Hound and the Phoenix already agreed, so the Court

of Seven was in accord. Their forces would pull back and let the Vroshir rampage until the pressures of chaos forced them to retreat back to their worlds.

Abidan would spread out more slowly this time, recovering surviving worlds and rebuilding others from fragments. From ten thousand worlds before Ozriel's departure, they would be reduced to...a hundred, perhaps.

Even her Presence couldn't speculate on the total number of lives that would be lost. At least those taken by the Vroshir would survive, but the Mad King and his allies would capture only those who could benefit them in some way.

Most would perish. And some of the worlds they lost would be vital ones.

She returned her attention to the map of the Way hovering in front of her. Sector 12 was entirely gray now, and other Sectors were darkening around it. Abidan had pulled back, leaving that region almost entirely undefended. One Sector in particular was surrounded, left entirely to the mercy of the Vroshir.

Sector 11.

With a heavy heart, Suriel reached out to the first world in the Sector: Iteration 110, Cradle.

Before the world was entirely closed off to the rest of the Way, she found a tiny piece of herself manifested in reality. She resonated with it, sending a message through the blue candle-flame inside.

It had to be simple. More simple impressions than words. *I'm sorry,* Suriel sent. *Hold on.*

She spared an instant of grief for the world. The Mad King, who had once been the hero Daruman, knew the significance of Cradle. He knew it was the birthplace of the original Abidan, and—perhaps more importantly to him—Ozriel's home.

Now, it was at his mercy.

Eithan gritted his teeth. "Cut it off."

Yerin grabbed his hand too tightly. "Are you sure?"

"Do it!"

With the chime of a tiny bell, Yerin carefully used the Endless Sword. And Eithan's glorious hair fell to the floor.

He gave a cry of pain, and Yerin patted him on the shoulder. "You looked like a yellow dog that climbed out of the fireplace. Your hair was suffering, and we eased it on its way."

"A mirror," Eithan croaked. "Bring me a mirror."

He could see himself through his bloodline power, now that they were hovering in the cloud fortress outside of Sacred Valley, but there was still no substitute to using your own eyes.

Yerin handed him his pocket mirror, holding it up for him so he didn't have to move his bandaged hands. She had left only two or three inches of hair. Barely enough to style.

He looked...well, he still looked great. A change in style could be refreshing sometimes.

But that didn't mean he wouldn't mourn the loss.

"Thank you. I just needed to see the damage for myself."

She patted him again, and he could see her struggling not to make some comment about having *real* injuries to see to.

Eithan himself had a brace on his neck and all four limbs, as well as scripted bandages around his entire midsection and no less than three medicinal pills in his system. If not for the scripts, he would feel like beetles were eating him from the inside out at the moment, but at least he would be healed in a few days.

But he wasn't the only one who needed attention.

Mercy and Ziel were both asleep, recovering from spiritual wounds. Little Blue had seen to them both, and Mercy would wake soon. She had strained her bloodline far beyond its limits, and would have suffered worse if she hadn't left the battle once her armor broke.

Her mother would be able to restore such an injury, no doubt, but then they would all be in the unenviable position of explaining to Malice why they let a Monarch's Overlady daughter face down a Dreadgod. If she recovered on her own, Malice need not be bothered.

Ziel had also pushed himself too far, but fortunately not beyond the restorative benefits of the Pure Storm Baptism. Eithan had performed the next stage—with his arms stiff as boards—and now Ziel slept with sparks of lightning madra playing through his spirit and over his body.

Orthos was perhaps in the worst shape, and his size couldn't be reversed until he woke up and was provided with more soulfire. He hovered over a hill outside like a mid-sized Dreadgod himself, drifting on green cushions of life aura guided by a script. Everyone had donated life-aspected natural treasures to the effort, and now his flesh was knitting itself together at visible speed.

Even Yerin had not walked away unscathed, though she'd recovered before everyone but Lindon. Veins of bright red madra covered her body, replacing broken flesh, including a chunk of her hip. If she had to fight now, she could.

Instead of mocking Eithan, Yerin stood and looked to the door. "Scream if you need more coddling. I'm going after him."

"You don't think he needs some time alone right now?"

"Been more than a minute since he's been alone at all."

Physically, Lindon was fine. He was suffering some after-effects from having Consumed too much of the Titan, but nothing he wouldn't wrestle through.

Loss was harder to handle.

"Beings such as Dross don't really *die*," Eithan said. "... except under truly extraordinary circumstances."

They could, however, change so drastically from damage like this that they came back with entirely different personalities. Which would not reassure Yerin, so Eithan didn't say anything.

It wasn't a guarantee, anyway. Perhaps Dross would recover and be perfectly healthy.

Eithan hoped so. He still had high hopes for Dross.

Yerin glanced at him as though she heard his unspoken

thoughts. "Doesn't mean he has an easy road to walk right now, does it? I'd contend he shouldn't be finding his way on his own."

"Nor will he have to," Eithan agreed, "but sometimes you need time to yourself first."

Her expression shifted subtly as she wrestled with herself, and Eithan could read the pain on her face. She knew he was right. She'd pushed through loss enough times herself.

While she was working to her own conclusion. Eithan left his bed. He didn't have much control over his body, so he looked something like a turtle righting itself after landing on its shell.

When he finally stood stiffly on two thoroughly bandaged legs, he congratulated himself on the victory.

"Doesn't count as alone if you pop out of the bushes," she pointed out.

"I can lurk without popping out. Besides, I'm not going to Lindon."

Yerin radiated such obvious skepticism that he thought he could see it in the vital aura.

"Lindon isn't the only person in the world. I do sneak up on others occasionally."

She gave his legs a pointed look. "You won't be sneaking up on a deaf brick."

"Ah, but you underestimate my legendary grace and agility." Eithan hobbled across the ground, his every step clattering on the floor until it sounded like the return of the Wandering Titan.

He paused at the door. He had used up his soulfire to heal himself and perform the Baptism on Ziel.

"Would you mind helping me with the door, please?"

Without a word, Yerin pushed it open.

⬡

Somehow, Jai Chen found herself leading a procession of several hundred sacred artists. Most were much older, and none had any idea who she was.

She led by virtue of being the strongest sacred artist present, and because Mercy had told everyone to listen to her. They had been about two hundred strong then, but the last time Jai Chen extended her detection web, she'd counted almost twice that.

Mercy had also left her with a medicinal pill for her brother, and now it slowly revolved in his spirit, but he still hadn't woken up.

Jai Chen hauled Jai Long behind herself on a stretcher that lay on a hovering construct. She'd been lucky to find that platform; at first, she had been dragging him over the uneven terrain, which couldn't have been good for his recovery.

The further they pushed into the black trees, the more dreadbeasts they'd encountered. Most wouldn't bother a group of their size, but some seemed to have no sense of self-preservation at all.

Fingerling flew around her, staying alert for more, even though he was at least as exhausted as she was. He sagged in midair, and his eyes regularly fluttered closed, but he kept shaking himself awake.

Now that the Dreadgod was gone, Jai Chen could turn back west again, but she didn't want to go back to Sacred Valley in that condition. Nor did anyone else who followed her, it seemed.

They had a plan for the Wilds, so she was clinging to it like a life raft.

But the plan let her down at the first step.

She called out a warning as she felt more sacred artists approaching, but when they emerged, she was the one to panic.

The forty or fifty sacred artists coming out of the trees wore blue, carried spears, and their hair was stiff and shiny as metal. The Jai clan.

Jai Chen and her brother had wondered about this. With

the clan being pushed out of the Blackflame Empire proper, it was possible that they would look for places to settle on the border of the Empire. Places that weren't really under Imperial supervision at all. Like the Desolate Wilds.

A woman with glistening black hair stepped up, her spearhead shining like a white star. "I am Jai Hara, of the Jai clan. Name yourselves."

There was deathly silence from the Sacred Valley side as everyone waited for Jai Chen to speak. Even Fingerling turned to her.

She shoved the panic down into her stomach. These people wouldn't know who she was. They couldn't recognize her; she wasn't wearing anything that marked her as having once been part of their clan, and she didn't have their Goldsign. Or any Goldsign at all, as she was still Jade.

They *couldn't* know, but she still trembled at the thought that they would figure it out.

"We came from the west," Jai Chen called, and she didn't like how her voice shook. "We're fleeing the Dreadgod. We just want a place to stay for a while. I...*we* have friends in the Sandvipers. Or the Purelakes. Are they still here?"

Jai Hara's face was as stiff as her hair. "We have barely enough for ourselves, but if you will tell us which experts you represent, we will know where to send our apologies."

Jai Chen's sense of danger spiked. They wanted to know if she was backed by anyone to know if she could be pushed around or not. If she said they were here on their own, they might even attack.

At first, she thought to say the Arelius family, since she could prove that relatively easily. But that would only ensure they attacked; it had been the Arelius family that had pushed the Jai clan out of the Empire.

Next, she considered the Akura clan, but she really had no idea who they were. Important, she gathered, but what if they were even worse enemies to the Jai clan?

Other than an outright, outrageous lie, she only had one idea left.

"We were sent here by the Sage of Twin Stars," Jai Chen said.

There were enough gasps and mutters from the dozens of sacred artists behind Jai Hara that she knew she'd said the right thing.

"A *Sage?*" Jai Hara repeated in astonishment. "So you're the...honorable Twin Star sect?"

"Yes," Jai Chen said immediately. "That's us."

She had spent enough years in the Desolate Wilds to know that Sages were only legends here, but they were legends widely told. She herself didn't understand how Lindon could possibly be a Sage—he had felt like an Underlord to her, and he hadn't acted with the aloof air of an expert she had always imagined from Sages—but as long as he could technically claim the title, she could use it.

Jai Hara had started conferring with someone behind her, so Jai Chen kept talking. "The Sage himself is close by. He was fighting the Dreadgod, but the valley to the west was destroyed. So we needed to find shelter for ourselves. Before the Sage comes to get us."

She was explaining too much, so she clapped her mouth shut before she dug herself a hole she couldn't dig out of.

Jai Chen *really* wished her brother was awake.

Jai Hara straightened herself up. "We have, of course, heard tales of the Twin Star Sage's heroism."

No, they hadn't. Jai Chen would have been shocked if Hara had heard the name before now.

But this was the kind of harmless lie that might soothe the ego of an expert and prevent enmity. Jai Chen understood.

"It is no surprise to us that the honorable Sage has come to defend us from the Dreadgod," Jai Hara continued, "but who is *that?*"

She pointed behind Jai Chen's shoulder.

With a jolt, Jai Chen realized that she hadn't paid attention to her spiritual sense. She was exhausted, but that was no excuse for a lack of vigilance.

Eithan Arelius drifted up, looking like he'd floated straight out of a healer's tent. He was sprawled belly-down on a white Thousand-Mile Cloud, wrapped entirely in bandages. His limbs all looked completely stiff, and his hair had been cut short and swept back.

He reached into a hole in the air, from which he pulled a long gray length of cloth. "I am here as another representative of the Twin Star sect. Let our banner stream behind us!"

Eithan let the cloth catch the wind, where it billowed out to display an unbroken stretch of gray. The banner was blank.

Jai Chen didn't want to say anything, but Eithan saw the look on her face and sighed. "You didn't give me time to get it sewn yet, but imagine how amazed you would have been if I *did* have a banner ready. Pretend that's what happened."

A cry had gone up from those of the Jai clan who had extended their spiritual senses. "Underlord!"

Ten or fifteen went down to their knees immediately.

But not most of them.

Eithan responded to their calls with a cheery smile. "Close enough!"

"They're going to recognize you," Jai Chen said, her voice low.

Most of the Jai remained standing, and they were not happy. Jai Hara herself spat at the foot of Eithan's cloud. "We know who you are. There's only one Arelius Underlord."

"That is not actually correct, but I do not represent my family. They make their own decisions." Some of the standing Jai clan glanced to one another.

"I embrace my true identity," Eithan continued. "Personal acolyte to the Sage of Twin Stars himself, and one of the founding members of the Twin Star sect."

He strained himself to hold the banner higher, despite the thick wrapping around his hands.

There was some fierce debate among the dozens of Jai artists in the back, but after a moment of struggle, Jai Hara begrudgingly lowered her head. "We don't have food to share, but you can rest behind our lines until the Sage comes."

As their crowd from Sacred Valley was ushered into the Wilds, Jai Chen whispered to Eithan. "Thank you. We just need a place to recover for a while, and then we won't impose on your hospitality anymore."

Eithan was lying face-down, his banner missing. Either the effort of holding it up had exhausted him, or he hadn't wanted to stay in such a strange position for any longer.

Now, however, the Archlord spoke straight into his cushion of dense cloud madra. "Impose? No, I simply ask that you give me a few days to prepare better accommodations than this. I couldn't let our new sect die out in the cold."

Jai Chen didn't know how to respond. On the one hand, having a sect backing them would solve most of their problems. She yearned to stop running and hiding, to settle down somewhere.

On the other hand, there was no Twin Star sect.

"I'm sorry, Archlord, but the sect...I was just—"

"Making it up? Every organization in history has been made up by someone."

"We don't have—"

"A headquarters? There has been quite a bit of real estate around here leveled in a recent disaster. You may have heard about it."

"My brother—"

"I'm not just looking for your brother." His head lolled to one side, and he looked at her with a single blue eye. "From you, Jai Chen, with no pressure from me, I would like to know: if we could provide you with a home, would you want one?"

She hesitated.

"No commitment," he assured her, "and pending your brother's approval. You could both walk away if and when you wanted."

"Yes," she admitted. "But it's hard for me to believe it isn't a trap."

She flinched as she said it. He was an Archlord, and she was doubting his given word.

He let out a breath of relief. "Fantastic! It actually isn't a trap this time; I just need someone who knows real sacred arts to sort through all these Irons to find some who might actually be worth teaching. It so happens that I have recently come into possession of a plot of flying farmland with plenty of sacred herbs and spirit-fruits to support the development of a small sect. So I appreciate you founding one."

Eithan dipped his head in what was probably supposed to be a bow. It was really just him pushing his face deeper into the cloud.

Despite her misgivings, Jai Chen giggled.

Northstrider crossed his legs and closed his eyes in mid-air, catching his breath and slowly recovering his spirit.

The clouds below him were torn apart, the landscape devastated for miles. An abandoned fortress had been reduced to rubble, there was now a bay where once had been uninterrupted coastline, and one small mountain had been leveled while another one had burst into its place.

"I'll have to have my maps re-drawn," Malice said with a sigh.

She drifted up next to him out of a cloud of violet essence. Her dissolving armor lit up the sky, but it was nothing compared to the red light that retreated north.

The Bleeding Phoenix, flying into the Trackless Sea.

Not fleeing.

[Behavioral deviation detected in the Bleeding Phoenix,] his oracle reported. [It acts according to unknown purpose.]

Northstrider didn't need the reminder. They both knew they hadn't driven it off; it was flying somewhere with intention.

"Do you think it's feeding to regain its power?" Malice asked.

"I don't know."

"Oooh, I know how much you love that." She was smirking, he was sure, but she had always valued useless conversation. He continued cycling, seeing to his spirit, categorizing how much strength the battle with the Phoenix had cost him and how long it would take to recover.

"He did this," Malice said at last.

"Yes."

It would be no mystery among the Monarchs who was responsible for the strange actions of the Phoenix. Only one among them even claimed to have any influence over the Dreadgods.

"He has gone too far," she said, and now he could feel her cold anger bleeding out into the world around her. "He's toying with forces that could be the ruin of all of us. What could he possibly expect to gain from this?"

Northstrider opened his eyes. "I will know soon."

Wearing more veils than he ever had in his life, Reigan Shen shoved his way through collapsed houses and upturned trees. He was still in his human body, and he was both sweating and breathing heavily.

He felt as weak as an Iron. It was like wearing a suit so tight that it had burrowed into his skin.

Even so, he wasn't doing the work himself. He may be a sacred beast, but he wasn't an *animal.*

Jade-level constructs pushed beams aside, dispersed soil, and lifted boulders so he could pass. More scoured the area, clearing the entrance.

It had taken him hours to reach this point, and *finally* the starting point was within reach. The last chunk of masonry rolled away, revealing a towering stone door. It was carved with the image of a gaunt, sunken human with many grasping hands, its eyes hollow and mouth open unnaturally wide.

This was Subject One, at least as he had appeared long

ago. A Dreadgod, though few knew that. The man who had become warped by hunger aura. The origin of their bloodline.

Shen's willpower was veiled, but still powerful. He commanded the door to open, and it obeyed.

With great ceremony and a hissing release of power, the Nethergate swung open.

Inside, a wood-paneled hallway was lit with flickering scripts. Finally, Reigan Shen had gained the wish he'd dreamed of ever since Tiberian's death: entrance to the western labyrinth.

Only the shallowest layer, to be certain. The bulk of the work was still left to be done, and the depths of the labyrinth would surely be locked down tight. Fortunately, he had the key.

Reigan Shen strode into the tunnel, on his way to retrieve his new weapon.

EPILOGUE

With his Remnant arm in a scripted sling, Lindon faced the Ancestor's Tomb. It had come through the Wandering Titan's attack more or less intact.

Part of its roof had caved in, one pillar was cracked, and it was covered with debris like a small town had dumped its garbage all over it.

But Heaven's Glory must have done their job well when they rebuilt it, because the Tomb still stood.

There were no security measures left around it, all of them having been destroyed either by the trembling earth or roaring winds, so he walked through the front doors of the Tomb easily.

Once he stood inside the open temple-like room, he faced down the sealed door at the other end. A mural of the four Dreadgods covered the entrance.

Lindon had learned many things from the Wandering Titan's memories. *Too* many things, he would say; it was impossible to process all the impressions, instincts, and thoughts. Dross had been going through them, but even for him, it was difficult to separate what had come from the Titan and what from Lindon's own mind.

Still, a few themes were clear. One was that the Titan had

detected its goal here. The one meal it needed. The source of hunger madra.

When it had arrived and felt nothing more of the sort, the Dreadgod had assumed it wasn't here. Like a dog chasing after a stick, only to never find it.

But Lindon had more than a few reasons to suspect the Dreadgod's prize was still here. Just locked away. Buried.

Besides, Lindon's arm had been strained and cracked by absorbing so much of the Titan's power. He needed more weapons of hunger madra if he wanted to rebuild it. And improve it. Scavenging from dreadbeasts wouldn't hold him forever.

He had to pick his way across a field of debris as he crossed the room; evidently some people had used the Tomb as shelter during the Dreadgod's attack. As it had been before, the inside of the Ancestor's Tomb was just a wide-open space lined with pillars.

At the end of the room stood an ornate door, sealed shut. The entrance was undamaged by the previous collapse of the building, which didn't surprise him. If it was part of the labyrinth below, it had to be made of stronger stuff.

Lindon had been reaching out for the door already, silence filling his mind where Dross' chatter belonged, but he stopped as he noticed something.

The door had no mechanism to open it and no clear script-circle, which meant he would have to use his authority to open it, but that wasn't what had seized his attention. It was a trace of someone else's authority over to the side of the hall, a little to the side of the door.

An indentation in space. Like an invisible bump.

Lindon's alarm went up immediately. Someone had torn space here, and if it wasn't him...

He should call for help in case there was something deadly on the other side. Dross could have done that.

The spirit wasn't gone. Not quite. He drifted in Lindon's soul, right around the base of his skull as usual, but Lindon didn't see details. His eye, his boneless arms. Instead, Dross felt like a loose cloud of dream madra. Like a two-dimensional copy of his former self.

Eithan insisted that it was possible to bring Dross back, but Lindon understood the nature of spirits. If Dross returned, there was no guarantee that he'd be himself anymore.

Lindon shook himself free. Dross wasn't here, but some of his passive enhancements to Lindon's mind remained.

He focused on the bump in space. It didn't feel like a tunnel to him, or a trap. It felt like a sealed void key more than a tunnel somewhere else in the world.

Though he supposed there could be anything *inside* the void key.

He stretched out a tongue of Blackflame, infusing it with his authority and using it to slice through space. It was much easier than when he had tried the same thing with only his will; when he commanded the world to **"Open,"** he cut through the barrier separating the spaces almost without resistance.

As soon as a doorway in midair unfurled, opening onto a huge room cluttered with various objects, he noticed two things more than any others: the art and the swords.

This room actually had walls, and on those walls hung brightly colored tapestries, long black-and-white landscapes painted on scrolls, framed portraits, even decorative lights and constructs of slithering color that were clearly designed only for decoration.

Between the paintings were swords. Some were elaborate and ancient, shining with power, while others were dull, pitted, or rusty. Some were just hilts, their madra blades having faded away to essence, and still others had Forged blades that were perfectly preserved.

A scripted cauldron sat cold in the corner, next to buckets, boxes, bags, and bundles of herbs, spirit-fruits, pills, and elixirs. Next to it was a rack of sacred artist's robes, all black, many of them nicked and cut.

Lindon's stomach twisted.

He noticed the second rack, filled with more black robes, all of them shredded as though by errant sword-slices.

And the rack of cycling swords next to them, all radiating sharp aura.

This had to be the Sword Sage's private storage space. It was the only thing that made sense.

But that was impossible.

"It can't be his," Lindon said aloud. "It's too old. The world would have healed up the entrance by now, and I would never have found it."

When no one responded, Lindon turned slightly over his shoulder.

"I'm talking to you."

An onyx statue of a curled-up panther sat next to the entrance, where there had been nothing a moment before. To be fair, the illusion was convincing, even to Lindon. But he had senses the inhabitants of Sacred Valley couldn't fool.

That, and Lindon had felt the Path of the White Fox following him before he opened the portal.

The onyx panther uncurled itself, its tail spreading out into five copies. The tails flexed out as the cat stretched, opening its jaws wide in a yawn, and as it did so it grew taller. Its snout extended, and its smooth surface melted to gray and then to a coat of white fur.

"You have traveled far down your Path, child," Elder Whisper murmured.

"So have you, I see. And you have kept that to yourself."

He did not hide the tone of accusation in his voice.

Elder Whisper prowled around Lindon. "I did not deceive anyone. At first, we taught our descendants to focus on one technique at a time as an adaptation to the suppression field. But memory fades so quickly, and time is the greatest liar of all."

"If you had the power to open this space, you could have helped us fight the Dreadgod."

"To face one of the four beasts with illusions is to face down a lion with a spider's web."

Elder Whisper kept an illusion of himself standing still and talking as his real form crept out beneath a cloak of invisibility.

Lindon traced the invisible one with his eyes. "That's how we beat it."

"When you lose what you fought to defend, and your opponent leaves you alive out of mercy, is that victory?" Elder Whisper sighed and let his illusions drop. "Perhaps it is. In any case, any victory against one of *them* is temporary. That is why I preserved this place."

Lindon swept his gaze over the isolated space. "Why didn't you take what you needed and leave it closed?"

"While I can visit Heaven's Glory unseen whenever I wish, it would be quite another matter if I were to drag a trunk behind me in my teeth. And the ability to open these spaces is quite separate from the power to create one of my own. In that, you have me outmatched.

"Sages avoid these lands. The last one to visit, the man who left this space, was asking forbidden questions. Which is the best way to find forbidden answers."

A purple-and-white flame kindled over a cylinder tucked away in the corner.

It was about as high and broad as Lindon's waist, and made of dull bronze metal. Scripts wrapped around the cylinder, and it took Lindon a moment to analyze them.

When he activated the scripts in the correct sequence, the cylinder fell away, revealing a tall rectangular box beneath. This one, he had to cut through with Blackflame.

Finally, a cube about the size of his head rested in the third layer. It throbbed and pulsed, and Lindon recognized the taste of the madra inside.

As he recognized the symbol on the top: the moon crest of the Arelius clan.

"The Sage brought this to our lands," Elder Whisper continued, "a tool granted to him by a Monarch. A key to the prison at the depths of the labyrinth. But he was not capable of delving deeply enough."

Lindon's will was enough to open the box. It wasn't made to keep people out so much as to keep something *in*.

If it was what Lindon suspected, he needed to be fast.

The box opened to reveal a shriveled, mummified, chalk-white left hand.

Appetites Lindon had absorbed from the Wandering Titan burned to life, and he longed to consume the hand whole, to tear it apart with his teeth and let it satisfy his stomach and his soul.

He slammed the box shut again. "We can't open this," Lindon said firmly. "It will drag the Titan straight back."

Elder Whisper sat on his haunches, tails waving smoothly behind him. "Wei Shi Lindon. Would you like to know how to kill the Dreadgods?"

THE END
of Cradle: Volume Nine
Bloodline

LINDON'S STORY CONTINUES IN

REAPER

CRADLE : VOLUME TEN

ＡＮＤ ＮＯＷ ＴＨＩＳ…

Lindon braced himself. Here they were, ready to return to Sacred Valley. The time had come.

Nothing between him and his family except a Dreadgod.

[Could be worse!] Dross pointed out. [There could be *two* Dreadgods.]

Eithan leaned over to whisper in Lindon's ear. "That, children, is what we call *foreshadowing.*"

Lindon felt Eithan's presence before the door to the second floor swung open, and Yerin was already yelling. "Not a candle's chance in a rainstorm."

Eithan folded his arms and looked at her curiously. "I've always wondered. How many of those do you have?"

"Not a pig's chance in a butcher shop," Yerin said. "Not a star's chance in daylight. Not a sheep's chance in a tiger den. Not a snowflake's chance in summer. Not a Copper's chance."

"A Copper's chance in what?" Lindon asked.

"Copper doesn't have much of a chance anywhere."

Eithan stroked his chin. "Do you make these up on the spot, or do you have an extraordinary memory for folksy idioms?"

"Sometimes I remember, sometimes I make 'em up." She shrugged. "Can't say it makes an inch of difference either way."

Lindon was impressed. "If you're making those up that quickly, I think you might be some kind of genius."

She snorted. "Not a snowball's chance in Hell."

Eithan and Lindon stood over the grimy pit, looking down into the hole where a Heaven's Glory building had collapsed. "If you already know what's down there, I would appreciate it if you would tell me," Lindon said.

Eithan grimaced. "Lots of grimy blankets, some destroyed tools, and a shallow sewer of human waste." He knelt and brushed his hand over an indentation in the rubble. "A halfling lay here." He moved to another dent next to the first. "And the other."

"What's a halfling?" Lindon asked.

"Hush, I'm dodging copyright." Eithan closed his eyes, tracing a trail. "They crawled...their hands were bound!"

"I'm certain you're making this up."

"Their bonds were cut!"

Lindon decided to ignore him.

Ziel stared down the Kazan Patriarch. "There's a big monster coming. It's called a Dreadgod. Come with us if you want to live."

"Okay, let's go," the Patriarch said.

They high-fived.

Orthos exchanged glances with Little Blue before he looked back to Yerin. "He does not feel like he's in danger."

Yerin's heart eased a little. "What *does* he feel like?"

Orthos gave her an odd look. "Like all humans. Soft but bony. I don't see why you'd need to ask me that, though."

Yerin's face heated. "Wait, no, I meant—"

"What a question to ask an old, lonely turtle. You would know the answer better than I would anyway, I imagine."

"I yield. White flag. Please stop."

Little Blue's laughter echoed like bells.

For the second time in a day, Lindon gripped the marble and prayed.

I don't know what to do. Help me.

The marble buzzed for a second, then stopped. Then buzzed again. On the third buzz, it was interrupted by a woman's voice.

"New marble, who's this?"

"This is, uh, Wei Shi Lindon? From Cradle?"

"Oh yeah, Lindon! Hold on one second, let me put you in here. Cradle...Kid...I...Saved...okay, I've got you in. Now let's make this quick, I'm roaming."

"State your desires," Northstrider said.

Yerin spoke immediately. "Infinite wishes."

The gathered Monarchs looked to one another.

Northstrider grunted. "Obviously we can't—"

"I wish to win the next tournament."

"That violates the entire spirit of the competition."

"Immortality."

"You don't need any more increases to your lifespan."

"The ability to grant my own wishes."

"That's advancement, and it's what we're offering you." Northstrider's eyes narrowed. "Where are you getting these ideas?"

Yerin pulled out a scroll, which unfurled all the way to the ground. "Lindon wrote it. I remember 'em all, but he thought you might want to read them. Next, I'm supposed to ask for 'points.'"

Northstrider incinerated the list.

WILL WIGHT lives in Florida, among the citrus fruits and slithering sea creatures. He's the author of the Amazon best-selling *Traveler's Gate Trilogy*, *The Elder Empire* (which cleverly offers twice the fun and twice the work), and his series of mythical martial arts magic: *Cradle*.

He graduated from the University of Central Florida in 2013, earning a Master's of Fine Arts in Creative Writing and a flute of dragon's bone. He is also, apparently, invisible to cameras.

He also claims that *www.WillWight.com* is the best source for book updates, new stories, fresh coriander, and miracle cures for all your aches and pains!

Made in the USA
Middletown, DE
14 April 2021

37552632R00209